β

# SKELETONS IN FRED'S CUPBOARD

# SKELETONS IN FRED'S CUPBOARD

**Fred Young**

Thomas Harmsworth Publishing Company

First Published 1995

Cover illustration: Dave Rudd

British Library Cataloguing-in-Publication Data. A catalogue record of this book is available from the British Library

ISBN 0 948807 28 8

Printed and Bound in Great Britain by
Bookcraft (Bath) Ltd

# Dramatis Personae

Fred . . . . . . . . . . . . . . . . . Me
Rose Higgins . . . . . . . . . . . my mother
Bob Higgins . . . . . . . . . . . my dad
Maddy . . . . . . . . . . . . . . Fred Holbrook's daughter
Fred Holbrook . . . . . . . . . . a Royal Marine
Mr Charles Pardy . . . . . . . . . my choirmaster
Mr Bertie Pocksome ('Poxy Bert') . . the Verger of my church
Charlie Baldock . . . . . . . . . Landlord of 'The
                                   Wheatsheaf'
'Granny' Litchfield . . . . . . . . midwife &c
Betty Holbrook . . . . . . . . . Fred Holbrook's wife
Freddie Holbrook . . . . . . . . Fred Holbrook's son
Edgar Holbrook . . . . . . . . . Fred Holbrook's son
Michael (Captain Cotter) . . . . . Bob's Company
                                   Commander
Fred Cotter . . . . . . . . . . . Captain Cotter's father
Lydia Cotter . . . . . . . . . . . Captain Cotter's mother &
                                   2nd wife of Fred Cotter
Hilda . . . . . . . . . . . . . . . Rose's sister
Rosalina . . . . . . . . . . . . . my sister
John . . . . . . . . . . . . . . . my brother
Bertie . . . . . . . . . . . . . . my brother
Leslie . . . . . . . . . . . . . . my brother
Michael . . . . . . . . . . . . . my brother
Ronald . . . . . . . . . . . . . . my brother
Charlie Dunn . . . . . . . . . . Bob's business colleague
Bert Campbell . . . . . . . . . . Painter & decorator
Gappy Lil . . . . . . . . . . . . Prostitute
Inspector Brown . . . . . . . . . Police officer
Sgt Jackson . . . . . . . . . . . Police officer
Constable Adams . . . . . . . . Policeman
Mr Streeter . . . . . . . . . . . Policeman
Mr Gapp . . . . . . . . . . . . . Bob's solicitor
Nurse Bowling . . . . . . . . . . midwife
Jock Fraser . . . . . . . . . . . . Bob's Army mate

Sam Somers . . . . . . . . . . . . . Maddy's husband
Gisselle . . . . . . . . . . . . . . my Jersey girlfriend
Henri Frenay . . . . . . . . . . . Gisselle's brother
Joan Cox . . . . . . . . . . . . . a Prostitute
Ernie . . . . . . . . . . . . . . . a Boxing Club mate
Lois . . . . . . . . . . . . . . . a lady's maid, my wife
Mary . . . . . . . . . . . . . . . Waitress wartime friend of
mine, my wife
Cynthia . . . . . . . . . . . . . wife of brother John
Veronica . . . . . . . . . . . . my daughter
Douggie . . . . . . . . . . . . . CID next-door neighbour
Percy . . . . . . . . . . . . . . Rosalina's elder son
Sally . . . . . . . . . . . . . . . Percy's wife
Teddy . . . . . . . . . . . . . . my son
Mrs Batch (Batchelor) . . . . . . The cleaner
Mr Conti . . . . . . . . . . . . a head waiter
Lydia . . . . . . . . . . . . . . my Canadian friend

# CHAPTER 1

King George the Fifth once said, 'I like to think of myself as just an ordinary fellow.' Soon after speaking these words a public house was built and named *The Ordinary Fellow*. And it was in that same town that Fred had first seen the light of day a couple of decades beforehand, when poverty, bugs, headlice, malnutrition and World War I (or The Great War, as it was then called) were raging.

This is the story of the days of not answering the door when the rent collector called, of barefooted children awaiting the emergence of their parents from the local pub at closing time to be given a penny to purchase potato chips for their dinner from the fish and chip shop; and of Mum and Dad 'having it away' almost in the presence of the kids, Mum's belly almost annually swollen; and of the disgrace of sister Fanny being in the 'Pudden Club' and not yet married.

Scarlet fever, diphtheria, consumption, pyorrhoea of the teeth, rickets were a way of life, all exacerbated, no doubt, by the chamber pots below the beds in which children slept head-to-toe like sardines in a tin.

They, too, were the days when some kindly neighbour would enquire of the family's well-being, should it be known that some disaster or other had befallen it, and when neighbours would donate a penny or two towards a wreath for a bereaved family, or a sum of money to a woman in need. The days when everybody thought they knew everybody else's business, and despite the frequent family feuds and punch-ups between them, a strange kinship and unspoken bond existed.

In each street a kind but hard-boiled woman seemed to have been placed by a weird and uncanny act of providence. She would always be at hand to help any family - and would do anything, from shopping for house-bound folk, to 'laying out' the dead for the undertaker, for in those days many folk died in their own beds at home.

There was the ever-nostalgic smell of the Sunday joint - roast beef and Bisto with batter pudding and baked potatoes, followed by rice pudding: 'It's my turn this week to have the skin off the top - you had it last week, you pig!'

Beef, beef! The least costly of all meat. A two-bob joint provided enough for Monday's dinner too, with bubble and squeak made up from the carefully-conserved cabbage and spuds from the previous day. Ah, the smell of that bubble and squeak frying in the pan will for ever stimulate the taste buds of lowly folk for the rest of their days!

Only posh families could afford the luxury of pork and lamb, and chicken was a dish spoken of with awe. Turkey was only for the very upper classes; but for the poor, Christmas dinner was provided by the slaughter of the rabbit, which had cost next to nothing to fatten up from the household scraps, and which was kept in the home-made rabbit hutch in the kitchen yard and allowed to grow to maturity.

Most families had a Singer sewing machine, foot treadle type, which was perhaps the most vital piece of equipment in the household economy. Not only hand-me-downs of growing brothers' and sisters' clothing were altered by Mums to fit their younger kin, but dresses, shirts, blouses, flannel under-wear, curtains and innumerable other items - which today are bought ready made - were produced with the expertise which shames the shoddy, badly finished but so-called 'quality' goods of today which cost a comparative fortune.

The females of those days spent their leisure time, apart perhaps from the usual weekly visit to the cinema and the Saturday night 'hop,' engrossed in knitting, crochet-work and dress-making from patterns, many of which were given free with such publications as *Peg's Paper* and *Red Letter*. In all haberdashery shops were to be found a wide range of plain and colourful rolls of cotton and silk for making dresses and underwear.

Every Mum made jam and pickles; every home had a mangle and front rooms displayed an aspidistra in their windows and some boasted a piano - usually in need of tuning.

Working class house toilets were outside in the garden, and emptied by the local council under disgusting and insanitary conditions. No household was equipped with a bathroom.

Mums and Dads were strict in the control of their children's manners and in the wearing of the 'Sunday Best.' Children were required to attend Sunday school in most families and take with them a half-penny for the collection, and their Star card. This was a small folded card which would be stamped by a star-shaped metal disc to leave the symbol signifying attendance. Woe betide he who failed to produce a stamped card when he arrived home.

The Sunday School Christmas treat was always awaited with joy. The entertainment of the Punch and Judy show, the gift of a toy and a bag filled with apples, nuts, oranges and sweets was one of the rare highlights of the year. The other was the Co-op treat at the local recreation ground when Mums and Aunties would be there to serve the sandwiches, buns and ginger beer. The kids, wearing their Sunday best, bearing a ticket of admission with their names printed on their blouses, would march in procession behind the local brass band to the festivities. There one was to see the never-forgotten spectacle of the Maypole dance, performed by small girls in pretty dresses, their hair decorated with flowers, and who danced, each bearing a long coloured silken ribbon to form intricate patterns on a tall decorated pole, to the rhythm of music.

If a child's parents could afford to spare six pence per week it provided for the Sunday School outing. This was in the form of a char-a-banc trip to the coast with sandwiches and apple lunch and tea with cakes.

These were the days of the traditional sepia-coloured family photographs, the 'musts' of pictures of babies for the family album and posterity. The days of bread and dripping and cabbage water, ('it's good for the complexion'), and brandy snaps and Fleed cakes and Saturday night baths in the galvanised household all-purpose two handled oval-shaped tub on the kitchen table. Each boy and girl awaited his or her turn to be bathed in the same water, which was given added warmth by the addition of hot water from the saucepan on the near-at-hand hob of the Kitchener fireplace-cum-cooker.

The saviours in supplying the mid-week money for essentials were the 'Uncles' - the pawnbrokers: the over-endowed gentlemen, for they displayed three balls - but nevertheless were god-sent to balance the economic budgets of many households. At their ever-receptive cubicle 'private offices,' the Mums would pawn their wedding rings and Dad's best suit on Monday mornings and redeem them on Friday evenings for a small interest payment. Should circumstances necessitate the pawning of blankets and sheets from the family beds, 'Uncle' would be generously helpful so long as they were free of fleas, bugs and other undesirables. Until these items were redeemed from the family budget, the nightly warmth of the bed was provided by the mysteriously ever-present great-coats of Armed Forces uniforms of the First World War which should rightly have been returned to the authorities at demob time. These heavy cloth items were ideal for allaying the fears of parents in the knowledge that their children would not be bereft of comfort and warmth. Mums would put the kids to bed with their small legs encased in the arms of the inverted coat, would wrap it around their little bodies and button it up.

These, too, were the days of the roistering preamble to General Election day when kids were encouraged by the simple inducement of a half-penny ice cream cornet to march behind a candidate and chant such ditties as:

4

Vote, Vote, Vote for Charlie Brown,
Kick old Conway out the door,
He's a nasty old man
And we'll kick him if we can,
And we'll vote for Charlie evermore.

At tea time on Sundays, lettuces and radishes would be pulled from the small rear garden to supplement the four-penny pint of winkles or shrimps. Saturday's special treat was a tuppenny piece of fish and a 'pen'orth' of chips shared among the kids.

Corporal punishment of the birch and cat-o'nine tails for those found guilty of physical assault did much to stem violence, and prison sentences of Penal Servitude with 'hard labour,' and 'hanging from the neck until you are dead,' if guilty of murder, resulted in half-empty prisons. No suspended prison sentences then; and public respect of the Police Force enabled policemen to execute their duties without interference by the self-appointed bodies purporting to understand the minds of criminals better than professional upholders of law and order. Elderly folk could walk the streets at night free from the fear of assault and robbery and there were no scenes of violence at football games. Nor was graffiti to be seen everywhere - the fear of the certainty of heavy prison sentences or the birch, or indeed both, saw to that.

When children played truant from school they were in constant fear of the school attendance officer lurking around the next corner of the street. The punishment for habitual truants was very often the sending of him to a reformatory school away from home and, unlike today, there was no 'little chat' by a highly-paid so-called expert on child psychology after which a kid is hoped to become a reformed character. Gilbert and Sullivan's 'Let the punishment fit the crime' was well observed.

Fred's father was a firm believer in this. He would grab his son's hair by the short tuft above his forehead and, with the words 'Bend over', remove his wide leather brass buckled belt and proceed to administer what he called 'Chastisement.' Fred would then be sent to bed to stay there until the following day with no food. When his father had gone to the pub his Mum would rub his bum with cold cream and urge him not to be a naughty boy again. And then, secretly, she would take him a basin filled with Oxo and cubes of bread soaked in it and tell her sobbing little boy not to tell his Dad and then kiss him goodnight. But, of course, his Dad did know and pretended not to.

These summary punishments were more beneficial to a child's future good behaviour than a dozen theoretical understanding little chats by people who had not been blessed with the gift of parenthood, and Fred's mother never forgot to forgive him with words of kindness and understanding.

All too many old folk were obliged to end their days in the workhouse. Should they be seen on the streets on the occasional days they were allowed out they were easily recognised by their drab, durable, standard-issue clothing. Many of these institutions boasted a Casual Ward to shelter one-night-only vagrants and the homeless, who were given a meal and a supervised bath. Many are now refurbished and have become hospitals bearing such names as St Stephen's, St James' etc. All of them had once been known as 'the spike.' They comprised a lunatic asylum and geriatric ward - the menial chores of cleaning, laundry, bed-making, cooking being done by the inmates. All maintenance, other than that requiring professional handling, was the duty of these inmates, and all those capable of working at the upkeep of these high-walled, sombre-grey and large institutions were set to work. Hence the name. Workhouse. Fred was to come to know this environment, and it was to leave an enduring impression upon his youthful mind.

The large-horned hand-wound gramophone was the popular medium of home entertainment and the playing of the fragile 78 rpm 'Winner' records was to be heard echoing from many houses. The 'Winners' - so called as the centre round label depicted a jockey passing the winning post holding aloft a gramophone record - was succeeded by the now familiar 'His Masters Voice,' the label of which is unchanged. 'Don't forget to change the needle.'

Amy Johnson and her husband, Jim Mollison, the history-making aviators, were household names, and the music halls and 'Cat's Whiskers' radio crystal sets, ('2LO Calling') gave the simple joys of life to the lower classes.

Classes. Great Britain was very class-conscious then, and the working class were led to believe that forelock-touching to the affluent was the right thing to do.

These were the days of A P F Chapman and Tich Freeman, Jack Buchanan ('Goodnight Vienna'), Horatio Bottomley and John Bull, Billy Bunter and *The Magnet*, *Everybody's Weekly*, *The Boy's Magazine*, with its outrageous stories of science fiction which have today been surpassed by fact, Richard Tauber ('You Are My Heart's Delight') and, many many years before Gene Kelly sang it, 'Singing in the Rain' was a popular song. The University Boat Race was always front page news on the *Star*, *Evening News* and the *Standard*, and days before the race - even in provincial towns and cities miles from the Thames - small celluloid dolls bedecked with light or dark blue ribbon were on sale to be worn on the great day.

Maddy was a girl who was, because of his love for her and hers for him, to become one of the four women to influence Fred's life. As a teenage girl she had become pregnant, but far from becoming an outcast with the stigma of unmarried parenthood, she had found the love and compassion of Fred's mother to help her over the stile of her despair; and to Fred, then a small boy, Maddy was more beloved than his sister. She would often take him to the penny bazaar - the very foundation of what was to become known internationally as Marks and Spencer - and to Woolworths (nothing over six-pence) for him to gaze upon the wonderful displays of articles.

The pleasant and undefinable smell of those stores Fred was, throughout his life, to associate with his beloved Maddy, as he did the feeling of his hand in hers.

The sense of values and respect for others may perhaps be measured in simple and small things. When a funeral cortège was passing, whether or not the coffin bore the remains of a familiar past person, it inspired the reverence of a halt of step and the raising of one's hat; but, sadly, not today.

To belong to a tennis club in those days of class distinction meant that one was of superior standing to a footballer; and at that time, to the uneducated, socialism was thought to be a high-class tea or cocktail party, or a sherry for important dignitaries, such as the mayor or the parson.

When Mum or Dad repaired the kids' boots and shoes on the three-cornered iron last, bought from Woolworths at the cost of a tanner, a great saving was made; for the cobblers, or 'snobs,' as they were known, were expensive, and repair material, such as leather, Blakey boot studs and such, were cheap. Fred's Mum always sealed the narrow gaps between new leather and the soles with heelball, and her finished job would last longer than that of the snobs.

For Mums and sisters the heart-throbs of the cinema were Rudolph Valentino, Ronald Coleman and Douglas Fairbanks Sr; and, for the Dads, it was Mary Pickford, Velma Banky and Ruth Chatterton. The kids looked forward to Saturday mornings when, for a penny admission, they would sit enthralled at the adventures of Tom Mix and Tony, his horse, and Flash Gordon or such serials as the Pony Express - 'To be continued in this theatre next week.'

Those predators on the gullibility of their fellow humans, the Salvation Army, were ever increasing in strength, and their pontificating assertions that they were God's true messengers, calculated to exploit the ignorance of unenlightened decent honest folk, was compelling. By the use of well chosen words and phrases they encouraged poor people to believe it was their bounden duty to God to throw ill-afforded coins into the many proffered tambourines and other collection receptacles. That vague but inherent sense that one feels one must always have in one's heart to help others is to the present day exploited by this fabulously rich organisation of Hot Gospellers.

It was during one of these many street collection operations that Fred was to receive his first insight into the un-Christian and unbenign behaviour which the exaggeratedly named 'Officers' of the purported Army of God were capable of showing. Pennies and half pennies were, to the urgent appeals of the senior salvationist, being thrown into the collection pot lying within the circle of the instrumentalists singing 'Lassies.' Some of the coins missed the target to roll into the gutter, whereupon the usual 'search party' was quick to retrieve the odd copper or so. Now Fred, his eyes ever alert for that rarely missed coin, bent down to pick up a halfpenny with the honest intention of throwing it into the collection pot. As he bent down he received a smart smack on the back of his head from a man wearing the uniform of the 'Army' who told him in most ungodly terms that 'kids are not wanted here and clear off.' Suffer little children to come unto me! Bewilderment, disenchantment, disillusion, disgust and, more importantly to his young mind, the disgrace of the inference of being publicly branded as a thief. Slowly he picked up his small frame from the pavement and then heard vulgar and expressive profanities emanate from a by-standing Royal Marine, who then matched his words with action by the process of pulling the peaked flat uniform hat over the brow of the ecclesiastical empyrean entozoan, spinning him around and kicking him with a well-polished boot in the backside. This act of chivalry attracted the attention of a nearby police officer who, having no doubt that justice had been fulfilled, turned his broad shoulders to the darkness of an adjacent alley and moved away from the scene of the crime.

Filled with humiliation and dejection, Fred slowly walked away from the crowded congregation, only to hear the sharp click, click of heavy boots behind him and to feel the gentle pressure of a large hand on his shoulder. He turned his face towards the massive frame of the Royal Marine who had dealt the summary punishment to the bully. He picked up Fred from the pavement and held him strongly but gently to his chest and said, 'Don't cry, Sonny. I know you were not trying to steal. I saw you throw all the money you found back into the pot; and just you wait and see, Jesus will punish him. Now be a good boy and stop crying.' He lowered Fred to the ground.

'I've got two little boys just like you at home and when they cry I put my hat on their heads and it makes them laugh - let's see if it works on you,' he said.

His uniform hat was similar in shape to that of present lower-deck naval ratings. On the black silken band bearing the gold-lettered name HMS So-and-So there was a brass badge depicting the globe encircled by a laurel wreath and the motto 'Per Mare Per Terram,' surmounted by a crown.

This gentle and compassionate man who, perhaps ironically, wore a uniform of similar colouring to the harsh salvationist, placed his hat on Fred's small head and with a flick of his fingers spun it as Fred would spin his whipping top. As it rotated on his closely cropped scalp he felt as if his head was being tickled. His tears, as if by magic, were turned to loud laughter; his despair of a few moments before forgotten.

His new-found friend picked him up and let him replace the hat to his head.

'What's your name, son?'

'My name's Fred.'

'Well, well, well, that's my name too, and I've got a boy with the same name at home, but he's in bed. And that's where you should be at this time of night. Where do you live?'

'Bryant Street,' said Fred.

'Oh! I know where that is. Come on, Cock, I'll take you home.'

He took the small hand into his own and made his way to

where the boy knew he was in for the belt for staying out late if his Dad was in. On the way they neared a fish and chip shop and the ever-appealing aroma pervaded Fred's nostrils. Bob Whitaker's fish saloon was the finest in the town and here one could sit and eat a 'tuppenny and pen'orth' from a china plate at the snow-white scrubbed tables upon which stood a large cruet of salt, pepper and vinegar. Fred felt a sudden tug on his arm and heard his guardian say, 'If you were my son and worried his Mum and me by staying out late, you would get a smacked bum and sent to bed with nothing to eat, so come in here with me.'

Young Fred had on many occasions been into the shop and bought a 'pen'orth' of chips and, wrapped in newspaper, he would stuff them down before he arrived home; and often he had gazed upon the plates of fish and chips passed over the high counter to be taken and devoured by customers at the, to him, luxurious table. But never had he had his vision fulfilled of being seated with knife and fork and filled plate. His hero told him to sit down, and in bewilderment Fred said, 'Where can I sit, Mr Fred?'

'Over there at that table,' he replied indicating a table in the corner. With a feeling of awe Fred slid his small buttocks on the edge of a chair and heard Mr Whitaker say, 'One and tuppence please,' and saw big Fred pass the payment over the counter.

The boy watched in wonderment as the big man approached him bearing a large plate in each hand covered with steaming fish and chips surmounted with white freshly-pickled onions. A threepenny and two-pen'orth of onions on each plate: never in all his childish fantasies did he imagine that such delight would befall him as, in a dream, he looked at the food before him and at the resplendent figure of the man, *his friend,* in the proud uniform of the men he had so often seen marching behind the pith helmeted bandsmen led by the magnificently-attired mace-bearing Drum Major on their way to Sunday morning church parade from the Royal Marines barracks. Fred would run from his church where he sang in the choir, jump on a tram and be just in time to see them swing out of the barrack gates.

'Well, come on Fred, sit up and eat your supper and don't leave any,' said big Fred interrupting his thoughts.

Fred needed no second bidding and with relish but with good manners did he quickly scoff all before him, and leaned his shoulders against the wooden wall behind him with that ecstatic feeling of satisfaction which comes after a 'blow-out' of a meal.

'It looks like you enjoyed that lot, Fred.'

'Not 'arf Mr Fred. Thank you very much,' said the boy. 'I ain't ever had any plate-load in here but I always wanted to. But my Mum and Dad ain't got the money for it. And my Mum said we would have if my Dad was not a lazy sod.'

'Hasn't he got a job, then?' said Fred senior.

'No, he ain't. But Mum takes in washing and ironing from the Wet Canteen at your barracks.'

Little Fred had the vision of his father lying in bed in his long-johns, smoking a 'Woodbine,' watching the smoke rising to the ceiling, when he would come home at dinner time at 12 noon and when his Mum would shout up the stairs, 'Come on Bob, the dinner's on the table; hurry up or the kids will be late getting back.'

'What's your full name and where do you live?' asked the Marine. Fred told him.

'Come on then, I'll take you home.'

'I'm gonna get a bashing from Dad.'

'And so you should, staying out like this.'

Taking the boy's hand, the Marine walked up the hill called Church Street, at the brow of which there was indeed a Norman church.

'I'm a choir boy in there,' said the boy, 'but I don't like it much - I want to join the Royal Marine cadets and be a Drummer Boy. Dad said I must do as I am told because he is a mate of our choirmaster and they get drunk in the Wheatsheaf.

'You shouldn't say such things about your father.'

'But it's true. And when he comes home he gets his belt off, and we all hide in the cellar.'

'Well it seems like you're in for some trouble when you get indoors,' said big Fred.

'Don't think he'll be there 'cos on Fridays he always gets drunk with Mr Pardy.'

'Who is Mr Pardy?'

'Our choirmaster.'

Big Fred was well acquainted with Mr Pardy with whom he often partook of the sustenance offered by the landlord of the Wheatsheaf, who had been christened with a similar name to the choirmaster. He then realised that this small boy was the son of that layabout he associated with himself on Friday nights and who was forever complaining about his non-apparent war wounds.

'Do you really sing in the choir, Fred?' he asked.

'Yes I do, and I have to sing alone, 'cos I'm what they call a boy soprano.'

'I'd like to hear you sing, Fred. Go on, sing. Let me hear you.'

'Nah! I can't sing in the street.'

'All right, then. The church garden gate's open, so go inside there and give me a tune. Go on.'

So saying, he gently pushed the boy into the churchyard, and watched him hide behind a large shrub.

'Go on, Fred. Let me hear you,' he called.

And then he heard the most beautiful sound of a boy's voice: *The Lord is my Shepherd, I shall not want. He leadeth me ...* 'The huge man's body shook with emotion, oblivious of the tears in his eyes, and of the passers-by who stood near him until the boy had finished his rendering.

He was brought back to his usually disciplined frame of mind by the ever inebriate-sounding tone of the voice of little Fred's choirmaster, Mr Charles Pardy, who was accompanied by the verger, Mr Bertie Pocksome - a most unfortunate surname for someone who sometimes had the unenviable duty of ensuring that the choirboys upheld the dignity of ecclesiastical practice, while not referring to him as 'Poxy Bert.' Mr Pocksome had once been the recipient, albeit not intended, of the charming chant:

> Amen, and so be it,
> Proxy Bert blew a fart
> but could not see it.
> But when he took a further look
> he found it in his prayer book.

'What's going on here?' he enquired in an authoritative manner, to nobody in particular. He then noticed a movement within the shadow of the shrub where Fred had hidden.

'Come out at once,' he called. 'I know who you are, you disgraceful boy,' he said with all the aplomb he could muster. 'And what do you think you are doing? Come out at once,' he said again.

Fred, in fear of the wrath of these gentlemen purporting to the upholders of Christendom, but knowing also that they were a pair of drunkards, made a rapid escape by the simple expedient of running in the opposite direction from them. He ran like the clappers from Hell, and disappeared over the rectory wall. Messrs Pardy and Pocksome became at once aware of mild applause at the escape of this vandal from consecrated ground. With dismay they sought the faces of the unbelievers who, to them, were those who failed to attend church, thereby failing to put a penny or two in the offertory box in order to maintain their existence as representatives of the Almighty.

'Hello, Charlie; Hello, Bert.'

It was to them the stentorian, familiar voice of big Fred.

The small gathering of people slowly dispersed toward the Wellington or the Wheatsheaf, to perhaps discuss between themselves whether or nay the vicar, the Reverend Vicar, was (and good luck to him if he was) continuing to bestow the divine-given gift of his hands upon the posterior of the devout Mrs Mulholland, whose dear husband left this troubled world, and left not only all his money to her, but the memory of his incapability of giving her a 'good seeing to,' and whether the Vicar had yet firmly re-established her faith in manhood.

'Little Sod, I'll box his bloody ears when he comes to choir on Sunday. I wonder what he was up to.'

'I didn't believe him when he told me he was a choir boy so I asked him to prove it,' said Big Fred, 'and that's exactly what he was doing, so go easy on him, Charlie.'

'Right then, I won't clout him, but if Bob's in the Wheatsheaf I'll tell him about it. That boy is a proper little bastard. He's always up to some bloody nonsense or other. I know it was him who stole my umbrella last week after I found it hanging on the altar with a notice on it: For sale, only two pence. And another time I caught him standing on a chair dropping newts in the font.'

'Why do you keep him in the choir, then?' asked big Fred.

'Only because he has the best voice we've ever had,' chipped in Bert.

'That's true enough,' said Charlie, 'but wait till his voice breaks and he loses his high pitch. I'll chuck him out then if he don't behave.'

'Well, come on, I'm dying of thirst,' said Bob. The trio sauntered toward the pub.

Going through big Fred's mind was the thought of the punishment that little Fred's father would no doubt mete upon the boy and a sense of guilt weighed within him.

'After all, it was my fault really,' he told himself.

'Charlie,' he said abruptly, 'please don't tell Bob about what's happened.'

He then recounted the circumstances of what had appeared to be another of the boy's escapades.

'All right, Fred, if you want that, then, I'll keep quiet, but I strongly advise you not to encourage him - the little bleeder don't need encouragement.'

They entered into the warmth of the Wheatsheaf, to be greeted by landlord, Charlie Baldock's, cheery 'Evenin, gents.'

The first figure for big Fred's eyes to fall on was Bob, the boy's father, standing at the bar in his usual place, and the thought struck him - 'I wonder if the kid's got home yet.' He quickly decided to go outside and look for him. Having excused himself to his drinking mates he stepped into the street. The first thing he saw was the lad's head peeping around the corner.

'Why haven't you gone home yet?' he asked.

'Is my Dad in the pub?'

'Yes he is, so off you go.'

'Thank you.'

The big Marine then noticed that the boy was minus one of his plimsoll slippers he had been wearing instead of shoes.

'Where's your other plimsoll, son?' he asked.

'It fell off when I jumped over the wall and it fell back in the churchyard.'

'Right, come with me and I'll find it for you. Come on.'

He took the boy's hand and led him back to the church and found the gate had been locked. This was no great obstacle for him and bidding the boy to stay where he was - 'And don't move 'til I get back' - he quickly climbed over the railings and was soon to return with the missing slipper.

'Get it on a bit sharpish and I'll take you home.'

'Thank you, Mr Fred. My Mum would have been worried 'cos I only got one good pair of shoes which I can only wear on Sundays. Mum always mends us kids' boots and shoes. Dad don't 'cos he says he gets backache.'

The huge man was filled with compassion for this well-mannered little soul, and the thought of his beer-swilling lazy father whose duty it was to put the needs of his children before his self-indulgence repulsed him.

They walked slowly along the cul-de-sac street and stopped outside a house, the door of which was ajar, and which was immediately opened by a woman uttering, 'Oh, thank God you're home. I've been so worried - where have you been?'

Picking him up, she kissed him.

'It's all right, Mum. Mr Fred's been looking after me.'

The woman turned her tear-moist face, and only then did she become aware of big Fred standing there.

'Oh,' she said, 'I beg your pardon. I didn't notice you.'

'That's all right, Mrs Higgins. He lost his shoe and I helped him to find it, but as it is rather late I thought I should see him safely home. My name's Fred Holbrook.'

'It's very kind of you to do this and I am very grateful, thank you so much,' she said.

By the light of the street lamp he looked into the face of this refined woman. He saw dignity. He saw faded beauty. He saw careworn eyes and suffering. And then she smiled. Transformation. She exuded a charm which was lost in the pitifully drab surroundings and yet, somehow, it seemed to Holbrook that the sun had suddenly appeared. She was a beautiful woman. How unjust is this life. He thought of her lazy husband and had pity for this extraordinary woman and reflected upon the comparison between her and his own wife, Betty. Betty was a hypochondriac and a constant source of anxiety to him - anxiety for the welfare of his young daughter, Madeline, and two sons, Freddie and Edgar. Betty was also of suicidal tendency.

Not a full day's leave passed without Holbrook travelling to Deal, his home town, to be with his family. Not that he missed his wife, for his long-suffering marriage was a disaster, and were it not for his widowed mother, now installed in his house, his children would have had to be moved to foster parents. Betty was a pathetic creature. Self-indulgent, lazy, permanently complaining of some imaginary medical condition and over-reacting. She was utterly selfish and self-opinionated, never stopped talking; she over-spent on clothing for herself and yet neighbours and unknowing folk thought she was a charming person. Holbrook also long suspected her of adulterous relationships with men, one of whom had been shipmate of his. He had long ceased to feel any deep emotion for her and sexual relations between them were of the past. But his children he loved and took care to let them know of his love. If only providence had given them a mother like Mrs Higgins, he thought to himself, and me a wife.

'Goodnight, Mrs Higgins,' he said, and walked slowly away to the Wheatsheaf.

He looked at the pub door and visualised Higgins standing at the bar inside and thought of the woman he didn't deserve as a wife and felt a sense of betrayal in contemplating the thought of being in the company of the bastard. 'Why should I feel this way?' he said to himself. 'I hardly know her.' But something had happened to Holbrook.

Something wonderful.

# CHAPTER 2

Rose Higgins had spent another day of drudgery. The bedside alarm clock awoke her at 6.30 am. She switched it off and lighted the candle, then lay back upon the pillow to steal a further few minutes in the warm bed. 'Goodness,' she thought, 'it's cold this morning. I'd better get up before I doze off.' Suddenly she became aware of Bob's hand creeping beneath her flannel nightgown. She knew better than to stop him. She didn't want another black eye. She'd had too many, and then there was always the embarrassment of explaining its cause to the children and neighbours. Rose was too proud a woman to admit she had married a lazy bully and pretended she didn't mind the almost annual state of pregnancy she found herself to be in.

Six children in eleven years and a suspected other one on the way, for she failed to see the signs of 'the curse' last month. Curse! God almighty! 'Curse?' To Rose it was a benediction. Twice she had been successful in using 'slippery elm', and once a miscarriage had saved her from another child, but the birth of a stillborn son, her first child, had grieved her deeply. She pretended to neighbours and friends that she had always wanted a large family, for her sense of dignity forbade her to admit she was a mere woman who had become the wife of a lustful, uncaring man. Not for her would be the stigma of an unsuccessful marriage. The very thought of her being the subject of ridicule and the topic of the ever-ready gossiping women of the street appalled her. Rose was not a snob nor a prude. Neither had she been raised in childhood and to womanhood in the same environment as she now found herself, but she resolutely held on to not becoming one of the women who knew, or purported to know, everyone's private domestic circumstances.

No. Rose had been brought up to respect the privacy of others, and although she was obliged to sometimes listen to gossip when shopping and bumping into neighbours (to her it was mannerly to listen and not to be rude) but none of what she heard was of interest to her. Also she had realised the necessity of choosing her words during the conversations, for she had seen the outcome of innocent observations made by participants of gossip, and then repeated to the subject of it out of context. The disgusting words used during the ensuing quarrels were intolerable to her.

She had met Bob during the First World War. He was a professional soldier and, after serving in India, had soon reached the rank of Sergeant-Major, as did many men later who found themselves promoted owing to the outbreak of war. They fell in love and, like hosts of couples during wartime, were soon married - many men never to return to see the children they had fathered.

Rose's father was the proprietor of an old-established laundry inherited from his father, and when she had left school Rose was employed in her father's office, but not before she had been taught the craft of laundry 'finishing.' This required expertise in the use of starch and gophering irons on the many lace items of female clothing, and the polishing of men's starched collars and shirt fronts and cuffs - an art she was, in later years, sadly, to be grateful for having learned.

Her father died suddenly. It was said he died of a heart attack but those nearest to him knew the cause of death was alcohol in which he tried to find solace after the death of his beloved wife, Mercy. The business suffered through his lack of control and after his death was taken over by his son, Jack, who had returned from the battlefields of France and Belgium where he had lost an arm. Rose bought the small house, in which she had taken two rooms just prior to her marriage, with the money her father had left her in his will.

What exciting days they were for her. She bought tasteful second-hand furniture, carpets, a piano and, wonder of wonders, a brand new forty-two stringed, mother-of-pearl inlaid zither. Her father had taught her to play the zither. He had been a gifted musician and had played piano and harmonium, concertina and harmonica. Also he had been an adept dancer, known to all as 'Lightfoot Hill.' She also bought the layette and cradle for the child she was carrying.

Bob had last been home on leave some months before and together they shared the happiness of the coming of their first-born. Would it be a girl? Would it be a boy? Names were chosen by the dozen. Neither of them spoke of their fears. The fears of all who were parted by the war. Parting was fear and not sweet sorrow.

Each time he had gone back to France he had given her a red rose which he had kissed, and she always placed one beneath the regimental cap badge on his helmet. On the train he would remove his helmet, kiss the rose and wave goodbye to her.

'God send you back to me, over the mighty sea, dearest. I love you so. God is above you. He knows how I love you. He will send you back to me.'

How many times had Rose played this prayer on her zither? 'Please God keep him safe.'

She was a God-fearing woman and since girlhood had attended Sunday school and church and now, with her husband away from home, she devoted her time to hospital and church voluntary activity. Everybody loved Rose. She was kind. She possessed her father's sense of humour and inherited his gift of music and dancing. In those days, before television and radio, the Music Hall was the venue of entertainment, the local being known as Barnards Palace of Variety,

21

purported to be the world's oldest. Rose never missed her weekly visit and her ability to memorise the words and music she heard enabled her to render it on zither, piano or harmonium to perfection. She was ever in demand to attend social gatherings but never did she lose her inbred sense of refinement and dignity. Wordlessly many had suffered the icy expression she would use in admonishing those guilty of vulgarity and bad manners.

Rose's baby was now almost due and at home every arrangement had been prepared. Hilda, her sister, was staying at her house with her and when the time came, quickly sped on her bicycle to summon the midwife. After many hours of pain a boy was born. He was dead. It was 5.30 am.

At midday a telegram arrived to advise Bob was missing, 'believed killed in action.' Poor Rose's world had fallen apart. Her many friends had gathered around her in sympathy. Hilda seldom left her side but Rose was inconsolable and when at last her emotions had subsided she seemed to be convinced Bob was not dead. 'Hilda,' she said, 'I know he's still alive.'

'Darling Rosie,' she replied, 'please don't torture yourself, and me too - we must help one another to be brave.'

Hilda's fiancé, Tom, had been killed in action during the first month of the war.

'But Hilda, I know, I know. I can feel he is still with me. He hasn't gone. I know.'

Three week's later a Captain of the Royal West Kent Regiment was standing at her door step.

'Mrs Higgins?' he enquired.

Rose nodded her head in affirmation.

'I am from your husband's battalion.'

'Please come in, sir.'

He was carrying a small brown paper parcel which he gave her saying, 'this belongs to your husband, and I thought perhaps you would take care of it.'

Rose slowly sat down in the large easy chair she had bought for her husband.

'This was Bob's chair,' she said quietly.

'Mrs Higgins, it still is Bob's chair.'

This huge man knelt beside her and shared her tears.

'It's all right, my dear, please don't mind me. Just thank God we still have him and I shall explain everything when you feel ready to listen.'

Hilda had been beside them and had heard what he had said. She moved into the kitchen to 'make a pot of tea,' she said, but only to empty her heart. 'Rosie, Rosie,' she murmured, 'I'm so happy for you, but where is my Tom?' She returned to the living room to hear the Captain say, '... now I had better introduce myself. I am Captain Cotter, but please call me Michael. Let me explain the circumstances of your husband's disappearance. We had been subjected to heavy attack, and after it had subsided we heard the cries of a man in obvious pain. Bob went to his aid in a shell hole, and was about to carry him back when the enemy guns opened up again. The attack was severe and many of us were killed and wounded. We were forced to take position further back the line and it had been assumed that Sergeant Major Higgins was among the dead. It was only last week at Base Hospital that we discovered him, for his clothing had been removed by the medics at Casualty Clearing station and somehow became mixed up with those of the dead.

'I'm sorry to have to tell you he received rather nasty shrapnel wounds to his back but, fortunately, his spinal column escaped injury and so he will be able to walk again. I have spoken with him, but I'm afraid at present he is suffering from shell-shock and he was unable to gather his senses sufficiently to hold a conversation. This is the reason for my bringing the contents of his clothing with me. The second reason is to tell you that he has now been shipped back to England and at present is in the Military Hospital at Aldershot.

'I know your christian name is Rose, for Bob often spoke of you in the trenches. You see, Bob and I served in India together and have known each other for many years and this is the reason why I sought permission from my Commanding Officer to be the person to break the good news to you. Rose, he is a very brave man and you can be proud of him; and also, although he does not yet realise it, he has been awarded the Distinguished Service Medal. The reason for this award is that not only did he save the lives of three men; he also machine-gunned twenty Germans.'

He paused, looked at the faces of the women and said, 'I should very much like to escort you to see him tomorrow, but I must warn you of the change you will see in him. This damned war has destroyed many of us. Destroyed us morally and spiritually, but please be thankful in that Bob's war in France is over for he is to be medically discharged. But what of the war in his mind? Only he can win or lose it. And so, Rose, you must help him to win.'

He left shortly after, with the promise of calling for them at 2 pm the next day and that he would arrange transport.

Rose and Hilda sat together in silent prayer for one knew the thoughts of the other, but it was Hilda who broke the silence.

'Come along, darling, we must open that bottle of port I brought you, now we have good reason to celebrate.'

Rose slowly got to her feet and began to sing, 'Let the great big world keep turning, for you have come back to me.' She cared not that the words were not in the order of the composer. She wanted to sing to the whole world. Her Bob had come back to her. God had sent him back to her. 'Dearest, I love you so.'

Rose had almost forgotten the parcel Captain Cotter had brought for her, and almost with reverence began to untie the string. On the crimson cloth of the table she slowly opened it. It contained her photographs. One in her wedding gown with Bob resplendent in uniform standing beside her and another studio picture of her which Bob had insisted she had taken for his wallet, inscribed with the words, 'For my soldier sweetheart from your English Rose.' In an envelope she found the remains of the roses she had placed under his cap badge with a note, 'There is one rose that will never fade in my heart.' In his small pocket diary he had written, 'Today is the day I may become a father - I hope my Rosie will be all right.'

He had a small gold necklace wrapped in tissue inside an envelope inscribed with the words 'For my baby.' His date for the birth was a week too early and Rose suddenly realised she would have to break the sad news about the birth to him. She found the letters she had sent him since their last meeting and made a mental note to put them in the mahogany box with the others she had sent him, the beautifully carved ornamental box he had brought back from India and which was kept on the bedroom mantelshelf. His gold watch given to him by her father was there but damaged, obviously by the explosion of whatever caused his wounds, as was the silver cigarette case she had given him for Christmas. 'Dear, dear, Bob, I love you so much.'

Hilda came into the room to find Rose in tears again but she knew they were the tears of happiness.

'Come on, love,' she said, 'we've got to get some things together. Tomorrow will soon be here. What should we take with us, do you think?'

'I can't begin to think of anything but I've just thought of a good idea.'

'What is it?'

'Let's have more of that port.'

'And why not?'

They were getting back to normal.

The following day Michael arrived in an Army car driven by a corporal. Its canvas roof had been folded back for the sun was shining. It was shining specially for Rose. She felt somewhat self-conscious as the driver saluted her as indeed had the Captain himself.

'Good afternoon, ladies,' he said and took the basket laden with items for Bob.

Soon they were on their way through the countryside. Rose

25

was on her way to see her Bob. She would soon make him well. She would make him well with all the love she would never cease to give him. All the doctors in creation were unable to give him what she knew he would thrive upon - her caring devotion to him, her understanding of his needs, her tolerance, her humour, her music, her laughter, herself. All those qualities which he had told her so often endeared her to him.

Alone she walked to his bedside. He was sleeping. She sat down beside him and tenderly kissed his hand. His eyes slowly opened and stared at her face in a fixed vacant strange manner.

'Hello, Bobby.'

He did not reply but continued to stare at her.

'Bobby, it's your Rosie.'

She heard him whisper her name over and over, but he showed no sign of recognition. She slightly raised her voice. 'Darling Bob, I'm here with you.' She kissed his face.

'Rosie, Rosie, where have you been? I couldn't find you, where have you been, my Rosie?'

'I've been searching for you Bobby, and now I have found you at last.'

She kissed his lips and felt his tears upon her face, her compassion for him stilled her tongue.

'But where have you been, Rose?'

'Darling, searching and searching for you, and now we have found each other we will never lose ourselves again.' His hand gently caressed her hair as he whispered, 'Rose, I can't remember anything at all but you. What has happened to me; where am I?'

'You have been wounded, darling, but soon you will be well again and at home with me.'

A shadow of a smile reached his pale features, his eyes seemed to concentrate on distant vague mystery, striving to piece together a jigsaw. His head was bandaged to cover his head wounds. Rose had heard from some of her acquaintances and friends of men who were permanently suffering from shell-shock and with loss of memory, of men totally mentally

26

disabled, men completely beyond medical aid and who would spend what was left of their lives in asylums for the insane. A silent prayer left her heart. 'God, thank you for letting him remember me.'

She became aware of Hilda and Michael at the bedside but Bob showed no sign of recognition of either, but held resolutely to Rose's hand. His mind seemed to tell him he had found the anchor which he must not weigh. He could not remember this man and woman, only Rose in an indefinable manner of affection. She was so important to him, he knew. She must not leave him, and with these thoughts he clasped her to him as a child to a mother.

Michael said softly, 'I'm afraid we must leave shortly as the ward sister has told me it is time to dress the wounds of the patients.'

Rose had resolved to stay in a rooming house nearby to be with him each day for as long as she was permitted. She prepared herself to go.

'Bob, we must leave you now, but I am going to find somewhere to stay in Aldershot and I will see you every day until we go home again.'

She kissed him and rose to leave.

'Rosie, Rosie, please don't leave me,' he sobbed. 'I shan't find you again. You mustn't go.'

He cried the tears of a child, and desperately clung to her.

'Darling Bob, I promise you we shall never lose each other again. And to prove it to you I have brought this.'

From the depths of her large handbag she drew a small box. It contained a single red rose and a picture of herself from his wallet and which she had put in a small silver frame.

'There you are, darling. Doesn't this prove to you that we shall always be together?'

Gently she passed the stem of the rose between the bandages on his forehead.

'Rose, I can remember the railway station.'

'Of course, you can remember the train you used to go away

on. But you've always come back to me, and now you have the rose again I shall come back to you. Remember we always said we must not cry but only smile as we waved to each other, so be a good boy and no tears please.'

She gently released his hand from her arm and kissed his head and walked from the bedside. At the door she turned and waved her hand. He waved back holding the rose to his lips and smiled, 'Bye bye, Rosie.'

'Bye bye, Bobby.'

He had come back to love her. 'Thank you, God.' Rose found Hilda and Michael seated on a bench in the corridor and told them of her intention of finding local sleeping accommodation, but Michael said that was not necessary as he had telephoned his parents who lived in a village a mile outside the town and who would be happy to have both ladies until Bob was fit enough for discharge.

'Michael, you are an officer, and surely your rank forbids you to fraternise with non-commissioned men.'

'Rose, the war has taught me many things, and one is this: when we face death every day there is no difference between us, and the simple lessons of life, to me, have been the most difficult to learn. Everybody who is incapable of learning are not worthy of contentment of mind. What I see in you and Bob is the aftermath of one of the constant storms of life - a rainbow - for were it not for the rain there would be no rainbows. Do not - please do not - offend my parents by not going to them because of wretched class distinction, for you will not find they are snobs, and they would almost disown me were I to become one. I am an only child and I realise the trauma of their concern for my safety and I love them as I did as a child. By the way, they met Bob one day when they came down to Dover to see me off to France, and have often spoken of the red rose in his cap. So you understand now, don't you, why they are anxious to meet the lady more beautiful than all the roses in the world, as Bob told them.'

The corporal driver stepped smartly from the awaiting car,

saluted and held the door open for them to enter. He was familiar with the route to Michael's home and needed no instructions. He pulled the car into the kerb outside a bungalow bearing the legend *Deldyfair,* which Michael explained was an anagram of his parents' christian names, Fred and Lydia. His parents were obviously watching out for them.

The front door opened as they alighted from the car and they were greeted warmly by a charming and beautiful woman and a silver-haired gentleman obviously much older than his wife. Rose could at once sense an air of tranquillity and devotion between them, a togetherness which exuded utter affection.

After introductions were over Michael and Hilda announced their intention of returning to Rose's home to collect clothing and other items required, but Michael's mother insisted that they must have tea before leaving.

'Let me show you to your room first and then we can settle down,' she said, and led them to a large bedroom containing a large four-poster bed, a marble wash, and two arm chairs.

'You'll be comfortable here and I'll light the fire for you a little later. If there is anything you need or anything we can do for you, please say so. Now come along and we'll have tea.'

'Mrs Cotter, I can't begin to thank you enough for your kindness, but thank you,' said Rose.

'Please call me Lydia and I shall call you both by your christian names,' she said. 'I'll show you around the house after tea.'

Michael and Hilda left, with strict instructions to be back in time for supper, leaving Rose, Lydia and Fred chattering small talk.

Rose studied Lydia and was struck by the beauty of her ever-sparkling brown eyes which were accentuated by her light hair. Her smile suggested the kindness of her inherent good nature. Although she was much younger than her husband it was refreshing to see the harmony between them and one could be forgiven for believing they were newly-weds. As

Lydia told her later, 'Freddie and I are true soulmates, and what a wonderful son we have produced between us.'

After the luxury of a night of deep slumber and pleasant dreams Rose was awakened by Lydia's knock on the door. Hilda slept on as always - she buzzed about the whole day long, and slept like a hibernating tortoise.

'Tea, my dears. And Freddie's starting to cook breakfast.'

'We never bother to bath until after we've eaten, but I've brought some hot water for you to have a quick wash.' Rose gave Hilda the usual shaking to rouse her and sipped her tea. Too hot, she thought, but nice. She got out of bed and poured hot water into the bowl on the marble washstand and washed her face. 'Hilda, hurry, get up, we are guests you know. Come along, get up,' she said.

Hilda slowly sat up.

'What's the time?'

'Eight o'clock.'

'It's far too early to get up.'

'You'd stay in bed all morning if you could.'

'You're right, I would.'

'Well, you can't. So drink your tea.'

Rose took the pins from her hair and began to brush it. Her crowning glory, Bob called it. Beautiful dark chestnut brown, it hung down well past her shoulders and as she brushed it to a luxuriant sheen her thoughts were in the bedroom of her home when Bob was on leave. She would sit on the side of the bed in the morning brushing her hair and he would pretend to be sleeping but watch her through half-closed eyes. When she was about to return the brush to the night table she would feel his arms encircle her waist and she would so willingly fall into his arms and be covered with kisses.

So deep in thought had she been, her imagination had produced a glow upon her cheeks which turned to a blush as she realised that Hilda, the very perceptive Hilda, had perhaps guessed what she was thinking. To confirm this Hilda said with a smile, 'Well, you won't have to wait much longer now, dear, will you?'

'Whatever do you mean, Hilda?'

'That expression I saw on your face couldn't mean anything else, but I understand!'

'Hilda, you are outrageous!'

'Be quiet, for goodness sake, and hurry! We mustn't be late for breakfast; it's rude.'

'Don't you think Michael is nice, Rose?'

'Oh, yes! He is really charming. And so kind in doing all he has for me,' she said.

'On the trip last night to collect our clothes, he told me lots about himself and his parents,' said Hilda. 'His father had been married before, apparently unhappily, but for the sake of holding his family together (he has a son and daughter he loves very much) he stuck it out with her until she died of cancer. The children had grown up and he had mistakenly thought they were unaware of his unhappiness.

'She developed cancer and only he had been told by the doctor that she had just eight months to live. He told nobody and nursed her to the end. Sadly it was during this time that she began to show the consideration for him that he so long wanted. It was only after she died that he discovered that his children had been aware for years of their mother's selfishness towards him. But, she had been a good mother to them and for that he was thankful.

'He met Lydia for the first time when he was on holiday with his daughter and fell in love with her at once but, it being his nature, kept it to himself, for he thought he had no chance of marrying her because of the age difference between them. Sometime later, when he was recovering from an illness they met again, and he found his love for her had grown. Still he was afraid to tell her for fear of her rejecting him.

'They found they had formed a companionship and promised to write to each other. Fred said, half jokingly, "Shall I write you love letters?" She replied that she had never received a love letter before and so he was able to pour out all his love for her. She loved his letters and all the love poetry he composed and sent her. Michael said she keeps them locked up. I'd love to read them Rose, wouldn't you?'

'Well, yes. Perhaps I would, but they must be very private and one should not pry.'

'Oh, I realise that, but you know what a romantic I am.'

The smells of breakfast pervading the air reminded them to hurry and they made their way towards its source to find Fred busy at the gas cooker.

'We always have breakfast in the kitchen. Sit wherever you wish,' he said, 'and don't leave anything or Lydia will tell you off.'

'Fred, you make me sound like a shrew,' said Lydia, suddenly appearing, 'I heard what you said.'

'Darling, you're not a shrew, only shrewd.'

'Dish up the food please, and less of your wit.'

'Certainly, Madam.'

This was typical of the happy aura which ruled this pleasant home and Rose envied them their relationship.

Michael joined them with: 'Good Morning! I've made arrangements with the hospital that Rose may visit Bob between 11 am and twelve noon; and from 6 pm to 8 pm each day. I also have had words with the senior doctor who tells me a very marked improvement has taken place in Bob's condition since your visit but, although his wounds are not severe, they may, psychologically, have a lasting effect. Only time, kindness, understanding and patience will help him. His advice is, to a certain extent, to treat him somewhat as one might treat a child, and allow him to find his own level of mind. It may take a long time, and perhaps not. At present it is impossible to tell, but the watchword is kindness.

'I shall give him all the kindness in the world and do everything I can,' said Rose.

'We all shall,' said Michael. 'Now I'm afraid we shall not have the luxury of a car for transport as I pulled a few strings in getting it yesterday, so it will have to be the bicycle or

Shanks's pony, but a mile is not far to walk. Sorry there's nothing else.'

'The walk will do no harm,' said Rose, 'and thank you again for all your kindness.'

'When your husband is feeling better I should like to meet him and, perhaps, we may find some way of bringing him here; we'll have to wait and see,' said Lydia.

'That would be lovely and I know he would want to thank you for everything you've done.'

'Does he like a drink?' asked Fred, 'because I firmly believe a drop of the right spirit is better than anything a doctor is likely to prescribe. Never doubt it - right Lydia?'

'Of course, dear. Whatever would life be without the bottle that cheers,' she replied. 'I should imagine absolutely ghastly.'

'You see, my wife and I agree on all the important things of life.'

'Especially that,' said Lydia.

After breakfast and washing up Rose and Hilda prepared for the walk to the hospital.

'It won't take you very long to get there,' Michael said. 'I suggest you should give yourselves half an hour prior to each visit and you'll be there comfortably.'

They stopped en route to buy flowers and cigarettes for Bob. Every street bustled with the presence of people in uniform: nurses dressed in starched hats and cloaks, the men in puttees and leather leggings, horse drawn army vehicles, motorised transport, ambulances bearing huge red crosses, men marching in columns with rifles slung over their shoulders, the tramp of heavy boots, men on crutches wearing the drop front trousers of service hospital blue, men in bandages, many bereft of an arm and, oddly, huge posters of a field-marshal pointing a finger above the words, 'Your Country Needs You,' as if those to whom he was pointing had time to spare.

Hilda insisted on waiting for a while in the corridor of Bob's ward allowing Rose to spend some time with him alone. Rose somewhat nervously went to him. His back was to her as she

entered. She wondered what he was doing as she could see
the movement of his arms. Cautiously she approached his bed
and then saw he was holding the now half-dead rose she had
left him and his other hand was clutching the framed photograph of her. Alternately he kissed one and then the other.

'Hello Bob,' she said.

He turned slowly toward her and smiled, his head tilted to
one side as if he was unsure of who his eyes beheld.

'Hello, my Rose,' he said. 'Please kiss me.'

She bent over him and kissed him warmly and tenderly and
felt his arms embrace her tightly as he did so long, long ago,
it seemed.

'You are much better today, darling,' she said.

'I believe I am beginning to remember things and then I
stop, but you are in everything.'

'You will start piecing things together soon, Bob, and if I
help you it will be easier for you. Tell me anything about what
you remember and perhaps I will know what it means to you.'

'Do you remember my sister, Hilda?' she asked.

'Er, no. I don't believe I do.'

'Well, dear, she came with me last night and came here to
see you and she is outside now. Shall I get her? It may help
you. I shan't be a moment. I'll go and get her.'

She hurriedly explained the position to her sister and returned with her, to see Bob intently watching.

'Hello, Bobbykins,' she said.

'Bobbykins' was her pet name for him which he always said
made him sound as if he were 'A bloody baby.'

He looked at her in vague concentration, and one could
imagine his mind trying to co-ordinate some distant spark of
memory with her face. His eyes suddenly brightened and he
coolly answered 'Hello, Hildegarde.'

'And you make me feel like a bloody German,' replied
Hilda, for that had been her stock reply to him.

The clouds were beginning to clear, and when the two left
him with the promise of returning later he was very slowly

34

emerging from the mist which dulled his shaken brain. During their visit later that day Michael joined them, whom he recognised at once. But he failed to comprehend the familiarity between them in the use of first names. To his disciplined military mind, to address a commissioned officer other than by 'sir' was a Court Martial offence for insubordination. The maladjustment of his mind had not yet allowed him to recall the occasional lapse of regulations during the heat and madness of battle. Albeit during their long association, overseas and home, the captain had, when out of earshot of others, called him Bob. He had never himself committed such an outrage of discipline, and to hear his own family doing so was strange, unbelievable, and, more importantly, wrong!

With love and perseverance, Rose slowly but surely cleared the fog from his stricken brain but she began to see a less gentle man emerging from the haze. He had somehow assumed a mantel of authority over her. In whatever he ordained, even in the most unimportant and smallest entity, he demanded his own way. His indulgence in Rose seemed to belong to the past, but her unwavering love and adoration of him sustained the conviction that, when he had fully recovered, he would become the caring and loving gentle Bob again.

His very mannerisms, verbal expressions and general demeanour were more in keeping with the barrack square, and she was to obey him for fear of incurring his wrath. She adhered to her task of rehabilitating him to his former self, placidly and with patience. His wounds had healed, and he would be returning home soon, medically discharged from the army.

His wounds had healed. Yes! But his mind? Back to the hated 'Bloody Civvy Street!' Thrown on to the pile of the 'army dodgers,' that mass of cowards who were lining their pockets with gold from the blood of his massacred mates. The bastards should be ordered to give the money to the widows and children of the men whose patriotism made it possible for them to become rich.

He was indoctrinated to a degree in his love of his country and the Army. Dogmatic in his belief that it was incomprehensible that the Government could tolerate and seemingly condone the barefaced fraudulence of 'the money-grabbing shit-bags in reserved occupations.' To attempt to reason with him would provoke obscenities and profanities Rose would never have associated with him before. This terrible war was destroying everything decent in life. 'Please God do not let it destroy the man I shall always love, no matter what you ordain.'

Rose and Hilda were unfailing in their twice-daily visits to him and wheeled him sometimes outside the hospital grounds to visit shops. It was during one such excursion that he demanded Rose buy a bottle of gin from a wine merchant's shop and which he took back to the ward with him. At their next visit they found the ward sister awaiting them in the corridor. She sternly advised them of hospital rules forbidding the taking of alcohol by patients. It appeared that Bob had shared the whole bottle of gin with his two immediate bed neighbours who had rejoiced in the singing of 'Colonel Bogey' and had scandalously and unmistakably made it plain that she was the object of their carousel. They had used the words of the barrack-room version of this resounding march and such behaviour was not to be tolerated. Apologising for his bad manners, Rose assured her it would not occur again, but inwardly rejoiced that Bob had not lost his infectious sense of humour, for this was reminiscent of his former self.

Having left the somewhat mollified lady they entered the ward.

'Good for them,' whispered Hilda. 'Bloody old dragon!'

Rose found that Hilda was less inclined to tolerate Bob's new image, and responded to his conversation in flippant style. If he was rude she would respond with rudeness and this resulted in his becoming less offensive, and very often she would be first in making rude remarks. This particular visit was one such an occasion.

After the usual greetings, she said to him, 'You bloody well let us down, didn't you?'

'What d'you mean?'

'You know damn well you weren't allowed to bring booze into the hospital, you crafty devil, and we've just been told off by that old cow of a head nurse because you got drunk and insulted her.'

For the first time since they had visited him he not only smiled broadly but laughed uproariously. Magic! When he at last controlled himself he said, 'Getting a 'blighty' has its compensations - she can't do sod all about it, for I'll soon be in Civvy Street. And you're right; she is an old cow!'

His whole manner was more pleasant when she conversed in his vernacular and Rose adapted herself to this mode of conversation, which he warmed to. But she was prudent in not over-pushing her luck. She found it largely successful.

It's an ill wind that blows etc ... for Rose had observed a relationship budding between Hilda and Michael, and on occasions the two of them had taken long walks together. It was obvious also to Fred and Lydia that their son had at last fallen in love. Michael had fortunately been posted from France to Aldershot and this was ideal for the peace of mind of his parents. This gave him the opportunity of living at home. He knew that he would later be transferred to Salisbury but that was not far away, and anywhere was better than the hell of France and Belgium; he had already been wounded on two occasions but, thank God, not seriously. Lydia had become fond of Hilda, as indeed she had of Rose, but Hilda had much the same sense of fun as did Lydia.

Since her meeting with Michael, Hilda's dead fiancé, Tom, had become a tender memory.

After it became clear that the engagement of Hilda and Michael was just a matter of time, Lydia and Hilda confided together on many feminine topics.

One afternoon, Rose had gone to visit Bob. Fred had gone for a haircut - what was left of it - and Michael was at the barracks, when Lydia said to Hilda, 'Come with me, I want to show you one of my treasures.'

In the drawing room she had brought a deed box and from a large envelope she extracted a sheet of paper.

'This is one of the many poems my Freddie wrote for me a long time ago, and I know he will always think of me in the same way. Please read it.'

Hilda was about to have her curiosity satisfied! It was entitled 'Loving My Lydia' and continued:

> Loving is living with beating heart,
> For she who fills ideals so tender
> Loving is sweetness and she is part
> Of my very breath, my soul and doth render
> Me to see in every scene her face.
> Her smile, her perfect brown eyes,
> Her darling lips and my heart doth race
> With thoughts and dreams, and in the skies
> I see no clouds but just the stars
> That in those eyes do gently sparkle
> For me to kiss and gaze in wonder.
> Loving is needing her warmth, her softness.
> Loving is pure in my desire for her.
> Loving is wanting her in precious abandon,
> To have and to hold forever.
> Loving is clean and bereft of lust.
> Loving is to kiss as the soft kiss of snow.
> Loving is the warmth of blood aglow,
> And loving is nearness of heart and mind.
> Loving is the mating of two souls and I did find
> My sweetheart, Lydia, to fill my soul

With love for her, and tho' apart
She is with me, she is here, she is real
For she *is* my heart.

It bore the message beneath, 'For my beloved Lydia' and was signed simply, 'Fred XO. England.'

Hilda was silent, deep in thought, and wanted to be loved as Fred loved Lydia and could not find her voice. She turned her face to see Lydia smiling and could understand the depth of devotion of the soulmates, as Michael had described his parents, and now was so sure he sincerely believed what he had told her.

'Thank you, Lydia. I shall always know now what deep love can be.'

Lydia carefully returned the poem to her box of treasures and said, 'Perhaps someday I may show you some more but, in the meantime, think on the words you have read and know you have seen the heart and soul of a very sincere man. Please believe me when I tell you he will ever mean those words. That is the meaning of love. Love my son as I love my husband and your love will be his strength and his love for you shall be your strength.'

Bob was discharged from hospital and, shortly after, discharged from military service on medical grounds.

Michael and Hilda were married six months later leaving Fred and Lydia to become a 'Darby and Joan' as they called themselves.

# CHAPTER 3

Bob found it difficult to settle down and adjust to the civilian way of life. He suffered severe headaches and depression and his lethargy was a constant source of concern to Rose.

His doctors told him that the headaches would decrease in time and his wounds should not overtax him. He was urged to find light employment, not only for psychological reasons, but more to the point, as far as Rose felt, for financial benefits. Her capital was slowly diminishing, a fact that she had delicately imparted. His disability pension, commensurate to his rank and length of service, was not sufficient to live on comfortably, despite the fact they owned the house and had no rent to find. His habit of drinking had increased, and with it money was wasted.

Rose began to worry. When would he pull himself together? When would he realise he was not on permanent leave? When would he start to consider her feelings? When, oh when, would it sink into his mind that she was eight months pregnant and begin to show a little care for her? She had been so tolerant with him, and her love was as deep as ever it had been, but she wanted to be loved. She wanted his affection.

When her baby was about to be born he suddenly began to return to his old caring self. When the time came to call the midwife he was beside himself with anxiety. She was an elderly lady known to all as 'Granny Litchfield.' She told him, 'Go to the Pub on the corner and stay there. I will come and get you

40

after the baby arrives, hop it!' Granny was the local street's gift to the community. It was she who washed and 'laid out' the dead, for many folk in those days died at home. The undertakers would arrive at the house with a coffin, and after measuring the deceased, place it on trestles in the parlour, carry the body downstairs and install it in the coffin. Should the body begin to putrefy prematurely, the coffin would be screwed lightly closed, not always successfully sealing off the odour of a rotting body. 'Chapels of Rest' were only for those with money to pay for them.

Granny was also the person who would pay house-to-house calls on neighbours to collect money for a communal floral tribute or, should a woman of poor financial means be widowed, a collection of cash to help her.

One of her self-appointed services was to help at childbirths. She would assist the midwife and launder soiled bed linen, help in general with domestic chores during a mother's confinement to bed (in those days a recommended ten days), and frequently would act as a midwife herself. And all these vital services for no monetary gain. Strangely, in every community of working class folk a 'Granny' was present. She was a confidante to all. She knew family affairs, and secrets, but to divulge them would, to her, be sacrilegious.

Rose had a very short period of labour and the birth was quick and easy for her. Her dread of a repetition of her first child proved to be unfounded and a beautiful baby daughter was born to her.

Granny Litchfield found Bob sitting alone in a corner of the saloon bar, deep in thought. Quietly she approached him and touched his arm.

'Mr Higgins, wake up and come and see your wife and daughter.'

He looked into her eyes and saw kindness and compassion and knew before he asked, 'Is Rose all right?'

'Of course she is. So is the baby. Now buy me a glass of stout and talk to me. There's a few things I have to say to you,' said Granny.

'Are you sure there's nothing wrong?'

'There's nothing wrong with your wife and baby, but there's a bloody lot wrong with you, and don't tell me to mind my own business.'

'What do you mean?' asked Bob.

'I'll tell you what I mean. I've known Rose since she was a child herself, in fact I've known her family for donkey's years. When you married Rose she was very happy and when you were reported missing her heart was broken and she spent her days and nights praying for you to come back to her. The way you have been treating her since, it might have been better for her had you not.

'Rose is a very sensitive and kind woman, and is not used to being treated like shit, and that's how you're treating her. And anyone can see it. She has looked after you better than you deserve. You're not the only man to come back from the war wounded, for Christ's sake! Start standing on your own feet again. You used to be a smart bloke and now look at you - a bloody lazy, boozy sod, and the talk of the neighbourhood!

'The first words Rose said when the baby came, and she knew it was alive - not like last time when it was dead and you were not with her - was, "Oh! Thank God. My Bob will be happy." Do you know, Mr. Higgins, I'm pretty hard-boiled, but I wanted to cry. Get yourself a light job and get your self-respect back and don't forget you have another mouth to feed. The midwife is going to wait until I get back, so buy me that glass of stout I asked for.'

Bob was grateful for an excuse to leave her to get her stout at the bar. During the course of his long army career - he was quite a bit older than Rose - he had been reprimanded by senior ranks occasionally, but never had he felt the humiliation from them as he did from the lashing from Granny's tongue he had just received. But Bob in his heart knew that she was right in what she said. He must smarten himself up. He looked down at his shoes. They needed to be cleaned. His creaseless trousers were a disgrace to him. He had not shaved for two days.

'I look what I am,' he thought, 'a lazy bastard.' And with this self-reproach he felt a sense of shame and resolved to improve himself.

He felt a sense of elation - 'I'm a father now! I must get home to Rose at once. Granny can drink her stout alone.' He took it to her, saying, 'Please excuse me, Granny, I'm going home.'

Granny leaned forward and said quietly, 'You had better dry your eyes and face before you see Rose.' Only then did he realise that he had been weeping.

'Thank you, Granny. I will try really hard to do what I know I must,' he said.

He walked quickly away and hurried to his front door. Inside he stood to listen to the cry of his daughter and her mother's soft crooning to comfort her. He heard the midwife approaching from the landing, bag in hand.

'Hello, Mr Higgins,' she said. 'Everything's fine. Nothing to worry about. And Granny will be back soon. She'll tell you what to do if anything wants doing after she goes home, and I'll come back to see your wife tomorrow morning. Good bye.' He closed the door behind her and timidly mounted the stairs.

He felt a sense of awe as he neared the half-opened door of the bedroom and, almost with reverence, slowly opened it to look inside. Rose was half lying back on the pillows with a bundle in the crook of her arm. She looked pale and wan, but when she became aware of him standing there, his unshaven face wet with tears, she smiled and said tenderly, 'Hello, my Bobby.'

He did not reply, but with bowed head went to her and sank upon his knees and buried his face on the bedcover, sobbing uncontrollably. With her free hand Rose stroked his hair and whispered, 'Please don't, Bobby. Today is a day to be happy and everything is fine, and we've got the girl you've always wanted.'

'Rose, I've been such a bastard to you, I don't deserve you and the baby,' he said.

'Nonsense, Bob! I know you have had a terrible experience and you are not yet fully recovered, but don't worry, darling, everything will soon be all right. Now, come on. Don't you want to see your little daughter?'

He slowly rose to his feet as she drew the shawl from the baby's face. Bob looked down at the tiny pink child and was filled with wonder and pride.

'Isn't she like you, Rose?'

'Do you think so?'

'Oh yes, very much.'

'But I can see you in her, too.'

She gently lifted the small bundle towards him.

'Go on, Bob, hold her.'

'I'm afraid to. No! I might hurt her.'

'Please let me see you hold her, dear. You're her Daddy.'

Very cautiously he took the baby from her into his awkward arms and smiled the smile that only a father, a proud father, can bestow.

'Shall we call her after you, Rose?'

'If we do we will probably get mixed up in the future.'

'Shall we call her Rosalina?'

'That's a pretty name, too. Yes. Rosalina. Nice name.'

And so Rosalina was christened.

During the next eight years Rosalina was followed by Fred, John, Bertie, with a couple of miscarriages between them, and then came Leslie and Michael and a near miss.

When sexual relations had resumed between them soon after Bob's discharge from hospital, gone was the gentleness and joy of hitherto. He became over-demanding, and Rose found herself less receptive to his advances; until after the birth of Rosalina when he, happily, reverted to his old affectionate self.

Bob found employment in the driving of motorised goods wagons and was proficient in the mechanics of them. Too, he

44

had resumed his pride in his personal appearance. He was a good father to his children and they idolised him. Rose worshipped him.

Granny Litchfield became almost one of the family, and when one day Bob sat with her alone, he said, 'Granny, I know I have you to thank for my happiness. Had you not brought me to my senses on the day Rosalina was born I think, when I look back, that I would have ended up in the gutter. But you saved me. You made me see what a bloody washout I had become, and I then realised what I was doing to Rose. I was destroying her.'

Granny looked into her glass of stout and said, 'Bob (she had long not used the "Mr Higgins" mode of address), you are right in only one respect in what you have just said. You were destroying Rose; but I simply reminded you on that day of something you knew in your heart was true, and you have been man enough to put it right. You pulled your own socks up and it's been worth it, so don't thank me. Just remember those days and I hope they never return.'

# CHAPTER 4

The war ended, and Great Britain was not, as many recognised, the 'Land fit for Heroes to Live in.' Political unrest rumbled, and strikes were beginning to occur. Oddly, the first strike took place before the war ended, and more strangely still, the men who struck were the very men whose responsibility it was to control political demonstrations. Even more strangely, the general public were behind them: the Police Force! They won the strike for (as the-then Prime Minister, Lloyd George, is later purported to have said) the country was very near to Bolshevism.

Smaller strikes had also occurred, and with the war not yet over, it was obvious that if these upheavals could occur during wartime in a country steeped in patriotism, even more violent demonstrations in the cause of industrial and economic betterment of the working classes would occur in peacetime.

The use of horses in the transportation of industrial and agricultural commodities was fast disappearing, and in their place motorised vehicles were growing in number. Motorcars were replacing other means of conveyance as individual transport.

Bob had toyed with the notion of embarking on business privately, and was saving what money he could afford towards the capital required, but with his family commitments it was a pitifully slow process. He knew he could borrow the amount required from his brother-in-law who had retired from the army with the rank of major, and who was now living in Hampshire, but his pride forbade him. So he resolved to find a partner with whom to open a motor-repair garage. This man would have to have as good a knowledge of motor mechanics as himself.

One day he confided his ambition to a colleague, like him a lorry driver, named Charlie Dunn. Charlie was well qualified in the workings of motor engines, and had been taught his trade in the army, having been a tank driver during the war.

Charlie was keen to join Bob in the venture and, more importantly, was able to scrape up his half of the capital. Bob had long before found the premises ideal for his purpose, should his ambition be realised: a long-disused blacksmith's forge. It had the very essential stone floor, vital to the use of the necessary heavy plant and vehicles in repair. And with a high ceiling and well-ventilated windows, huge doors and easy access to the road, no more amenities were required. Dilapidations were not serious and Bert Campbell, an old army mate now in private business as painter and decorator, offered to refurbish the place for a very low fee. Another mate promised to install the electricity system cheaply.

Bob and Charlie opened a small bank account and bought 'War Surplus' items of plant and tools and general impedimenta. They prepared to open for business.

Bert Campbell did a fine job. Not only did he paint the legend 'Higgins & Dunn' on the facade of the doors, he also inscribed the words, 'All Motor Repairs, Bicycles and Motor Bicycles Repaired, Wireless Accumulator Batteries Recharged, Punctures Repaired, Paraffin Sold.'

Came the great day of opening. Bert insisted on being the first customer, but payment was refused.

Business began to thrive, and within a month they were working at full tilt, and were beginning to build a reputation for good workmanship. Should customers demand their vehicles to be repaired quickly, they was told they would be ready only when they was properly repaired, and if that was not quickly enough to suit them they could take their business elsewhere. 'No shoddy repairs here,' they were told. This policy slowly paid off and soon their reputation was established.

It was the custom of Bob and Rose to take an evening out each week when Granny would attend to the children. As was usual, a visit to the music hall was most important to Rose. On the way home after the usual visit to a public house they would take home fish and chips for Rose and Granny, Bob taking home jellied eels from the 'Eel and Pie Shop.' Rose thought eels were ghastly!

It was during one such excursion that Bob decided to collect an outstanding account from a man who had asked him to call as he had been ill and unable to get to the garage.

After leaving the first house of the theatre they took a short tram ride, collected the money, and decided to have their usual few drinks in a nearby pub. They were somewhat shocked at the sight of Charlie Dunn at a secluded table deep in conversation and hand in hand with a lady whom Rose would describe as 'rather common looking.'

Being the diplomat that she was, and knowing Charlie to be married and the father of three children, and also knowing that his wife was six months pregnant, Rose quickly turned to the door with Bob following, leaving Charlie unaware that he had been 'caught out' in what was obviously an illicit friendship. 'Christ, the daft bastard!' said Bob. 'If he wants to do that sort of thing you'd think he would have enough common sense to take a bloody bus ride out of the way for a few miles.'

'I never did trust him with women,' said Rose.

'Why not?'

'Oh! I don't really know, really. It's just a feeling one gets about people,' she said.

Little did Bob realise that she had once slapped Charlie good and hard when he had crept up behind her, cupped her breasts in his hands and pressed his body hard against hers. She had threatened to inform Bob, and she would certainly have done so had he ever offended her again. However, such was the extent of her obvious sense of outrage that he had got the message, and after apologising, kept well away from her after that.

'Well, it's not our business what he gets up to as long as it doesn't affect the garage,' said Bob.

'I suppose not,' said Rose, 'until somebody comes looking for him and then it *will* affect the garage.'

'Well, I'll not let him know we saw him,' he said.

'Perhaps you should. It won't do business any good if you have trouble there, and that woman looked very much like an "old tom,"' said Rose.

They boarded a tram and alighted to visit their usual pub, and no more was said about 'Dirty Dunn, he's Dunn 'em all,' for this was the reputation Charlie had, of which Bob was well aware. What perturbed Bob was that Rose had been correct in her assessment of Charlie's companion. She was an 'old Tom' and frequently seen to emerge from the local 'bag shop' with a half-drunken male companion to disappear with him in the direction of the park. This park, during the hours of darkness, was the haunt of ladies prepared to endow 'short times,' 'quick flips' and other sought-after services at varying monetary rates. Charlie had, he saw, been hand in hand with this prostitute and prostitutes cost money. And money, not a lot, had been disappearing from the till in the garage. When Bob had mentioned this to Charlie he had at once said it must be George, the young lad they employed as a learner, and so he was fired for 'twice in one week arriving late for work.' The shortages had ceased since then, until recently, but Bob was convinced that the new boy was honest. He had purposely placed a marked one pound note on the rear seat of a car, in for repair. The mark was a minute dot and almost indiscernible, and Bob put the boy to work on cleaning off oily fingerprints on the bodywork after repairs were completed. The boy did not open the car door but called Bob who had deliberately disappeared into the office.

'Mr Higgins, there's some money in this car,' he said. Bob gave him half a crown for his honesty.

Bob decided to have a word with Charlie who had lately also been less industrious at work.

'I know you're very fond of hole, Charlie,' he said, 'but can't you find anyone better than 'Gappy Lil' to sit in a pub and hold hands with?'

Gappy Lil was so called as she lacked a front tooth, allegedly lost in an accident at home, which may or may not have been true. But her loss of tooth had been observed by the neighbour who had assisted her to her feet after her mother had thrown her from the front door to the charming accompaniment of, 'piss off and don't come back, you dirty little whore.' This fond farewell was followed by a bag containing clothing. A bag for a bag, one may observe.

'Who's been talking to you, then?'

'I saw, myself.'

'She may be able to put us in touch with somebody to our mutual advantage,' said Charlie.

'I want nothing to do with any of the type she mixes with and you're a bloody fool to expect me to. What's wrong with you? You must be barmy. She can only bring trouble so whatever you have in mind, forget it as far as I'm concerned,' said Bob.

Charlie was unabashed.

'She knows a bloke in charge of transport at the Motor Works and he can let us have all the stuff we need for next to nothing,' he said.

'I don't give a monkey's what he can let us have. I want nothing to do with it,' said Bob.

Charlie began to show annoyance and said, 'Look here, I got half share in this place and I've got a say in what goes on. Don't come the bloody sergeant major with me. You're not still in the army.'

This was the first disagreement of their partnership, but unpleasant though it was, Bob's intuition told him it would not be the last, although he resolutely adhered to not condoning doing business with any friend of Gappy Lil. The matter was dropped and business carried on, outwardly harmoniously; but an undercurrent of disunity existed.

Bob told Rose what had happened. They discussed the possibility of buying Charlie's share of the business.

'I'm sure Michael would lend us enough to do so,' she said, but Bob demurred, saying that he had already sounded Charlie out to no account. And so the state of affairs continued.

Charlie left the garage when and as often as he pleased, sometimes saying he was on his way to the wholesale suppliers and returning with spare parts paid for in cash and producing the appropriate receipted bill of sale, printed on the official billhead paper of the regular suppliers. Often he gave no indication of his destination but Bob suspected it was either Gappy Lil or some other feminine attraction.

Bob wondered how long this unsavoury atmosphere would persist. It was reflected in a decline in business which was, he knew, partly due to national economic conditions. But had Charlie pulled his weight, things would not have been as bad as they were.

His headaches were beginning to return and with them the irritability of his pre-Rosalina trauma. Rose saw it coming and with it her hatred of Charlie Dunn heightened daily, for he was destroying her beloved Bob. Her frustration was reflected in her manner toward the children. She found herself raising her voice to them; her normal patience was quick to snap; she slapped them at the slightest provocation and slept fitfully.

One evening she heard a loud knocking at the door and opened it to find two policemen standing in the porch.

'Good evening, madam,' said the one bearing the stripes of a sergeant.

'Good evening,' replied Rose, who instinctively knew their visit was of impending disaster.

'Does Robert William Higgins live here, please?'

The use of Bob's full name brought terror to her heart.

51

Not 'Mister,' but Robert William Higgins!

'Yes,' she faltered.

'Are you his wife?'

'Yes.'

'Is he at home?'

'Yes. Won't you please come inside?'

Bob was asleep in his special chair at the fireside, the kids in their night clothes playing at the table. The sergeant said quietly, 'You'd best get the children out of the way.' Bob slept on.

Rose could hardly trust herself to speak, and by signing to the children in touching her lips to indicate silence, pointed to the ceiling.

'Go to bed,' she whispered.

They looked in awe at the uniformed men and did as they were bidden.

She gently touched Bob's arm. He awoke at once. 'I dropped off, dear, what's the ...?'

He stared questioningly at the policemen and looked at Rose and saw her ashen face.

'What's wrong?' he asked, and rose to his feet to put his arm around her shoulder.

'Mr Higgins, I want you to come with us to your garage. We wish to search it, and we have a search warrant to do so,' said the sergeant.

'Whatever for? What are you looking for?' Bob asked.

'We have reason to believe you have stolen property on your premises, property belonging to Jasper Motor Works.'

'That bastard, Charlie Dunn. I'll kill him!'

'Oh! Then you know of why we are here?'

'He told me of stuff going cheaply, but I forbade him to bring any to the garage, the fool.'

'Why did you not report it to us?'

'Sergeant, he's my partner - more's the pity!'

'Any person involved in the theft is an accessory.'

'Not me. I told him I wanted nothing to do with anything

52

to do with stealing.'

'That's as maybe,' the sergeant said. 'But get your coat on and bring your garage keys with you.'

He indicated towards the door with his arm.

Bob kissed Rose and told her not to worry and that he would be back soon. They left the house.

Rose hurriedly attended to the children and went in search of Granny Litchfield. At the garage doors two more policemen were on guard as Bob opened the small wicket gate inset in the main doors and switched on the lights. The sergeant summoned the officers on guard to come inside and he closed the door behind them.

'I want you to stand here and not move,' said the sergeant, and nodded to one of his men to see his instructions were adhered to. Systematically the others searched the place. Every drawer and cupboard was examined.

'Here we are,' said one man, and pointed to the contents of a parcel he had opened. It contained the spare parts Charlie had purchased from the suppliers two days before. Bob breathed a sigh of relief. 'Is that all you were looking for?' he asked. 'That's not stolen - I've got the receipt for it.'

'Where is it?,' asked the sergeant.

Bob made as if he were about to walk to the office but was told to stand where he was.

'Tell me where to look for it, and *I'll* get it.'

'On the hook bill-file hanging on the wall.'

Sure enough it was there, but the sergeant impounded the whole file and, after taking charge of the spare parts, bade Bob to the door and after switching off the lights, locked it.

'Stay guard on the door, Jones, until you're relieved,' he said, and to Bob: 'You must come with me to the police station, Higgins.'

Bob had lost the title of 'Mister.' Slowly he was walked to the police station, escorted by two policemen who, unnecessarily to his mind, each held an arm. He was told to empty his pockets, and he was thoroughly searched. In a small room he was told to sit down at a table where several receipts from his supplier and the open parcel of spare parts were displayed.

'My name is Inspector Brown, and I want you to answer my questions truthfully,' said the man at the table.

'Yes, I will.'

'My sergeant tells me you said you paid for these goods; but I know it is a lie.'

'Well,' said Bob, 'they were paid for by my partner, is what I really meant.'

'And this is the bill of sale for these items?'

Bob took the paper from his hand and checked the spare parts with the list on the receipt bearing the name and address of the supplier.

'Yes,' he said. 'It's all in order.'

The inspector looked pensively at him and said, 'How long have you been receiving stolen goods - a month, two months, or much longer?'

'I have never knowingly received stolen goods from anybody and, as regards these items, surely the receipt proves they were paid for.'

The inspector pointed to the remaining bill heads and said, 'They don't prove payment at all, for if you look at the top right hand corner you will see a serial number. These pieces of paper were removed from the duplicate book of which the copy sheets are blank.'

To prove the point he produced the bill book, the corresponding numbered pages of which were blank.

'You may as well know that your partner has been arrested and charged with receiving stolen property and was caught in circumstances which he cannot defend. He has signed a statement involving yourself and he swears you were in full accord with what he called a "little fiddle." Also I will tell you the man responsible for removing the blank pages is an assistant, or I should say *was*, as he has now been sacked and is also under arrest. The transport foreman at Jaspers has confessed he has been stealing and supplying goods to you and your partner as well as four others, and all have confessed and are under arrest. You are the only man not to own up. You are involved in this conspiracy up to your neck and you will be wise to do admit it.'

Bob was in despair. He could only deny these accusations, and pleaded with the inspector to believe him. He told him of the situation at the garage - of the theft of money from the till, of Charlie's attempt to shift the blame onto the boy and finally of Charlie's original contact of the foreman via Gappy Lil. The inspector inwardly believed Bob's story, but six men had signed statements involving him equally as themselves. He had observed that none of them had mentioned Gappy Lil but they were all married and were perhaps more in fear of the wrath of their wives than of the law. He would question her and see what happened.

Bob was charged with receiving, and signed a statement dissociating himself from those whom, he said, he had never knowingly met, Charlie being the only person arrested whom he knew. Nevertheless, he was installed in a cell and told that his wife would be informed.

He stared transfixed at the limed walls caging him. His head throbbing, he thought of Rose and the kiddies and started to cry. His world was falling apart. He was unable to control his emotion and wept as an abandoned child. Then he heard the door open to see a man in civilian clothes with a man in uniform holding a large bunch of keys, gazing at him contemptuously.

'Sorry you've been caught, eh, Higgins?' asked the plain-clothes man.

Tears streaming down his face, he turned away ashamed, but filled with hatred for his interrogator.

'I'm speaking to you Higgins, answer me,' he said.

Bob could hardly raise his throbbing head but replied, 'I haven't done anything wrong.'

'Ah! That's what they all say.'

'But I haven't.'

'Bloody liar! Why don't you own up and stop snivelling like one of your bleeding kids?'

The mention of his children in such a derogatory manner inflamed his rising rage. Bob was a powerfully built man who, through his many years in the army, and the fitness required of his rank, coupled with the strength needed for mechanical repairs, was no weakling. He feared no man.

'Shut your big mouth before I take your head off,' he said and rose to his feet.

'Threatening me, are we?'

Addressing the uniformed officer, Bob asked, 'Who is this bastard?'

'Detective Sergeant Jackson.'

'I don't give a sod who he is. He'd better not refer to my family like that again.'

Jackson, no doubt, would never have dared address Bob in that manner, had he not had the policeman as back-up.

'I'll talk to you any way I choose to, you bloody crook,' he said. 'And if I say you were snivelling like one of your bleeding kids, then you were.'

Bob stepped quickly forward and grabbed Jackson by his lapel, simultaneously delivering a heavy blow to his face which he followed by a series more severe to his body. Such was the surprise and speed of Bob's action that Jackson's companion had no opportunity of preventing the thrashing, and by the time he had gathered his wits, Jackson was a bleeding hulk on the cell floor. Bob said, 'He asked for that, but don't worry, I won't be any more trouble,' and sat on the hard bunk.

The policeman called for assistance and they were joined by the inspector.

'Jesus Christ! What happened?' he said, looking down at the unconscious Jackson.

'Higgins did it.'

'I know that, but why?'

'Jackson backed a loser this time, sir, and got what he asked for,' nodding towards Bob, who sat, his head buried in his

56

hand. 'He was too quick to stop, sir.'

The inspector knew of Jackson's habit of provoking the tempers of prisoners and felt no pity for him. He also strongly, but privately, felt like shaking the hands which dealt the justice he could not outwardly condone. This miserable pile of rubbish on the floor, to him, was a joy to behold, but it was hard luck on Higgins whom he firmly believed innocent of the charges against him. Too, he had made his mind up to personally dig deep into this case, and his first interview would be of Gappy Lil. He felt genuinely sorry for Higgins, for he knew he would have to charge him with 'assault and battery' on a police officer which, he knew, if proved, would mean a prison sentence. Poor bastard! He well knew of the unpopularity of Jackson among his colleagues and decided to try a little subterfuge to perhaps help Higgins, and at the same time not becoming involved noticeably.

'Constable,' he said, looking squarely into his eyes and winking his eye very briefly. 'Constable, did Sgt Jackson provoke the prisoner by using his usual practice of pushing at him very roughly?'

The constable got the message, for he too was grateful to Higgins, and felt the same compassion for him as did the inspector. Returning the slight wink he said, 'Yes, sir, several times. He also insulted his children and used obscene language.' Speaking in Bob's direction, he said, 'Is that correct what I've told the Inspector, Higgins?' Bob too, despite his throbbing head, had got the message and replied, 'Yes, the cocksure pig! He shouldn't be a policeman. He should be chucked out and made to work in a dog-house.'

Jackson was slowly regaining consciousness and moaning in pain.

'Get some help and a stretcher and get the surgeon here,' said the inspector.

The constable returned accompanied by a sergeant, who grinned widely.

'I hope his injuries are not too serious,' he said in a sarcastic tone.

Blandly the inspector said, 'Yes, sergeant! I'm quite sure everyone will agree with you,' and left the moaning Jackson to the capable and heavy hands of his sorrowful fellow officers. Later the sergeant returned bearing a large mug of strong steaming tea and a statement form.

'Higgins, drink this. You need it mate. I've just spoken to your missus and told her not to worry too much,' he said.

'May I see her, please?'

'Sorry, old son, not tonight. I've got to charge you for what you did to that bastard, but if it's any consolation to you, we're more sorry for you than for him. But that's between you and me, so don't repeat what I've said. I think the boss is on your side too, but he hasn't said so. I've only told you this to cheer you up, so keep it to yourself.'

Having taken Bob's statement of what had occurred in the cell, 'according to the Book of Solomon,' as he had said, he asked if Bob wanted something to eat. Bob thanked him but said he didn't feel like eating.

'Higgins, I am going to bring you a sandwich and I want you to eat it. Your missus is worried about you and I promised to look after you and if you don't eat you'll feel worse than you already do. So take my advice. I've seen hundreds of men like you locked up for a time. And I appreciate what's going on in their minds. Few of them want to eat, but those who do always feel at least a little better. Your body needs it.'

Bob's frustration and genuine sense of injured innocence, his throbbing head and concern for Rose, and the kiddies overwhelmed his whole being. He was no weakling, just a tender hearted husband and father entangled in the web of Fate's machinations. He had recovered from his physical wounds of war, but his mind had been shattered.

He had fought so hard to adjust himself so as to be worthy of the priceless affections of those he loved, but he knew he would not win the battle of his will to regain what he had left behind in No Man's Land. Fleeting and vivid visions came to his memory of foreign men's terror-stricken faces beneath their pot-like helmets and heard the screams of dying men. Men he was killing. They told him there were twenty. Twenty men who, but for him, might have gone home to have their dearest ones place a rose on their caps. For murdering twenty men they called him a hero and gave him a circular piece of metal to prove it!

The sounds and flashes of exploding shells, the crack of rifles, the chattering of machine guns and the cries of men maddened in fear of death, throbbed through his pulsating head as he collapsed on the hard cell bunk in tears. He had always known Rose had been aware of his unspoken war. She knew of his endeavour to win. She loved him. Without her he was worthless. She kept the spark of hope alive in him to win. And yet he knew that some day he would fail her. He could end it all, but could not bear to be the reason for the misery he knew Rose would suffer without him. 'But I'm not worthy of her,' he told himself. 'My beautiful English Rose. I love her so much.'

He felt the sergeant's hand shaking his shoulder.

'Cheer up, Higgins,' he said. 'Drink this cocoa and eat these.' He had brought a tin plate bearing corned beef sandwiches and a large enamel mug.

'Is your head troubling you?'

'How do you know?'

'Your missus told me and why.'

'I'm sorry I'm such a baby.'

'No you're not, mate.'

'Thank you'.

'Come on, have some of this and you'll feel better. I'll stay here with you for a while as I'm here all night.

'Bob appreciated the kindness of this man and found himself nibbling at the sandwiches.

'What's the time, please,' he asked.

'Half past one. I know you don't feel like sleeping but you must. Put this in your mouth and swallow it. I scrounged it from the surgeon. It's a sleeping pill.'

'Thank you, but I never take those things.'

'Put it in your gob and swallow, please. I promised your missus I'd take care of you, so don't let me down, and when I can see you've eaten that grub I'll leave you to it. Take your time. The boss knows where I am, and it's all right with him.'

The wisdom of the sergeant's insistence in sustaining his bodily needs was slowly bearing its reward at his realisation of a lessening of the turmoil within his mind.

'You'll be able to see your missus tomorrow after you've appeared in court, but I can't give you any hope of going home. You'll probably be remanded in custody for a week and I hope for your sake, not for his, for he's had it coming to him long enough, that Jackson is not too bad. He's been detained in hospital with a broken jaw, broken ribs and severe concussion.'

Bob was feeling the effect of the drug. He well knew when he'd hit that bastard that he had murder in his mind. 'Well,' he thought drowsily, 'I won't be charged with that.'

'Where will I be taken?,' he asked.

'To a remand clink. Probably Canterbury. I shan't be here in the morning, but the boss will: to give evidence about yourself on the assault charge and also the receiving one. All the others will be in court with you, but try to keep yourself to yourself. Don't show any signs to the court people of any regard for Charles Dunn except contempt. Now, when I go off duty I'm going to see your wife so tell me what you want her to bring in when she comes. You will be allowed to wear your own clothing while in detention until your case is completed and you don't have to eat the prison grub. So I'll mention it to your missus. It might help to let her know what to expect rather than having the shock of it. Also I'd better tell you that the constable who was in the cell when you clouted Jackson 'in self defence' will be in court too.'

'What will he say about me?' asked Bob.

'You heard what he said last night, and that's what's on the statement he's made and signed. Now, take some of your clobber off and get some sleep. You look knackered. Good night.'

Bob felt knackered, and the sleeping pill dulled him to sleep within minutes.

He awoke to hear a voice saying, 'Higgins, wake up!'

He opened his eyes and wondered where he was.

'Christ! A nightmare,' he thought, but gradually oriented himself to his surroundings.

'I thought you were bloody dead. I been shouting at you for long enough. Here's some tea. I'll be back in five minutes to take you for ablutions if you want to. It's now seven o'clock.'

'When can my wife see me?'

'After you've been in court.'

He was a constable Bob had often seen walking his beat outside the garage and who had always addressed him as 'Mister' - but not today. He was beginning to feel like an outcast, a bloody criminal!

His head started to throb again, and with it came the mental torment he had fought against for so long.

'God help me, God help Rose, God help my dear babies! Is there a God? If there is, why is this happening to us?'

He heard the key in the lock as the cell door opened.

'Come on, Higgins,' he was ordered, and was shown the ablutions for prisoners.

'Have you used the cell jerry?'

'No.'

'Right, get on and get yourself washed.'

'I need a shave.'

'I can see that, but it isn't allowed. Don't take too long. The rest of the prisoners have to get done. The night duty sergeant left orders for you to go first. You must be in favour. The place usually smells like a shithouse, as well as being a shithouse after some have finished.'

He moved near to Bob and whispered, 'I'm sorry if I seem nasty, Mr Higgins, but those other sods in the cells can hear me and we are not allowed to show favouritism. Got me?' Bob nodded.

'Thanks, Mr Streeter' - his name.

In a loud voice he said, 'For Christ's sake get a bleeding move on, Higgins. I ain't got all sodding morning to waste poncing about with you lot,' winking an eye.

He led Bob back to his cell, slammed the door behind him with more force than necessary and shouted, 'Right, you next, Dunn, and get a move on. So sorry you can't have Gappy Lil here to give you a wank this morning 'cos she's in bed with your brother,' goading him.

Bob was sure Streeter was enjoying his chance of revenge as Charlie Dunn, who - before he had gone into the partnership and when lorry driving - had once dropped him in the mire by not warning him, when he could easily have done so, of the approach of his sergeant whilst he was having a buckshee pint of bitter at the back door of a pub.

He heard the voice of Streeter again. 'Oh, I'm afraid I forgot, Dunn, you'll have to wait 'til last. By the time the others are done the karsy will be smelling beautiful for you and will remind you of your sweet Gappy Lil. Jones next!' Streeter was having a ball!

This interlude had the effect of stimulating Bob's spirits, and when they were called to be taken to the upstairs courtroom his head had ceased to throb. He saw Rose sitting in the small public gallery alone. Poor Rose, a pathetic dear soul. His lifeline. His saviour. His soulmate. How he loved and worshipped that wonderful woman to whom he had brought only grief. And standing in the dock beside him, these men who were responsible for her presence. Men not worthy of walking in her shadow. His bitterness was to be seen in his eyes. Rose knew the hell he was suffering, realising the danger of his impending collapse of composure. She drew her fingers to her lips beseeching him to retain his dignity. Bob saw her sign and brought his mind back to what was asked of him.

'How do you plead?'

He did not hear the clerk of the court, so enraged was he with the men responsible for his plight.

'Not guilty.'

In turn, each and all of his so-called conspirators pleaded guilty and were sentenced to six months prison with hard labour. Charlie Dunn had broken down, his cries from below to be heard in the courtroom. 'Serves you right, you bastard,' thought Bob. Normally a compassionate man, he would have applauded a sentence of six years.

He was now alone in the dock in readiness to attempt to verbally defend himself, but Inspector Brown asked for a remand for seven days in order that he could, 'complete my inquiries, sir.' This was granted, and the further charge of assault to which Bob pleaded, 'Guilty, but in self-defence, sir,' was - again at the request of the inspector - remanded for one week. Bob was escorted to a small room, an official in attendance.

'Sit down, Mr Higgins,' he said civilly.

Bob wondered at the welcome restoration of his title. He was 'Mister' once more.

Inspector Brown came into the room, dismissed the guard, sat down and said, 'Mr Higgins, I've got a present for you. Read this.'

He pushed a sheet of paper toward him and Bob at once recognised it as a statement form. At the bottom he saw the familiar signature of Charlie Dunn. Charlie had retracted his avowal of Bob's participation in the thefts and had admitted Bob's condemnation of them.

'I went to work on him after the station gaoler had given him a taste of what to expect as treatment in clink. I told him I knew, or rather suspected him of lying, and reminded him of the possibility of my asking for a remand for further inquiries. I pointed out that the magistrate was empowered to impose a sentence of six months maximum, but, if the case were committed to the assizes, he might receive three years. He opted to tell the truth, and so that charge against you has, of course, been withdrawn. The assault charge, in the eyes of my seniors, is a different matter, for Sergeant Jackson's condition is more serious than it was at first considered; but I promise you I will do my very best to help you.

'You've been very unfortunate and largely a victim of circumstances. But I want you to understand that you have my sympathy. Also I have a feeling of personal guilt and blame myself to a large extent for not pursuing my instincts that Dunn and others were lying; but that's how things are, I'm afraid. I've given instructions for your wife to be with you alone in this room until transport is ready to take you to Canterbury. I shall have words with somebody there in authority to ensure you are not treated as a 'run of the mill' remand prisoner. That's the best I can do for you. By the way, you may wonder, as Dunn had confessed to your innocence, why you were included to stand in the dock with them. I want you to realise that you will be in front of the self-same magistrate next week on the assault charge. He will now have an impression on his mind of you and this, I hope, will be favourable in the understanding of your outburst against Sergeant Jackson.

'Now, if he should consider the case is out of his power to impose a heavy enough sentence he will commit you for trial to a higher court.' Tongue in cheek, he went on: 'Now you must adhere to what you have said in your statement in that you acted in self-defence and lost control of your self-composure on having heard the disgusting and obscene words he used in reference to your children. Further, there will be the substantive evidence of Constable Adams whose account of the incident concurs with your own and who will be present in court to give it. That's the lot and I wish you well, but remember, this - this conversation hasn't ever taken place. Understand?'

'I was in the Army for many years,' said Bob. 'Inspector, if that is not enough to tell you this conversation never happened, I don't know what is.'

Smiling, the officer said: 'Sit down again and I'll find your wife. Good Luck,' and he was gone.

The door of the small room opened. He heard a voice say, 'This way, Mrs Higgins.'

She came to him in that graceful, dignified way that belonged only to Rose as the door closed behind her.

'Rosie, Rosie, I'm so sorry, dear,' he said.

'Bobby, please don't cry. This is not your fault and I'm so proud of you.'

'How can you be proud of me?'

'I know what you did and why you did it.'

'Who told you?'

'No matter who told me, Bob, I mustn't tell you yet.'

He understood her, and realised how kind these hard-boiled men had been to her and the compassion they had shown.

As ever, everybody loved his Rose.

'They're going to take me away from you again.'

'It won't be like before, Bobby. This time I know you are coming back to me, and this time, too, I won't have to go to hospital to see you, will I?'

'No. But, Rose, next week they may send me to prison for a long time and what will happen to you and the nippers? I'll go bloody mad thinking of you all.'

'Bob, darling, you mustn't worry. Remember we all love you, and if you have to go away I shall manage somehow, and I shall have Granny with me. She is in need of us for she cannot get about easily now. I know you'd do it for her, darling, so last night she insisted on staying with me, but she can hardly walk up the street. She can share the room with Rosalina. Is that all right, dear?'

'Of course, Rose. I won't worry so much if she's with you.'

'I posted a letter to Hilda and Michael today.'

'Goodness, I wonder what they'll think of me.'

'I've explained it all. I waited until your case was over and managed to add a postscript to it. I posted it outside here a few minutes ago.'

65

'Bobby,' she went on, handing him a small suitcase, 'in here are the things you will be allowed to have at Canterbury, enough for a week, and I've put some money inside in case you need it.'

'Rosie, you've always looked after me like a mother,' he said, holding her closely.

'And you've always looked after me as if I were a little girl,' she said.

His thoughts went back to the day of Rosalina's birth and he told himself again, as he so often had since that day, of how much she mothered him. Without her there would be no life for him.

'Bobby, I picked this from our garden this morning.'

From her handbag she drew a red rose. Poor Bob shook with emotion and love for her. He was, he knew, just a child. A child ever in need of her. Whatever he did, whatever he said, she forgave him. And now he would be without her.

'Bob,' she said, 'please remember our old motto and no tears, just smiles,' as she placed the rose in the buttonhole of his jacket. He did not answer her but felt her soft lips gently kiss his unshaven face.

They stood in tender embrace and heard a respectful knock on the door. It was Constable Streeter who said, 'I'm afraid you must leave now, Mrs Higgins.'

'Thank you, sir,' Rose said respectfully. She took Bob's hand.

'Come on, dear. See me to the door like a gentleman,' she said, as he followed her the few steps to the door. He bent his head forward to kiss her lips, 'Good bye, Rosie, and don't worry.'

'Bye, bye, Bobby,' she said, smiling, as she left the room.

'I've been detailed to escort you,' said Streeter.

'Well, at least we're not strangers, are we?' said Bob.

'No, but I can't say I don't wish it wasn't necessary, especially over a bastard like Jackson. This won't do his career any good, I can tell you. Whatever happens to you, he's in trouble, I can assure you.'

Bob was escorted to the station yard and boarded the awaiting 'Black Maria.' Streeter sat beside him and took his pipe and pouch from the folds of his tunic.

'This is one of the perks when you're detailed for station gaoler,' he said, 'and sometimes you need it. D'y know, sometimes a lot of blokes shit themselves at the thought of going to clink. Thank Christ, I've dodged having to escort Dunn and his mates to Maidstone clink. If you want to smoke you may. There's only you and me. Here you are. Here's your smokes. Your missus slipped them to me afore she went out. I've met her before, you know. A long time ago she used to play the piano and that lovely big zither she had, at the church hall. Has she still got it?'

'Yes,' said Bob.

'She makes that thing speak, don't she?'

'Oh yes! She still plays it,' said Bob.

'Bleeding gifted she is, and don't she sing nice?'

Bob thought once more: 'Everyone likes Rose.'

Streeter chattered away the entire journey and Bob guessed the object of it was to distract his mind from the trauma of his impending imprisonment.

'Don't forget, you're not a convicted man,' said Streeter, 'so don't allow the warders to treat you like one. They'll lock you up, of course, but hang on to your belongings and if you want anything within reason from outside ask for it. If they refuse, you can demand to see one of the bosses. They're not a bad lot of blokes in there though, and it's a cushy clink compared with Maidstone. Just think, by the way, of Dunn and mates handcuffed on their way there. A nice thought, eh?'

Bob was grateful for the companionship but found no consolation in Dunn's misery. They had once been good friends, but he realised, too, that friendship is often like money, easier made than kept, and that the law cannot punish where it cannot persuade. Perhaps now he had learned the lesson. Despite what had occurred, and knowing he was in trouble through Dunn's lies, his inherent compassion over-ruled hatred.

'I've never known Inspector Brown taking such trouble with a case before as he has with yours. He must be clapped out; that's the trouble being on night duty. If you pinch someone, you've got the job of appearing in court in the morning. But Inspectors usually dodge it,' said Streeter.

At the prison, Streeter left him in the hands of the prison staff. He was again searched and his small case examined. He was allowed to keep the contents with him, with the exception of his ivory-handled open razor, being told that he could only use it in the presence of a warder. Rose had included two clean shirts and long-john underwear, soap and towel, a tin containing her home-made fleed cakes, and another of her brandy snaps, of which the reception warder, with a smile, said, 'You can do without one,' and stuffed it into his large mouth.

Later he was taken to a cell to be visited by the senior warder who told him, 'The best way to pass your time here is to read. Don't sit and mope. It doesn't do you any good. Here's a list of books. Pick out one, and I'll see you get it.'

They bought him his unappetising midday meal with the Sexton Blake novel he had chosen.

'You are entitled to request food to be bought in from outside but you have to pay for it yourself. So if you don't fancy what you've got, say so, and we'll get what you want,' said the warder.

'No thanks, I'm not hungry,' Bob said.

Left alone he dipped the large piece of dry bread in the gravy of what looked like after-birth, reluctant to chance eating it. He was grateful for the fleed cakes Rose had packed and the two pounds cash she had put into an envelope. He would send out for something next time. Later they bought him two thick slices of bread and margarine and a small piece of cheese with a tin mug of what he thought was coffee but what turned out to be cocoa, which tasted like tea. He was told that he would get nothing more before breakfast. He ate the food and settled down to read on the bunk, which proved to be less hard than it looked.

He began to feel the chill of the distempered walls and found, when he had climbed into bed, the blankets thin and inadequate to compete with the cold of the cell. He donned a pair of long-johns and put his socks back on. He spent a restless night listening to the night sounds of the prison and thinking of poor Rose and the kids. He told himself he must, for their sake, not allow his bitterness to get the better of him, and allow his will to capitulate to his conviction that one day he would lose his reason. His nightmare. 'I must fight it.'

Morning came with the banging of cell doors and the shouting of warders, the clinking of keys and the sounds of tin cell pots being emptied, and with the stink of stale urine. The cell door was opened loudly.

'Right, Higgins, come with me. If you've got soap and towel bring it with you,' he was told.

'I want to shave.'

'That will be attended to. Come on.'

He followed the warder, passing a communal washing area, to see many men stripped to the waist watched by warders demanding, 'No talking.'

'In here, Higgins.'

He found himself in a small cubicle equipped with metal wash basin, wooden tub half filled with warm water and was told to remove his clothing and bathe himself in the tub. Naked, he soaped himself and rinsed off with the provided metal jug. Having dried himself and dressed to the waist he asked the watchful warder for his razor which was produced from his tunic.

He felt somewhat refreshed when he was escorted back to his cell where he complained of the thin blankets to be told, 'Hard luck mate. You should have behaved yourself, and you wouldn't be here.'

He had experienced many such power-bloated men like this man, and knew of the futility of argument with them, and recalled Streeter's advice. 'You listen to me, mate. I'm not a bloody convict yet, and I'm not prepared to argue with a cocky twat like you. Now get your boss, or I'll shout for him. Clear off!'

This short delivery was rendered in true sergeant-major style, and with somewhat crestfallen ego the warder marched off to the cheers of the more permanent residents of that unhappy abode. He heard the laughter and voices applauding his outburst, and his experience in the art of the understanding of men, learned over many years, told him of the unpopularity of the recipient of his oration.

He got two extra blankets.

Breakfast came in the shape of what appeared to be a fresh and steaming, but anaemic, mass accompanied by a tin mug filled with what was purported to be tea and tasted of treacle. He cared not to discover the taste of the main course, but ate the bread and margarine which was also served to complete this culinary masterpiece.

A more civil warder accompanied him on a fifteen minute walk of exercise around the prison yard after its evacuation of the convicted men. When, at the point furthest from the likelihood of being overheard, he said, 'You're getting quite a reputation - bashing self-important detectives and cock-sure warders.'

'They both asked for it.'

'I don't doubt it. I've known them both for years. I hope you don't get convicted on account of Jackson. You did to him what many coppers would have liked to do themselves. You have every right not to be treated as an inmate at present, so just you ask for what you want.'

'Christ, the grub's grim. How do I go about getting something decent to eat?' Bob asked.

'When we get back I'll tell the senior warder you want to see him. Tell him you would like to have your dinner sent in every day you're here. He'll send to the pub just outside and it will be ready to be collected at the same time every day. You get a good dollop of meat and two vegetables and a sweet. It only costs a bob a day. Oh, I forgot, it includes a jug of tea.'

'Thanks for the tip.'

'No sweat, but now stop talking.'

Back in the cell later, the Chief Warder agreed to arrange the mid-day meal for him and told him to ask for any further needs, such as tobacco. This lessened Bob's discomfort.

On his third day he was told he had a visitor.

'Oh no,' he thought, 'it must be Rose.'

He hated every notion of her in these degrading surroundings. This environment was so very unlike anything remotely associated with her. He should have forbidden her to visit him.

'Is it my wife?,' he asked.

'No, it's a Major Cotter.'

'Good old Michael! Thank God,' he thought. Not his Rose.

'He is accompanied by a Mr Gapp, a solicitor.'

He followed the warder to a sparsely furnished room to find the men waiting for him. Introductions over, Bob asked Michael of Rose's welfare and thanked him for his kindness in coming.

'Look, Bob, I don't have to tell you not to worry regarding your family. Hilda's with them and we'll both stay until this affair is over. I want you and Mr Gapp to sit down and discuss your problem and I'll just sit and listen.'

'Tell me exactly what happened and what was said,' said Gapp.

Bob knew he must not deviate from what was on his statement and recounted the incident 'according to the Book of Solomon.'

'I made enquiries as to the medical condition of Mr Jackson who is, I have to tell you, liable to be detained in hospital for at least another week, which means you will be further remanded. I will endeavour to get the remand non-custodial but, and I must be frank with you, I don't hold much hope for it and so you must be prepared to return here. You must understand that assault of a police officer, no matter what the provocation, is a much more serious offence than that on a civilian. You are very fortunate in that you have a very reliable and immovable witness in Constable Adams. This is of tremendous value. I have no doubt in my mind that, as you acted in self-defence, your case will be heard more sympathetically than not. Also, the mental provocation, in that the obscenities used by Jackson were extremely unbecoming of a police officer. Too, the whole manner of his interview with you and the rest of his phraseology was not in accordance with proper police interrogation ethics. In view of these circumstances, when the time arrives when Jackson is able to attend court, he will no doubt be represented by his own solicitor. I shall ask you to take the witness stand and ask you various questions, which means that Jackson's man will be prepared to do the same. I advise you to consider your replies carefully for he will endeavour to make you contradict yourself. I have been made aware of the serious wounds you received during the war, which I understand have the recurring effect of your nervous system sometimes being troublesome. Do you wish me to use this in your defence?'

'On no account, please,' said Bob.

'I think I understand, Mr Higgins. Only in the extreme would I refer to it, but you must not forget the responsibility you have for your family; but I shall not, hopefully, need to. I shall see you in court next week, and now I will leave you to have a chat with the Major.'

A very brisk, down-to-earth and obviously competent man, he shook hands with Bob and with a nod to Michael and 'I'll wait outside for you,' he left.

Before the days of generous legal aid to all, Bob was perhaps understandably concerned about the fee of this able, experienced advocate, and wondered if he could afford the cost. 'More bloody worry,' he thought. 'When the hell will it all end?'

'How are you, Bob?' he heard Michael ask.

'Oh, you know how I am. I'm worried sick about Rose and

72

the kids. I'm grateful for your kindness, you know I am, but I can't help thinking of them all the time I'm stuck in this bloody hole. Michael, please promise me that Rose does not visit me. She's not to come here. She's not to become contaminated by the stink of this poxy place.'

'I'll promise, Bob. She wanted to come with me but, knowing you, I guessed you would prefer her not to, and made the excuse of Mr Gapp's presence.'

'Thanks, Michael. How much do you think his fee will be?'

'There's no need to concern yourself on that score, Bob. I'll attend to that. I owe you my life.'

'Rubbish! You owe me nothing.'

'You got me back to the trenches. If I had been left there I wouldn't be here now and you know it. And I'm not the only man either.'

'Bunk, Michael!'

'Have it your own way. But Gapp is a friend of my parents and his costs will be nominal. So that shouldn't worry you too much. He's a shrewd man and, don't tell him I told you, but he is toying with the idea of getting Jackson charged with what he considers to be an unprovoked assault on a gallant shell-shocked man who has been decorated on the field of battle fighting for his King and Country.'

'Well, for God's sake, Michael, don't let him.'

'He is a very professional man, Bob, and he simply wants to rub every advantage home and, as he so rightly points out, the circumstances of your presence in the cell are due to a now-convicted felon, and a liar to boot. I can assure you, Bob, that his professional reputation is sacrosanct to him, so whatever you say, if he believes the case is not going in his favour he will use any ploy to assure his success.'

'Michael, I am so grateful to you in getting him. Is he a local man?'

'Not likely. His offices are in the Strand in London. My parents phoned him, and he was down like a shot.'

'I don't know what to say, Michael, but thanks.'

'Now, don't let's talk any more about that. Rose wants to know if there is anything you need.'

'Well, it looks as if I shall be sent back here again, so please tell her very gently for me and ask her if she'll pack the same stuff as before for me.'

They spoke together of mainly unimportant subjects for a while and Michael reluctantly took his leave saying, 'I hate leaving you Bob, but I know Mr Gapp has things he wants to pursue in this matter, so I'll say good bye for now, and try not to worry.' He lowered his voice as he knew a warder was near the half-opened door.

'Take this. It'll cheer you up a bit. Put it in your pocket quickly.' He left the room.

In the semi-privacy of his cell Bob found 'good old Mick,' as he was called so long ago in France by his men, had given him a half bottle of gin. 'Christ, I can do with some of that,' he thought.

The following day he was somewhat taken aback when the senior warder told him to give him the bottle when he had emptied it - 'to dispose of myself - we're not daft in here, y'know.' With a grin he left him. Inspector Brown had kept his promise of 'having a word with someone in authority.'

Bob was taken back to court where he was once more remanded; this time for a further fourteen days. He learned that Inspector Brown had been instructed by his superiors to oppose bail.

The local press made much of the case, and speculation as to the outcome was made in many quarters. Poor Rose was subjected to a variety of overt blank faces, smiles of condolence and outright sneers when on shopping excursions. The kids, too, were the butt of other children's cries of 'Your Dad's in prison, your Dad's in prison, your Dad's in prison.' That bitter hurt that only children can unfeelingly inflict upon each other. Rose and Hilda took them to and from school and they were kept indoors. Only Granny Litchfield, walking stick in hand, stayed the tongues of many adults with sly and meaningful references to the skeletons in their own family cupboards.

Two days before the next hearing the garage, which had remained locked since Bob's arrest, was gutted by fire. Three boys, it was later discovered, had gained access by forcing a window at the rear and indulged, as boys are apt, in smoking Woodbines in the seclusion of the small office where scrap paper had been accidentally - they swore when caught - ignited and, unable to extinguish the flames, they had hurriedly left.

Michael and Rose, realising that the impact of this shock would no doubt result in the near total mental collapse of Bob, implored the police to refrain from informing him of the event until after the case had been resolved. In this they agreed to comply.

When he was brought to court Bob at once noted the absence of Rose in the now rubber-necking, filled-to-capacity public gallery. He saw Sergeant Jackson sitting in the well of the court.

'You bastard,' he thought. 'I should have killed you.'

Hate welled within him for this man who had created this injustice, this unhappiness to his beloved Rose. His head began to throb and he told himself he must not lose his self-control or he would be finished.

The stipendiary magistrate listened to the details of the charge, looked towards Bob and said, 'What have you to say?'

Bob repeated almost verbatim the words on the statement he had signed. He had no qualms of conscience in perjuring himself. He cared not for the future of Jackson's career. He felt it was his duty to see that this bastard was stopped from imposing the indignities upon other humans which his power of warrant gave him. In his eyes, and obviously in the eyes of his colleagues, he was an outrage; and it was all too apparent that he was despised by all.

'Who else was present during this incident?'

'Constable Adams, sir,'

'Call Constable Adams.'

Bob discovered that Adams had perjured himself to a much higher degree than he had, and, judging by the expression on Jackson's face, one could be forgiven in believing he was in a state of near apoplexy. Jackson took the oath. During his career he had taken it so often that he could recite it in his sleep, but now he required the prompting of the court clerk to complete it. His self-composure was approaching nil, for he blurted, 'It's a bloody lot of lies!'

'You will conduct yourself in a proper manner, and you know better than to use profanities in court. Now, please let me hear what you have to say in a manner becoming a police officer.'

He floundered.

'They are liars, both of them. Before I had the opportunity of introducing myself to the prisoner he struck me on the jaw with the cell chamber pot and then struck me with heavy blows to the chest and kicked my shins.'

'Did he tell you he was unjustly arrested?'

'No. He just came and hit me.'

'Anything else?'

'I woke up in hospital, that's all I remember.'

The magistrate looked at him long and hard, and told him that that would be all for now.

Mr Gapp stood up, sheets of paper in hand, and said, 'Sergeant, you realise the penalty for perjury, no doubt, and yet you have committed perjury. I have here a list of the injuries you sustained by my client's hand, and which he does not deny. They are: a dislocated jaw and severe bruising of the ribs. My client, as you see, is heavy in build. He requires boots - he never wears shoes - of size eleven and, should he have kicked your shins, the resulting injuries would have been included in the list I am holding. This list bears the signature of the two doctors who examined you at the hospital. It also states that, on your admittance there, you were perfectly conscious. Also, I have a statement here (he waved a sheet of paper) signed by the two ambulance men who took you to the hospital, in which they state clearly that you were conscious when they arrived at the police station; you were conscious throughout the journey to the hospital, and you were conscious on arrival there. This leads me to have no doubt whatsoever that you have just committed perjury. This being so, I have no doubt in my mind that your account of what occurred is a tissue of lies - further perjury. Do you deny pushing and striking Mr Higgins?'

'I didn't lay a finger on him.'

'Did you refer to his wife and children in any manner at all?'

'No.'

'And for no reason whatsoever, my client attacked you?'

'That's correct.'

'And your colleague, Constable Adams, an officer who has served nineteen years in the police force has committed perjury in order to assist a prisoner, a prisoner who an hour before had been charged with a very serious offence. Is this what you are alleging, Sergeant?'

'Yes.'

'Do you not agree that to anybody your accusations sound outrageously preposterous?'

Jackson did not answer.

Bob thought, 'Gapp has done some homework!'

The magistrate had already made up his mind.

Adams, to himself, said, 'Gotcha, you bastard!'

Inspector Brown thought the same.

Gapp addressed the magistrate.

'My client is a man of honour. He is a local businessman. He is a man honourably discharged from the army with war wounds. He was a professional soldier, and was decorated on the field of battle with the Distinguished Service Medal, and he is not a liar. Thank you, your Worship.' He sat down. Almost simultaneously, the magistrate said, 'Case dismissed.'

The public gallery applauded. Bob's mind seemed to explode as he collapsed to the floor.

He opened his eyes, and felt the tang of smelling salts

pervade his nostrils and throat. They had taken him to the small room where he had said goodbye to Rose, and here she was now, rubbing his hands. She had often seen him in this condition, and knew a doctor would not be necessary. She had told them, but, they sent for him regardless; and here he was administering the sol volatile.

'Major Cotter has driven his car into the yard. He's ready to drive you home if Mr Higgins feels fit to walk to the yard.'

'Thank you, Doctor. Would you kindly stay here for a moment while I speak with him?'

Rose hastened to Michael and said, 'Do you think you should drive past the garage. He's got to be told at some time or other. It might be best to get it over and done with, rather than drop another bombshell when he's getting better. He's sure to ask me something concerning it soon.'

'Yes, I agree. It will be for the better, and I shall be with you should he become ill again.'

Michael drove slowly past the garage. He heard Bob sobbing in the rear passenger seat and saw in the mirror that Rose had cradled his head beneath her chin, stroking his greying hair.

'Poor blighter,' he breathed, almost in tears himself.

Since speaking in court Bob had been silent. He asked himself over and over again if his words of vengeance would haunt him, and should he detract them to avert ruin for Jackson? Would they be on his conscience for ever? But if he did, what would happen to Rose? Basically, he was an honest man and in his dilemma saw the shattered face of the man his words had destroyed, but through the haze of his trauma he saw the same face sneeringly repeating 'your bloody snivelling kids' and told himself he would always recall the face he despised. He was home now sitting in his big chair, a free man he told himself, and sod Jackson!

Granny had been to the Bottle and Jug bar of the Ordnance Arms, returning with beer and stout, 'to celebrate,' she said. When Constable Adams called at the house he, too, raised his glass to a 'notable victory,' for he bore the tidings of 'the whole bleedin nick' rejoicing in the knowledge of Sergeant Jackson being 'asked to resign.'

Rose quoted 'Jure Divine.' Adams said 'by the Book of Solomon.'

# CHAPTER 5

The garage remained closed and Bob's will to win his fight was fast fading. Mr Gapp had attended to the monetary intricacies of fire insurance, payment of debts, moneys legally belonging to Charlie Dunn and other affairs.

The world recession was destroying the morale of working class people throughout Europe and the Americas.

'Buddy, can you spare a dime?' was the appeal of men unable to find employment to sustain not only themselves but their dependents. In America men became hoboes, drifting from one place to another, destitute, hungry, unwashed and uncaring. In Britain men in similar positions became tramps, vagrants, beggars, street musicians, match sellers. They, too, drifted from one workhouse to another, where they were communally bathed and deloused, given a meal, one night's shelter, one shilling and told to move on.

The workhouses were filled to capacity with the men who had fought the bloodiest war in history. Each morning at eight o'clock these 'heroes' were to be seen in pathetic single file emerging from the workhouse gates. The more fortunate, those with homes, would pass on the opposite side of the road to avoid contact with them, and stand to stare and discuss with their fellows in unsympathetic vein the plight these men were obliged to endure. Are not critics like the dung-removers of rich men's horses? Has it not been said truthfully that life is judged with all the blindness of life itself? Humanity has ever seen the smugness of the 'haves' and the despair of the 'have nots.' In this Shakespeare never wrote more meaningful words than: 'He that wants money, means and content is without three good friends.'

Rose was feeling the financial pinch again and finding it difficult to make ends meet. Bob had gone to his old employers in search of a job but had been turned down. They had heard of his breakdown in court and now, being aware of his unstable condition, did not think it prudent to risk his collapsing whilst driving one of their vehicles. His general lack of health, too, was apparent. His hair had greyed rapidly, his hands trembled slightly and his alertness seemed to have deteriorated. They did, out of kindness, offer him a menial job of cleaning the vehicles and keeping the yard tidy but, wordlessly, he walked away.

He began drinking heavily, and lost his temper quickly and easily with the children. Rose was becoming more concerned with her inability to buy household necessities and realised she must find a rented house and sell the present one in order to live on capital. Bob's dole allowance, as for all the unemployed, was miserably low. If a man applied for 'relief,' a supplementary allowance to feed his undernourished dependents, he was subject to the dreaded 'Means Test' which meant he must sell articles classed as luxuries. Perhaps during his days of employment he had bought a piano or gramophone and other musical instruments or other such items not - in the opinion of those responsible for this unspeakable injustice - needed. He would be obliged to dispose of them for cash. Should he not own such luxuries his home was inspected by an official to ensure that his claim was legitimate. Many a treasured luxury was sacrificed and many a treasured luxury was hidden in the house of a friend not liable to become a victim of this diabolical law.

Long queues of men were to be seen outside the towns' Labour Exchanges, a misnomer as there was no labour to exchange, each day. On 'dole day,' when the meagre allow-

81

ances were paid, extra police personnel were required to control the wrath of those paid less than expected by the frequently high-handed, 'holier than thou,' pay clerks. Fights were the norm on such days and many a frantic poor soul found himself under arrest, to be carted to the police station to cool down, and to be released without being charged by the sympathetic police.

This earth, this realm, this England, was green but not pleasant, for it was a country of extreme riches and extreme poverty.

The General Strike gained nothing for the participants. The commandeering by the strikers of a Schweppes mineral water horse-drawn wagon, filled to capacity with bottles, was the weaponry used to bombard the Houses of Parliament. The strikers were halted by soldiers of the Brigade of Guards and the ensuing fracas became known as the 'Battle of Westminster Bridge.' This Sceptred Isle was set in a sea of tears, and extreme riches and extreme poverty remained.

This was the environment in which Rose, the kind, gentle lady, was engulfed. She had easily found a small house to rent in a terraced cul-de-sac. The ground floor comprised two rooms and kitchen with a small garden and an outside lavatory. Upstairs there were two medium-sized and one small bedroom, but not gas-lit as was the lower floor. There was also a coal cellar.

Granny had died a few months earlier. Rose felt her loss deeply but perhaps, she told herself, she would have been unhappy here.

Bob was occasionally able to get a few days casual employment but always complained of his back paining him. She had no doubt in her mind it was untrue, as she had witnessed his gradual lethargy. However, she told herself she must persevere with him and that time would heal him. But she knew in her heart that the imprisonment had blighted him for ever. Sexual relations were now of scant pleasure. He had reverted to his pre-Rosalina coarseness and Leslie and Michael arrived all too

82

soon. He became over-demanding and on three occasions when she had expressed disapproval he had been brutal. On these occasions he had afterwards sobbed bitterly and begged forgiveness, and Rose, the ever compassionate Rose, would mother him despite her bruised face.

The unknowing would shoulder her with the blame for his apparent laziness but not knowing her love for him. Only she understood his mind. Only she knew his basic kindness. Only she knew of the deep love he had for her and their children and she cared little for others' opinions of the man they saw and thought to be an uncaring lazy drunkard. She knew he was at heart none of these things. He was a tragedy of humanity to be pitied and loved. She knew he was aware that he was drinking to excess and he had endeavoured to lessen this habit, and had now reduced his nightly excursions to the corner public house to twice-weekly visits.

Rose had been lately laundering the linen of a few people who could afford her expertise, to supplement her household expenses, and much to Bob's credit, when he discovered this, he was appalled and ashamed. He very reluctantly allowed her to continue when she told him not to be embarrassed as she liked to be able to help him have his 'little enjoyment of a drink.' In this she was sincere as she realised it was an outlet for his troubled mind. 'But Bob, I don't like you when you get drunk and upset, dear. Please don't get drunk; you're a sod when you do.'

She had, since moving to this area, found herself using the odd profanity occasionally, but she was more concerned about the speaking habits of the children, which sometimes provoked her to admonish them, although she appreciated that the reason was that the locality was rubbing-off on them. She nevertheless strove to correct them and still found time to take an interest in their education by teaching them elementary subjects. This was reflected in their school reports, with the exception of Bertie's, who suffered with ear trouble.

She took them to church each Sunday morning. Freddie

had joined the choir. He sang solo soprano beautifully, and she was very proud to hear the comments of praise for his voice, but he was not, she knew, the angelic cherub his blonde hair and peach complexion suggested. He had tasted Bob's belt all too often for his many outrageous escapades.

She was glad to have Sunday afternoon to relax when they were at Sunday school - or at least when they should have been there - for she suspected that Fred had purloined the metal star die used to stamp their attendance cards (and she had, in fact, been told this by the ever tale-telling Rosalina).

Rose made the children's clothes on the treadle Singer sewing machine, and the 'Sunday Best' the boys wore were pressed and clean when they set out. But on their return they appeared as ragamuffins, and she was thankful that Bob would then be enjoying his Sunday afternoon nap and would not see them. She didn't tell him.

Apart from boyish squabbles, they were happy to be together and woe betide other boys if Bertie was subjected to their bating. Fred and John joined a boxing club, of all things, and all too often Rose would find a mother of a boy who had suffered at their hands at the door complaining of the damage to her son's face. Even if Bob found out about this, it would not result in a beating for the boys, as Bertie was not a strong lad and had, since birth, been a source of anxiety to his parents. Indeed, he was the only one of them who had never felt Bob's belt.

They had taught them to be mannerly, which indeed they were, but they were no softies. Their father had taught them not to be, but they *were* little sods, and Fred the worst of the bunch. His solo escapades were almost legendary, often shocking, sometimes disgusting.

Rosalina had well passed into womanhood, being the only girl of the family and with it, perhaps felt a sense of isolation. She had assumed an air of watch-dog, and seemed to enjoy the punishment suffered by her brothers through her spiteful tales of their misbehaviour. When they retaliated her high-pitched indignation was a joy to their ears as they made themselves scarce. On one occasion her 'Amami' shampoo was replaced with a mixture of mustard powder and flour. Happy days!

The boys never informed on each other. They were true brothers and, although Fred was usually the culprit or the instigator, he was never betrayed. Nor did he betray another.

To keep them clothed meant money and was time-consuming. Rose bought oddments of cloth from the stall market draper to make trousers, shirts, underwear and even jackets, but shoes and boots were a problem, and these she would repair herself from sheets of leather she bought at Woolworths at threepence for a piece measuring one foot square. The cheapest footwear were rubber plimsolls at ninepence per pair and very durable. These she bought to lessen the toil of the near bi-weekly need of boot repairing.

The kids' appetites were enormous, but she managed to feed them well on the cheapest food available and they seemed content with what she gave them. A two-pound loaf of bread was fourpence, potatoes were a shilling for fourteen pounds, ox liver tenpence a pound, herrings five pence a pound and corned beef ten pence. Beef was the cheapest meat and, apart from the half a crown joint for Sunday - the left-overs were kept for Monday to be served cold with a mountain of hot 'bubble and squeak.' She bought the cheapest cuts at sixpence per pound to make pies and puddings. Eggs were a penny each and new-laids a penny farthing. She bought a gallon of dried peas and would soak the quantity she needed for the next day in water overnight. Luxuries were few but the children were never hungry. For Fred, the days were to come when he was to learn the meaning of Rose's words, 'never waste the bread which God has provided.' He was also to learn that youth is a time of errors, manhood a constant fight, and maturity is to laugh at the tears of the past and seek the fulfilment of dreams.

Despite being well fed the boys appeared to be slim, but Rose attributed this to their constant mobility. She was proud of their large bones and knew they would mature into good physiques. Nevertheless they did give the impression of being underfed.

Bob had gone to the Wheatsheaf. It was Friday night. Rosalina was shampooing her hair, and Fred had gone to choir practice and should have returned an hour ago. Rose was used to his not coming home immediately when he knew his father would not be home to remonstrate with him; but he should have got home by now. When a further half hour had elapsed she became worried, and looked along the gas lamp-lit street several times. She left the front door ajar and hurried there as she heard the sound of heavy boots on the pavement. Fear gripped her heart, to leave just as quickly as it had come, when she also heard the piping voice of her (secretly) favourite son. 'Thank God the little bugger is all right,' she breathed, 'but I wonder what he's been up to this time.'

When she saw him, his usual perky self, she was at a loss whether to scold him or embrace him. She embraced him. Then she became aware of the wearer of the heavy boots she had heard, listened to the reason for his presence and thanked him for his kindness. She had heard Bob speak of him, and knew of his domestic problems which he divulged to Bob one night when he was drowning his sorrows in the Wheatsheaf. He had drunk too much on that occasion and had emptied his heart to all within earshot. Bob had taken him to the tram stop and thence on to the servicemen's hostel. Bob realised he would have been arrested by the naval Picket Patrol had he been seen by them in his drunken condition. He had never thanked Bob. Perhaps he did not remember, and Bob did not remind him.

Holbrook, for it was he, had told Fred he would not mention to Bob what had occurred, and Rose hoped he would keep his word. She always feared that Bob might go beyond the limits of chastisement once he had taken off his leather belt. He was showing no signs of improvement. She knew he had head-aches, and his vision troubled him, but she could not convey to the boys the awful details of their father's malady. They were too young to understand, and when they asked why he never tried to get a job she would give various reasons or, if she was depressed, as often she was, because 'he's a lazy sod.' But she ever reproached herself for this.

Rosalina was beginning to understand it all, and for this Rose felt less of an island. She could confide in her more as she was now at work, strangely enough in a laundry, and now becoming mature.

It was some months later when Bob told her of the suicide of Holbrook's wife and death of his mother. Holbrook had been fortunate in having a relative to take care of his two sons, but his daughter, now seventeen, was in only-temporary shelter with a friend. Holbrook had asked Bob if he and his wife would consider having her to stay with them on a permanent basis. Bob told Rose it was to be her decision, and she, at first, was loathe to shoulder the responsibility of someone else's child. She had quite enough to do with her own, she said, but Rosalina welcomed the thought of a room-mate and Rose decided to agree, on the understanding that she must conform to the household rules.

And so Madeline entered the fold. She was an attractive girl. Her hair long and light brown, her eyes blue-slate, her complexion fair and her figure beautiful. What Holbrook had not divulged was the fact that she had inherited some of her dead mother's questionable feminine qualities. She over-dressed, over-used cosmetics, was untidy and would sometimes smell strongly of alcohol on returning from an evening spent with one of the many boy-friends she had acquired in a short time. She was cunning, and when she at first visited the house prior to her settling in, she appeared demure, wore no make-up and dressed soberly, but once firmly established, the reverse side of the coin became very apparent. A particularly bad habit, to Rose, was the display of her beautiful legs to almost the thigh when relaxing in an armchair in Bob's presence. Rose had no doubt of the deliberation of it. In the privacy of Madeline's room, which was a shambles, Rose remonstrated with her and was promised it would not occur again.

Madeline was also an inveterate liar, and many were the squabbles and quarrels between her and Rosalina through her lies. She began to arrive home late, sometimes after midnight, and Bob told her that she must behave or get out. This brought tears but Rose was quite aware that this girl could 'turn the tap on' at will to receive sympathy from a man.

A few months later Rose could see the signs which she had expected, but dreaded, and demanded the name of the father. Madeline said it was a man unknown to Rose, who thought it was more likely that Madeline was unsure of which man it was. Holbrook, when informed of his daughter's condition, was outraged. He considered himself fortunate in having her accepted into the Higgins home and had warned her to conduct herself decently. He was aware of the inherent short-comings she possessed and had hoped the influence of Rose would change her. He realised now that she was the shadow of her mother.

Rose was kind in that, despite being pregnant herself, she would see Madeline safely through to the birth, and thereafter try to rehabilitate her. They tried to find the name of the father, but to no avail, despite the fact she would be in need of money to support her and her unborn child. Holbrook wanted to thrash the father's name from her, not for the purpose of exposing him but to be prepared to start legal proceedings for a Paternity Order after the birth. Rose guessed the reason for her evasive and unreasonable behaviour was that she was unable to say with certainty who the father was. Too, she realised that this selfish and conceited liar would not be above naming a man not guilty of intimacy with her. Such was Madeline. Rose's informant was Rosalina, who imparted the gossip among the girls of the town. It appeared that Made-line's promiscuity knew no bounds, and she would probably become a candidate for the 'Bag Shop.' Bob blamed himself for suggesting helping Holbrook in giving Madeline asylum in their home, and insisted it was entirely his fault.

Despite Rose's efforts to alleviate Bob's worsening troubled mind, she seemed unable to reach him, and when he assured her that it was his firm conviction that he was responsible for all the years of her unhappiness and that she would be better off without him, she feared he would leave her.

Madeline eavesdropped on these intimate conversations, unknown to them.

Rose had her baby, a boy named Ronald. He was a puny small thing, and the midwife was concerned for his survival. Underweight for a normal child, and feebly responding to nourishment, he lingered on.

When Madeline came to be in labour Rose took advantage of her pain and urged her to tell her the name of anyone who might be the father. Madeline told her of two men.

'Who else Madeline?'

'I won't tell you.'

'Why not?'

'I mustn't.'

'Tell me his name, you foolish girl.'

'No, No.'

'Is it someone I know?'

Madeline felt another contraction approaching, screaming, 'I mustn't, I can't.' Even in labour her inborn cunning did not desert her and she continued to repeat, 'I mustn't.'

Had the midwife not arrived Rose felt she would have discovered the mysterious unnamed probable father. She left Madeline in the care of the midwife. She had a more important worry. Bob had disappeared.

Two nights before, she felt him leave their bed. He had not used the chamber pot. Rose had assumed he had needed to use the outside toilet and had returned to sleep. When the alarm clock sounded she found that he had not returned to bed. His old army rucksack was gone and with it his razor and other small items together with his everyday clothing, his best still in the cupboard. She hurried to the room Rosalina shared with Madeline. 'Get up quickly, your Dad's disappeared,' she said. Madeline pretended to be sleeping. It was Sunday and Rosalina did not have to go to work that day.

Downstairs, Rose told her that she was going to the police station. 'When the boys get up, give them their breakfast and tell them they are not going to church, except Fred - he must go to sing. Give the baby a change of napkin and feed him with the bottle. If the boys ask where I am, tell them I've had to go out with Dad. Tell them anything you can think of.'

'Mum, what should I do if Madeline's baby starts to come?'

'Send John for the midwife and tell him to run and get back home at once.'

Rose went to the police station and was told that as Bob had not broken any laws she must understand that the matter must be regarded as a case of desertion. It was the police station where Bob had been charged so long ago. She asked for Inspector Brown, but he had long gone. Only Streeter was still there, but he was off duty. Rose went to his house and told him of Bob's disappearance. He knew of his mental fight and promised her he would unofficially undertake the task of finding him. Telling her to go home, he promised to let her know what he could if he found him.

Frantic with worry Rose awaited Streeter's visit. He was dressed in plain clothes when he came. Kindly he told her that he had used the methods usual in such a search for a man who was wanted on a criminal matter but to no avail. He hastened to point out that should she fear he was intent on taking his own life he would not have taken with him the daily-used items she found missing. The only trace he had found of him, and this was a positive identification, was that he had bought a single railway ticket to Tunbridge Wells early that morning, and was recognised by the ticket clerk who knew him well. Monday morning brought a letter from Bob post-marked Tunbridge Wells and enclosing thirty five-pound notes. It read: 'My Darling Rose, I love you and shall always love you but I shall never be any good to you. I have tried so hard to be worthy of you but it will never be. I have dragged you down and down and but for your loyalty to me I would have taken my own life a long time ago. Please, my Rosie, I want you to believe me. I shall not take my own life, for you have told me it is a wicked thing to take what God has given. I know you are able to look after the children, for you always have, with little help from me, and you have looked after me as one of them. I will send you the money each month from my pension but I must keep some to live on; and I will try hard to find a job. You will be far better off in not having me and my bad temper to worry about. Please forgive me for all the bad things I have done to hurt you, but Rosie, you have always known that I don't mean them. Please don't worry about me any more but please think of me sometimes and never forget I love you. Please kiss all my babies and make sure they know I love them. When they are older they will understand, as I hope Rosalina will when you show her what I have written. Good bye my Rosie. Bob.'

Hilda and Michael had emigrated to Canada. Dear Granny Litchfield had passed on and Rose had only her teenage daughter, Rosalina, to confide in, but her strength of character would carry her through, with her inborn practicality and logic the keystones to survival of mind.

She heard a renewal of the loud screams above and returned to Madeline. Perspiring in the labour, and the pain of birth now fast approaching, she saw Rose enter the room. With closed eyes and clenched jaws she was able to emit, quite clearly to the ear, the words, 'It was him, it was Uncle Bob, it was Uncle Bob' and, with a final push downward of her abdominal muscles, she produced a son.

Rose froze in her step, speechless with shock. Stunned, she lowered herself to a chair, oblivious of the midwife's announcement to the mother of the sex of her child. A loathing of this travesty of humanity overpowered her. A loathing she had never hitherto experienced in her entire blameless life. A hate foreign to her nature overwhelmed her. She wanted to exterminate this destroyer of decency with her own hands. Shaken and ashen-faced she found herself sitting at the table downstairs. She had sent the children to the park with sandwiches and told them to stay there until she came for them. She had not wished them to hear the sounds of labour. Baby Ronald was quiet in his cot by the Kitchener cooker fireplace, Rosalina was kneeling beside her mother, glass of water in her hand. She had stood at the foot of the stairs and heard Madeline's words, and had the sense to disbelieve them, but her beloved mother, she knew, would be distressed.

'Mum, please drink some water,' she said. Rose looked at her humbly and said, 'Did you hear what Madeline said?'

'Yes, I did. That's why I came and brought you down.'

Rose did not remember coming down, her head was in a whirl.

'Mum, mum! You mustn't believe her. It's not true. I shall never believe it.'

'And I shall never believe it either, but why did she say it?'

'Because she knows that Dad has gone away and is not here to deny it. She's evil, Mum. I know her better than you think I do. I share a room with her, more's the pity, and if you knew half of what she speaks about, and what she gets up to, you and Dad would have thrown her out long ago. Some of the things she has told me I am too embarrassed to tell you and I know how worried you have been about Dad since he started blaming himself for her being here. I didn't want to worry you more by telling you.'

'What can she gain by telling such an awful lie?'

'I don't like saying this, Mum, but she knows you are soft-hearted and you would blame yourself for Dad's mistakes and feel that you must look after her. The crafty bitch knows you would feel it was your duty and you would allow her to stay here with her baby. She knows her own father doesn't want her - who would? She's rotten, Mum, and I hate her for what she's said about Dad, and I hate her for hurting you.

92

She's not going to get away with it. I'll see to that, the bitch.'

Rose was shocked to hear her daughter speak as she had never heard her speak before and eyed her with surprise.

'Sorry, Mum, but working with so many girls and grown women has taught me a lot of naughty words and expressions. At least I am grown up enough now to know that cows like her are shit!' pointing her index finger to the ceiling.

Well, well, thought Rose, her daughter had grown up. She had not until now realised it, and inwardly thanked God for her welcome companionship.

They heard the midwife descending the stairs and stood up, anxious to see her reaction to what she heard. She entered the room and closed the door quietly behind her, and with fingers to her lips said, 'She's half asleep.'

Nurse Bowling was a woman well indoctrinated in the harsh and cruel ways of life, and her experiences had taught her many of the good and bad facets of human nature. Above all, she had learned prudence, a fact of which Madeline had not been aware in her effort to acquire a witness to her avowal of her child's father's name. Nurse Bowling had known the Higgins family as a cut above the level of many working class families, despite their surroundings and shortage of money. She also knew of the struggle Rose had had in raising her children decently with a husband who was ill and unstable. She had long admired Rose and had attended at the birth of some of her children and, in her book, that meant more than many things of life. The girl upstairs, she thought, was a misfit in this household and if she were allowed to stay disaster would be the outcome, she knew.

'Mrs Higgins, I want you to know I did *not* hear what that girl accused your husband of, and I promise you, if I had, I would never divulge it. Please rest assured of that,' she said.

'Thank you so much, Nurse. Please sit down and have some tea.'

'Thank you, Mrs Higgins. And you should have a drop of brandy.'

Raising her voice, she shouted to Rosalina in the kitchen, 'Bring in two glasses, please love.'

So saying, she delved into her maternity bag and produced a half-bottle of Hennessy's. 'Always good for the soul,' she said with a wink, 'and by the way, the baby is bright ginger.'

Sipping her brandy, Rose said, 'Nurse, the brandy is good for the spirit, but you, Nurse Bowling, are good for the soul!'

Placing her hand over Rose's, the nurse said, 'Now don't you worry any more, I shall keep an ear open, and should I be able to solve the mystery of the real father I'll whisper to you. In the meantime let that girl up there know well and truly that you don't accept her word. Now, I'm off - I'll drop in tomorrow morning.'

Rose climbed the stairs to the bedroom where the new mother and child were lying. Ever compassionate, her wrath for this child-mother had turned to pity.

'How do you feel, dear?' she asked.

Madeline pretended to be sleeping.

'Open your eyes, Madeline. I know you are awake.'

'I feel very weak.'

'It's always like that at first, but you'll soon feel stronger. Would you care for a cup of tea?'

'Yes please, Aunt Rose.'

'Here you are then, I've brought you one.' Rose leaned forward to raise the pillows beneath Madeline's shoulders and kissed the girl's forehead.

'Come along, dear. Drink some and you'll feel better.'

Madeline had never received such tenderness as this from her own mother. Such kindness was unknown to her. A wave of guilt and shame for what she had planned in her mind overcame her, and tears came to her eyes as she hung her head and sobbed. She felt Rose's arms about her, heard her say, 'Have a good cry, dear, it helps sometimes,' and could feel the gentle hands stroking her hair. After so long she had found the kindness and care which she had yearned for and never found. She had sailed into the haven of love and understanding and knew that Aunt Rose was her sheet anchor. A strange love filled her heart for this woman, who should have condemned her for her wickedness, and she knew this new-found love would endure.

Rose dried her tears and bathed her face and forehead with a moistened flannel and brushed her hair.

'Now let's look at our new little man,' she said as she crossed to the far side of the large bed Madeline shared with Rosalina.

The child was indeed bestowed with the most flaming colour of hair Rose had ever seen and, had she entertained the slightest suspicion of Bob being the sire of the newly-born, her fears would have left her as she beheld the tiny infant. As she studied the small features she saw none familiar with any man of her acquaintance and wondered idly who really was the father - but she had no doubt it was not Bob.

Madeline had begun to weep again. Rose quickly went to her, soothing her with motherly crooning and patiently cradled her head.

'Aunt Rose, please forgive me for saying it was Uncle Bob. He was always kind to me. I'm so wicked to have said it. It wasn't true. He told me often to behave myself, and said if I didn't I would get myself into trouble, and now I have. I'm so ashamed.'

'Madeline,' Rose said, 'I'm not going to lecture you and let's not discuss it any more. I can understand the dilemma which has possessed you, and of your father's concern in finding the father, but now is not the time to worry about that. You must not worry about anything at all except the new little fellow, and this is your home and his for as long as you wish. We will all share what little we have, but if we all have love for each other we will be rich in what is important to us all.'

'But I know Rosa hates me.'

'Darling, for a little while I hated you myself, but that has passed, and so it will with Rosa, as you call her. You will find that when she learns that you are not as black as you have allowed yourself to appear, and she can see for herself, as I can, you will be as sisters and love each other as such.'

'Aunt Rose, I'm afraid of my Dad. I dread the thought of him coming here and shouting at me.'

'When he comes, Madeline, I shall ask him to conduct himself in the proper manner he should in a home which is not his. If he does not, I shall make it quite clear to him that he is not welcome to return,' said Rose. 'Now let me attend to you and then we can attend to the baby.'

She called to Rosalina to heat some water and bring Fullers Earth, napkins and the towelling she had prepared.

Rose heard her daughter ascending the stairs and left the room to take the items from her. Rosalina could not fail to comprehend the unspoken message of the demand for silence she saw in her mother's eyes. Those eyes her children understood and obeyed without question.

'Come and help me, dear,' she said aloud.

Together, Rosalina in silence, Rose chattering in kindly endeavour, they attended to the comfort of Madeline. The task completed, Rose, ever the diplomat, decided to clear the air that Rosalina's presence was causing. Encircling Madeline's shoulders with her arm, she said, 'Rosalina, Madeline has told me that what you heard her say is untrue, and I have forgiven her for saying it. And perhaps if you realise how genuinely sorry I know she is then you too will forgive her. Think of what worry she has had with her mother gone and her father a less kindly man at heart than your own. She fears that you hate her, but I know she is in need of your love as she is in need of mine. You will both make me very happy to see that love grows into a lifelong affection for one another, and throughout your lives, remember that hatred is the cancer of the mind, which destroys all that God has taught us.'

Two young women, she thought. Which of them would benefit spiritually in future years from the tragedy of today? *Domine dirige nos!*

She had placed some house bricks in the kitchen oven to be used as bed warmers when wrapped in cloth, and saying she must go to the park to bring the boys home, bade Rosalina fetch the bricks for Madeline's bed; then she set out for the park. When she later returned home she smiled in the warmth of her heart to hear the chattering of female voices in pleasant animation from the room above.

Rose knew that the next hurdle to overcome would be the survival of her baby Ronald, but feared he would be taken. Barely a month before, Dr Hoby had told her that the baby's heart and lungs were weak. It seemed to poor Rose that worries were everlasting, and now Bob had gone she felt alone. But then she reminded herself of her new-found companionship with Rosalina. She will be my strength, she thought, and prayed that the fullness of time would bring Madeline to them both to share what the future held. She had not told Madeline of her feeling that *her* baby, too, gave the appearance of lacking the robust movements (with the exception of Ronald) that she had seen in her own children. She decided to speak to Nurse Bowling about it next day.

But now the boys were clamouring for food. She took the large plate of thick brawn which she had made from the shelf at the top of the cellar steps (where she had put it to cool) and set about slicing it into thick wafers to put between the slices of cottage bread and margarine. Boyish hands were everywhere hoping to stuff a stolen piece into their mouths should she avert her eyes for a split second, but Rose, wise to the ploys of little boys, gave them scant opportunity to supplement their share.

Later that evening Holbrook called to see Madeline. Rose made him understand that she would not tolerate his threatening manner and, should he persist in harassing his daughter, she would ask him to leave. To her surprise he said the reason for his visit was to console her regarding Bob's disappearance, and asked if there was anything he could do to help. He didn't want to see his daughter nor the 'bastard' she was going to have.

Rose looked at him with contempt and said, 'Thank you for

your concern for my welfare, but don't you think your daughter is worthy of a little thought? She is a child in need of affection, in need of parental care. It is the duty of us all to foster their love. I seldom speak as I do now, but you should search your soul and ask yourself if you have been a good father. It is her misfortune that her mother's mind was unbalanced and it is, too, her misfortune that her father did not care about how she grew up. Of course she would emulate her mother's mode of life. She thought it the accepted practice. You are an intelligent man and you watched her grow and try to behave as her mother and you did not attempt to stop it. Now it is too late, and the 'bastard' she is going to drop, she did today, and I'll thank you not to use vulgar expressions in my presence. As you do not wish to see your daughter and her child I will ask you to leave - at once.'

Rose walked to the door and held it open, fixing her withering stare to him, and said, 'Kindly leave.'

Holbrook was not as lacking in parental responsibility as Rose had made out, and she well knew it, but she considered that a little nudging of his conscience would remind him that a child is always in need of its parents' love and respect throughout its span upon this earth. She knew that she had crushed him but she felt it her duty for the sake of them both, father and daughter.

He stood before her, uniform cap in hand, bewildered at the measured and modulated home truths Rose had subjected him to.

'Rose, I don't want to leave,' he said.

'Well! What *do* you want?'

'I love Madeline - I love my sons. My married life has not been happy, and I want you to understand that. Despite that I have always tried to keep a home together for the children.'

'I know that. Bob told me often about your domestic burdens, and frequently expressed his concern for you. It was at his request that your daughter, a stranger to us, do not forget, came to this house. It might interest you to know that

Madeline's pregnancy was the final straw in the years of unhappiness Bob thought he had brought me. That is the reason he has gone away - to lessen the burden on me. Think of that, Fred Holbrook! My happiness has been to be with him, for I love him, you see. And since his awful experience during the war he has never been the same man. Did you know he was decorated on the field for bravery for saving the lives of men, and for killing twenty Germans single handed? In destroying those men he has destroyed himself. Did you know that? No! I can see you did not. There are many things you do not know of him. But know this: he would stand by his children if they were in need of his love. He has sacrificed his own happiness because he wrongly believes he is not worthy of them. Don't do that to Madeline. Show her you love her.'

How wrong I have been in thinking Bob was a lazy layabout, thought Holbrook. It was wrong to take him at face value and wrong in believing he was a bad father and husband. His common sense should have told him that a wonderful woman like Rose would know him differently to become his wife and still love him. 'Well, Fred Holbrook, do you wish to see Madeline?' He heard Rose speak in that wonderful way he never ceased to admire.

'Yes please, Rose.'

Looking into her eyes, he, too, saw a message. A message telling him to show compassion to Madeline. Rose, he thought, spoke with her eyes!

'Well, I'll just pop up first to see if she's decent - I shan't be a moment,' she said.

Upstairs, Madeline had heard her father arrive and the hubbub of Aunt Rose's voice; and she knew by its tone that she was admonishing him. She awaited him with trepidation.

Aunt Rose came into the room with a smile upon her face and said, 'Everything is all right now, dear. Your Dad's coming up to see you. I've had a little chat with him and told him there's nothing to worry about. Now be a good girl and be kind to him for me.'

'Are you sure he won't start on me again, Aunt Rose?'

'I'm very sure. Bye bye. I'll come up when your Dad's gone. Come along, Rosalina, let Madeline have a 'heart-to-heart' with Mr Holbrook.'

Madeline saw the change in her father's face from what she had come to fear. He knelt at the bedside and took her hands in his. He was gentle as he asked, 'Are you feeling all right, Maddy?' He had not used her childhood name for so long and she felt the nearness to him she had thought had left her.

'Yes, Dad. I am sorry for the shame I have brought.'

'I'm sorry for not guiding you and it's as much my fault as yours. But now we must try to forget. We have the future in which to look for happier times. I suppose we all should benefit by our mistakes in life, and I believe that you and I will.'

'Let us thank God we have Mrs Higgins, Maddy. She is an angel, and I sincerely mean that. We have her to thank that we are still the father and daughter we should both feel that we are, and we must never forget that. Poor woman, she has enough troubles of her own, and yet she has helped us to love each other again.'

'Dad, please try to understand. I know it's wrong of me to say it but within a few hours I have come to think of her as my own mother and I know she will look after me more than my real mother ever did.'

'I know that, Maddy, and I'll leave her some money to buy whatever you need. I know she will need it but knowing her she might be too proud, so take this and pretend it is yours.'

He took his wallet from his pocket and gave her twenty pounds and said, 'You'll need it.'

He rose to his feet to look at his grandson. He saw the auburn head, the closed eye-lids and tiny clenched fists and felt a strange sense of accomplishment, pride and wonderment. He reproached himself for his use of 'bastard.'

This small human being was his blood.

'What shall we call him, Maddy?' he asked.

'You choose his name, Dad. I want you to.'

'Would you mind if we call him after my brother, your Uncle Jim?'

'James. Yes, that's a nice name. So that's it, Dad.'

Jim was Holbrook's only brother. He had gone down with his ship during the war. Little Jimmy's days, too, were to be sorrowfully few.

When Holbrook left Madeline gone were the undercurrents of mutual arbitrariness. A bond had been welded. A bond of rekindled unspoken dependability. Rose was happy to see him smiling but felt she must tell him of her fears for the newborn's survival. She told him as kindly as she knew how and was saddened by his reaction to it as she saw his smile turn to dismay.

'Does Maddy know?' he asked.

'I'm not sure, but if my fears are correct Nurse Bowling will break it to her - very kindly, be assured.'

'When is she coming again?'

'Tomorrow morning about ten o'clock.'

'I'll get a day's compassionate leave and come here.'

'Thank you, Fred. I'm sure she will need you.'

Bitterness had been replaced by endearment and for that Rose was thankful despite the circumstances. After he went she left Madeline alone, happy in her new relationship with her father.

Rosalina's voice could be heard in high-pitched indignation. The boys were in the cellar, now grandly known as the 'gymnasium.' It had had various titles. At one time it was the venue of a Magic Lantern show to be followed, in the progress of advanced technology by a candle-lit, hand-turned film projector, the legal ownership of which was known only to the projectionists, and they were not telling. This venture was brought to an abrupt finale when the one and only celluloid reel was ignited and - but for the ensuing noise of the audience scrambling for the exit (the coal flap through which they had been admitted for the price of one half-penny each) and the smell and shouts of *Fire!* and the timely arrival of the fire brigade (Rose and Rosalina) armed with life-saving buckets of water - the house would have gone up in smoke. Anyway, at present the cinema was the 'gym.' The boys had equipped it with their father's old kit bag stuffed with stones and paper and suspended it from the ceiling, calling it the punch-bag. Other refinements included two pairs of boxing gloves, dumb-bells, skipping ropes and a chest expander. The mystery of the origin of these superb appointments was never solved, but it had been noticed by the delicate Bertie that, prior to the weekly visits of Fred and John to the boxing club, the cellar coal flap would be unbolted from within, so that any such items might, for instance, pass straight into the cellar without having to pass through the house, past the eagle eye of Rosalina and Rose.

On their return home, and after a non-suspicious time had elapsed, Fred would make an excuse to go to the cellar. Bertie noticed that after Fred's return the cellar coal flap would be found to be firmly bolted again.

Bertie was the cashier at the 'gym' and was responsible for the receipt of one-halfpenny from each of the 'club's' members, the sum total to be divided by the resident 'officials.'

Rose preferred them to play among themselves rather than with many of the street's children. Several were ragamuffins, neglected by their parents and undernourished. Both mothers and fathers spent the money they should have spent on their children in the Wheatsheaf and were to be seen staggering home at closing time followed by their often bare-footed offspring.

Rose had a constant battle in cleaning her sons' heads of the tiny crab-like lice which infested them. Each night, in turn, they would sit at the kitchen table for their mother to comb their hair with a very fine tooth-comb downwards towards a sheet of newspaper; and should lice appear the scalp would be massaged with paraffin oil and shampoo with Sunlight soap. On occasion, she would find bugs - the boys called them 'steam-tugs' - or hopping fleas, known as acrobats, which had been transferred to their clothing from their playmates from other families. If this type of insect was found, shirts and underclothing would be put in the 'copper,' the coal-heated built-in washing tank, filled with household soda and water for boiling. The outer clothing was hung on the garden clothes line where any remaining lice would die for lack of body warmth.

Despite the multitudinous chores of every day, Rose would often take her zither from its hiding place - a zither forbidden to all on pain of punishment - and play for the 'Higgins Choir.' *Yes, We Have No Bananas, Roses of Picardy, I Passed By Your Window, It Ain't Gonna Rain No More, Singing In The Rain* and other popular songs of the day were to be heard by neighbours, and Fred's solo soprano of *The Bells of St. Mary's* could be heard at the end of the narrow cul-de-sac.

On Sundays, each boy, to his disgust, was obliged to don his straw boater attached by black fine cord to the lapel of his light-blue-striped blazer that Rose had made, wear his calf-length leather black Wrinkin boots and black velvet trousers and follow his mother to church. This procession would be watched by the boys' playmates who were not averse to getting a silent but visible rise out of them. On occasion their behaviour provoked John, a rather quick-tempered lad at times, to break ranks and attack an offender, knocking him to the pavement using the most un-Sabbathlike words of 'piss off,' an act for which he was severely punished at tea-time by the stopping of his share of the winkles and shrimps with watercress, regularly served on Sundays. And for John the replacement of it by bread and dripping was a bitter blow. The mother of the boy responsible for one of John's lapses of discipline was somewhat indignant when after that week she called at the house complaining of John beating up her 'little Ernie' three times in as many days. But the children of the street had been taught a lesson and therefore the desired respect was shown to this elite parade. *Docendo Discimus.*

Rose hastened to investigate the cause of Rosalina's cries.

She had been sitting by the fire with the cat on her lap, she said, when she heard odd sounds coming from the door leading to the cellar. She had opened it quietly to discover 'that little sod Fred hacking away at the brawn on the shelf with a filthy penknife with his mouth already full of it.' Rose called to the depths of the cellar, 'Fred come up at once.' Silence. She descended the steps to find the cellar empty of budding athletes. From the front door there was no sign of him nor his brothers. They were taking advantage of the absence of their father, she told herself, and that would never do. It was past 'coming in time' and they knew it. If she was to be able to control them she must start at once with severe punishment. She went indoors to ensure that the 'Charlie Chaplin' cane was hanging on its usual place on the gas bracket (for it had been known to disappear when one of them was due for its use).

Eventually, shame-faced they timidly filed along the passage from the front door, Fred in the rear, fearing the worst when he saw that icy look on his mother's face. Holding the cane casually across her lap she said, 'Upstairs and in bed at once the lot of you.'

'Mum, I want my Oxo,' said Bertie.

'No Oxo tonight for any of you. This will be your support tonight,' she said, brandishing the cane. 'Go up, get your clothes off. Get into bed,' menacingly adding, and holding the cane aloft, 'and when you are in bed, I'm coming up.'

She had never severely caned them before and was reluctant to do so now, but knew she now had to be both father and mother to correct them. And thrash them she did. When she left her howling sons to dwell upon the prudence of good behaviour she returned downstairs and wept. After a while she returned to massage cold-cream on their burning buttocks, later to take them their usual mugs of hot Oxo and bread. She kissed them all goodnight after they had promised not to be naughty again and returned downstairs to weep once more.

Nurse Bowling arrived earlier than expected the next morning. Rose told her of her patient's change of heart and of the happy reunion of father and daughter, and spoke of her anxiety for the child.

'That's the reason for my coming early. I was of the same mind when I left you last night but you had enough on your plate then. I want to examine him and, if I think I should, I will get hold of Dr Hoby before he leaves his surgery to start his morning rounds.' Dr Hoby's examination confirmed the worst. Little Jimmy died during the afternoon in his mother's arms. It took much of Holbrook's and Rose's gentle persuasion for her to relinquish him.

Little Ronald died the same evening in his cot. Their tiny bodies were laid side-by-side on the table in the front parlour, a room used only at Easter, Christmas and special occasions, and covered with the white satin shawl which Rose's mother had given her many years before. That night Rosalina slept in her mother's bed alone. Rose and Madeline shared her bed. Two bereaved women each comforting the other. The tiny white coffin which held both babies was placed in the glass hearse drawn by a single plumed black horse followed by a carriage drawn by two black horses containing the four mourners. They were laid to rest in the children's section of the town's cemetery.

The Higgins boys had been good boys and they too wept. The whole street had been told that Bob was ill and taken to Woolwich Military Hospital.

# CHAPTER 6

Bob closed the front door quietly behind him. It was 5 am and Sunday morning. The few men lucky enough to be in regular employment would not be astir this morning. He had carefully planned ahead and would go to Tunbridge Wells to the home of an old army friend and get permission from him to have his monthly pension sent to his address and then collect it later each month. He did not wish anyone to track him down, and would be free to send Rose money to help towards the upkeep of the home he was not worthy of living in.

He had considered taking his life to render Rose free to marry again and benefit from the reliance of someone to take care of her, somebody she deserved, but knew she would blame herself for his suicide. He hoped she realised that he had taken his razor only to shave with.

At the street corner he turned and looked back to see the gas street lamp outside his boys' bedroom. He could visualise them! Three in one bed, two in another. He thought of their little heads and cropped fair hair. And Rose. What would she think of him? He hoped his letter would help to explain. He fingered the two letters in his raincoat pocket - one for Rose, the other for the pension people. He would send them from Tunbridge Wells when he had the permission from Jock Fraser, his army mate, to use his address.

And Rosalina? He prayed that none of Madeline's feminine crudeness and unchaste behaviour would rub off on her and remembered Madeline's sexual invitations when she was alone in the house with him. She would sit in the chair opposite his at the fireside, exposing her beautiful legs to the thighs, revealing her firm white young flesh and looking invitingly at him. He was conscious of his lust for her many times and, on one occasion she had stood before him adjusting her suspenders. She neared him and her hand strayed towards him. He had stood back and slapped her face before he quickly left the house, but he knew he had nearly succumbed to his urge, as he had so often almost done with her. Bob had many shortcomings but sex with women other than Rose had never been one; but it was very difficult not to be sexually aroused by the wantonness of this attractive young woman.

Bob was neither shocked nor surprised to learn that Madeline was in 'the family way' and silently thanked providence his conscience was clear, except perhaps he should have warned Rose of her. She would have known how to deal with her and wondered why he had not - was it his shame in allowing Madeline to be aware of her success in stimulating his sexual impulses? Holbrook should have taken her away from the house - anywhere, Bob cared not - when he first learned of his daughter's condition. But no, his house was left to bear the stigma of an unmarried mother as one of its inmates. And it had been the kindly Rose, his Rose, who had insisted in seeing the poor girl through her trouble.

And it was my fault in taking pity on Holbrook's plight, thought Bob. The bastard must have been aware of his own daughter's character, must have known that her demure feminine lady-like manner when introduced to them was a charade. If he had warned him and Rose that she was in need of rigid guidance he was sure Rose would have bettered her. The whole street was gassing, gossiping and sneering, deriding his genuinely lady-like and dignified Rose! The gossiping sluts didn't give a damn about the pregnant girl. Some of their own daughters had been well pregnant when they had married and some had obtained Paternity Orders from the men who had refused to 'give the kid a proper name.' What these filthy, lazy cows were enjoying was what they thought would be the end of the reign of the 'Duchess' as they two-facedly referred to Rose among their unwashed selves - the end they thought of the Sunday perambulation to church 'dressed up to the bleeding nines.' However, Bob knew that apart from circumstances arising to cause her non-attendance, she would appear to be totally unaware of them except for the stone faced 'Good mornings' to those rubber-necking at their front doors. Through all the years of worry he brought her she had never complained, but his humiliation was the final straw, and he had to get away from her to allow her not to have any more fear of his instability.

He made his way through the silent streets towards the railway station. The only people he saw were milkmen and railwaymen. He bought a one-way ticket to Tunbridge Wells and went below to the platform and awaited the train. The ticket clerk recognised him but it was of no moment, he told himself. He was informed that, it being Sunday, the train would run later than on week days. He waited ninety minutes and picked up a discarded Saturday evening *Star* to read. Unemployment figures were rising, politicians were, as usual, blaming each other for it and much space was taken up by the debate on the possibility of there ever having existed a straight banana. The popular song of the time was recorded on the 'Winner' gramophone records and was entitled *I Have Seen Almost Everything But Never a Straight Banana*.

When he alighted from the train he asked directions to Jock Fraser's address. He had never been free to accept the invitation of a reunion with him and it was with alarm that he was eventually greeted by a stranger in response to his knock. He was told that Mr Fraser had moved house to a small village miles away, named Milton. The man was reluctant to give Bob his new address and only after he produced proof of his identity in the form of his army discharge papers was he informed of it and how to get there. A change of two buses was required and a long walk but he finally arrived at a small thatched cottage. The door was opened by Jock's wife who, asking him to wait, called for her husband busy tending the rear garden. He waited to be greeted by 'Christ, it's Bob Higgins, come in.'

Bob made the excuse of having been in the locality and decided to 'look you up so we could have a drink together,' but at the first opportunity told him he wanted a private talk. It was Jock's habit to visit the local pub on Sunday mornings and his wife thought nothing unusual when he announced his intention of having his 'Sunday pint'.

'Come back and have a bit of dinner, Mr. Higgins.'

'Call me Bob; and thanks, I'd like to.' He was hungry.

'Call me Eleanor.'

'Right, and thanks again.'

He outlined his request to Jock who, somewhat mystified for the reason, agreed, but asked, 'Do you mind telling me why?'

Bob decided to be honest in his answer and told him the whole story. Jock knew of the circumstances of Bob's medical discharge - he had been one of the men who owed his life to him - and was prepared to repay him in any manner he was able. He sympathised and admired him for his sacrifice. He had met Rose on the platform of the railway station when they had embarked on the journeys back to France. He remembered the touching scenes of the placing of the red rose in his helmet. In admiration the whole battalion would watch Rose, who never appeared to hear Johnnie Howson playing *Roses of Picardy* on his mouth-organ. Poxy, bloody war!

Jock invited Bob to stay with him for a while until he felt more settled in his mind, but Bob had made up his mind not to burden others again. His headaches had become more frequent, the throbbing sometimes more violent, the vision more pervasive and his fear that the explosion of his mind would result in utter despair for Rose made him determined that she should not suffer when it finally came. Leave the mess for others, but not for my Rosie!

He posted the two letters and boarded a bus to Margate, and slept on the seat at the rear of 'Dreamland,' a very tired man. Autumn, he awoke shivering with cold, and made his way to a sea-front café, the only one left open as the season for trippers had ended.

He had planned to move around the area of East Kent and not stray beyond easy reaching distance of the Fraser cottage in order to collect the voucher for his monthly pension. As time went by he became familiar with all the venues of cheap hostels for men and, with the passing of time, his nervous system deteriorated. Each month Jock Fraser saw this once proud soldier become a worsening shadow of himself. As the years passed he saw him sink to become visually a vagrant, a tramp, until his voucher ceased to arrive and Bob ceased to call for it. He knew his haunts and attempted to locate him, but he had vanished.

# CHAPTER 7

Each month Rose's envelope arrived from Bob. Each month the postmark was different from the previous one. Rose knew the full amount he received, which was shamefully low, but knew it to be in keeping with policy on the treatment, by changing Governments, of the men who had been promised a better standard of living after they had won the war for them. Yes, for Them with a capital 'T,' for the men who had done so had hardly benefitted at all. The only advantage that they had gained was the passing of the days of forelock-touching; no longer were the rich held in automatic awe by those of lowly birth. These latter had acquired a strength in unity, and strikes were the order of the day. Nobody was morally a winner, but the strikes did point to the eventual ending of extreme class distinction. And so this meagre pension awarded - 'awarded' was surely a misnomer, she thought - was the 'reward' for the shattering of human beings.

The sum in the envelope regularly caused her to wonder how he was maintaining himself, for it left precious little for him. In each one was a small note bearing the words 'God bless you all,' and as time passed the handwriting became more spidery.

Hilda and Michael wrote to tell Rose of their impending first visit since their migration. They were horrified by her plight. Rose had tactfully warned them in her letters not to expect to find her new locality on a par with her previous one, which they knew well and adored.

Rose was embarrassed to welcome them from the street along which they had walked. The usual nosy-parkers were at their doorsteps, no doubt discussing the well-dressed lady and gentleman they had seen knocking at the Higgins' door. She had become familiar with her neighbours' lack of manners and they withered at her glance of disdain, but to her visitors their blatant stares were an unwelcome experience.

Rose was now obliged to undertake the washing and finishing of more families' clothes and much space was required to hang, dry and air the miscellaneous articles of their linen. The garden clothes line was insufficient for her needs and cord was stretched across the kitchen and living room. She did not tell her sister she was also cleaning the houses of three of her clients, but Bertie did, much to her chagrin.

Michael had established a thriving business in Vancouver and Rose took great interest in his achievements. Alas, Hilda was unable to have children. Had she been, Rose knew their education and environment would be of a standard she would have wished for her own. Her own were happy but had become inured to their lowly environment and, sadly for her, accepted it as normal. Often as she scrubbed the laundry of more fortunate folk on her zinc corrugated wash-board and stoked the wash copper and stirred the contents with the thick wooden pole copper-stick, she prayed for better things for them. Hilda and Michael had become affluent and were generous in returning from a shopping expedition laden with goods far beyond the means of Rose's meagre purse. Boots for the boys, trousers, socks, underwear, toys, food and presents for Maddy and Rosalina but Rose stubbornly refused the money they urged her to take.

'I can manage, but thank you,' she said in her best manners.

Michael told her they must return to London where he was negotiating some business, but would return the following week and stay at a local hotel before returning home.

The boys were enthralled by the stories of Canada their

112

uncle and aunt told them. Leslie and Michael were the two youngest and found companionship in each other, as did the two eldest, Fred and John. Not that the two groups were apart from one another. These bunches of mischief were held together in a fraternal bond, but as happens in many large families, an unarticulated tendency to separate into pairs often occurs, and so it was with the Higgins clan. But Bertie ever clung closer to his two elder brothers, and had thus grown to know that he was safe from the taunts of 'old deafy, old deafy' from other kids if he stuck close to them. Woe betide those who derided their delicate and backward brother!

When Hilda and Michael returned, the boys were given money by Michael and packed off to see Tom Mix at the cinema. This, he told Rose, was so that he could be free to discuss an important proposal.

'This may sound to you rather selfish,' he said, 'and what I am about to say you must consider very seriously. As you know, Hilda and I are unable to have children of our own and have talked at length together of adoption. We have decided against it except that we, both of us, should he happy and proud to have the privilege of taking home with us two of your sons. We would regard them as our sons, we would educate and prepare them for an adult future which, darling Rose, is beyond your reach. And Rose, most importantly, they will be wanted and loved. They would keep the name of Higgins and will never be allowed to forget that you are their wonderful mother. They will write to you regularly and send you photographs of themselves as they grow so you can watch their progress. We would ensure that the existence of their brothers, of Rosalina and Madeline does not fade from their minds and we will bring them back should they become homesick and unhappy.

'Rose, I have said that you may think us selfish. Well, perhaps we are in wanting to take from you those you love, but we envy you the love the children have for you, and we would want them to love us as they love you.'

Rose bowed her head as she sat, her slightly greying hair reflecting the light of the sun as it shone through the window. She remained silent. Then she raised her face to them and said as a tear left her eyes, 'It must be their decision.'

Hilda sat beside her and placed her arm around her, but did not speak. Rose was aware of making another sacrifice. Michael had branded himself as selfish but, Rose thought, would I not be selfish to deny my sons what I cannot provide? Deny them the future I have dreamed of their having; wish them to remain within their present environment to mature in the mind and morality of it, to become part of it, simply because I love them? Yes, because I love them, I shall let them go if in their adventurous dear minds they would care to.

She felt their eyes on her as she faced them.

'Thank you, both. But now you must tell me which of the boys you have in mind.'

'Any two,' said Hilda.

'I warn you both that whoever chooses to come is a devil without a tail. But their one redeeming quality is that they are well-mannered, and they are more liable to punishment for a lapse of manners than for naughtiness,' said Rose.

And so the decision was left in the lap of the Gods, or perhaps in the hands of satans!

The boys arrived home smelling suspiciously of chips, no doubt purchased from the pound note Michael had given Fred for the cinema tickets and monkey nuts. The change was ceremoniously handed to the donor, who checked it, saying, 'There's nineteen shillings and a penny here.'

'Yes, I know,' said Fred.

'But isn't it twopence halfpenny each to get in?'

'Yes.'

'And a penny each for the nuts?'

'Yes.'

'And a penny each for an iced cornet?'

'Yes.'

'Well, that lot comes to one and ten pence ha'penny.'

'Yes, but we got in for nothing. Only Bertie bought a ticket and once he was inside he let us in through the fire exit. He always does.'

'Why isn't there an odd ha'penny in the change then?'

'Oh, we tossed up for that.'

'It still doesn't add up properly,' said Michael.

Rose intervened saying, 'I've told you often enough that you are not to do that, it's dishonest.'

'All the other kids do, Mum.' Bertie piped. 'Fred gave Uncle Michael all the change back so that shows we're honest, Mum. Michael raised his eyes to the ceiling and thought: There's no answer to that.

The time had arrived to sound them out. They were due for bed, and were likely to use any excuse to stay up longer - for instance, by listening to what was being said to them.

'Who would like to go back to Canada with Uncle and Auntie?' Rose asked.

The voices of Bertie, Leslie and Michael answered in unison, 'I would.'

Fred and John looked at their mother in dismay.

Fred spoke for them both:

'What, without you Mum?'

'Yes.'

'Why?'

'Because Auntie and Uncle would like you to.'

'How long for?'

'Until you are older.'

John spoke for them both this time, 'No, not without you, Mum. No!'

'If you're not going I don't want to,' said Bertie, meaning his two bodyguards.

All eyes turned to the traitors. They were enchanted with the thought of sailing across the ocean on the big ship and then the train and seeing the mountains and cowboys and Indians and cattle. Rose gave the wordless command of silence, with her eyes, to the patriots.

'Listen to me carefully.' All the family took heed when she used that tone of voice. 'If you go, you will grow up there and I won't see you for a long time, but Auntie and Uncle will look after you and take you to a new school. They will give you a nice room for just the two of you and with a bed each and that will belong to you both, so you must keep it tidy. There is a real bathroom and the lavatory is indoors, and it is a big house. But once you get there you must stay for a long time until you have grown up to be big men. Do you understand?'

'Why can't you come Mum?'

'Because I must stay here and wait for Dad to come home from hospital.'

'Will you look after us, Auntie?'

'Of course I will, dear, and Uncle.'

'Have you got a dog?'

'Yes, we've got two.'

That settled it.

'Now the pair of you go to bed,' said Rose; and looking at Bertie ... 'and you.'

She knew the others understood that they were to remain as she escorted the three to bed. As Rose tucked them into bed she wondered if they would recall this room with nostalgia, or would all the happy boyish times pass from their minds? Would they remember her kissing them goodnight? Would they remember the nursery rhymes they insisted on her reciting before she blew out the candle and went downstairs? They were going to a better life and for that she was happy, but God told her she would see them again before he took her.

'Boys, before you go to bed, I wish to tell you the reason for Leslie and Michael going to Canada,' she said. In matters of serious contention she demanded their close attention, and would explain in succinct detail the matter for discussion.

'You have heard me try to explain to your brothers that they will be going to a new school and that school will cost a lot of money. They will be taught many subjects which are not to be learned in their present school so that, as they grow, they

116

will acquire a knowledge of many worthwhile things which will enable them to qualify for employment of high degree. As they progress their salaries will progress and they will be able to afford to buy many nice things. Now do you understand?'

'Yes, Mum, but we would rather stay with you,' said Fred.

'Thank you, my dear boys. You are older than them, and you, I know, appreciate that they do not properly understand that I cannot afford to do what your Uncle and Auntie are so kindly going to do for them. When they grow old enough I hope they will not forget what has been done for them. Now I want you both to make them feel how lucky they are and you are not to discourage them from going. We shall all miss them very much but, remember, it is for their own good. Please promise me you will not say nasty things to them because they are going away. Now promise me.'

'I promise, Mum.'

'I promise, Mum.'

And both kept their promise.

It was arranged that Hilda would stay at home to tend the remainder of the family while Michael, Rose and the new emigrants went to London to make arrangements for their departure to Canada. Rose would wear her very best clothes and she took them from her dress cupboard to hang on the garden clothes line the day before the journey in order to eradicate the smell of the mothballs she had left in the pockets.

Rose dressed carefully for this first excursion from home for a long time, and tastefully applied Pompeian bloom to her fine delicate skin. She had retained her beautiful complexion by nightly application of Ponds Vanishing Cream which she used after washing her face - a ritual she would practise no matter what the tribulations of the day had been. Bob would often stroke her forehead and say, 'Like your bottom, dear, not a wrinkle!' She thought the occasion warranted the rare luxury of a touch of her small bottle of Chem-el-Nezim perfume, and she also placed a tiny heart-shaped tablet of Parma Violets on her tongue - extravagances she had not allowed herself for so very long.

Michael had ordered one of the taxis from the newly-opened car hire office to take them to the railway station, 'to give the sightseers of the street a red-letter day,' he said. And he much appreciated the look of surprise of the booking clerk on learning of the address the taxi was to pick him and the three other passengers up from at eight-thirty the next morning.

He and Hilda left their hotel early to arrive at the house. Fred opened the door to admit them. He and his two brothers were dressed ready for school, faces and hands washed, hair brushed and neckties straight. They would return at dinner time to appear as scallywags, only to be reformed as clean lads for their return to their lessons. Rosalina and Madeline had feigned 'an upset of the stomach' to excuse them from work for the day and, as previously arranged, Fred and John rose early to take a message of illness to each of the girls' employers. Not to have done so might have proved hazardous, for jobs were not in plenty and employers wielded rods of iron with the tight fists which kept wages very low. Michael and Hilda were amazed at Rose's tasteful ensemble and Michael expressed his sincere admiration with, 'Rose, I have no idea how you have kept so utterly beautiful.' Hilda silently agreed - not in the least jealous of her husband's compliments. Rose loved him for his words.

Children were in the street dawdling their way to school when the hired car reversed along the narrow street, the sound of its engine the signal for the opening of front doors by the inquisitive snoopers with their ever self-righteous airs of 'it's my bloomin' street as much as yours - I pay my rent and I'll stand at my open door as much as I want to.' Many of them were in arrears with their rent, the cash having gone across the bar at the Wheatsheaf. Eyes goggled at the sight of the uniformed chauffeur holding open the door of the shining Morris. Michael had deliberately asked for the best car, and tipped the clerk five shillings to ensure its presence - 'to put

118

the icing on the cake,' he had told him. Open mouths joined the goggling eyes at the appearance of 'Lady Bleedin' Muck,' another of the charming titles which Rose had had bestowed on her by her endearing and delightful neighbours. As she lowered her head entering the car, not wishing to spoil the angle of her hat, Michael, resplendent in his pin-striped trousers and black jacket, and bearing a silver-knobbed ebony walking stick and light pigskin gloves, escorted the boys in their Sunday best to the off side of the vehicle.

As the shining black vehicle moved slowly away to the stares of the street-side audience, Rose waived her silken gloved hand in regal fashion to them. This was the pre-arranged signal for Michael to raise his bowler hat in gentlemanly style. And as the car turned from sight, groups of tongue-wagging females formed to venture a guess as to the reason for the spectacle they beheld. They could hear the hilarious female laughter emanating from the Higgins house but were entirely oblivious to the fact they themselves were the butt of the hysterical sounds within. They were not to know that Hilda, Maddy and Rose were discreetly viewing the scene from behind the lace curtains of the front parlour, nor that their degenerate behaviour was up to its usual degenerate standard.

Old habits die hard and the passing of time had not erased Hilda's taste for a glass or two of port. Her copious shopping bag was the source of two bottles, together with cold meats, fruit and salad vegetables for lunch (she had long ceased to call it dinner). But bread, milk and other items were needed and this entailed running the gauntlet of those gossips, and suffering their reference to that 'bleedin' stuck-up lot.'

The hard-boiled Madeline had been gently mellowed by the influence of Rose's kindness and a mantle of refinement had replaced much of her former behaviour. She had absorbed the strength to shun the past, but she was unable to restrain her hatred of the neighbours who derided her beloved Aunt Rose and she had no hesitation in letting it be known. On two occasions she had scratched the face of a woman and torn the hair of another. Rose had attempted to persuade her to ignore them ('you must be the lady that you are, and not allow them to drag you down to their level'), but this was something she was quite unable to do. The sluts were left in no doubt that Maddy was not a Rose, and they got used to avoiding triggering her anger.

To them Rose was a mysterious woman who was not prepared to become one of them, and this was the rock bottom reason for their puerile hostility (they knew little of Rose's affairs). And so it was Maddy who was prepared to run the so-called gauntlet.

From behind the lace curtains Hilda and Rose watched Maddy purposefully stride directly through a cluster of females, deliberately shouldering her way. She could have simply walked on to the street but resolved to use the pavement.

'So, out of my way, you lot of horse dung,' she said and paused in her step to observe their reaction. True to form they dispersed into their homes, slamming the doors behind them. More laughter from the Higgins house!

When the boys came into dinner they made short shrift of the unusually large and varied meal. It was nice to come home to find two giggling pink-faced sisters, and a smiling Auntie; and to smell that special medicine they were drinking, and to go back to school with twopence each in their pockets.

In London the other half of the family were having lunch - not dinner - in a restaurant, being served by waiters. Michael was proud to take his guests to the 'Criterion' in Piccadilly Circus and as they sat he marvelled at the poise of Rose and impeccable table manners of the boys who were to become his 'sons.' He would very much have liked to have known what the other diners were saying of the lady and boys. He had observed the discreet glances and pleasant smiles and wondered if they would ever have believed the background of Rose and her children were they to be told. He doubted it. Each time a plate was placed before them or an empty plate removed there was a 'Thank you, sir' to the waiter from the boys.

They arrived at Charing Cross station and strolled across Trafalgar Square to Canada House where Michael explained the purpose of his visit. Rose signed official documents and after leaving the building they crossed Cockspur Street to the offices of the shipping line to arrange the passage to New York for the boys. With childlike wonder they gazed at the red 'General' solid tyre buses and the mixture of petrol-driven and horse-drawn traffic and the mass of people. On returning to Charing Cross Michael telegraphed a message to his home giving the date of his arrival, with two guests who would occupy the 'Windsor Room.'

When Hilda had seen Rose's poor circumstances she agreed with Michael not to embarrass her by speaking of the true extent of his success in business. He had now expanded and employed five hundred people, and had large investments in other spheres of industry, their home being commensurate with his standing. Their intention had been to invite the entire family to emigrate and pay all expenses, but they were unaware of Bob's absence. They knew that Rose would always wait for his return and would not have agreed to their taking all five boys.

Two weeks later the whole family were standing on the boat train platform at Waterloo Station. Michael guessed Rose's thoughts, for here she had stood before when she and other soldiers' wives made the short journey from their home towns to bid farewell to their husbands. Here had been the scene of the gathering of the battalion and of the rose ceremony, the sound of Johnnie Howson's rendering of *The Roses of Picardy* which Rose had pretended not to hear. On this day, too, Rose forbade tears. 'We must all smile,' she said. But when the size of the train had diminished to a tiny dot tears could be seen on their cheeks. That train was to take the boys and the Cotters to Southampton where they would board the liner *Aquitania* bound for New York. There they would entrain for Ontario and begin their journey on the Canadian Pacific Railway across the vastness of Canada to their home in Vancouver.

'Farewell, my boys! God has told me he will send you back to me "over the mighty sea," dear boys. I love you so!'

Rose knew that God had not promised to send her Bob back to her but God would tell her when He took him.

Home was perhaps a little less noisy, but Rose wished it so. Her thoughts were with her two youngest for a long time, always wishing them to appear with their darling filthy faces and hands, crying for Mummy to kiss a tiny cut to make it better. Long gone were those days, but to her, all her children were her babies.

# CHAPTER 8

Maddy was now twenty-two, much more worldly-wise, her beauty unblemished, and still unmarried. She had taken to heart the wisdom of Rose's tactful teaching, and despite her natural feminine needs of sexual fulfilment had successfully retained what she called her virginity, but sometimes it had been a near, very near thing.

Rose, the ever understanding Rose, would listen with interest to the frank recountings of her romances and the lurid details of overtures of the young men who clambered to escort her to 'hops' at the Casino dance hall and other venues of entertainment. Maddy, was very selective and no candidate for her company was considered unless well-dressed and, more importantly, well-off. If they were unable to afford the best seats in the cinema or theatre she had no compunction in making them aware of the affront to her dignity.

Maddy had become as hard as nails with young men since her previous tragedy and had learned what men regarded as fair game was not 'love all.' She knew the father of little Jimmy and frightened him no end when she threatened to enlighten his wife. He was ginger-haired, as were his son and daughter and when one evening, in the company of the baker's son, sitting in the bar of one of the better public houses she saw him with two cronies, she had no doubt that she was the object of the sly grins and whispered conversation. She boldly walked to them and said, 'Has this carrot-top told you that apart from him having my body he is the father of the baby resulting from it? Has he told you he promised to stand by me, but kept away when I needed money? Has he told you he was engaged to his present wife who has now two kids as ginger as my baby?'

Then, facing Ginger, she said, 'If I ever learn of your slandering me again you can expect me at your front door with a birth certificate and photographs of a baby with ginger hair and, unfortunately for him, the image of you.'

She had neither of these, but he was not to know that, nor were the many customers in the now-hushed saloon. That was Maddy! And because she felt regret for the discomfort of her escort, on returning to him said loudly, 'Come along, Cousin Bill,' and, turning at the door, called, 'Good night, Daddy.'

Fred loved her and she adored Fred. Rosalina thought him detestable. The feeling was mutual. It was to Maddy he went if ever he had boyish secrets to share and it was to Fred she would give secret presents of toffee and chocolate. One day she had made him a kite from sheets of newspaper and as he excitedly - string and kite in hands - ran outside to fly it, he fell, his forehead crashing on a corner of a heavy wooden chair. His head was swollen to the extent of causing blindness. Maddy was heartbroken but the doctors said it would pass, as it did. Maddy would run home from work to sit with 'her little blind boy' and tend him to the extent of leading him to the outside toilet and guiding his hand to the sheets of newspaper to clean himself. When his eyesight returned she took him to the music hall and bought him some chips on the way home.

One day Fred was closely examining his private parts. The entire region had become inflamed. He was too embarrassed and ashamed to tell even his lovely Maddy, but she had sensed something unusual was plaguing him. She voiced her concern to Rose who, too, was aware of his uncharacteristic mood and had repeatedly asked him to tell her the reason. He had gone to the lavatory and remained there until she became worried and brought him indoors but still he would not tell her what was wrong. 'Maddy, I am very worried in case he has been up to something again. If anyone can get the truth from him it's you. He simply won't tell me.'

Later that evening Madeline winked at Fred, raising her eyes to the ceiling, the usual signal to follow her to her room when she had a secret present for him. Sitting on the side of the bed, small bag of tiger nuts in hand, she heard him slowly ascending the stairs. He would normally run. Tears were streaming from his eyes as he stood in the doorway. He very seldom cried, and as he ran to her arms she embraced him in compassion. She allowed him to sob as she had never heard him cry, and gently she persuaded him to tell her his secret.

She unbuttoned his braces and lowered his short serge trousers to behold an area of angrily inflamed flesh and realised he must be taken to hospital at once. Telling him she must break their pact of secrecy, she called for Rose. They bathed him and applied ointment and bandaged him around his middle region. It was difficult for him to walk and Maddy insisted on using the old upright perambulator from beneath the yard table and, bidding Rose to stay at home, wheeled him to hospital. Years later dear Maddy was to wheel Fred to that same casualty ward alone again.

Maddy held his hand as a doctor and nurse treated him and shrouded his penis with thin boracic lint. They told Maddy that he must be circumcised within a few days when the inflammation had receded. Dr Hoby, much to John's disgust, arranged for the brothers to receive similar treatment on the same day, and so it was Maddy's hand that Fred held as the anaesthetic mask covered his face, and Rose's hand John's. It was Maddy who wheeled the vomiting Fred home and put him to bed, and it was Rose who put John there.

To Rosalina the entire episode was disgusting and was completely Fred's fault, of course! Her opinion of him was, she believed, vindicated when, after his complete recovery from the 'major' surgery, he had deposited a penny-worth of white fizzy sherbet powder in the bottom of her white chamber pot. When she used it just before going to bed the foaming chemical prompted screams which brought Rose and Maddy running to her. When the mystery of the cause of the effervescent phenomenon was solved, Rosalina failed to understand why Rose and Maddy were falling about with laughter and declared, 'That little sod Fred should have had his bloody head chopped off instead of his cock!' Fred and John were pretending to be sleeping when Rosalina burst into their room to wreak vengeance, but she burst into hysterical tears when her upper reaches became saturated by the jets aimed on target by her water-pistol-packing dear little brothers. Rose, striving to restrain laughter, pretended to smack their backsides, and Maddy took Rosalina into her arms to comfort her, biting her lower lip to hide her humour.

But Fred could not countenance unkindness to Maddy and until her death many years later he loved her as he never loved his sister. She was his sister.

Two years later Maddy met the man she was to love, and be loved by, throughout her life. Sam was a foreman bricklayer, and when they were married shared his widowed mother's house, but Mr & Mrs Samuel Somers waited to have their twins, a boy and girl, until he had built with his own hands a bungalow on the outskirts of town. Like Rose and Bob, they were soulmates.

When Rosalina married a Royal Marine the boys secretly clapped their hands at the thought of her leaving the house to take up residence in married quarters and were chagrined to learn that her husband would share her room at home. The boys wondered if he realised what a cow she was, and not the sweet girl she appeared in her white bridal gown. They disliked her even more when they were told by Rose that they were to be smartened up with fancy clothes to become ushers in juvenile clothing which did nothing to acknowledge that they were on the threshold of manhood. It was only to please their mother that they finally agreed. It was a happy day for them when she finally took residence elsewhere, and the once-crowded house now consisted of Rose, two boys in early youth and Bertie in puberty, and who would require his mother's tender care for the remainder of her life.

Fred and John continued with their boxing and succeeded in representing their club at regional contests. Rose was not enamoured by their interest but never attempted to dissuade them. When Fred joined the cadets of the Royal Marines she was proud to watch him in the forward line of the junior band playing the side drum, but he persisted with his boxing and competed successfully in the inter-cadet services contests.

Fred then gave up the cadets to become a grocery delivery boy after school hours and all day on Saturdays to earn money to help his mother. John delivered bread for the same purpose. Rose was granted an allowance for bread and hobnailed boots for the boys and twice-weekly they would go to the local workhouse gates with the voucher for five loaves which they would bring home in the white linen-bag Rose made. But the boys were a source of concern to her when they would bring home bags of coke and coal, potatoes and other goods, although she was grateful for them. No amount of questioning would provide her with a satisfactory answer as to their provenance. The boys had discovered that coal and coke, fallen from the wagons of trains in the freight area of the station was left where it had fallen and the porter had no objection to these well-mannered boys taking it home to their 'poor mother.' What he never saw was their taking the fuel from full stationary wagons to supplement that which had fallen off accidentally. The spoils were quickly loaded onto the four-wheeled barrow and taken from sight, and when one - namely Bertie - walked the forty yards to thank the porter, the others would push the loot to safety. 'What nice boys,' the porter used to think.

The potatoes were easier to come by, for a potato merchant's yard had a wall alongside the rows of open trucks, stacked with sealed bags tied at the neck, ready for dispatch to the wholesale market. Fred would climb the wall and with a scout's knife cut the string of a couple of bags. As the trucks left the yard the vibration would cause the contents of the unsecured bags to fall into the street where awaiting hands rapidly transferred them to the barrow - and away!

Every penny the boys earned from the jobs they did was brought to Rose and she would ask them how much she should take. Always the same reply, 'How much can we have, Mum?' and they would be happy with anything she said. Often they would buy her a small bunch of flowers or a small paper bag of her favourite bulls-eyes.

Rose wondered what the future held for them. Already John had said he wanted to join the Royal Navy; and she wanted Fred to further his education at a higher school. He had sat for a scholarship and was now awaiting the result. She had no doubt of his success and encouraged him to study. His ambition, he said, was to reach the top of the profession he would choose. 'When I'm old enough to know what I want to do.'

Fred had taken a new part-time job with a butcher delivering meat, and each Saturday morning he rose at five-thirty, washed, made slices of bread and dripping to take with him, and would be at the shop at six o'clock to work until, apart from an hour's dinner time, seven in the evening. Too, he would be at the shop at nine o'clock on Sunday mornings to deliver Sunday joints to those without means of retaining the freshness of the meat, for few folk possessed refrigerators. He was happy to take Rose the money from the tips given him for this special service, tips ranging from two pence to six pence and sometimes a little more. But he was happiest on Saturday nights when his boss, Joe Ransom, a very strict but very kindly man who paid him generously, packed a mutton cloth with a large joint of meat, sausages, pudding beef and chops. 'Take this lot home and give it to your lovely Mum with a big kiss from me.' Always the same message.

Fred would carry the bag over his shoulder and go home very tired and very happy to dump his perks on the living-room table for Rose gratefully to inspect. He would proudly give her his wages and felt like the family breadwinner. After, he would soak himself in the long tin bungalow bath his mother had prepared for him in front of the Kitchener fire range. The only difference was that nowadays she was careful to avert her eyes from his nakedness, and he, too, conscious of his puberty, covered his maleness with his hands.

The coming of youth had taken his soprano voice and he declined Mr Pardy's request to remain in the choir as tenor, happy to be free to study during evenings and work Sunday mornings. The Sunday Higgins church parade had long ceased, and Rose now attended Evensong.

The eagerly awaited examination results vindicated Rose's expectations of her son. He won top position of the five chosen from the twenty candidates entered, but she was saddened by the knowledge that he would not benefit from his achievement. He knew that, were he successful, he would be unable to attend school till the age of sixteen; but Rose admired his resolve to 'let them know I'm as good, if not better than that lot.' 'That lot' being the sons of parents able to afford the required school uniforms, sports wear and other extras. Parents who did not require their sons to earn a wage to support themselves and contribute to the household budget. The school leaving age was fourteen. Fred was thirteen, with nothing more to learn from the school curriculum, and was given special dispensation to leave. He was taken on full-time by the butcher and received ten shillings a week plus tips and a mid-weekly supply of meat added to the usual weekend bag. He told his mother he would one day buy his own shop, and this he did intend to do, but it was not to be.

John, too, was well eligible to enter a similar examination when he attained the appropriate age, but shunned it. He intended to receive his mother's permission to apply to enter the Boy Service of the Royal Navy. Rose's consent was given. When the time arrived his mother and brothers said good bye to him at the Boys Recruiting Office, whence he was taken to Shotley, near Harwich, to become Boy Wireless Telegraphist Higgins. Farewell my son. Farewell another of my babies, come back in your smart uniform. He did.

# CHAPTER 9

Fred Holbrook had fallen in love with Rose at their first meeting and although she had sensed it for some years she gave no indication of it. He was a good man, she knew that, but for her, Bob had been her only lover and, despite her womanly physical needs, had remained faithful to him. Several men had shown interest in her, and lesser chaste women in needy sexual and monetary circumstances would have succumbed to their polite offers of 'assistance.' Her intuition told her that Bob would never return but she prayed for him each night, as did her children when she blew out the bedside candle. The pension money had arrived regularly through the years, the address written by unfamiliar hands, telling her that now his nerves were deteriorating and, had she been able to discover his whereabouts, she would have gone to him and brought him home.

Holbrook had spent many hours and days over a long period searching for him on her behalf to no avail. Before the two younger boys departed for Canada, Rose and Rosalina had accompanied the boys on the annual Sunday school outing to Herne Bay. Bertie had seen a tramp watching them from the corner of a nearby street, and told his mother. She saw similarities to Bob in the gait of the figure. Head averted, he vanished from view. She ran after him, but he had gone by the time she reached the corner. Later that same day a policeman's attention was drawn to a small crowd of people clustered around a dirty looking tramp sitting on a park bench weeping bitterly.

Fred Holbrook and Mr Pardy next day searched Herne Bay for him and at the police station were told of the incident but could get no clue of him. Pardy and Holbrook agreed not to tell Rose and their persistent searches failed to find him.

Also monthly, Rose received an envelope bearing the eagerly-awaited Canadian stamp. Always the letter enclosed photographs of the two boys. Though they were on the opposite side of the world she was able to watch them grow, and now, in the late 1920s, they looked as little men sitting astride two white ponies. Their small heads were turned directly to the camera, right arms in salute, faces wreathed in smiles; little notes in tiny envelopes enclosed within the large one told her of their progress from childlike indecipherable scribble to, 'Dear Mum, today I rode Sammy, my pony,' and gradually she was to see them grow into youths and men.

As the years passed their letters to her were sent by their own hands, telling her of their progress and scholastic achievements. She wept alone on the day she received Leslie's letter telling her he was about to enter University, with the rejoinder, 'I'll make a doctor out of myself yet.' Later in his letter he said, 'Mike's better than I am at learning, so he'll no doubt take over one of Uncle Michael's places.' She also wept for her Fred, who had proved that he too might have entered a University.

Often Hilda filled in the details the children omitted. Rose would reply - sending back the money Hilda had sent in the form of dollars. She would write, 'I have asked you so often to not send me money. The letters and photographs and the good welfare of the boys are the treasures you have provided.'

Hilda slowly acknowledged defeat but Rose found the presents of modern feminine clothing very acceptable. It gave her much pleasure, too, to know that Fred and his now-Canadian brothers corresponded, and it amused her to learn that Fred wrote he would visit them some time in the future. How he could possibly do so she had no notion, and told herself it was just wishful-thinking. But visit them he did.

Rose recalled the time she thought she might lose Fred. He had complained his throat was sore and her usual treatment of his sock bound around the neck, which had hitherto been successful, did not work, and Fred had developed a temperature. She asked Dr Hoby to call and, unable to visit immediately, he examined the boy during the afternoon, by which time he was comatose. He diagnosed diphtheria, but was unable to arrange transport to the local isolation hospital because, being Sunday, an ambulance was unavailable. All residents of the household were forbidden to leave the house, he instructed, for fear of infection to others. He told Rose to come to his house should Fred have difficulty in breathing, when he would return and perform a tracheotomy. Telling her to keep away from others, he promised to visit next morning should she need him.

Fred remained unconscious until six o'clock next morning, his temperature slightly lower. Rose sat beside him the entire night through. When Dr Hoby came he took a swab from the boy's throat for scientific examination before the ambulance took him to the Fever Hospital where he was taken to a ward to join the many patients in similar condition. The hospital was sectioned into three isolation blocks to care for those infected with diphtheria, scarlet fever and typhoid. The only visitors were relatives of those in danger of death, amongst whom was Fred. Dr Hoby drove Rose to the hospital where she was clothed in an antiseptic gown and mask and taken to the oxygen tent in which Fred's bed had been placed. He had lapsed into a coma; his temperature had risen. They told her to fear the worst should his temperature remain high or rise further. Again she sat beside him all night and it was dawn when she saw him open his eyes and heard him croak, 'Mum, where am I?' Her fervent prayers had been heeded. She took the cool hand of her favourite child and then knew he would come home.

Fred was put in isolation for four weeks, the house was

fumigated and his brothers kept from school. A decade was to pass before insanitary conditions then prevailing were to be improved, conditions from which mainly children fell victim.

Christmas would be easier for her. Each year it seemed the portals of life were opened and closed for her. Bob had gone. Jimmy came. Ronald had come before him. Both had gone together, to God. Leslie and Michael had gone. Maddy and Sam had come. John had gone away. Rosalina had gone and now her first and second and then her third child had come to join Maddy's twins. She would be invited, she knew, to Rosalina's or Maddy's house to join the Yuletide celebrations and, with her two remaining boys, would accept. But the ever-present reflection of Bob, her soul mate, would prevent her, she knew, from proper attention to those she loved.

'Bob, my Bob! Where are you this Christmas Day? I know your heart is with me. You know my heart is with you. Others cannot understand the meeting of souls - meeting to never part. Mine and yours are here today to say "Happy Christmas, Grandma!" and "God bless, Grandad," the tiny ones you have not seen, but who have learned to love you, my Bob, by the love they know you have for me.'

John had come home on leave, and as was the custom, was in uniform. (Indeed it was forbidden for lower-deck personnel to wear mufti). It was with passing thought of Bob that they returned from the Wheatsheaf. Both boys were now of an age which allowed them to purchase alcohol from the Bottle and Jug bar, and with a bottle of port for her, and a bottle of sweet brown ale for themselves they made for home. Later they would attend a party at Maddy's house, which always culminated in a boisterous but happy 'knees-up.' This Christmas was to be no exception.

Sam drove Rose home early in his brand new Austin Seven, which he had just purchased at a cost of £75, with Bertie sitting beside him; Fred and John to walk home, probably a little mellowed and, if not drunk through over-indulgence in the plentiful supply of the brown ale they had acquired, near to being so. Maddy's parties were legendary in that there was never a dearth of liquid sustenance nor of the music provided by her plentiful supply of gramophone records, John's playing of the piano (he was a very welcome guest at any venue boasting a piano) and even Fred's harmonica renderings.

Sam's 'party piece' never varied. Standing on a chair dressed in his long night shirt, back-to-front, straw in mouth, a battered trilby hat with the brim turned down, a lavish smearing of Maddy's face rouge on each cheek, he would parody to near-perfection 'nissed as a pewt,' Leslie Sarony's popular depiction of an archetypal country bumpkin - 'There was an old man he had three pigs, pigs, pigs, iddilly digs, sussanas a funical man.' The refrain of a short raspberry and whistle he had rehearsed to perfection, and he never failed to create the desired effect. Well imbibed, his guests would fall about with laughter and tonight was no exception. And laughing helplessly, Rosalina fell against a fellow female guest of large proportions who fell upon a male guest, who fell upon Sam's chair, the result being a mound of semi-inebriated humanity from beneath which came the cries of pain of Fred.

They carried Fred, crying loudly at the pain he felt in his left thigh, to an adjoining room. He was examined by an ex-Army medical orderly who purported to be knowledgeable in the functions of the human frame. After much pulling and pushing, bending of joints and physiotherapy in the form of the thumping of thigh muscles by the thick side of the palms of his hand, the former stretcher-bearer declared the patient fit to be carried home by his fellow revellers, and despite his lapse into unconsciousness. The journey home was not un-eventful, for within a few yards of the house Fred was accidentally dropped from the shoulders of his willing but incapable bearers, which resulted in further cries of agony from the now-conscious youth.

Maddy instructed him to be carried and put on the large bed she shared with Sam, and when her guests departed - amongst whom was Rosalina, whose sisterly concern was expressed with the words 'Sod him, let him get on with it. I'm not going up to see him,' - she tenderly removed his clothing. Knowing it would cause him pain to attempt to dress him in Sam's pyjama trousers, with the care of a mother for her child, she covered him with her night dress, gently pulling it over his head and shoulders.

Sam knew of the love between Maddy and Fred and understood his wife's kindness in her maternal wish to stay with him in the bed to comfort him in the manner she had since his childhood. He too loved Fred and knew that, next to his mother, his wife meant the world to this growing young man.

That night and the ensuing twenty days and nights remained in Fred's mind for the rest of his entire life - a combination of pain and gentle kindness. Maddy, his wonderful, sweet, kind, precious Maddy and her good, caring, affable husband Sam were to Fred more than mere relatives; and his deep affection for them endured.

Boxing day, and a further day of agony.

Despite Maddy's request to the local doctor to examine him he refused, it being a Bank holiday. She had no difficulty in persuading Sam to drive to Fred's panel doctor, Dr Hoby, to try to get him to see him. But the patient was outside his catchment and medical protocol forbade his attending him.

It was only after the payment of half a crown that the local doctor diagnosed a pulled thigh muscle and recommended massage, and the expertise of the ex-stretcher bearer neighbour was regarded as provident, despite screams of pain from the patient.

Rosalina's loudly expressed opinion was: 'He's putting it on. He's malingering. He's pretending to be suffering. He should have his backside kicked.' And twice weekly for three weeks the past-retirement-aged doctor would attend to collect his fee of half a crown to utter the immortal words, 'treatment as before.'

The doctor was, no doubt, inclined to agree with the diagnosis of Fred's beloved sister but medical protocol and

135

two half crowns a week bade his silence. Maddy was alone in her conviction about Fred's agony. 'Tonight Sam is going to the British Legion Club and if you can stand the pain I want to get you to the hospital. Can you slide on your back downstairs? If you can manage that I can get you there,' she told him.

Maddy dressed him in trousers, socks, slippers and pullover and placing a mound of pillows beside the bed eased him to the floor, pulled him by his armpits to the head of the stairs and, despite his moans - shutting their pitiful sound from her mind - eased him slowly down. She must not abandon her task, she told herself. I know he's sinking. He was visibly losing weight and had become pale and ashen. His cries had diminished to whimpers.

Maddy summoned all her strength to lift him into the old Victorian wicker bath chair she had borrowed from an elderly neighbour; and wrapped him in blankets as a mother would a baby in a perambulator, gloved his hands and enshrouded his head with scarves. She pushed him through the bitter winter's night to the hospital three miles away to the same casualty department she had taken him to, as a child, when he was in need of care.

Given morphia and X-rayed it was discovered that Fred's femur, at its summit, had been pulled from its socket in the pelvic frame. Encased in plaster of Paris he was ordered to remain in bed for six to eight months and, because no more treatment could help him, he was transferred to the local 'lying in' hospital situated within the precincts of the workhouse. He was installed in a geriatric ward to become the only youth among thirty-four patients. Here he saw incontinence, senility and death each day and night, an experience which broadened his youthful mind; and with this came a maturity far beyond his years, which strengthened his belief that in life dependence lies within oneself, for the aged are without money, unwanted and deserted, as are the afflicted young. Fred realised that he would be afflicted for the rest of his life. In that hospital bed, surrounded by unvisited old men, he resolved to face his future alone and to be a burden to nobody. Was this the mirror of his own dear father?

Rose visited him daily, appalled by his disgusting surroundings. She complained of them to the authorities to no avail. Maddy, more forthright, created scenes at the Town Hall, wrote letters to the local press and vehemently expressed her indignation to her Member of Parliament, but all her efforts were fruitless. After many months a new doctor was posted to Fred's ward who at once directed the Matron to move him to the small annexe. Here he was later joined by a young man his own age. Charles was terminally ill and aware of it. His courage and stoic character inspired Fred to surmount his own depression and when Charlie died, his hand clasping Fred's, he left his spirit within his ward mate. Tillie, the kindly nurse, knew Charlie's span on this earth was drawing peacefully towards its close and, at his request, had pushed the two beds together, and despite the fact she was off duty, she stayed with him and his assembled family to the end.

Tillie was wonderful. When, shortly after Charlie's death, the plaster cast encasing Fred from armpits to left ankle snapped at the femur apex region, it was Tillie who came to him in response to his cries of pain and it was she who undertook many kindnesses to maintain his spirits, some of which were beyond her line of duty.

When the day of his discharge came, walking sticks in hands, Fred experienced the gold of human kindness and the obscenities and indignities of death. Serenity in the death of Charlie. Indignity in the excrement of shattered bodies of old unwanted men who had fallen from their beds to die unattended by the solitary overworked night nurse: scenes indelible upon his youthful mind forever.

Unemployment was yet rife - young people were working sometimes in adult work for juvenile wages. Fred knew his chances were abysmal. Joe Ransom was kind enough to supply Rose with meat each week while Fred had been away, but butchers' work then entailed the handling of heavy hind- and fore-quarters of beef, and this was now beyond the capability of Fred.

Fred refused to allow his sticks to become a lifetime hindrance and persevered in walking long distances. Having gained strength he was able to discard one of them. However, nobody was prepared to employ, even in the most sedentary, humble capacity, a cripple. The word 'cripple' he hated throughout his life and referred to other unfortunates as 'lame.'

Fred saw a notice advertising a 'strong boy wanted' in the window of a newly-opened fish and chip shop and, realising that he would be turned away, snapped his one remaining stick across his knee. His limp did not go unnoticed by the proprietor but he got the job at ten shillings per week with two meals in the twelve hour day of six days per week. The proprietor, too, had a very pronounced limp and perhaps his heart ruled his head. Fred's job was to peel potatoes, chip them and cut fish in varying sizes, making batter and moving hundredweight sacks of potatoes.

Weekly his leg grew stronger and his industry was rewarded by an increment of two shillings per week. His ability to use his fists had not left him and once, in the absence of the owner and manager, deposited into the street with ease two objectionable customers. This aroused the interest of several female employees; also the owner's wife.

Fred had not hitherto been bereft of the pleasures of sex, his initiation being with the verger's daughter in the appropriately named 'organ loft,' and later, the stallion-like pleasuring of two hitherto maiden spinster sisters; and Tillie, the nurse, who had applied her soft, healing hands to tenderly massage the rigidity of his ailing body. And yet throughout his entire life he was the seduced and not the seducer. Always gentlemanly with ladies he was an oddity to many of his male friends. The teaching of his mother to 'always be respectful to ladies' never left him. But this did not deflect him from the numerous amorous adventures which befell him, that in the fish and chip shop being no exception.

Fred first fell to the wiles of a vivacious staff member named Betty, who had expressed to him her fear of walking home alone in the darkness after her day's work, and invited him to escort her. Pure in mind he was happy to do so, and at her suggestion sat on the grass of the now-deserted park. He was somewhat embarrassed as she laid back gently tugging him to her; and was amazed to discover what articles of apparel she was *not* wearing. She became as an animal possessed. She was twenty-five, her husband a Petty Officer serving on the China Station. Fred was sixteen, but having tasted, he found he enjoyed the flavour, and partook of the elixir with relish at the same spot on further occasions. Perhaps it was fortuitous that her husband returned sufficiently early to be with her when she produced their 'prematurely' born son, a son remarkably resembling Fred whom he had never met. Her husband was, as she, dark haired.

The second lady was Barbara. She, too, was married. When she asked him to replace a washer on her dripping kitchen tap, her husband being engaged in tomato-gathering for the season in the far-away Channel Islands, Fred was happy to oblige. When he had satisfactorily completed his task she insisted upon taking him on a conducted tour of the house. In the main bedroom she bent forward to place each hand on the hem of her dress, and in one swift upward movement revealed rather more than he had expected. Thereafter Fred executed services for her which required the attention of his fast-expanding field of expertise. Always on Sundays.

Fred's youthful manhood had not gone unnoticed by the owner's wife, whose demands of him, though cautious, were frequent. She was thirty-five and proved to be more lustful that the two younger women. But Fred coped. However, the harem door was closed to him when the unattractive cashier, Gertrude, from whom he had successfully avoided more than the odd kiss, blew the whistle on him to the owner, acquainting him with the adultery of his wife. Despite his own known liaison with a waitress next door, he gave Fred the sack. But more important to Fred than the loss of the amenity was the loss of the job itself.

Rosalina, a gossip as ever, heard the news from a member of the staff, a friend, and sped to impart the tidings to Rose before Fred had summoned sufficient courage to go home and tell her himself. With the familiar verve of yore, Rosalina branded him: 'The dirty little sod, he'll end up bad. You mark my words!'

Rose simply placed her hands on his shoulders and said, with a smile and a slow shake of her head, 'Freddie, you're growing up.'

When Maddy was told by Rose she laughed like a drain.

In those days, were a person to be fired for nefarious reasons, he was not allowed dole; but here Fred was fortunate in that his late employer was loathe to supply the real reason for his dismissal, and reported it as a necessary reduction in staff owing to loss of trade. Now over the age of sixteen, Fred qualified for the higher dole allowance of eight shillings, six of which he gave to Rose. She had ceased to launder others' clothes and supplemented Bob's pension by working in the houses of the more affluent as a domestic cleaner. Bertie was a perpetual source of concern and was shortly to leave school with no hope of employment. John made her a small allowance from his pay; so now a little sunshine filtered through her economic gloom. Rosalina 'could not see her way clear' to help her mother's budget. Maddy, sweet Maddy, was generous with both purse and love.

Fred, after few weeks, found employment as House Boy at a small hotel eight miles from his home. The wages were four shillings plus tips with full board and bed with one half day per fortnight off duty. The working conditions proved to be of Dickensian slavery, the tips non-existent and, at the behest of his mother, he picked a quarrel with the manager's wife, threatened the bullying husband and went home. During the night of his return he was awakened by the weeping of his mother and hastened to her room. She was sitting on the edge of the bed, face in hands. He sat beside her to comfort her and held her close to him.

'Mum, please tell me what's wrong.'

She continued to weep. Fred at a loss to understand the cause said, 'Please Mum, I shall cry too if you don't tell me.'

Her head was buried on his shoulder when he heard her say 'Your Dad has God to care for him now. He promised me He would tell me when He took him and He has just told me.'

Knowing his mother's deep conviction to Christianity he took her hands into his and said, 'You will not worry any more Mum, I'll look after you.'

'Fred, I will be happy when you are happy. You have your life before you and, through it all, God has told me you too will shed many tears, but the happiness you will find after those tears will be yours alone and, though by that time I will be with God I shall see you and be happy too.'

Her room was now the one in which the boys had slept as children, and by the light of the street gas lamp outside its windows he helped her into her bed and went downstairs to make her some tea. The time was now three-thirty as he wondered at the strange power which had also convinced her of his father's death. Despite his mother's belief in Christ she had not ruled the family by the Bible. Hers was a simple heartfelt worship. Never had she entered into tirades of religious fervour nor over-used long biblical quotations. Even the Higgins Church Parade, she told them, was to discipline their minds to the fact that we were, all of us, the children of God.

To others, perhaps, her life had been one of toil and tears, but to Fred's mother it was the will of God in his wisdom. She possessed an indefinable strength of mind, the gift to lessen the burdens she carried within her.

Fred placed the cup at her bedside table and asked, 'How do you feel now, Mum?'

'I'm all right now, dear, I shan't cry again.'

'Tell me, Mum, did you dream about Dad?'

'No, son. I was sleeping and I felt your Dad's arm around me and that was a message from God' - a measure of the family's trust in Rose's beliefs and that they should accept it without question. But the question was: Where is he? Rose's reply to it was, 'Not far away, I know,' spoken with utter conviction!

Tomorrow would be Saturday and the early mail delivery would bring news, she said, and of course it did. Among the Easter cards came a large envelope by registered post addressed to Mrs Rose Ellen Higgins. As she sat in Bob's big chair and opened it she looked at her sons with the well-recognised message of her eyes demanding silence. She drew forth his pension book and a single sheet of typewritten paper. It was headed Sittingbourne Town Hall and referenced to Robert William Higgins.

Dear Madam, The above named man was admitted to the casual house of Milton Institution on Thursday last at 7 pm. All casuals must bathe before admittance to the dormitory and during this process he collapsed and was transferred to the Medical Ward where he died at 3.05 am the next day. This letter and contents have been sent to you on the instructions of Mr John Fraser, the resident of the address beneath the Pensioner's name on the pension book.

There are no other effects but the clothing which I feel should be disposed of by the staff of the Institution. Should you not contact this office within three days of the above date, the deceased will be interred by Parish funds.

The letter was signed by an indecipherable hand but the meaning of it was plain. Bob had become a tramp, had gone to the Workhouse for a night's shelter, had collapsed and died and within three days would be buried in a pauper's grave. Rose drew from the envelope a small package bearing the message, 'To be opened by my wife after my death.' Inside she found the old photographs of the children and that of Rose and himself, and inside a small tobacco tin a faded red rose and a sheet of paper bearing his now very spidery handwriting. He had written:

My lovely English Rose. I have never stopped loving you all and thinking of you. I saw you all one day and I nearly came to you but I ran away because I am no good. Sometimes on Sunday mornings I hide in the bushes of the church to see you and when I see how beautiful you are it makes me feel unhappy. I promised you I would not take my own life but many times I have wanted to; and then I remember you once told me it is wicked and anything wicked annoys God. I don't want God to be angry with me when He takes me with him to wait for you to be with me again. When you read this letter I shall be waiting for you, my darling Rose. Your Bobby.
P.S. Please Rosie, no tears and only smiles X.

Sadly she handed both letters to Fred who, having read them, handed them to John. Bertie sat and cried. Fred reflected on hearing his mother's cry in the night and wondered once again the strange power which sent the message of death, as she had estimated the exact time to have been five minutes past three.

Fred was grieved to realise his father was to be ignominiously cast into the earth and resolved to attempt to make it not so. Bidding John to stay beside his mother he kissed her forehead and said, 'I'm going out for a while. John will make you a cup of tea. I won't be long.'

He walked to Mr Pardy's house a few streets away to find him at home reading. He had not met him since he had left the choir but was not ashamed to plead with him for help.

'Come in, you don't look well. Is your leg playing you up?'

'No Mr Pardy.'

Seated in Pardy's parlour he told him of Bob's death and asked him to loan him money for his Christian burial.

'Fred, you have always been a little bastard, but I forgave you a long time ago when I saw you trying to help your Mother after your Dad went away. He was a friend of mine and I told myself that if I ever met him again I would withdraw all I have said about you. You have humbled yourself in coming to me, of all people, but it tells me that for some reason or other you know that I am not a tyrant. Yes, I will help you. Now, go back to your Mother and tell her I shall call on her in half an hour.'

'Mr Pardy, thank you. One day I shall pay you back.'

'I don't want it back, son. You may find it hard to believe but I too am a Christian. Now go home.'

On the way home Fred saw Sam's familiar car parked outside the barber's shop and was about to enter when Sam came out. He told him of his father's death. Sam had never met Bob but knew of the family's regard of him. Maddy had told him of her past and of her shameful behaviour, but he loved her and knew of the happiness Rose had created for her. He had money. He would pay the funeral expenses and be proud to do so. Why had Fred not come to him first, he wondered. 'I am of the family. It is my duty to do so.' Such is the milk of human kindness. An hour before - despair - now peace of mind.

Sam, with Fred, drove to his home to break the news to Maddy, and together they returned to Rose to find Pardy sitting with her. He had lost no time in contacting the authorities at Milton with instructions, by telephone, to delay interment pending his arrangements. Sam drove Pardy and Fred there later that day.

The sombre grey building symbolised its institutional function of provision for the impoverished. Its aura of pauperism was reminiscent of the institutional hospital in which Fred had spent so long. My father here! His youthful indignation did not blind him to the kindness of Pardy, a man he had in the past deliberately enraged. He had, despite his boyish bad behaviour, sensed he was kinder than his facade of despotism

144

suggested, and inwardly he vowed to repay him in some manner, he knew not how.

They were led to a small whitewashed stone building used as a mortuary. The smell of death pervaded Fred's nostrils as he recalled the tiny white coffin which had laid upon the table in the parlour at home. An odour which he was never to forget and which he was to smell again and again. The shelves around the walls of the room contained plain wooden coffins. Marked on each lid in blue chalk was a name or a date and hour of day and the description of male or female. The attendant, a bearded, austere, elderly man enquired the name of 'the body' for identification and 'by whom.' Pardy told him that Fred was his next of kin but they wished to be together when the body was viewed. Sam stood at the door as the attendant unscrewed the lid bearing Bob's name and swivelled the top end to reveal a bearded ashen face.

In death his father's features closely resembled those of the large framed photograph which hung from the wall in the parlour at home. He turned to see Pardy gazing in a strange manner at his father's face, slowly nodding his head in affirmation, and looking at Fred for agreement. Together, simultaneously, they said, 'Yes, it is him.' Pardy put his arm around Fred's shoulders and they left the room, telling the attendant, 'Mr Higgins will be called for this evening.' Outside Pardy said, 'Fred, it is a long time since you saw your father but you recognised him at once. How did you?'

'He looked just the same as his picture at home. Mum told us it was taken in India many years ago and he had to get permission from his Commanding Officer to wear a beard.'

Mr Pardy said, 'This may sound strange to you, but he looked very much like a young man, but I had absolutely no doubt at all that it was my old good friend Bob Higgins. I'm overwhelmed at the peaceful smile on his face.'

Then Fred was aware of the sob in his voice as he spoke. Looking into his face he saw not the face of a harsh exacting choirmaster but that of a benign kindly but grieving gentleman, head half-bowed in sadness. Replacing his bowler, Pardy told them of the arrangement he had made with an undertaker in Milton and asked Sam to drive them there.

In the small office Pardy wrote out a cheque to cover the funeral costs and enquired if the burial plot had been allocated at the small local cemetery. The undertaker had carried out Pardy's telephoned instructions and told him the cost of the land and, as Pardy picked up his fountain pen to write a further cheque, Sam's large hand fell upon his. 'I insist that Maddy and I pay for it and later we will have a memorial stone made,' he said.

Pardy reluctantly agreed and then suddenly became the choir master Fred knew of old. Abruptly he rose from his chair and said to the undertaker in a voice Fred knew so well from the many choir practice sessions he had attended, 'I want Mr Higgins removed from that stinking hole at once.'

The sudden transformation of his manner astonished the man, who seemed only able to nod his head in assent.

'I shall wait here until you do, and I haven't got the remainder of the day to waste. Now jump to it!'

He did, and within thirty minutes returned, Bob's body having been transferred to a polished brass-handled coffin. Explaining the need to later use his professional expertise 'to present the deceased in more refined dressing for respects to be paid by his family and friends,' he said that they were welcome to visit between 10 am and 8 pm until the day prior to the funeral.

It was with a sense of accomplishment that Fred returned home with Sam and Pardy. He had little money, and yet he had been instrumental in providing a burial for his father which he knew his mother would want for him; and watching her face as she was told of it confirmed to him the gladness of her heart. She turned her face to Fred but did not speak with her lips. Her eyes gave him his reward.

The next day Sam drove Rose and her children in the small crowded car to see Bob. At the undertaker's parlour Rose paused to look at them with an unspoken message in her eyes that she would like to visit him alone.

As she saw his face, it seemed to her not to have changed from that of so many years ago, and the whimsical smile took her to those days when he would return home unexpectedly from France. She would hear a knocking at the front door of the nice house she had bought, and when she opened it she would find him standing there burdened with his kit-bag, and khaki canvas bags. And always that same, gentle smile and the words, 'Hello, my darling English Rose.' Here, it seemed, she could hear him again.

'Hello, my Bobby,' she whispered, and as she gently kissed his cold lips she felt not their coldness but the warmth of their eternal love.

'Wait for me, my darling Bobby. We shall meet again,' she said as a tear left her eye. 'And now our babies will come to you.'

She walked slowly from him to open the door, and word-lessly bade them enter. John, as had Fred, recognised him from the picture at home. In turn, they each kissed the cold forehead and said, 'God bless you, Dad.'

Rosalina did not kiss him. She later said she was nervous of a dead body, but said 'Good bye, my Daddy.'

Rose walked to him and said, 'You see, Bob, we all love you and I shall return to you.'

Silently they boarded Sam's car and were driven home to find that Maddy and Holbrook had laid out the large living-room table for tea.

An air of finality, but not deep sombre unhappiness, per-vaded them as they discussed the forthcoming burial. Maddy made her familiar secret signal to Fred, casting her eyes to the ceiling, and with a wink of her eye ascended the stairs. As when a small boy he followed her to her old room, to find her waiting for him sitting on the bed. Beside her were two brown paper parcels. Opening one she said, 'Try these on.' 'These' were a pair of the new-fashioned winkle-picker shoes. Fred, like most youths, had little money to spend on the clothes they would dearly have liked to possess, and it was thus with almost child-like glee he found them to be a perfect fit. He kissed Maddy.

'Thanks, Mad,' he said.

'Now, then,' said Maddy, 'try this on,' opening the other parcel.

She had bought him a new suit from 'Burtons.' He had never owned a suit before. To him the thirty-seven shillings and sixpence she had paid for it was a fortune. Overwhelmed with gratitude and love he cried tears of happiness, 'Maddy, Maddy, I love you', he said.

'I love you too, Fred. Now I'll close my eyes whilst you try on the trousers!'

Hastily he donned the trousers and shoes, waistcoat and jacket. A perfect fit. He told her to open her eyes. She saw the suit had transformed him from semi-youth to near-manhood and stood to admire him. She knew how much this meant to him, but to her it meant much more. She had always loved him more than her own blood brothers and to see his excited face filled her with affection and nearness. And she knew he loved her as she would have wished her brothers to have loved her. To them she knew she was the black sheep of the family. But she belonged to Aunt Rose's family, the home of penury, but a home rich with love, compassion and laughter. The tears and the joys were shared by them all in harmony of heart.

'Maddy, how do I look?'

'You look marvellous!'

'Did you buy it for me so I would look smart at Dad's funeral?'

'Yes.'

'Why isn't Rosalina nice, like you?'

'She is really.'

'No, Maddy. Nobody except Mum is good like you are.'

'I didn't use to be good until I knew your Mum loved me and now I'm not bad any more, Fred.'

'Maddy, I love you more than Rosalina.'

'You mustn't say that Fred, ever. You would make your Mum unhappy if she heard you.'

'No, I wouldn't tell her, Maddy, but now I am growing up Rosaline still treats me as if I'm still a boy; but you understand me better. What a cow she was when I got the sack from the chip shop. She seemed to be pleased I was in trouble but you understood and laughed. I know I shouldn't have done all those things with those girls but I couldn't stop myself once it had started and I liked doing it anyway. But I can tell *you* about anything. You always understand me. When my leg was hurt, Maddy, you were so kind to me. You've always been kind to me. Next to Mum you're the kindest lady in the world. Maddy, I want you to know that to me you are my real sister and not Rosa because I really love you like I know I should love her, but I can't, and I know I never will. So please always remember, Maddy, you are my sister.'

She put her arms around his broad shoulders and said, 'Thank you, Fred, and you are my brother and all through my life I will remember today. If ever you are in need, you know that I am here to love you and help you. As you grow older the years may take you away from here and you will marry. None of us know what is before us, and you will make mistakes as I have. I have been fortunate in finding real love, but remember this: before you find it you will find many heartaches and sadnesses. When you feel unhappy please remember these moments to remind you that what I have said is said from my own unfortunate heartaches and sadness, which God and Aunt Rose helped me to overcome. If I am not here to help you God will send somebody to do so; to help you to be happy as He did for me when he sent Aunt Rose to make me happy.' She kissed his cheek and said, 'Come on now, let's go downstairs and show you off.'

Everyone, with the exception of Rosa, agreed he looked very smart. Her opinion that 'it makes him look too old' was greeted by general dissent. Maddy and Fred said nothing but found each other's eyes to agree, 'Yes, she is a cow.'

On the day of the funeral Holbrook and Pardy hired a taxi to transport those who were too many for Sam's car, which called at the house to pick them up. The usual rubber-necks had gathered to hazard their guesses as to what was going on in the Higgins house. None of them had been told. Strict secrecy had been imposed. But at the sight of the indignant Maddy, bearing down on them, and hearing her demand of 'push off back to your rat holes, you nosy lot of filth!' the street, to the slamming of doors, was rapidly emptied. To her it was desecration on this day to allow that they could make a topic of their tragedy, albeit they knew not of its nature. But her hatred of them knew no bounds.

The night before Maddy had told Sam she wished to make a visit to the parlour of the undertaker with Rose: just the two of them, and he understood. She had told him, before they married, of her falsely accusing Bob as she gave birth to her now-dead Jimmy. He drove them there and waited outside as the two women entered together.

Maddy saw the serenity of his face and asked silently for his forgiveness as she put her fingers to her lips to press to his; and Rose understood the meaning.

'Shall I go now, Aunt Rose?' she asked.

'No, darling, please stay. I know he has heard what you have prayed for.'

Rose took a small napkin from her handbag and from it she took two roses, one red and one white. They were made of satin. She had made them.

'Maddy, I have made this for you to put beside him, for now you are a pure girl and he would want to take it with him for you to know of his forgiveness.'

His hands had been crossed upon his breast. Gently Maddy kissed the white rose and placed it on them.

Rose took her symbolic token of their love and she, too, kissed it before she placed it by his face. With a final long gaze at him she said, 'Farewell, my Bobby, till we are together again.' Together they slowly left him.

And now, as Maddy verbally attacked these unknowing gossips, the scene of the evening before was with her. Her blind hatred of them welled-up within her. Little did they realise she had murder in her heart.

Fred, in his new suit and shoes, and John, resplendent in his Number One uniform, with its gold wireless-telegraphist badges, and trousers pressed sharply crossways, went to the undertaker's parlour before the coffin was loaded into the high glass-sided hearse bearing their father to his last resting place. Unknown to their mother, they took the medals their father had worn at the last 11th November Remembrance Day when attending service with their mother (and at which Fred had sung soprano solo 'Oh, for the wings of a dove'). They also took a Union Jack loaned from their boxing instructor, which they knew he kept in his store room for Empire Day (knowledge they had acquired when they had 'borrowed' the equipment for their 'Gym' in the cellar at home.

Together they draped their father's coffin with the symbol of his service to the Empire and placed his India Frontier Campaigns and Great War medals upon it, the Distinguished Service Medal at the nearest right.

Maddy had sewn on the black arm bands they wore. Rosalina was 'too upset' to do anything. Mr Pardy and Fred Holbrook were joined by the much-maligned Mr 'Poxy' Pocksome in their tribute to Bob, and the memory of them together at the graveside, as the clergyman uttered the funeral service, was to remain with Fred for the rest of his life. His boyhood perception of his father and drinking cronies took on a new dimension. Here was the dawning of his understanding; of a fellowship of manhood that he had thought only existed within the minds of boys.

Before the coffin was lowered into the grave Fred Holbrook, dressed in his uniform, ceremoniously took Bob's medals from the coffin and handed them to John. He then carefully folded the flag and as the coffin was lowered, they both, in disciplined style, brought their heels together and saluted as Rose tossed a red rose to the depths of the grave.

They returned home to find the previously arranged funeral refreshments had been provided by Pardy's sister and Pocksome's wife. Such was the kindness of those from whom it was least expected.

Rose had borne herself with the dignity of the refined lady she had never ceased to be, in surroundings of near-poverty, and her few words of expression of her sincere gratitude to those responsible for the dignified farewell to the man she loved were voluminous for their brevity. But she wept as she read that the cause of death of her beloved Bob was malnutrition.

# CHAPTER 10

MEN REQUIRED FOR TOMATO
PICKING. MUST BE OVER THE
AGE OF EIGHTEEN. ACCOMMO-
DATION AND FOOD PROVIDED.
MUST BE PREPARED FOR THREE
MONTHS' CONTRACT. PASSAGE
TO CHANNEL ISLANDS FREE

A blind eye was turned by officialdom when this annual request for labour was posted on the notice board.

Fred, aged sixteen, entered his name on the list, as did many, under and over the specified age. His pink complexion and blond hair but broad shoulders were deemed by the agent charged with the selection of the candidate as satisfactory qualifications for engagement. He looked healthy and physically fit! And when the required papers and contract were completed no mention was made of his limp.

Rose packed his portmanteau case with what she thought would be his needs. She had not attempted to dissuade him from pursuing what he described as 'making a start somewhere.' She knew him well enough to understand his sense of physical inferiority and his determination to overcome it, and she had faith in his doing so. But such was her inherent maternal anxiety that she felt a natural motherly loss in this step towards independence, as indeed she had done with Rosalina, and then John (although not with Michael and

Leslie).

Together with twenty-four others of varying ages Fred boarded a *Tillings and Stevens* omnibus to Poole in Dorsetshire. After a meal they were conducted to a coastal ship and were told by a loud-mouthed seaman in a dirty blue jumper to have their papers of engagement ready for inspection. Having passed inspection they were herded aboard to join a mass of men en route to the same destination, exactly where was vague to all. The Channel Islands were far distant lands to this band of unseasoned travellers.

The lucky passengers were those who boarded the vessel first. They were ushered below decks to make room for those of Fred's, and other parties, for no sooner had the ship cast off than a heavy downpour of rain soaked those who - unlike Fred and several others who had taken cover in lifeboats covered with tarpaulin - were on the upper deck.

Many were violently sick as the ship rolled and tossed in the choppy sea, and when a seaman, after what seemed like an eternity, distributed thick sandwiches of meat wrapped in grease-proof paper, eating was far from the mind of most. Fred took the opportunity of swiping more than his ration and secreted several packs in his pockets. But he took just one of the enamel pint cups containing thick treacly ship's cocoa.

After another eternity the ship put into St Peter Port. Most men thought the journey was thankfully over but Fred, remembering his geography, knew they were now in Guernsey, with another twelve miles or so to reach St Helier, Jersey. At St Helier they were conducted to their sleeping quarters, a derelict but hastily and economically refurbished church hall, the floor of which had been covered with coconut matting, camp beds lining the walls.

Most were so tired and exhausted they were prepared to flop down, fully clothed, to rest, the journey having taken, since boarding the bus, nineteen hours. Fifty beds, two tin tanks filled with warm water for washing, no soap nor towels, and three cubical septic outside-toilets constituted the appealing delights of Fred's shelter for the ensuing weeks, and in which, after a very few days, the odour of unwashed feet, clothing and bodies became strong.

Each man was given a small tally book in which the tallyman entered twice-daily the holder's measured picking. At the end of each six-day week, on request, a 'sub,' or part-advance of cash earned was allowed. Fred, intent on taking home the large part of his earnings at the end of the season, lived frugally, but the men 'subbed' the limit allowed in order to spend it in the local hostelries. They would arrive back drunk, and fights and disturbances were frequent.

Whores were in plenty, but many men took the cheap small boat journey over to France, thirteen miles away, to visit the state-registered and more-hygienic brothels. They were unaware of the need for passports, and were smuggled ashore for the cost of two shillings per man, half of which went into the pocket of the local gendarme.

Fred worked hard. His tally book showed his earnings to be higher than many grown men's and, bronzed by the sun, and filled healthily in body by his diet of tomatoes, bread, cheese, root vegetables and very cheap red wine, he was chosen to continue employment after the tomato season ended, in digging the crop of potatoes.

His lame leg strengthened, but the slight limp remained. This new experience of individuality greatly broadened his outlook on life, and here he became the object of attraction to a man of homosexual tendencies. Not being aware of the oddities of humanity he, at first, wondered why a particular individual found pleasure in frequently stroking his nether regions. When this man approached him, making a few specific suggestions, Fred told him to clear off, and when that failed to achieve the desired effect, Fred followed expedient of a less verbal nature, and laid him out with a single blow.

The news quickly spread to his employers and the man was sacked and dispatched to Weymouth, being forced to pay his own transport home. But the community had learned that the youth with the yet-unshaven face was no push-over.

Before leaving for work early each morning Fred would call at the baker's shop basement to buy his bread, which was baked by a brother and sister. The sister, Gisselle, was as her brother, half-French. A widow, her fisherman husband had drowned during a storm, leaving her pregnant with her only child. The baby, a girl, was born a deaf mute, and was now four years old and in the care of her mother-in-law in Cherbourg on the mainland. Gisselle, now twenty-nine, was tall, big-boned and dark haired with deep black-brown eyes, a little over-weight, but very open-hearted.

Sunday was rest day. The Channel Islands were not yet the holiday centres of today and shops closed, giving the air of a true Sabbath. Fred, taking his usual stroll away from the stink of his residence found himself in a narrow rural lane when he heard a female voice calling, 'Froddee, Froddeee.' He recognised the accent of Gisselle calling him and walked in the direction of the voice to find her standing in the small front garden of a cottage.

'What you do 'ere, Froddee?' she asked.

'Nothing, just walking.'

'You 'ad déjeuner yet?'

'No, not yet, Gisselle.'

'You come ave it wiz me?'

'Where at?'

'Ici, avec moi ...' She made a gesture to indicate 'here.'

'Oh, thank you,' he said, as she opened the small wicket gate to admit him saying, 'You come.'

She led him to a kitchen smelling of the nostalgic Sunday cooking of dinner at home. She added more cutlery - the wooden table was laid for one - and beside it placed a glass.

'You like wine, I know. I see you drink in field when come spy on you.'

Indeed he had acquired a taste for the local wine shipped from France which he received illegally from the wine shopkeeper in exchange for a basket of tomatoes or potatoes.

156

'You spy on me? I have never seen you,' he said.

She laughed and told him that when she left the bakery each morning to go home to bed she would walk a little to get some fresh air and, being resident the whole year, she knew of the changing pattern of venues of the crop-gathering. When one plot was exhausted, the position of the next she knew by heart: year in and year out.

'Why do you spy on me?'

'Ah, I come see your boddee,' she laughed.

She saw the look of self-consciousness on his youthful face and said, 'Gisselle is naughty girl, huh?'

He smiled and asked, 'Are you?'

'Sometimes,' she laughed, and then pointing to the table said, 'Sit.'

From a cupboard she took a litre bottle of red Burgundy and poured two large glasses.

'You drink with Gisselle, huh? Santé!'

'Good health,' he said.

She went to the oven and removed a large sizzling joint.

'You like agneau?' she asked.

'What's that?'

'It is lamb.'

'Yes, thank you.'

She made a sauce of wine, herbs and arrowroot.

He had been used to Bisto and wondered if his taste would appreciate the weird concoction she was preparing. Nor had he before tasted the spinach mixed with dandelion leaves she served him on a large plate piled with slices of meat and jacket potatoes covered with butter and cream. It was his first home-cooked meal for many weeks and she watched him devour it with relish as she refilled his wine glass.

'You eat like man. I like see you eat,' she said.

She saw his satisfied appreciation of the meal and produced a bowl of fruit and camembert cheese. She helped him to a large piece of cheese, and put an apple on the plate with it. He looked at her questioningly - he had not before tasted this

157

unusual ripe cheese.

'I show you, Froddee,' she said, and standing beside him cut a slice of apple and cheese, placed them together and said, 'open your mouth,' and popped it in.

'You like 'eet?' she asked.

'Very nice.'

'So you geeve Gisselle leetle kees, huh?' and bending him down, planted her lips on his.

'You want some cognac now?'

'What's that?' he asked, thinking it might be the French word for sex.

'Brandy,' she said.

'I've never tasted brandy.'

'I give you some. Eet is good weeth the café.'

They had drunk the bottle of wine and Fred was beginning to feel delightfully mellow as he sipped the brandy. She told him much about her life and of her loneliness since her husband's death. She was obliged to work in order to send money to France for the maintenance of her daughter who was receiving tuition in sign language in Cherbourg, a facility not available in Jersey at that time. She asked him of his own background and expressed her disgust at the living conditions he was obliged to endure in the dormitory.

They sat and talked for a while and had a little more brandy. She was amused and touched when he got up, telling her to remain in her chair while he washed the dishes in the sink, drying them very carefully, and stacking them where he guessed they belonged saying, 'I have to earn my keep.'

It was now mid-afternoon and she told him that he must go to bed to get some sleep before she went to the bakery to begin her night's work. As he prepared to leave and thanking her for her kindness, she stood before him, her height on a par with his and said, 'You kees Gisselle goodbye, huh?' and encircled her arms around him to kiss him open-mouthed. As she pressed her thighs against him she was in no doubt about how he felt about her.

'You come sleep with me, Froddee? Come, come!'

She really meant it when she had expressed disgust for his communal living conditions, and invited him to live in the luxury of her small home for a few weeks before he was to leave the island, an offer he declined saying, 'I should like to Gisselle, but people would learn of it and you would get a bad name.'

'I do not care for thees pipple 'ere. Dey are nuzzing to me.'

'Your brother would know of it,' he said.

'Poof! 'e 'as two mistresses and 'is wife a lover. Me, I 'ave nobody since my 'usband die and 'e nevair make love to me like you make love to me.'

He would very much have preferred to live there but feeling he should pay a contribution towards his lodging, money he planned to take home for his mother, he considered it his duty to refuse. His living was frugal but sufficient for his needs, his stamina good, and his resolve to waste not a penny prevailed over the luxury of good food, a comfortable bed and the softness and warmth of a likeable and passionate woman. He also intended to keep some of his earnings to finance his future.

His future, Fred told himself, was in London, and not in his home town thirty miles away. To arrive there penniless, friendless and bereft of shelter was not his intention. Carefully he had noted in his small notebook addresses of very cheap men's hostels he had learned of from his colleagues, many of whom were Londoners. He was told that the most likelihood of employment was in public houses and small hotels where staff were required to live on the premises. The wages mentioned were much higher than those of the Dickensian hotel, which his advisers considered to be unbelievably low. He asked why employment was easier to find in such places and was told that single men and women could adapt to the long split day of opening hours, conditions not acceptable to those with a home and family. Keep to central London and the West End, they told him, and 'keep yourself to yourself ... be a loner.'

Many of the men were obvious 'ne'er-do-wells' but most were like himself - in Jersey to work hard and have the satisfaction of providing money for their loved ones; and this was another purpose of the tally book 'subs.' Men would 'sub' each week and send money home by registered post, the remainder to be the great fortune taken home with pride.

Fred made many friends among these men, and as he was by far the youngest, they adopted a fatherly attitude towards him and protected him from the influence of the 'bad 'uns,' as they were referred to. But after he laid out the 'Brown Hatter' they had become aware of his self reliance.

He had taken his mouth-organ with him, and sometimes was accompanied by a man named Ernie with his ukulele, much to the enjoyment of their mates, one of whom told Fred to take it to London with him, 'to earn a crust at busking, if you're hard up.'

Fred did not realise at the time the wisdom of the advice!

As if she had read his thoughts, Gisselle said: 'I do not want you to pay money to leeve weeth me, Froddee. I like you to be with me.'

'How can I live with you and not pay? That's unfair!'

'Poof! I 'ave plenty money from insurance when my 'usband die and 'e left money for me and I 'ave good job in the bakery. I would not take money from you when you are working hard for your Mama. I want you to stay weeth me please. Please make me 'appy for a leetle while before you go back to England.'

Fred had formed more than a passing friendship with her on his visits to the bakery, where she had often given him more than his payments warranted, plus the occasional bottle of wine. He liked her as a person now. And after knowing her so intimately, he relished the sincerity of her friendship - the nearness.

After dressing they sat together on the long sofa and drank a little more wine. She spent a short time in the kitchen and returned to place a key in his hand. Taking his hand, she said, 'Froddee, chérie, please go to the 'ostel and collect your belongings and bring them 'ere. I 'ave left you food and wine to take to the fields tomorrow and you come to the bakery to get bread in the morning and kees Gisselle 'allo.'

'Gisselle, are you sure you want me here?' he asked.

She gesticulated expansively with her hand saying, 'Please, please stay 'ere. Make me very 'appy.' And then, shrugging her shoulders and frowning with a questioning tilt of her head, 'Ah! You theenk I am bad woman?' her face showing a sadness, which reached his heart as he rose to his feet and stepped towards her.

His youthful yet protective senses stirred within him, an overwhelming compassion urging him to embrace her as a small girl.

'No, no, no, Gisselle! You are a nice woman, please don't speak like that,' he said holding her tightly.

Her head was resting on his shoulder as he reflected on the few other women he had known intimately. For them he had never experienced such closeness and affection. Had he fallen in love with Gisselle - so much older than he, he wondered? He did not know but felt he wanted to be near her. He experienced a strangeness he had never felt with a woman before. Not with his mother; not with Maddy. And they were the most important women in the world to him. He only knew that Gisselle had somehow become important to him. And despite the afternoon of passionate harmony he did not regard her as wanton.

She told him, quite truthfully, that since the death of her husband she had not had sex with any man, despite the many overtures made to her. But she wondered if this polite young Englishman believed her. She felt she should feel shame, but did not. She had seen him arrive with the rest of the field workers and noticed his limp. She had watched him from a distance toiling in the sun. He never seemed to cease, except to slake his thirst from a bottle which she had at first thought to be water. She later learned from the wine shop girl of his daily purchase of the cheapest wine, and followed him to watch him buy his never-varying frugal meal of cheese; and yet he was the healthiest-looking of the whole contingent.

When he called early each morning for his bread, she often managed to secrete more than he would ask for and, together with a bottle of wine, had it in readiness for him. Hearing his limped step on the pavement above she would excuse herself to Henri, her brother, and hasten up the steps to meet him, refusing the money he held in readiness. One day he offered to bring tomatoes for her. She knew he used to do this in exchange for wine from the wine shop. And she would say, 'non, merci, you kees Gisselle instead,' and each morning he timidly kissed her gently on her cheek. She fiercely drove from herself the urge to kiss him passionately, but knew she wanted him; wanted him as she had never wanted a man. Now, this afternoon, she unashamedly told him of her aspirations. He was embarrassed, and she saw the blush on his fresh, now sun-goldened face, and sensed his inability to reply to her when she asked him if he, too, felt the same attraction to her. He then admitted that he did. And she knew that her feminine intuition had been right. Mingled with her desire was a deep maternal compassion, and it concerned her that this clean young man was obliged to co-habit with a mass of men much older than he. Sometimes during the night she had even taken a break from her dough-mixing to walk past the open windows of the hostelry to sniff the pungent odour of the unwashed bodies within.

She had already told Henri of her intention of persuading Fred to take the spare bedroom in her cottage, and he had replied in the typical French manner of simply shrugging his shoulders and pursing his lips, 'Oui, Oui.'

And so, that Sunday, she watched for him taking his usual walk. She knew the exact time he would go by and had prepared more food than usual, allowing him to pass the window from which she watched from behind the lace curtains

162

before going out and calling him. She told herself she must not seduce him, but she knew she would. And now that she had told him her intentions, he simply kissed her and held her close as she wept in shame.

'Gisselle, please don't cry,' he said, kissing her tears. 'You are a good, kind, lovely girl and you make me want to cry too. So please kiss me.'

He walked with her to the bakery and promised he would pack his belongings and return to her cottage. The dormitory was empty. His mates were out drinking or walking, but as he emerged from the door he encountered the agent who looked quizzically at his suitcase. Fred merely smiled as the agent looked in the direction of the bakery, fully understanding the reason for his departure, saying, 'You lucky young devil; I've been after her ever since her old man was drowned. But good luck, and goodnight.'

Fred awoke next morning, the early sun shining through the open window, the perfume of the garden flowers wafting in, and no stench of feet, his toughened frame relaxed upon the softness of the huge feather-filled palliasse cover. He fingered the silken-light summer duvet covering him. He had never slept in such a bed as this. Its huge expanse, roofed by a heavy tapestry, was held by four posts of beautifully-carved wood depicting nude female figures bearing posies of flowers.

Luxuriously he bathed in the cold water she poured into the huge wine cask and dressed in his work clothes. He found she had packed him fruit and camembert cheese, a note inside telling him to take the meat she had left prepared on the cool slate shelf in the cellar. He found standing beside the meat a litre of white burgundy with a note over its neck 'Freddie.'

Gisselle heard Fred's footsteps on the pavement above and sped to meet him with croissants, butter and rolls. She had put a small knife in the box containing the butter and after he had kissed her cheek she told him to take care of it as it had belonged to her father.

'Gisselle, you are looking after me like my mother and

163

Maddy,' he said.

'They look after you because they love you. And I look after you because I love you,' she said. He softly kissed her lips and walked away.

When she returned home she found he had tidied and swept the kitchen and found he had left a vase of red roses he had picked from her garden. He had attached a note 'For the Rose of Lorraine,' and her thoughts went back to the story he had told her of his father and mother. 'The Rose of England' Fred's father had called his wife that. And now his son had named her 'The Rose of Lorraine.' Gisselle had never loved her husband as a wife should. She had succumbed to the constant urging of her relatives to 'get married before you become too old to attract a man.' Jean-Pierre had been coarse and inconsiderate. When he was lost at sea she felt no great sense of loss. Now, for the first time, she felt all those things for this man-youth that she had yearned to feel for a man. She wanted his body. She wanted his love. She wanted him to know of her love. She wanted him beside her constantly, and she wanted him to protect her from life's hazards. She also wanted his children, and all the happiness she knew she was not to have. And as she sat alone with her tears, she resolved to have her life's happiness during the next three months before the crop harvest was over and he would leave her life forever.

The injustice of life was their age difference. For a man to marry a woman much younger than himself was, perhaps, not regarded as unusual; but for a woman to marry a man much younger than she, was held to ridicule, and yet deep, lasting love can prevail in either instance. Sexual relationship is unimportant compared with the tender love between two beating hearts, and she knew in her heart that Fred loved her tenderly. She also knew that he wanted her not for her body alone, but for her nearness and care although, perhaps, he was not sufficiently mature in life to understand her concept of love. Content in her new-found happiness she slept. She

164

awoke to the touch of his lips on her cheek and the aroma of coffee standing on her bedside table. In the muzziness of half sleep she stretched her arms around his shoulders and held him close to her, wanting him. She smelled his freshly-soaped hard body and whispered something to him in French.

'I don't understand what you are saying, Gisselle.' he said.

She whispered in English, 'Eet is the same in every language, Froddee: make love to me.'

And so the days of her 'onaymoon' went by. She knew her life would become empty again when he left her, but she told him he must go, despite his saying he could not leave her to be alone. She knew it was from his heart when he told her he loved her. She would cherish these days with him always but she could not allow him to impair his future by remaining with her. There were not the opportunities here for him to reach the horizons she knew were his ambitions and she told him, too, he must not return to the island again for she would not be there.

He asked her her plans, but she did not tell him until the night before he was to embark on his journey to England that she would be joining her small daughter in Cherbourg. He wept bitterly when she told him she was going to sell the cottage and move to France to have his baby.

Fred had done many jobs and repairs to the cottage. He had cultivated her garden, loved her with tenderness and passion, found companionship with her and, on one occasion, protected her from two foolhardy fishermen he had heard speaking of her in an insulting manner, inferring she was 'baby snatching' in having him. He trashed them both in a manner that frightened her, and threw them from the small bar which they sometimes visited. Yes, his cool rage had frightened her in its harsh ruthlessness but she was proud of him and now she would have his child to complete all those things he had sought. The future would matter not.

On the last night she told him of all these things and said, 'Froddee, you 'ave many things to learn about life and as you grow older you too will 'ave your ideals, but you will 'ave to wait for them and sometimes you will cry.'

He said, 'That is what my mother and Maddy told me.'

'You will find there are a lot of wicked people, Froddee, and many of them are women, and it will be the women who make you cry, but one day you will love somebody like you love your Gisselle but, mon petit, it ees good for us to just love somebody once while we live, so don't cry for me as I shall always be 'appy now,' she said.

'Will you write to me, Gisselle?' he asked.

'No, Froddee, but when our baby come I send you picture, huh?' she replied.

They said goodbye at the small garden gate, and Fred, remembering his father's and mother's remark: 'No tears on parting,' placed the red rose in her hand and whispered, 'For the Rose of Lorraine,' and kissed her softly. He did not look back and she entered the cottage. He never returned to Jersey.

# CHAPTER 11

When Fred returned to the cul-de-sac street of his home the usual flea-bitten hags were clustered in their customary small cliques, gossiping to each other in low tones, occasionally rewarding each other with Judas smiles. But his thoughts were of the leafiness of the quiet cottage and Gisselle. He loved his Mother and all her goodness of heart. He loved Maddy and her humour and gentleness but he could not live in this street again, and his resolve was strengthened to leave for London.

Come what may, his confidence in himself had matured to an independence of resolve which surmounted his lameness. Now he could run, now he could dance (Gisselle had helped him). Now he feared no man in the knowledge of his ability to fight with his fists and win. Now he had learned the meaning of warm love and its deep emotional rewards. The physical facet of it he supposed was necessary to the chemistry of human nature, but not vital. Gisselle had taught him that. She loved him, of that he had no doubt, but she had sacrificed her happiness in her wish for his successful future and that was the true meaning and depth of love: unselfishness. Dear Gisselle.

Fred opened the door to hear no sound of welcome. He entered the warm old living room to find nobody there. He had written telling his mother of the day and time of his return and could not understand her absence. Then he heard a stealthy foot-fall behind him and felt two hands covering his eyes.

'Guess who!' said a female voice.

No other voice in the world could imitate Rose's, but he played along with her.'

'I've no idea,' he said.

'Naughty boy, you've forgotten me already,' she said.

'He turned to embrace her, now head and shoulders above her and, smiling, said, 'Hello, Little Tich.'

Surprised at the development of his frame and by his suntan, she stood back to admire her son.

'You look so much like your Dad did as a young man. I can't believe it's true.'

Toiling for five months in the open air had bleached his hair and broadened his already wide shoulders. He had also gained in height, but Rose saw in his eyes a maturity beyond his years, an expression of manhood and self-reliance. She knew her fears over his lameness were over.

Suddenly two more figures emerged from the coal cellar door. Bertie and his wonderful Maddy. Bertie simply smiled and said, 'Hello, Fred,' but Maddy threw her arms around him as he picked her up like a child to kiss her.

'Now who's the little one, heh?' he said, swirling her.

'I can't believe it! Put me down, you brute!'

'No,' he said.

'Aunt Rose, get the cane to him.'

'You fight your own battles,' said Rose.

'Give me another kiss and I'll put you down.'

She did, but still they clung to one another in mutual joy.

They prepared tea in the front parlour 'as today is a special day,' Rose said.

'First let me give you each a present,' said Fred. And opening his case he produced two hand-crocheted silk lace shawls, one each for Rose and Maddy, and a glossy coloured thick book on the Channel Islands for Bertie. For Rosalina he had a box of lace handkerchiefs. She was not present as she 'had other things to do.'

Fred whispered to Maddy, 'Handkerchiefs for her snotty

nose.'

When they had finished admiring the craftsmanship of their presents he told them of the French lady who had made them. Off-handedly he said, 'Her name is Gisselle.'

Ever-perceptive of Fred, Maddy slowly brought her eyes to his, and said, 'Ooh, la la, you dirty old man! You've been at it again, haven't you?'

'And what's that supposed to mean?'

'Oh come on! Tell me all about her, you little ram.'

'You're disgusting!'

Rose smiled. She had missed this bantering dialogue, and it was guaranteed to amuse her.

'Not as disgusting as you - I've hit the nail on the head again.'

'You've got a dirty mind, Maddy.'

'Not in front of Mum, eh? You don't want her to think you are the licentious little sod you really are, do you?'

He could not control the gradual blushing he could feel upon his face. Rose had seen it, and restraining her laughter said, 'Maddy, don't be so unkind, he's a good boy.'

'What, him? I bet he's left a few buns in the oven over in Jersey.'

Rising to the bait, he said, 'No, only one,' smiling.

Rose knew that look, and so did Maddy, and both stared at him in semi-belief.

Gisselle had fashioned a shoulder bag for him, made from a length of dark twill, in which she had put two tin boxes, one containing food for his journey; the other, she had tied tightly with red ribbon, having admonished: 'Not to be opened, plees, Froddee, until you get 'ome.' Rose and Maddy, with the inherent curiosity born in all women, watched as he slowly opened the box, eight inches square, to reveal an iced cake encircled with tiny red roses. In the centre were two hearts, a name beneath each: 'Freddie and Gisselle' with a sealed pink envelope at the side. In it was twenty pounds and a note, 'From your Rose of Lorraine for my brave Freddie.'

He ran from the room to the garden toilet, the sanctuary of his boyhood, to hide his emotion. It was his Maddy who came to sit beside him on the broad wide cover as he shed the tears of a child. He told her of Gisselle. He told her of their close relationship, of her age, her kindness, her sorrows, her sacrifice and her pregnancy. 'But Maddy, it wasn't dirty,' he said, and she believed him. She knew him better than any other and loved him as her own. He asked her to tell his mother, but never Rosalina, and he told her of his intention of going to London and the money he had saved.

'Come on, Fred, I'm sorry I pulled your leg. You know I would never want to hurt you,' she said.

'I know that, but if we ever joke again about girls, please never say Gisselle's name in fun, Maddy.'

'I promise you I won't, love, so don't think about it,' she said.

When they returned to the house Rose busied herself. She knew Maddy would enlighten her and she knew that Rosalina was not to be told of the confidences between them. This saddened her but she was also aware of Rosalina's lack of thought for others' feelings. Rosalina had known of Fred's expected return home today, but could not be bothered to greet him.

Fred had now overcome his emotional lapse and was keen to show his Mother and Maddy his earnings.

'You two ladies must help me to get my money out of my private bank, please,' he said, mysteriously. He pointed to the left top of his trousers.

'Get some scissors and turn your backs,' he said, as he removed his trousers and sat with his legs hidden under the table. Inside his trousers Gisselle had wrapped his money in brown paper, stitched cloth around it, and then sewn the package to the inside fabric. 'This ees so nobody robs my Froddee,' she had said, her precaution well-founded in view of the reputation of the annual seasonal workers, amongst whom thefts were commonplace.

Rose said, 'How kind of the lady to go to this trouble.'

Inside were one hundred and thirty-seven pounds plus another envelope bearing his name. It was from Henri, with a note: 'Freddie. Here is thirteen pounds to bring your money to a hundred and fifty. It is for lifting all my bags of flour for me - my poor old back! Good luck, Henri.' Fred had often shifted the heavy bags of flour to help him - Henri was often so drunk that he was incapable of lugging their weight. He blamed a severe, non-existent backache.

Fred had 'subbed' weekly to send Rose money, and when he pushed across the table towards her a hundred and thirty-seven pounds saying, 'This is for you, Mum,' she was dismayed.

'I have to tell you something, so it might as well be now. I am going to London to find work. I know I'll not find a job here so this money will take care of you until I find a job and send you some more. I will keep the money from Gisselle and Henri for myself until I find a job. You are not to worry about me as I have proved I am quite capable of taking care of myself.'

Rose knew it must happen but had not been prepared for the suddenness.

'Please stay a little while with us Fred,' she said.

'Just four weeks, Mum. Is that all right?'

'Yes dear,' she said.

She thought he intended to leave almost immediately but she would have him to love for a while. He was, apart from Bertie whom she was obliged to almost mother, the last of her children to leave her. John was now serving on the cruiser, *HMS Courageous,* and would not be home for another six months. She continued to receive the monthly letters from Leslie and Michael but had resigned herself to not seeing them yet (although she knew she would one day).

Her main worry was for the future of Bertie. He attended the Juvenile Employment Bureau regularly twice weekly but his hopes of finding a job were very slim.

Rosalina was living in the married quarters attached to her husband's barracks but had had problems with her neighbours, and Rose had little doubt that her daughter's spiteful tongue was responsible. She had asked Rose if she would consider sharing the house with her 'if Fred did not return from Jersey' (which she hoped he wouldn't) but Rose politely told her that she saw no reason why he should not come back; but would consider it. Rosalina now had three children and Rose reflected on the days when her home resounded to the laughter and tears of her own children. 'Perhaps it would be nice,' she thought. She was ever the kindly Rose, ever availing herself in helping others and ever being saddled with their troubles.

Fred Holbrook had many times asked Rose to marry him. He would take her away 'from this rotten street to somewhere nice.' But she said simply, 'Thank you, Fred, but no.' She had no doubt he loved her but she still loved her dead Bob and would feel a sense of his betrayal should she marry again. Her son, Fred, understood when she told him. His sister had scoffed, 'You're daft to turn him down.' Rose never mentioned it again.

Rose discovered that much of the disparaging stories of Maddy's escapades prior to the birth of Jimmy were figments of Rosalina's imagination and that Maddy was a dear, kind woman who showed her much kindness - sadly, much more than her own daughter, who took her for granted. Everybody loved Maddy, but few loved Rosalina. As young Fred once observed, 'I pity her husband. I don't wonder that they're always rowing.'

Fred said goodbye to his mother early in the morning of his departure. She rose to pack him some food and cook him breakfast, wondering when she would see him again, imploring him to come home should he not find work before his money was exhausted. Fred caught the workmen's train to Charing Cross. In his pocket was a street-map book of central London that Maddy had bought him.

He had carefully checked the addresses of the men's hostels given him by his ex-Jersey mates and compared them with the map, his intention being to find the nearest to Charing Cross. It proved to be in Covent Garden - price: one shilling and a penny per night. He had been advised to use this hostel as it was council-owned and supervised, and here one slept in a cubicle of one's own and not in a dormitory where one's belongings were at the mercy of the elements (thieves) while one slept. The extra cost of three pence compared with other hostels was well worth the money.

Fred's friends had told him to find the Lyons Corner House just outside the quadrangle of the station where one could deposit one's case for threepence. A case had to be collected before midnight on each Sunday and then re-deposited, where it could remain for threepence until the following Sunday. Very handy if you want to hide a bit of 'bent' property - as good as a safe deposit bank, he had been told!

Fred took his requirements from his case and carried them in a brown paper carrier-bag. He found the Corner House exactly as he had been told. He received his ticket on payment of threepence.

Fred had been a good listener. He found the hostel more easily than he had imagined and, forgetting the still-early hour, was told to return after mid-day to book his berth for the night. He had bought the *Morning Advertiser*, the organ of the Licensed Victuallers, to find it full of advertisements of jobs of all kinds relating to public houses, clubs and hotels. Managers and Assistant Managers, married couples, Head Barmen, Cellarmen, Barmen, Learner Bar Staff, Barmaids, Potmen, etc, in venues, many of which were totally unknown to him.

He wandered through the maze of Covent Garden from Drury Lane and Bow Street to St Martins Lane to find himself in Trafalgar Square. He looked down Whitehall towards the Houses of Parliament, places he had only read of. 'Now I am here I shall make it my future,' he told himself.

173

He remembered that Michael and Leslie had been here with his Uncle and Auntie before they went to Canada. They had come home full of all the wonder of London. But he said to himself, 'I am going to live here. I am going to work here. I am going to become part of it!'

He found a vacant bench-seat and opened his *Advertiser* to the Situations Vacant pages, and wrote on a paper pad the addresses of those bearing the postal areas he had hitherto only read about in his local newspapers, and where the lower-paid jobs appeared - 'Potman and Barman - Learner. Live and Sleep in.' Some had the added legend, 'Good food and wages.'

He cared not what work was entailed: he was prepared to scrub floors, clean toilets, wash-up glasses and china - all the chores he had done at the sweat-shop Dickensian hotel for peanuts. Here he noted the wages were vastly higher. He decided to try his luck. He had with him the required government insurance cards - one for employment stamps, the other for sickness stamps, the cost of which in those days was equally divided, the employee's half being deducted from his earnings. He opened his street map and found that a job for Bar-Learner was vacant in nearby Villiers Street. He walked across the Strand and saw the pub almost at first glace. He straightened his tie before he knocked at the half-opened door marked 'Saloon Bar' and heard a male voice reply 'Come in.'

As he entered he removed his cap and walked to the shirt-sleeved young man standing behind the bar.

'Whatcher want, mate?' he asked.

'I have come in answer to the advertisement in the *Morning Advertiser.*'

'Wait a minute, I'll get the governor.'

Fred heard him call for a Mister somebody, saying, 'There's a kid here with a gammy leg after the job.'

Fred froze in indignation. The manager appeared and walked through the bar-flap toward him.

'Good morning,' he said.

'Good morning, sir.'

'Sit down, son,' he said, and wrote down the answers to his questions about Fred's antecedents. When he had completed them he said, 'Right, let's see you walk.' Fred walked across the bar and back and was aware of the supercilious grin of the young, but older-than-himself, man behind the bar. Incensed, Fred said quietly, 'Do you see anything funny?'

'No! Just watching you hop along,' he replied.

'Right mate, just watch how quick I can hop,' he said, as he bounded across the bar to jump into a sitting position on the bar top and simultaneously grabbed the man by his hair to smack his head upon the counter.

'You rude bastard! I should teach you a lesson in manners and thrash you, but you're not worth the trouble,' Fred said.

This incident had taken just seconds, and as Fred turned towards the open-mouthed manager he picked up his cap and bag and thought, 'I shall have to learn to ignore people's bad manners,' but knew he would not.

As he walked towards the door the manager said, 'Just a minute, son, I apologise for him. He deserved what he got. But you can have the job if you want it.'

'Thank you, sir, but no. I couldn't work with that man.'

'All right, then, it's up to you. But I don't think you're wise as I'm sure he won't trouble *you* again,' he said.

Fred shook his head and left to reflect: First application, first fight, first chance, first refusal. What a pratt I am!

Fred applied for two more jobs that morning and felt the eyes of each prospective employer dwell on his limp, and their polite declinations of employment was for this reason.

He returned to the doss house and booked his cubicle for the forthcoming night. He then went to the fish and chip shop.

He had eaten the sandwiches his mother had packed him, and now sat in Lincoln's Inn Fields to eat his fish and chips, which he noted cost two pence more than at home for a smaller portion, and a cheese roll was threepence as against twopence.

As he wandered along Holborn towards Tottenham Court Road he worked out the mathematics of his capital and his daily budget, and then the weekly, remembering to subtract twopence, there being no publication of the *Advertiser* on Sundays. Incidentals, such as soap and toothpaste etc he included in an overall percentage in a monthly assessment. It was imperative he should maintain a smart appearance and must not allow himself to become down-at-heel.

In London for just a few hours he had seen many of the down-and-out types already. Who were they? Did they have a home and family somewhere? Did they have their mothers, Maddys and Gisselles to love them, and did they wish they were with them as he did?

Many were young men already becoming old in mind and showing the symptoms of losing self-respect. Dirty, unshaven, unwashed, stooping to pick up cigarette ends from the pavements and gutters, unable to find a job and now perhaps not caring to.

'Fred, Fred, don't become one of them. Keep your self-respect, keep yourself clean! Keep your spirit and waste nothing. Don't become a Micawber. Keep on looking and make something turn up. Sod your leg: forget it, and keep trying. You are only on your first day and you have already turned down one job because it didn't suit you.'

Maddy had given him a dozen letter cards, stamped and addressed to his mother. 'Promise me you will send one every week to her, Fred.' As the weeks dragged by he was now down to his last one, and his last three pounds. He had tried hard and was now beginning to feel the rigours of malnutrition and despondency, but knew he must not give up. Sometimes he had raked around waste paper bins in public places at night and had given himself sustenance from discarded wrapped sandwiches or half-eaten apples and he had not slept in a bed in order to conserve his dwindling capital.

One night Fred was accosted by a prostitute in Hyde Park were he often slept on a bench. He had only eaten one cheese roll during the whole day. He told her not to waste her time on him, but she persisted in talking to him.

176

'What's a nice boy like you doing sleeping rough?' she asked.

'I'm out of work.'

'I've been watching you for the past week. You've spent the nights here, haven't you?'

'Yes.'

'You can come home with me, if you like,' she said.

He turned his head towards her. In the light of the park road lamps he could see she was much older than he, her face not over-painted as were many of her kind. He saw her smiling at him.

'Look, love, I know you've got no money and I don't expect you to give me any, but wouldn't you like a nice bed to sleep in and some grub?' she asked.

'Are you pulling my leg?' he questioned.

'No, love, I'm serious.'

'But what about your, er, er, customers?' he asked.

'Oh, don't worry about that. I sometimes don't come out to work for a week or more. I get browned off with them and I never take anybody to my flat anyway,' she said.

'Where do you take them?' he asked.

'I only work in the park here,' and indicating with a nod of her head: 'over there in that clump of trees.'

'What! You mean you lie down there on the grass?' he asked.

'Not likely! I never lie down with them. So they can't get their real money's worth. But they get so worked up that they think they do.'

Fred laughed for the first time in weeks. Really belly-laughed. The manner was so matter-of-fact. She went on to explain the secrets of her craft and left him looking at her in admiration. If only Maddy were here to listen she would be in hysterics, he thought. And if she had seen me playing my mouth-organ in the doorway of Aquascutums in Regent Street to earn a few bob she would be in tears.

The girl interrupted his reverie: 'What's the matter, love? You look so sad, all of a sudden!' she said.

'I was only thinking of somebody I love - my sister.'

'Well, don't be sad - what's your name?'

'Fred. What's yours?'

'Joan - and now tell me, do you want to come home?'

'Yes please, Joan.'

She lived in the ground floor flat of a house in Shouldham Street, behind Edgware Road. Completely self-contained. He was pleasantly surprised at its home-like atmosphere. It was the first domestic room he had stood in since leaving home and, looking around him, he was filled with a sense of home sickness, a feeling he had fought against so often. He knew that if he returned to the sanctity and love of home he would never return to London and that must not happen, for London with all its riches and poverty would smile on him some day. When? Ah yes, when?

'You're looking sad again, Fred. What is it, love?'

She took off her coat and stood near him, touching his arm and looking intently into his eyes.

'Oh, just thoughts, you know,' he answered.

'Take your coat and shoes off and tell me about your thoughts.'

He looked into her face. She did not look like a whore. Not at all like the many over-painted, brazen, foul-mouthed women he had seen so many of here in London. She spoke in a more natural, feminine way.

Many whores had accosted him. He had kept himself smart in that he carried spare white clean detachable collars, his toothbrush and paste, his shoe polish and brushes, and often he found a cleaner-looking carrier-bag which he exchanged for his old one. So the street-walkers had no idea of his shortage of cash. He chose to ignore their soliciting: 'Looking for a naughty girl, dear?' and his silence often provoked obscenities, which at first shocked him, coming from a woman. But this girl, Joan, a self-confessed whore, was utterly unlike his concept of a whore. She was kind and seemed genuinely anxious to help him. She knew he had no money,

178

so why was she prepared to help him for no regard?

'Come in the kitchen with me,' she said.

He followed her to a small compact kitchen equipped with a Frigidaire and white gas cooker.

'What would you like to eat, love?' she asked.

'Anything, Joan. Anything at all.'

'Look Fred, I'll tell you what: you go and have a nice bath and I'll be cooking you something for when you're done.'

He stood before her, his hands upon her shoulders and said, 'Joan, why are you being so kind to me?'

'Well I don't really know, but there's something nice in you, and now shut up and have your bath.'

She led him to a real bathroom!

'Have you pyjamas?' she asked.

'Yes, in my bag, I'll get them.'

'Stay where you are. I'll get it.'

She ran the water from the cold tap and turned on the hot from the large copper geyser as he probed into the bag.

'Fred, don't be shy with me, and empty your bag.'

She took it from him and up-ended it on to the small bathroom table. It contained his daily impedimenta, together with two soiled shirts, underpants and socks. She stood for a moment looking at the pile of his belongings.

'Is this all you've got, love?'

'Oh, no,' and he told her of his case in the Corner House.

'What's in it?'

'Just a few spare clothes for when I find a job.'

'Look, get your clobber off and get into the bath. Go on, don't be shy,' she said and left him.

He had never been in a real bath, and the utter luxury of stretching full length was heaven. He washed his hair after he had cleaned his teeth and, semi-blinded by the rinsing of soap from his scalp, he did not see the door open when she entered.

'I've come to wash your back, love,' he heard her say as he quickly covered himself. She made no comment as she soaped his back and flannelled it; and afterwards she rinsed his head and back.

'All right, now, love?' she asked.

'Thanks, Joan. That was lovely.'

His thoughts were in the cottage, and the way Gisselle would do the same for him in an upturned wine cask. He was not betraying her, was he? She would understand, Gisselle understood everything.

'You've gone quiet and sad again, love. Pack it up and let me hear you laugh like you did in the park.'

'I'm sorry, Joan.'

'I should think so, too. Stand up and I'll dry you, come on.'

'Oh no, Joan! I can manage.'

'Do as you're told, and cover your dick if you're shy.'

She was a second Maddy to him. She pulled out the bath plug, and as he stood, dried and shy, she powdered him with talc, giving him the puff 'to do your cobblers,' she said.

He started laughing, real laughs. He had not felt so uninhibited for so long. She may be a whore, but she was a woman of compassion and kindly humour.

'There's your pyjamas - they're clean, but that other lot I've put in to soak to wash in the morning. Hurry up! Your grub's ready,' she said as she hurriedly left him.

He smelt the aroma of cooking food. It's for me, he thought. How on earth does one repay a woman such as Joan? I have nothing, she knows I have nothing.

London has no regard for people with nothing, and yet this woman, frowned upon even by the self-righteous adulterers who use her body in lust, and by society, is the kindest of all the teeming mass of humanity I have encountered. 'Some day, Joan, I don't know how, but some day, Joan, I will try to repay you, but I know there is no way of fully repaying your kindness of heart for, as Mum says, "only God can repay."'

She cooked him the first steak he had eaten in London with three fried eggs and chipped potatoes. She cut bread, buttered it for him and followed it all with a whole tin of pineapple chunks and a cup of cocoa.

'You've eaten it all up like a good boy,' she said, as she put the used plates into the kitchen sink, with the rejoinder, 'Sod that lot, it can wait till the morning to be washed up. Come to bed and tell me all about yourself.'

'Joan, er, er... I can sleep on the settee.'

'Why? Do you think I'm going to rape you?'

He could feel that awful blush starting again and turned his head away from her.

'Fred, your neck's turned red,' she said, and put her arms around him from behind saying, 'I don't remember the last time I had somebody to cuddle me in bed and if you think I'm going to waste the chance tonight you're wrong, so don't mess about and come and keep me warm.'

Strangely, as he climbed into bed and put his arms around her, drawing her close to him, he felt only a strong inclination just to kiss her face and draw her even closer. To him she was not a whore, but just a woman to protect, a clean and warm-hearted girl in need of affection. Her coarse expressions belied the heart that beat in kindness. Her profession was but a myth of imagination, a pure woman to be loved as such. She stroked his head and said, 'Tell me about yourself, Fred.'

He told her of Jersey, but not of Gisselle. He considered that was sacred. And of his mother, Maddy and brothers. He told her of his inability to find a job because of his lameness. And then she spoke the kindest words he had heard since leaving home.

'I don't understand, love. When you walked here from the park I never noticed you limping. You are big and strong. I'll get you a bloody job. Don't you worry, darling.'

'But, Joan, I *do* limp, and that's why I can't get a job. I've been everywhere, and although most places are polite, some are blunt and tell me why they don't want me.'

'Rubbish! I'll get you fixed up, love, so give me a kiss.'

He kissed her lips gently, without passion, and she kissed him back.

'That's the nicest kiss I ever had, Fred,' she said quietly.

He said, 'Joan, I'd like to know about yourself, and if you think I'm rude in asking, I'm sorry.'

'How old are you?' she asked.

'Eighteen.'

'I'm twenty-five, and bred and born in London: Battersea actually, and I'm really a waitress. I still do part-time waiting but when I want to treat myself to something I can't afford I do a bit of pashing in the Park to earn a few extra quid, but I never walk the streets and I never bring anybody home. I want you to believe me when I tell you that I have never had sex with anybody I've taken money from. I went out with a bloke for three years. We were engaged and were getting married when I found out that he was going with my best mate. I don't mind telling you that it hurt me and he was the only bloke I had ever been with. He destroyed my faith in men and so now I get what I can out of them, and if I get the chance, I sometimes nick their wallets when they are coming and they don't notice me doing it. There, now I've told you.'

He was quiet and did not know how to reply to such candour.

'Well, you've gone all quiet again. Have I shocked you?'

'No, Joan, I think you're lovely,' he said.

'Say that again, Fred - please, it was nice,' she whispered.

'You're lovely, Joan.'

'Fred, I'm beginning to feel randy.'

He didn't answer.

She said, 'Have you gone deaf?'

'No, I heard you.'

'Well, you're not a queer are you?'

'No!'

'Give me another one of those nice kisses.'

When Fred awoke he found Joan still sleeping in his arms. The bedside clock told him he had slept for nine hours!

He wanted to get up, yet hated to disturb Joan. However, after a while he gently disentangled himself from her and he went to the kitchen. When he returned he found she had not moved and, not disturbing her, he returned to the bed to embrace her again and to sleep. God, it was great!

He felt her fingers running through his hair and opened his eyes to find her face close to his, smiling. 'You lazy bones,' she said, 'do you know the time?'

Looking at the clock he found he had slept a further three hours 'I'm sorry, love, I was so tired,' he said.

'Don't matter. It's Sunday today,' she said. 'Kiss me like you did last night.'

He kissed her and said, 'You're lovely, Joan.'

Later he said, 'Stay where you are and I'll bring you a cup of tea.'

'I ain't had one in bed since I left home,' she said.

When he took it to her she said, 'How would you like to be my ponce?'

'What's a ponce, Joan?'

She realised his naivety but could not equate it with his manliness. He was a country bumpkin maybe, but I bet he could be a handful in any trouble, she thought.

She *had* noticed his limp but his powerful body exuded strength and virility.

'A ponce is a bloke who looks after a girl like me.'

'What, er ... goes out to work for you, d'you mean?'

'No, you daft bastard! He protects me if I get into a row with my clients; and I give him what I earn.'

'If I saw anybody hurt you I'd look after them, but I wouldn't want you to pay me for it,' he said.

After she had fully explained the duties of a ponce he expressed his disgust saying, 'If you think I'm that sort of a bloke you are insulting me. I'd sooner sleep on the park bench.'

'I didn't think you would, Fred, but it would be nice to have you here. I'm sorry if I've annoyed you.'

'Joan, do you mind if I stay here just for tonight and I'll go tomorrow,' he asked.

'Look, love, I told you I'll get you a job and I will. Perhaps not for a little while, but I will, so in the meantime please stay with me and let me look after you.'

'That sounds like me poncing on you,' he said.

'I'm not going whoring for a while. I've got some bookings for part-time waitress work and, like I told you, I don't always go out on the game so you needn't think I'm out bashing.'

'If I thought you were lying to me I'd go right now, Joan. It's none of my business what you do but I can't help thinking, now I know what a decent girl you are, what a pity it is that you think all blokes are the same as the one who let you down. By the way, I've got to go to the Corner House to exchange my cloakroom ticket.'

'I'll come with you, love. I want to walk along holding your arm.'

I must be going soft, she thought, but something about him worried her. She had seen him and watched him at night put newspapers underneath his body to keep the draught out between the slats of the bench he slept on. She often stood looking down at him as he slept, his carrier-bag as a pillow beneath his blonde head. Always the same bench. She guessed he chose it to be sheltered by the overhanging trees when it rained. Once she had stopped and was about to awaken him and invite him home, but her nerve had failed her and she waited until she could pluck up the courage, as she had done last night. Now that she had brought him home she decided to look after him, and could not bear the thought of his leaving her with no place to go except the park or some such place.

'Yes, I must be going soft. Am I?' Or was there something his presence stirred within her, to want him to be with her, something she had not thought possible since that two-timing boyfriend had destroyed her faith in men? She did not know but she was sure she would not allow him to go before he had got somewhere to go to, and in this she would help him.

He must have been hungry last night. She had cut a thick slice off the beef she had intended to roast today, but to watch him eat it had been a joy. And she had been loved by him in a manner new to her, and which she knew she would ever recall. He was not lustful, uncouth nor brutal. He had treated her as a child and with respect as a woman, and yet he was a mere eighteen but with attributes of a mature lover. She would never forget him. She did not know that he would never forget her. She did not know that they were to meet again. She did not know that he was to help her when she herself was to be in need of comfort and care.

Together they boarded a bus to the Corner House and collected his case. She insisted that he did not leave it there. Holding his arm they walked down Northumberland Avenue to stand, arms around each other's waists, to stare across the Thames downstream, the *News Chronicle* neon lights illuminating the Oxo and Shot towers.

He showed her the venue of the Silver Lady soup van which arrived regularly each night for the down-and-outs. The queue was already beginning to form where he had so often waited himself. He did not mention the scuffles for the right of 'first come, first serve' to commandeer one of the benches for the night, benches which ran along the entire embankment from Westminster Bridge to the Kingsway tram tunnel, nor of the punch-ups he had had in holding on to the bench he had taken for himself when some unknowing persons had thought the young lad with the limp was of no account, and easy to shift. It was for that reason he had taken to sleeping in the comparative seclusion of Hyde Park.

When they returned, to leave the bus at Marble Arch, she said, 'What about a nice drink, love? I'll treat you.'

He said, 'I've got three quid left to last me 'til I'm fixed-up, but I can spare a drink for us, Joan.'

'All right. Just one, then,' she said.

They went to the small local at the end of her street. He bought her a gin and orange and himself a brown ale, the first alcoholic drink he had had in London, he confided to her. She laughed and told him that it was the first time a man had bought her a drink in the three years since leaving home. They sat together at a small corner table holding hands beneath it. She liked being with him. He treated her as a lady. He would hold her elbow as she boarded and alighted from the bus, and when they walked along the pavement he would walk on the side nearer the curb. She had never been out with a bloke like him before. It was nice, too, that when she said she was going to the Ladies he would rise to his feet as she left and returned. It made her feel important and she wanted to kiss him. When she washed his soiled clothes he insisted on wringing them dry, 'because you've only got tiny hands.'

'You've not told me your full name, Fred,' she said when they had got back to her home.

'Fred Higgins. What's yours?'

'Promise me you won't laugh if I tell you?'

'Promise'

'Cox.'

She saw the grin disappear as quickly as it had appeared.

'You sod - you promised,' she laughed. 'Very appropriate, ain't it? But I'll tell you this much: yours is the nicest of them all.'

He laughed with her and wondered what made this girl so open and uninhibited and looked into her smiling, jolly face. Her hair was a light brown, her eyes large and dark brown, her mouth generous, her face broad and pale. She had attractive legs and was of medium height, her bust firm and one would find it difficult to imagine her profession to be other than the waitress she was.

He wondered what her future would be and hoped she would leave prostitution, with all its hazards, behind her, for at heart she was not a whore of the sordid type. Being with her belied the general belief that all prostitutes are worthless. He learned now not to despise them for she had shown him what she had not spoken of - compassion - a quality not normally associated with prostitutes.

'I want to be quite sure when you are ready to take a job, Fred. I won't start looking for one for you for a few days. Don't worry, love. I've got plenty of connections through working in the catering lark and could probably get you fixed up tomorrow, but I want you to stay with me and keep me company - selfish, ain't I?' said Joan.

'I don't know about that, Joan. All I know is that you're kind and good to me and I'll pay you back with my wages, but I'll never be able to thank you for what's come from your heart,' he said.

'Sometimes you talk as if you're older than you really are, but you embarrass me when you say things like that, love.'

'I don't mean to.'

'Never mind - I like it really,' she said.

A 'few days' stretched to nearly two weeks, during which time she paid for seats at the Holborn Empire to see Max Miller and at the Plaza to see Bing Crosby in *Sailor Beware*, fed him meals of man-size proportions, and washed his clothes. She hoped it would last, for she was a happy woman, although he was unaware of the change within her. But she knew he would leave her and tried to prolong the day. She tried to tell herself she had not fallen in love with him, but knew she had.

When one night he told her of Gisselle, she experienced a new emotion - jealousy. He did not tell her in a hurtful manner, but simply mentioned another lady who had been kind to him. She wondered if he was lying to her to save her feelings when she asked him if they had sex together. 'Oh no!' was his reply, but where had he learned to make love as he did, she wondered? If it *was* her, she was an expert teacher!

'Joan, I must tell you. I'm starting to feel like a ponce without paying for everything. I must get a job, dear. Please help me, I can't go on like this, taking from you all the time.'

Always when he had something serious to say, if they were not in bed, he would stand, as now, with a hand upon each of her shoulders and look her squarely in the face with those blue eyes she had learned to love.

'Fred, please don't leave me,' she pleaded.

187

'Little Joan, I don't want to leave you, please believe that. But I must get work and make a start at being somebody. What am I now? Just a bum with nothing except a lovely, kind girl, who deserves to be a queen, and who spends her money on me. Don't you know what you mean to me? Don't you think I have a wish to perhaps make you admire me? When we are in bed we talk and I empty out my heart to you and tell you that I am thinking about giving up and shamefully going home as a loser. You have changed all that for me, Joan. You have given me back what I was losing: self-respect and spirit, and I can tell now that I am falling in love with you, and if I don't get a job I have no right to love you, so please try to understand me. I must leave you, but I hate the thought of your going back to the park. You're too nice, too sweet to do those things you've told me about. You don't belong there, Joan. God, how I wish I could do something to stop you becoming a real old whore, for that is what will happen, and it makes me sad to know it. So please get me a job, Joanie. Help me to get a start.'

He could see her tears beginning to moisten her eyes as he embraced her.

'Oh Joan, please forgive me for saying that. Don't you see it mustn't happen to you? I know you're older than me, but I look on you as a helpless little girl I want to look after, and the thought of your doing those things in that bleedin' park pisses me off. Pisses me off, because I can't stop you.'

She could feel his body trembling with emotion. She had never heard him use a bad swear word before and realised his deep concern for her. His outburst had told her of his maturity of thought as she sobbed in his arms. He picked her up as a child and gently laid her upon the settee and knelt beside her. 'Joanie, please don't cry,' he said.

She didn't recall the last time she had cried, and she had not been called 'Joanie' since her childhood; and his tenderness for her she had never known from anybody.

Joan's own parents had never shown much affection to their children and constantly rowed and fought. She had been glad to get away from them and they were not sorry when their kids cleared off.

But why can't I keep the first person who is kind to me? she asked herself. She was not annoyed, as he thought, when he referred to her as being a whore. Her tears came from his words telling her of his wish to protect her. She had never had somebody who wanted to do that. But she realised she could not keep him and that he must leave her, and that she must try to forget him, although she knew it would be impossible. She was seven years older than he, and yet she felt as a child with him.

She felt his handkerchief drying her tears and his own as he kissed her softly saying, 'I'm sorry, I'm so sorry, Joanie. Please forgive me.'

She clung to him and said, 'I'm not crying because of what you said. I'm crying because you care for me. Nobody has ever said things like that to me before, and I don't want you to go away.'

'I don't want to go, but you know I must,' he said.

'Promise me you will stay with me for another two weeks and I promise you I will have a job for you to go to by then. Please say you will, Fred. Please.'

'Joanie, that's a long time, darling, to let you keep spending your money on me,' he said.

'Will it make you happy if I promise not to go on the game any more; an honest promise? I swear to you I will keep it.'

He sat back on his heels and looked into her eyes and believed her words as he held her hands and said, 'Yes, it *will* make me happy.'

'Then I promise you I shall not do it again.'

'Thank you. You *have* made me happy, Joanie.'

Pointing to the far corner of the floor she said, 'Go over there and lift the corner of the carpet back. Go on!'

Mystified, he did so to discover hidden beneath it what looked like a brown paper underfelt. But under it lay a mass of flattened large white five pound notes. He had never seen as much money in his life except perhaps at the Labour Exchange on dole days.

'Good God, where did all that come from?' he asked.

She was smiling when she said, 'Some of it I found, some of it I saved and some of it I nicked.'

Her candour was pure humour.

'Tell me about it,' he said.

'Well, when I work as a waitress sometimes the tips are very good and I am able to save quite a bit. Then one night coming home on the tube a bloke sitting next to me was drunk, and he got up and slipped and fell across the floor. There wasn't anyone else there so I helped him up and held the doors back for him to get out. When he'd gone and the train was moving I spotted his wallet on the deck. I bunged it in my handbag a bit sharpish until I got home and found in it two hundred quid and a packet of french letters and nothing to show who it belonged to - so that was mine then, wasn't it? Then one night in the park I saw a toff come out of Grosvenor House, cross over Park Lane and come over to where I was sitting. I could see he was a bit over the top and I thought, Hi, Hi, he's gonna be good for double fare, and he was! So I took him over to the trees and told him to pay up before the nonsense started. He was wearing a dinner suit, all silky lined, and when he took out his wallet to give me the quid he'd agreed to pay he had a job to find a single quid. All the rest was the big white money. It made my mouth water. Anyway, I did the usual, but I also tipped his wallet out of his pocket onto the grass, and as he was composing himself I pretended there was a copper coming. That always gets rid of them quick. He was away like greased lightning. So I just picked up the wallet and came home to count it.'

'How much was in it?' he asked.

'A hundred and thirty-eight nicker. And before you ask, his business cards, which I put down the karsy and pulled the chain,' she laughed. 'Wicked, ain't I?'

'You're a little lovable thief,' he said.

'Come and kiss me and I'll tell you something.'

He kissed her. 'What are you going to tell me?'

'I've bought a bottle of Booths gin and four pints of brown ale so tonight we can have a little session at home. I won't cook anything tonight but I'd like to go down the road and get some fish and chips. When we've had it we can have a few drinks and I've got some Jack Hylton records we can dance to. How about it?'

Fred was to remember that night for the rest of his life. He had told her of his choirboy days and, late in the evening, both mellow from their drinking, she asked him to sing for her. Bing Crosby, then a young man, was the equivalent of a top-of-the-pops star. His latest record, which she did not have, was *June in January*. It was now January, and Fred changed the 'June' to 'Joan.' Holding her to him he sang,

> It's Joan in January
> Because I'm in love
> There'll always be Spring in my heart
> With you in my arms.

Through the years, whenever he heard that tune, his thoughts went back to that night in Shouldam Street and the little angel prostitute, Joan, who on that night turned her back on her sordid past.

Joan kept her promise and three, not two, weeks later he started to work in a high-class pub as learner barman at twenty-five shillings per week with full board and lodging, with a monthly small bonus from stocktaking surplus results. He was allowed one day off per week plus one Sunday in every four. The food was good, his private room cosy. From the darkness and shadows of the Whores Parade of Hyde Park a flower had come to him to colour his grey garden and an angel had showered him with the sunshine of London.

# CHAPTER 12

Fred settled into his daily routine as a barman with enthusiasm, listening intently to all teachings, albeit of varying quality. Some said. 'Do things this way,' others 'that way.' And he was fast becoming a student of human nature, careful to pretend to benefit from all instruction. And his aptitude for absorbing and learning was exemplified by his ability to perform his duties stylishly.

He was gratified by the compliments he received from the boss and his wife, who were managers for an expanding subsidiary of a large brewery, and from the representatives who made 'courtesy' visits bi-weekly (but whose visits were intended to keep staff, including the manager, on their toes). From boyhood he had had the value of good manners drummed into him. It was quite natural for him to use 'sir' and 'madam,' even to the uncouth users of the Public Bar! And some of the old ladies who were regular customers of the saloon bar thought him 'a very nice young man.' Some of his male colleagues called it 'crawling'!

Nevertheless, his clean and smart appearance, good manners and his dedication did not go unnoticed by the manager and the 'courtesy' visitors, and after two months he was deemed sufficiently experienced to be a qualified barman, and received an increment of half a crown.

Fred had become acclimatised to the frequent, 'what happened to your leg?' request. His usual curt reply was 'accident,' which, coupled with a half-turn from the questioner and poker face, cut out the likelihood of further details being asked. The 'guv'nor' and 'missus' had, of course, learned the reason and never referred to it again except in a pleasant manner when she said, 'Fred, you are the best and quickest of all the bar staff and you've surprised me and the guv'nor.'

He knew he was. He had seen his male and female colleagues slopping beer from glasses, leaving the bar top running with liquid, and failing to mop up or empty ashtrays or collect used glasses to wash them in the under-counter sinks. Instead they would stand chatting, sometimes being called to order by the manager or his wife. It never happened with him, not because he was attempting to make an impression but simply because he knew it to be wrong to stand idle when there was obvious work to be done. But Fred wanted more than bread and butter money. He had now proved himself. His horizons had become broader and ambition gave him the incentive to look for a higher position, which entailed the learning of the art of good cellarmanship. And when the assistant cellarman left suddenly he asked to be considered for the vacancy. Once again the spectre of his lameness, now less noticeable, reared its head when the manager said, 'You realise, don't you, the heavy work involved. I don't think your leg would stand up to it, Fred.'

There was no cellar-to-bar lift and the heavy wooden beer bottle cases containing two dozen bottles and weighing forty-eight pounds each were carried by hand. He said, 'Give me a trial, sir. I know I can do it.'

The morning session was over and the pub closed. The bottle shelves were in need of refilling for the evening session. The head barman/cellarman had to hump the boxes from the cellar himself and was not too pleased at the thought.

'Do you want a hand, Jack?' Fred asked.

Jack, a nice enough bloke, but apt to be misleadingly surly said, 'Won't it hurt you?'

Fred did not reply. He walked past Jack and disappeared

through the cellar door to return bearing a case in each hand. They were astounded. He got the job.

He enjoyed the heavy work, his physical fitness growing daily. In those days of heavy wooden casks, which had to be rolled on to sturdy oak stillions, strength, apart from know-how and knack, was essential. But to Fred it was bliss to use his strong body and, too, his leg benefitted from the exercise. He learned eagerly the intricacies of the art of presenting the beer free of cloudiness, used filters and finings, kept the pipes and suction engines clean and took a personal pride in the cellar itself.

Jack was a fair-minded man and openly told Fred, after a few weeks, 'You're the best bloke I've had, and I've told the guv'nor.'

Fred got a five bob rise in wages. Always on his day off he would go to Joan's house with some flowers and chocolates. She would be waiting for him dressed in her nicest dress, perfumed and always smiling. He loved being with her, hold-ing her hand as he proudly told her of his progress. She would listen with interest, not telling him of his child within her; and his look of dismay when she told him she was leaving London to take a well-paid permanent job in Bristol nearly caused her to tell him the truth. She would simply move home to a different part of London and not burden him with the respon-sibility she well knew he would assume should he learn the truth. She loved him and wanted him to rise to the pinnacles they would speak of in their pillow talk.

Joan knew enough of the sordid side of London and could have paid for an abortion, but she wanted his child. She kept her promise and no longer prostituted her body, and strangely looked back in shame. She felt she would still be doing it were it not for his peace of mind, yet resigned herself to leaving him to mature and succeed. She had not told him that beneath each corner of her carpet hid sums of money larger than that he had seen and she had no fear of financial difficulties. She had intended, had her heart not ruled her head, to save for her old age, but now she intended to move into a furnished room, have her baby and then buy a small confectionery shop.

'Joanie, must you go? You are my only friend in London and I love you. Please don't go.'

'It's no good asking me, Fred. I love you too, but it will not be fair when you get older. I'm seven years older than you and if we were to marry you might hate me in years to come; and I always want to remember you love me. I have always had the feeling, and I don't know why, that women are going to cause you heartaches, and it won't be until you're much older that you find someone to really love. As long as you truly love her you will then be happy, and I know what it means because just to love you is enough to make me happy, as you too will be happy just to love somebody.'

'Joanie, you are the fourth lady to tell me that - first my Mother, then Maddy, Gisselle and now you.'

'Fred, what you don't realise yet is that there are a lot of wicked women about and women are attracted to you. You don't realise it because no woman has done you dirt but, believe me, they will, so please watch out.

They parted tearfully and he did not, in his naivety, realise its significance when they made love for the last time, and he patted her tummy saying, 'My goodness, you're getting a belly on you through eating too many of my chocolates.'

She said she would forward her new Bristol address to him but knew she was lying. For a long time he pined for her and once went to Bristol to ask for her at various large catering houses, not knowing she was just across the Thames from where they had stood with arms around each other's waists, it seemed, so long ago. Once a month he went home. He had never been able to persuade Joan to accompany him. She was shy, she said.

Fred's mother always refused the money he wanted her to have. She still had the money he had left her and wanted him to have it. She was comfortable now, and Bertie had been taken on as house-boy at a high class school where he now lived.

Rosalina had got her way and was encamped in her mother's house. Fred had mixed feelings this. On the one hand his mother was not alone, but on the other he knew she would be saddled with Rosa's children while she would be free to pursue her many gossiping meetings. But Maddy was always there to meet him and join him in the tap room of the Wheatsheaf for an exchange of confidences.

'Found yourself some crumpet up there, Fred?' she asked.

She listened with interest when he told her of Joan and how she had rescued him from the park. She understood when he told her of her sideline in the park and how he had persuaded her to give it up.

'She must be in love with you,' said Maddy.

'She's older than me, but I love her, and now she's gone away, but I'm getting over it, I only wish I knew where to find her,' he said.

'I think she's left you because you've rung the bell again, Fred.'

The possibility struck him as a fierce blow, and the recollection of her white, slightly swollen belly and his joke of eating too much chocolate filled him with a sense of dishonour. He told Maddy, who said, 'Well, there's not much you can do about it, but she must be a good soul to do that.'

'She is Maddy, she is.'

'You'll have to try to forget it - perhaps I'm wrong.'

He thought of Gisselle and wondered whether he had sired a son or a daughter. She had promised to send him a photograph to Maddy's address, and when he asked her if she had received it yet, she doubled up with laughter, saying, 'Jesus, Fred, by the time you're twenty-one do you realise you will be the father of three children, all bastards.'

'How do you mean three, Maddy?'

'That sailor's wife you used to do it with at the fish shop had a baby the image of you, and I've seen it,' she said.

'You must think I'm awful, Maddy.'

'No, I don't. It just makes me laugh, that's all. But don't worry, I shan't tell anyone except Sam, and I know he'll have a good laugh himself and say "Good luck to him."'

'It's funny to me, though - I've not chased anybody, Maddy.'

'Oh! You will, and then your troubles will start. I told you a long time ago that women will cause you grief, and you won't be happy for a long time. You'll have to wait.'

Back in London he further proved to be an asset to the management when two loud-mouths were asked by the guv'nor to leave the premises. As usually occurs, a silence fell upon the bar and conversation ceased, so that the dialogue between the offenders and the manager could be heard. Their use of four-letter words and their threatening manner was obviously shaking the nerve of the governor. Not a large man, he was not capable of defending himself from the severe shoving from the louts, and nobody was prepared to help him. Fred eyed them, weighing-up their aptitude for self-defence, and knew he could take them.

He vaulted over the bar and stuck his fingers in the eyes of one man and jumped on the toes of the other, smacked their heads together, and let one of them have a full-blooded clout in the teeth before throwing him out, returning to find the other cringing on the floor. Unceremoniously Fred grabbed him by the hair and dragged him to the pavement outside where he kicked his knee-caps, leaving him howling in pain.

Fred had not spoken during the fracas, and when he returned to the bar he again vaulted the counter and began doing the trivial chores of wiping the bar, etc.

The guv'nor called him into his office. He thanked him for coming to his rescue, 'but you surprised me and everybody else,' he said.

'What did you expect me to do? Stand there and see you done over, sir?'

'But you bloody nigh killed 'em. Where did you learn that stuff?'

'When I used to box, sir.'

'You used to box?'

'I still can, sir.'

'I don't doubt it from what I have just seen you do. You're full of surprises. Have a drink on me.'

'A brown ale, please sir.'

Shortly afterwards Fred was transferred to another branch as head barman/cellarman, with another rise in wages, and a position next in line for assistant management. The location, a working class district south of the Thames, proved a wise choice by his employers, now aware of his hidden ability to subdue the frequent disorders which occurred there.

Fair skinned, Fred began to shave once a week but had retained his boyish complexion, which misled the unsuspecting over the power of his physical assets.

Fred's boxing instructor, an ex-naval heavyweight champion, had taught Fred a little Ju-Jitsu coupled with a few tricks not in the book: tricks of extreme brutality which Fred often now used. News of this soon spread, and brought a lessening of disorder. A busy house, a large bar staff was employed, the larger proportion being female, who were segregated, room-wise, from the sleeping quarters of the males. After a burglar had disturbed them one night Fred was asked to sleep on their side of the building to afford them an assurance of safety.

Here Fred was to receive his first lessons in the business of feminine will. On his very first night he was awakened by the head barmaid pretending to have been disturbed by an un-usual noise. When he returned from his investigation and after finding nothing of a contentious nature, he found her in his bed, saying she was too nervous to sleep alone and he, having endured the severity of celibacy since Joan, now a sweet memory, at once sympathised with this poor nervous lady and jumped in beside her to afford her the succour he was em-ployed to provide.

Within the next few weeks hardly a night passed when his services were not called upon by the several ladies it was his bounden duty to protect, each and all aware of their turn.

When Fred heard the first rumblings of the resultant tempest, he quietly handed in a week's notice to the manager, swearing him to secrecy on pain of Fred divulging to his wife the nature of his extra-mural behaviour with a married lady customer.

So back to the dosshouse and the Corner House cloakroom. But now Fred had plenty of ready cash in his pocket and money in the bank. Now too his hands were firmly on the reins of the Chariot of London's stampede. He joined a boxing club and became mates with Ernie, who introduced him to the semi-professional halls where he later had a number of bouts, losing only one: to a man three stone heavier and years older than he, and that only on points. Ernie introduced him to fairground boxing booths where he took on all comers and became known as 'Fred the Leg' but nobody referred to his limp disparagingly without receiving physical retribution for their lapse of good manners.

He became a toughened young walking tailor's dummy, fastidious in his dress and appearance but yet a doddle for designing ladies.

During a meeting with Ernie in a West End bar, they were given the 'come-on' by two attractive young ladies. They joined them at their table. They said they had been 'stood up' by their boy-friends, which proved to be untrue - late perhaps - but not 'stood up,' a fact made patent by the appearance of two husky young men who told them to push off. Not wishing to cause a disturbance, but aware that they were well capable of guaranteeing the *status quo* of civility, they left, only to find they were being followed by the cock-sure boy-friends, who made the error of misjudging them, shoving Ernie roughly: a mistake they would never forget. The ensuing short fracas on the pavement of Piccadilly Circus resulted, within seconds, in one assailant flat out on the pavement, and the other, Fred's attacker, under a London bus.

Fred turned, but into the arms of a policeman, whom, to

his horror, he knew, through drinking with him in a local pub. But Fred did not remain to say 'Good evening' and disappeared rapidly into the bowels of the London Underground. Coincidentally, Ernie lived with his mother in Shouldham Street, a few doors away from Joan's old house. It was to this house that Fred fled. A panic-stricken fugitive from the might of the law. Ernie's mother was out when he knocked. But Ernie knew where Fred would make for, and a few minutes later arrived to open the door for him.

Ernie told him he did not wait to see the consequences of Fred's handiwork, and he too had sought refuge on the Tube.

Ernie had a relative in the Merchant Navy whose home town of Liverpool was where Fred found himself next day, armed with a letter of introduction, and a hope of assistance in finding a berth as a crew member on a ship bound for Canada. The other side of the world was not far enough away in the circumstances.

Now with a Seaman's Ticket, Fred was taken on as sick-bay attendant on a freight ship bound for Vancouver. He didn't mind the many unpleasant chores. He had done them before: scrubbing-out and cleaning, but he was surprised at the number of seamen and seniors sea-sick during the first days out.

The first stop was Rotterdam, then through the Kaiser's Canal from the North Sea, and into the Baltic to Stockholm, and back via the Kattegat and Skagerrak to Trömso in Northern Norway. Then Murmansk to Archangel, and then the long run over the top of Russia to the Bering Strait; into the Bering Sea and on to Vancouver Island, after Queen Charlotte Sound.

Quite unexpectedly, Vancouver reminded Fred of home: its general aura, not unlike what he was used to in England. The unloading of agricultural machinery and cattle gave most of the crew time to go ashore, the first stop being a café because the food aboard ship was diabolical, unless one bribed the so-called cooks. Fred's intention had been to stay in Canada;

he knew his Uncle Michael would arrange any formalities necessary. But before he had completed the whole of the outbound trip he made a decision to return to England to face the music. The thought of deserting his Mother and Maddy prayed on his mind and he felt a coward. But a shock awaited him as he was paid off. He was told the ship would not return to Liverpool for two-and-a-half years and during that time would make several round trips to Hong Kong from Vancouver. His shipmates had taken for granted that he was aware of this, and had not at any time referred to it.

His priority now was to locate and surprise his brothers, now many years apart. Would they recognise each other, he wondered? He had seen pictures of them and it was more probable that he would recognise them than they him. He bought a street and locality guide, pin-pointed their address, and was wandering about the broad streets near his goal when his attention was drawn to two young men looking in a menswear shop window.

They wore dark trousers and jumpers, each topped by a long-peaked cap. Their backs were towards him but both bore a strong resemblance to his brother John's rear outline. As young boys the Higgins children used to 'go exploring' in the thick woodlands on the outskirts of town, sometimes losing each other in its density. When this occurred they would make contact with one another by shouting 'Higgins.' Would they remember? He shouted! As one, they both spun around. There was no doubt. They sped across the road to embrace each other in brotherly reunion. Passers-by halted to hear in an English accent 'Hello, Les! Hello, Mike!' and 'Hi! Fred, Hi! Fred,' their features unmistakably denoting blood relationship.

The opulence of their home was in sharp contrast to their humble beginnings and yet they remembered their old home and family. Photographs, and their mother's illuminated religious texts adorned the walls of their separate large bedrooms, each with bathroom attached.

Both boys were at the University of British Columbia, Leslie studying medicine, Michael economics. Fred thought of how the future might have been for himself had money been more plentiful, but he had long decided he would one day create his own success, unaided and in his own manner. Fast he was becoming mature in mind, his life as a loner hardening him to the brutality and selfishness of humanity, and knowing too of the rarity of compassion. He was his own person. The resolve to win would not change his inherent inability to plunder the misfortunes of others. He had found that kindness was the key to peace of mind. When his kindness was mistaken for weakness he was not bitter and vindictive but regarded it as a lesson learned.

His aunt and uncle were to remark on his likeness to his father, and when Fred unexpectedly arrived at his office with his brothers, Michael said, 'Good Gracious! I thought I was looking at a ghost.'

Having heard the story of Fred's hurried departure from home, Michael was willing to help. Now an influential man, he said he would try to arrange Canadian citizenship for him, but understood Fred's feeling that he should return to England to face the consequences of action under the law. Fred would sail for Hong Kong and jump a ship to England via the Suez Canal.

The trip was to be a long and tedious one. Many dog-legged and zig-zagging routes were to be taken, and contrasting climates to be endured before Fred found himself landing in Malta. His ability to cook was to be largely responsible for his being accepted as crew on the various ships it was necessary to take, and it was not before Malta that Fred had his first punch-up since London.

Whenever a port was reached Fred was at a loss to comprehend the minds of many of his shipmates. Men married with children would speak of them and proudly show photographs of them, yet always after the usual bouts of drinking, would either pick up a prostitute or visit a brothel, and this sometimes resulted in attempts by the ever-present seaport thieves to rob them. One shipmate was picked-up by a Maltese girl, a decoy for two men who were in the business of robbing people like him. Drunk and incapable of defending himself he was lying in an alley when Fred, searching for him, came on to the scene. The girl was going through his pockets, the men holding him to the ground. Fred kicked the girl violently, and butted one man with his head, kneeing his stomach while he hit the other. The girl ran off, but not before he had grabbed her handbag. The two men proved to be the normal feint-hearted types when meeting their match but Fred ruthlessly kicked and punched them to unconsciousness. With his mate, now somewhat sobered, he robbed them of every penny their pockets contained, stole their watches and rings, stripped them naked and, after rifling the woman's handbag, returned to the ship to share the spoils.

Algiers, Gibraltar, through the Straits and into the Bay of Biscay, and then to Tilbury to face the music.

Fred had sent letters and postcards to his mother and Maddy from every port at which they docked, and having established the day and approximate time of his arrival in London, had written to Ernie arranging a rendezvous with him in the London pub they sometimes used in the Strand.

Ernie was waiting for him in Yates Wine Lodge, and after heart-felt greetings had been exchanged, Fred told Ernie of his intention of going to Bow Street Police Station to give himself up.

'No need to, mate,' said Ernie. 'That bloke you laid out on the road in Piccadilly was unconscious when the bus passed over him. It did not touch a hair on his head!'

Fred stared at him in disbelief. But Ernie produced a newspaper cutting to prove his words. He explained that he had been unable to contact him as Fred's changing whereabouts were impossible to follow. Fred wondered if his journey had really been necessary. But he knew that his travels had broadened his entire outlook on life.

No longer would Fred be able to hold his future to a pattern. He had ambitions and would try to achieve them, but his now fatalistic attitude told him that the steering of a set course would not be easy to maintain.

He found jobs in pubs and clubs, now much easier for him to obtain, and gradually he became more selective, and would think nothing of leaving if something did not suit him. The doss-house was the best in London, and although he often thought of taking a small flat and furnishing it he decided to wait. He had his fair share of feminine comforts but had not yet met a girl he could equate with Gisselle or Joan.

He regularly paid a visit home, but Rosalina had assumed what she thought was authority over the house. Although his mother did not appear to take much notice of this, it rankled with Fred. And always Rosalina seemed to enjoy talking of others' misfortunes. For instance, she had much to say of the fact that John had 'done a bunk' from his ship, a fact he was well aware of, for he had come home to assure his mother of John's well-being. John had come to him in London and Fred had sheltered and fed him and got him a job but he was not going to give Rosa fodder for her tongue. John had become tired of the Navy - said he did not really know his own mind when he joined (too young to know).

Fred could not contain his indignation when Rosa said 'The bloody disgrace of it when the Naval police come here looking for him with all the street looking on.'

'Well, if you don't like the place what the hell are you doing here? It's not your home, so shut your row and don't forget this is still my home if I choose to come back. You are taking advantage of Mum, so push-off if you don't like what people who belong in this house get up to,' he thundered. As in days gone by tears came to Rosa. 'Stop him, Mum,' she appealed to Rose.

Fred wrote every week afterwards, but kept away. He knew his mother was upset by family quarrels although she never took sides, and she knew that Rosalina was a cow.

John eventually returned to his ship wearing his uniform which *ipso facto* meant that he had not deserted but had merely been absent without official leave. He later joined the RAF under a different name and then deserted again to join the army which he enjoyed.

Fred had long wanted to become a cocktail bartender and in this sphere of catering he excelled such that in later years became head bartender at first class hotels and famous clubs in the West End of London. His work sometimes took him to the town houses and ancestral homes of the British aristocracy and nobility and the homes of millionaires, tycoons and the rich who spent money as water and yet would argue over the cost of trivial items. A good bartender, he never appeared to hear the conversations between people of world acclaim, conversations involving millions of pounds; and many slanderous statements concerning others of their ilk. He sometimes bought shares to a modest degree in companies he had heard favourably mentioned.

When he attended private homes for house or cocktail parties in areas such as Mayfair and Belgravia, much of the preparation would be done in kitchens and pantries where he would rub shoulders with butlers, footmen, cooks and maid servants. Here he met Lois, an attractive ladies' maid.

He formed a romantic liaison with her and after a few weeks spent nights with her in small hotels. She introduced him to her married sister and other relations. He found her rather possessive of him and he began to believe he was in love again. Not in a sweet way as with Gisselle and Joan, but he supposed he should think of settling down and getting married. He was now tenant of a small flat in South Kensington and had a fair bank account which he was ready to share. He had taken a number of girls there but had not found one whom he wished to 'come home to.' Even with Lois he was not over-enthusiastic. He had told her he shared the flat with a friend, as he feared her possessive nature would result in her taking him over completely. The cost of the occasional room to spend the night with her was safer, but he became rather involved with her family, and when she announced she was pregnant he could not escape the consequences, and fatalistically accepted her proposal of a quick marriage.

He did not love her as he would have wished but hoped perhaps it would develop and he would find domestic happiness in the warmth of family life and companionship. Rapid preparations were made for the wedding and, though he would have preferred a church wedding, Lois wanted to be married by special licence at a Registrar's Office. It was in this office that Fred discovered that she was seven years older than he. She had lied to him when he had asked her age on their first date, although he had wondered about it. He had dismissed it from his mind, but now his discovery raised an uneasy sense of betrayal. He felt trapped and toyed with the idea of calling off the wedding and told her so.

'What difference does it make anyway?' she asked.

'More than you think,' he replied, and he thought of Joan and of how he wished he could find her. He would marry her with love, and she was seven years older than he. Had it not been for her pregnancy he would not have married Lois, but reluctantly he did to save her the disgrace of bearing a fatherless child.

Once married he saw her in a new light. She was slovenly at home, shy of housework and not pregnant. She pretended to have unexpectedly resumed menstruation, disappointed though she was. He resigned himself to the fact that she was a habitual liar. He was not mentally equipped to deal with her type, and became very disillusioned. He simply hoped she would improve. He took her home and although she and Rosalina found conversation easy, he did not fail no notice the restraint of his Mother and Maddy.

It was Easter and he had days off work. He asked her to accompany him again to visit his mother. She declined, saying that she had arranged to meet her sister, but had no objection to his going alone. At the railway station he suddenly recalled that Maddy and Sam were to attend his father's grave with his mother and would probably drive on to the coast after. Fred, not wishing to return home at once, called on Ernie and his mother.

He arrived back at his flat early to find a bicycle standing in the hall which he recognised as belonging to a friend of Lois's family. Hearing no sound of conversation and finding the drawing room empty, he stealthily went to the bedroom. As he slowly opened the door he saw a mass of male and female clothing on the floor, and the cries of dismay of the occupants of the bed as they became aware of his presence. They rushed out of the room in fear of his wrath. But he did not attack them. He walked away to sit in the drawing room. His world was shattered.

Fred heard the man hurry from the house, and when he entered the bedroom to pack a case with clothing, Lois had dressed and was sitting on the beside, weeping. He did not speak and left the house not knowing his destination. He stood, case in hand at the street corner in tears, no longer a confident young man, but now a bitter pathetic boy who wanted to be near the good women who loved him. The small cosy home he had built was now, to him, a tarnished berth of degradation. He found himself in Shouldham Street, standing by the house where Joan had given him comfort, when Ernie's mother touched his arm. Her maternal instinct told her of his need of care, not knowing the tragedy that had befallen him. She led him to her house where she held him to her and he sobbed as a boy. She made him a bed on her living-room sofa and next morning urged him to 'go back and chuck her out.' He knew this, in hindsight, would have been right but he said 'No.' In truth, he felt that had he returned, he would have been incapable of controlling his emotions, and knowing his own ruthlessness when provoked, decided to leave her to herself.

Fred took a furnished room in Pimlico run by a weird lady who insisted on two weeks rent in advance and 'no women visitors.' Fred wasn't likely to entertain women, he assured her, as he wasn't interested in them. This led her to assume that he was homosexual. 'And no men friends either,' she said. He told her that he would not sleep there that night as he would be away on business. He went to Maddy and told her about the situation with Lois, knowing she would tell his mother, but he did not tell Rosalina and so give her a topic to gloat over.

Maddy did not remind him of her prophecy of the wicked women he would meet but as she looked at him she saw the youth of yesterday, and she knew she should not over-sympathise with him but gently tell him he should not forget the lesson.

'Not everybody's like her, Fred. You know that. Just be careful next time,' she said.

'There won't be a next time, Maddy.'

'Oh yes there will, Fred, and I have something for you,' she said handing him a letter. It bore a French postage stamp marked Cherbourg.

Fred's heart raced as he opened it to find no address inside. Just a picture of a little fair-haired boy smiling at him. He turned it slowly over and read Gisselle's handwriting, 'My name is Frederick Higgins Frenay.' Beneath she had written 'My Mama is the Rose of Lorraine.'

Maddy took it from his limp fingers and knew of his sadness when she told him.

'But this is to show you that somebody still loves you, Fred. Not every woman would be as brave.'

'If I could find her I would go to her.'

'That would be wrong of you. Don't you realise she would tell you where she is if she wanted you to know.'

'I just can't understand women. To two of them I owe so much: and they love me and disappear. And for one I've provided a home and she has crucified me,' he said.

He returned to London to resume work next day, his thoughts of Gisselle and his son ameliorating the shock of

208

Lois' betrayal.

A few weeks later he received a letter from the staff entrance time-keeper that there was a man there asking for him - a police officer. In plain clothes, it was an officer of West London Magistrates Court who handed him a summons to appear in court. Lois was suing him for desertion and was applying for a Maintenance Order against him.

In court he told the Stipendiary Magistrate the circumstances of his leaving her, which she denied in her typical ladies' maid, indignant, self-righteous, lying manner. Fred was fortunate in that the magistrate was a professional and not an easily-persuaded Justice of the Peace. He examined her statements carefully, telling Fred that if he could prove his allegations he had grounds for divorce in a civil court. However, the issue before him was of a different nature, and he had no alternative to making an order against him. He reminded him that the law provided him with the right to return to his home if ever he chose to do so - this order being for maintenance of his wife and not a separation order. Fred never availed himself of this privilege but paid the Order weekly into the court.

He had no witnesses to substantiate an application for divorce. She never wanted to remarry, content to take his money and, over the years, applied successfully to the court for increases due to gradual inflation. Fred was to pay her until her death forty-one years later!

In Germany, the Nazi party had taken control and the rumblings of war were beginning to be heard in Europe. Air Raid precautions were being prepared in Great Britain. Shelters and anti-aircraft gun emplacements, the issue of gas masks and recruitment of Civil Defence personnel were the priority. Warning sirens were tested, windows blacked out, bus, tram and tube train windows covered with an adhesive cloth mesh to prevent blast splintering, and in many large buildings house-Civil Defence squads were formed.

Fred was employed at a large West End hotel where he was

mobilised in its ARP unit, and he also registered with Westminster City Council's unit. He had volunteered to join the Merchant or Royal Navy but was turned down when his slight limp was noticed. Ernie joined the Territorial Army and was away from London on the Sunday morning that war was declared. Fred was lying in his bed in Pimlico recovering from tonsillitis.

When the sirens sounded after the announcement of the war, the panic of his fellow boarders resulted in screams to keep cool from the landlady from the depths of the coal cellar where she was the first to take cover. Instructions were given by the controller of the house ARP unit to report to the hotel at once following the declaration of war. Fred, having not eaten for a week, dragged himself from bed as the All Clear sounded. No bombs had been dropped, no planes had been heard: the warning, merely an announcement to those who had not heard the 'Umbrella Man's' (Neville Chamberlain) declaration.

Fred had acquired a taste for alcohol. He poured himself half a tumbler of Scotch, raised his glass to nobody in particular, and downed it in one gulp - the first liquid to pass his lips in a week. He lay in bed the entire seven days with no attention from the weirdo landlady who only knocked on his door to ask for rent. She knew of his illness. He made a mental note for revenge.

Fred washed, shaved and dressed, feeling the benefit of the whisky. He went to the nearby café to eat his first meal and afterwards reported to the hotel. Most of the men of the unit were married with families. Arrangements had been made for them to spend two nights a week at the hotel on a rota system but Fred was invited to become permanently resident for the duration as he was unattached. He accepted. Not only would he save in rent but would also be fed, have no transport costs and, more importantly, he would be doing his duty in perhaps saving life and property if the bombs began to fall.

Fred returned to Pimlico to pick up his belongings. The

landlady, being partly deaf, did not hear his knock on her half-open door. He could hear the sound of splashing water and put his head around the door to behold the landlady's wig hanging on the bedpost and she, completely bald, washing. He quietly entered, lifted her wig from its place and left the house to hang it on the basement iron railings. In all its luxuriant ginger glory he left it to be retrieved by the panic-stricken owner glaring from the window. Revenge!

The 'phoney war' after the fall of Poland, and the annexation of her eastern regions by Russia led many armchair politicians to believe that Hitler would now climb down - he was hemmed in by the Russian army and the combined might of the French and British Empire forces. When in the Spring of 1940 Hitler successfully invaded the Low Countries, culminating in the debacle of Dunkirk, the awful truth of the danger of invasion of the British Isles became a possibility.

# CHAPTER 13

With the fall of France Fred's mind was ever with Gisselle and his son. Although years had passed and Fred had grown from youth to manhood, she had created for him a dream of what he had imagined to be normal life with a woman. Through Lois he knew disillusionment. Joan he loved, and his short time with her had done much to reveal the existence of feminine goodness of heart. He had abandoned his search for her but not the hope that she would return to London and perhaps trace him. He wondered if she had been pregnant, and if so did he really have another child. Were it true, it would now be six years old and perhaps evacuated from London to the comparative safety of the countryside with thousands of other children taken there.

Fred's best friend Ernie lost his life during the evacuation of Dunkirk, his mother to mourn his loss, as she had his father, killed in France in World War I. She later died from grief.

Homeless, their countries overrun by the German hordes, many continentals found refuge in Great Britain and joined the armed forces representing their motherlands. In London many unusual uniforms were to be seen and many foreign tongues heard. Pubs were never empty until the ration of alcoholic stock ran out. And with husbands and wives separated by war service, many adulterous partnerships thrived. Years later when America entered the war and sent its fighting men to England venereal disease thrived. Huge notices were posted on advertisement hoardings with the large letters in ominous black 'VD.' It was wondered if the bill poster was a man of humour or an avid right-winger who was responsible for posting in Theobalds Road the notice 'VD' next to 'I got it at the Co-op.'

Rose at last moved from the cul-de-sac to a small house in more sedate surroundings but not before her faith had been rewarded by the visit to their mother of Captain Leslie and Captain Michael Higgins of the Canadian Army. Her belief in God's message had been fulfilled: Leslie a doctor, and Michael an engineer.

Bertie was evacuated with the entire boys and staff to a school in the West Country. Rosalina's husband was in the war service abroad and she occupied the new house with her mother. John had escaped from Dunkirk and, now a sergeant, was serving with the Royal Artillery and instructing recruits in Scotland.

The German air force, unable to sustain a daytime bombardment of London, in September 1940 subjected the capital to the full might of the Luftwaffe in the hitherto greatest number of bombs dropped on a single city in an attack, which lasted every night from dusk to dawn until the following April. Two nights were to provide the only exceptions, Christmas night and one other, when rain clouds engulfed the entire area of Northern Europe.

Fred was in London for every day and night to see death in all its horror. When not on duty at the hotel he was on the streets in charge of a squad of men whose main purpose was to rescue trapped victims and enshroud the dead in emergency sackcloth which each man carried. Known officially as a 'Light Rescue' party they were known to the firemen and ambulance colleagues as 'The Body Snatchers.' Bodies were enshrouded as they were found, sometimes fully clothed and whole, sometimes in pieces; and lined side by side to await dawn and the 'All Clear' siren when they would be removed to the Civilian War Dead van and taken to the make-shift mortuary and body cleansing post where the clothing and contents were placed with the body for facial, or any, identification. Victims were often found embraced in death denoting the knowledge of a bomb they knew was falling upon them to end their lives.

The saddest though, to Fred, were the many tiny children whose parents (often now dead also) had not the courage to evacuate them to safety. Was it lack of courage or, more humanly, simple parental love in wanting their loved ones near them?

Sometimes, when a particular district was the obvious target for concentrated attack and casualties were high, units were transferred to assist the hard-pressed personnel. It seemed that Waterloo railway station and adjacent factories were the target one night when Fred's unit was ordered 'over the water' (across the Thames). A large candle manufacturing factory and furniture depository were ablaze. The area, now the site of the Royal Festival Hall, was a working-class district of Victorian houses dotted with several small shops. A large number of houses had been demolished, the blast severely damaging nearby houses in which people were trapped. The 'Heavy Rescue' teams, responsible for the temporary shoring of heavy debris covering victims, had reported the sounds of life beneath one of the shops, and to this Fred's unit was directed.

The raid ended at dawn and, with daylight rescue, operations were somewhat easier. It was known that two women and a child were in the reinforced shored-up basement which had partly broken the fall of furniture dropping from the collapsed upper floor of the shop. As leader, it was Fred's job to locate the position of the debris-covered victims and, if possible, to ascertain the extent of their injuries if they were alive. He found an elderly woman in a semi-conscious condition pinned beneath a fallen floor joist. The further end had fallen across a face-down woman beneath whom he could discern the body of a child. Both were dead, he knew, but must be released and enshrouded. When the injured woman had been removed, now fully conscious but protesting her removal

214

from her family, the dead were next for attention. The joist now removed, Fred called for shrouds.

The back of the woman's head was covered with dust and plaster debris. As he turned her over to reveal her face he looked at the dead features in awe. He was looking at Joan! Fred's colleagues thought, as had happened to other men in similar occupations, that his nerve had broken as he fell weeping, holding the face close to his while removing his steel helmet. Beneath her was a small boy he knew to be his son.

The 'Incident Warden' was called and Fred led away by a colleague. He sat on a pile of debris in the street. He took the silver whisky flask he carried from the breast pocket of his tunic overalls and put it to his lips. It held the equivalent of a third of a bottle, but he gulped it down in two draughts. It was his habit to share it with his mates but they knew it to be better used. They realised a tragedy had struck him and placed the bodies away from his sight.

Later that morning he traced the survivor to the Brook Drive hospital. She was a Mrs Goulding, a widowed aunt of Joan's, who had lived with her since Joan had bought the shop. She had not been badly injured and shock seemed the worst of the result of the blast. She was able to speak to him of Joan. 'She came to see me at my flat in Kennington Road and told me she was pregnant. I could have fixed her up with an abortionist but she didn't want to know. I told her not to be daft but she wouldn't listen. She was about four months gone when she came to me and she'd already bought the shop. She asked if I would go and live with her. Well, I thought about it a bit. I'd always got on well with Joan; she was the only one of her family I did get on with, even though her mother is my sister. But I couldn't make her out. She said she knew who the father was, but had left him because she wanted to let him better himself. I have never heard of anything like it, but he gave her money the to buy the shop so I suppose he was a decent bloke,' she said.

'She told you that?' he asked.

'Yes, she did. But I couldn't make out why he never came to see her. When I asked her she told me he had gone back to the Channel Islands - that's where he came from.'

'It was me,' Fred told her.

'Is your name Fred Higgins?' she asked.

'Yes.'

'She called herself Mrs Higgins and the boy Fred.'

Fred told her the full circumstances of their friendship, omitting where they had met and what Joan had called her 'sideline,' and how he had searched for her. He later went to the mortuary and officially identified her and made arrangements for her funeral. Mrs Goulding's husband had been buried at Streatham Vale cemetery. She had paid for plot rights, intending to be laid to rest in the same grave, and expressed the wish that Joan and 'Little Freddie,' as she called him, should be buried there.

There were the only two mourners at the graveside when Joan's coffin was lowered to rest, followed by the tiny white casket of his son.

The London blitz took its steady toll of victims. Hardly a building in the whole vast area was spared of blast or demolition. The tube stations, normally the safest of shelters, became almost homes for thousands of Londoners. Balham tube station suffered the worst of any, due indirectly to enemy action. A bus was accidentally driven into a bomb crater, fracturing the water main and drowning many in the comparatively shallow shelter beneath.

But after April 1941 the raids became less regular, horrific in their intensity though they were. The last, but most terrible of these, took its toll on May 10th, 1941. The hotel in which Fred was employed and was resident housed many important dignitaries of governments in exile and was the headquarters of the foreign press correspondents.

Many large gatherings of exiled nationals were held in the large hotel ballroom, usually attended by the Head of State. King Haakon, the gentleman monarch, General de Gaulle and

King Zog of Albania, with his retinue of gorgeous women, were among the many wartime figures to be seen rubbing shoulders with their fellow countrymen of all walks of life. For such functions, a long bar was erected along a wall. From behind this bar Fred and his colleagues dispensed drinks for sometimes 500 men and women, all chattering in their native tongues.

The 'Four Fs' was the abbreviation of 'Friends of The Free French Forces' and it was during a gathering of its members that Fred was told that a gentleman at the far end of the bar wished to speak to him. He recognised the figure from his youth. It was Henri Frenay. As they greeted each other in typical French style, Fred's mind was taken back to the bakery at St Helier, to Gisselle, the flour bags, the aroma of baking bread and Henri sitting at the corner table dressed in white with the ever-present bottle of wine before him.

At the declaration of hostilities Henri had disposed of the bakery and returned to France and, being over military age, had been rejected for service. So he was employed as a civilian in an army bakery outside Paris. When the invasion of France began he returned to Cherbourg and waited to see the outcome, old enough to recall the over-running of France in World War I.

Gisselle had taken her son and daughter to Switzerland when it became more and more obvious that the Allied forces were inadequate to stem the German advance, and Henri was taken with many other evacuees abroad on a large barge which landed at Southampton. He now worked in the canteen kitchen of a large munitions factory in Swindon and donated part of his earnings to the 'Four Fs.'

Henri told Fred that it was he who had returned his letters. Gisselle had implored him to do so, but should Fred have returned to St Helier seeking her address he had been made to swear on a Bible not to give it. And now he would not give the address in Switzerland either.

'No, Freddie. I must keep my promise. It all happened a

long time ago and she is happy now. Perhaps you would both be disappointed in each other if you were to meet again; so remember it as it was.'

'How is she off for money?' Fred asked.

'She has plenty, and does a lot of work at home with her lace. She selects clients with plenty of money.'

Fred remembered the exquisite shawls she made for his Mother and Maddy; work of a high artistic standard.

'Perhaps, Freddie, after the war we will all meet again and when I write to her I shall be so happy to tell her we have met. We must just hope God spares us through the war.'

Henri gave Fred his address and wrote a short note of authorisation for the 'Four Fs' to provide his whereabouts should they lose contact.

Later in the 'Coal Hole' in the Strand they met for a farewell drink. Henri answered Fred's numerous questions of Gisselle and his son but Henri would not break his promise.

The war dragged slowly by, with Russia locked in bloody battle on the Eastern Front. Singapore fell. John escaped and was transferred to the Eighth Army in North Africa. And although the balloon barrage of London was a constant reminder to its people of the war, the terrifying dusk-to-dawn hours of whistling bombs and explosions were gone. The black-out was still rigidly adhered to, but those who had fled the capital were now trickling back like rats who thought the ship once-sinking was now buoyant.

Fred registered for military service at St Martin's Lane, and was later medically examined. His limp was hardly noticeable and this enabled him to be interviewed for category grading. It was only when leaving the small interview office that his limp was observed by the officer who had placed him in Grade I; and he was ordered to undergo *strict* medical examination, Fred was reassessed to Grade III, but not exempted from call-up. His wish was to join the Royal or Merchant Navy, but that was not to be.

Maddy was in a munitions factory and Sam a fireman. Rose had joined the Hospital Service and was proud to wear her large badge of office - happy to entertain patients. Rosalina, with three children, was happy to remain at home, and happy to leave much of the housework to Rose when she got home, so Maddy told Fred.

Many men who condemn women in general will, if they are honest, admit that their condemnation springs from an unhappy experience with only one woman. Fred was not of that ilk, and when he met Mary he thought he had found the woman he had been searching for. She was beautiful, smartly dressed and with a pleasing personality. He fell deeply in love with her, and she with him and within a short time they were sharing her small flat at Brixton.

Fred hated leaving Mary alone on the night he was obliged to be on stand-by duty, often changing with mates for day duty and often bribing his seniors to be excused duty. The danger of air raids was not ignored, indeed often a lone aircraft would drop the odd bomb to keep the ARP on their toes. He was quite frank with Mary. He told her of his broken marriage and of the alimony, but she 'didn't care about that,' she said. They were happy together; Fred paid the rent and bills and gave her house-keeping money. She, too, was a waitress, and when she was obliged to register for an occupation of national importance Fred got her the job of waiting on governmental ministers, including Winston Churchill - a post considered as being helpful to the 'war effort.' At least it saved the girl from becoming a trainee heavy-industry or munitions factory worker, in which she would have been hopelessly lost.

D-Day and the Normandy Landings came. Leslie and Michael, with many Canadian soldiers, lost their lives during the first month of this offensive. Rose, the fatalist she was, mourned them as a mother, but was proud to know her sons had died with honour.

London was now subjected to the first of Germany's 'secret weapons,' the 'Doodlebugs,' the V1s. And it was one such bomb which trapped Fred in the basement flat in Brixton. They had taken cover in a cupboard beneath the staircase so that, should the house collapse, no furniture would crush them from higher floors. Fred had taken the precaution of taking emergency food and drink, two torches and a referee's whistle with him. The whistle proved to be their saviour.

When the bomb exploded many people nearer to it lost their lives immediately, many were injured to die later, and many, including Fred and Mary, were trapped beneath the rubble which a few seconds before was their home. And some died from drowning in the water cascading from the fractured water pipes or were electrocuted by live metal.

Fred's experience during the blitz had taught him of these added dangers and his first action, after reassuring himself of Mary's safety, was to turn off the electricity and water supply which were controlled from within the cupboard in which they were now imprisoned. Within this tiny space Mary, four month's pregnant, aborted. He cleansed her with water from the bottles he had taken with them, using part of her under-wear as a flannel and, in the light of a torch, used his shirt as a sanitary towel. Fortunately, the haemorrhage subsided and for many, many hours he blew the referee's whistle in an attempt to attract the rescue parties he knew would be looking for survivors.

Fred had often seen human resilience to death when taking part in rescue operations of people who had been trapped for many days, and he knew that their lives depended on directing help towards them. Sustained by whisky and biscuits he maintained the morse SOS on the whistle, to be rewarded at long last by answering whistles. Mary was taken out first, Fred to follow unaided, to be taken with her by ambulance to hospital.

A few days later Fred and Mary arrived at his mother's house to temporarily occupy the spare bedroom. Welcomed by his mother, Fred should have known better than to take Mary to live under the same roof as Rosalina. Mary, a cockney, was not prepared to tolerate the innuendoes and snide double-meanings of Rosalina.

'Some people should know better than to live in sin.' 'Some men make it their pastime to get girls pregnant.' 'Lots of women have got no dress sense,' or 'a lot of women use too much make-up and look more common than others.' All such remarks, calculated to embarrass Mary and Fred, ended in a 'punch-up' between Mary and Rosalina, his sister receiving the treatment he and Maddy had for so long wished to administer themselves. Happily Rose was not present to see her daughter slapped good and hard, nor to listen to her London expressions and invective. Mary chose well the timing of her attack. Rosalina ran from the house in panic leaving her three children behind to the mercy of she-cared-not-who.

'Right, Mary. Upstairs and pack the bags. We're off!' Fred said.

Fred had plenty of cash and intended to find a small hotel when Maddy arrived laughing. She had passed Rosalina unseen, and heard her outpourings to her cronies: enough to get the gist of what had occurred.

'Wasn't it a pity I missed it!'

'We're not staying here, Maddy. I'd wind up killing that bitch,' said Fred.

'She's got a black eye,' said Maddy smiling. 'Come and stay as long as you want with me and Sam.'

It was good to be with Maddy and Sam. Their happiness did much to ensure an atmosphere of family nearness for Fred and Mary. Their children added to the feeling of being wanted. Their interest in, and goodwill towards, the couple were to be treasured by Fred all his life.

John had met and married Cynthia before going overseas. Fred had met her a couple of times since the wedding and was somewhat perturbed to hear from Maddy of her friendship with a married colleague - a man with a reputation for specialising in comforting women with husbands abroad. Fred's instinct was to sort him out and warn him to keep away from his brother's wife, but Maddy said no.

'Let them get on with it. If she wants to do that sort of thing you won't stop her. Leave her alone, she'll come to her senses.'

Mary and Fred returned to London. Fred had been commuting daily and looked forward to not having to make the journey each day. He had obtained a small flat in Balham, luckily not too badly blasted, and on which repairs had made habitable. And although no new furniture was being manufactured (all human effort being devoted to making essentials for victory) it was fairly easy to buy second-hand. Many homes were somewhat dilapidated, families still separated with children evacuated to the countryside, their men in the armed forces fighting abroad, wives waiting to pick up the threads of normal domesticity.

The Eighth Army had defeated the German and Italian armies in North Africa and Italy had been invaded by Allied Forces when Fred received a letter from his mother to tell him that John had lost a foot at Anzio. She said she would keep him informed of any further news. Three weeks later he saw a small paragraph in a newspaper, 'The first wounded men from Italy were landed at a West English port last night.'

Armed with his brother's army number Fred approached a War Office staff captain resident at the hotel and from him, later that day, learned that John was among those wounded. The captain arranged special permission for Fred and Mary to visit John at the hospital in Cambridge in which he and others were now lying.

Fred's joy at meeting his brother again after so long was turned to sadness when he saw him, his leg amputated to the upper thigh. His head was swathed in bandages, beneath which his hair had turned to snowy white. But he was still smiling in the same old disarming way which endeared him to all who knew him.

John was later transferred to Roehampton. Still Cynthia did not visit him. She was well aware of his home-coming: she had been officially informed by the War Office. So Fred made it

222

his business to find out why not. Fred and Mary visited John often in Roehampton and, as his condition improved, were allowed to take him with them for a long weekend. Four days beforehand Fred sent a telegram to Cynthia informing her of this fact and requested her to phone him at the hotel. She did not. Incensed by her behaviour, he went to the house she shared with her mother to be told, 'She's out for the evening.'

Maddy hinted of the place she knew Cynthia and her man friend spent their time drinking, and here Fred found them. He approached the table they shared with another man and woman.

'Cynthia, will you come outside please,' he said quietly.

Her face turned white. She knew the reputation of her husband's brother, and looked at her companion appealingly.

'She doesn't want to, mate,' he said.

'Do you know who I am?' Fred asked.

'No,' he said.

'I'm her husband's brother.'

'Oh, I see.'

Fred had no axe to grind with the man. If he was the type who found his pleasures with willing women but knew when to stop, that was all right, but if he wasn't he would learn.

'Well, Cynthia, are you coming outside or do I have to drag you there?'

'Yes, I'm coming,' she said.

'Say goodnight and goodbye to your friends.'

Her companion shrugged his shoulders and said, 'I'm sorry, mate, I didn't realise.'

'Please bear this in mind. Her husband has lost his leg and needs her. If I find out you meet her again socially I shall come back and have more than words with you,' Fred said menacingly.

'Truthfully, mate, I honestly didn't know,' he said.

Fred thought the opportunity to belittle her in the presence of her friends should not be missed as he said, 'She knew he was back in England, minus his leg and with head wounds, and for nearly a month she has not troubled to see him. I have come down from London to get her to stay with him at my house for the week-end. She knew he would be there but couldn't be bothered. What do you think of her now you know?'

He heard the gasps of disgust as he guided the tearful and humiliated Cynthia to the door.

Petrol was rationed, but if one knew where to get it, like many commodities in short supply it could be purchased at a very inflated price. Penalties for such abuse of the strict emergency laws were imposed regardless of one's standing, and were usually a prison sentence and heavy fine. Even the much-admired and popular Ivor Novello received and served a prison sentence, but to Fred, his brother's happiness was more important than a thousand Ivor Novello reasons for breaking the law. He paid well over black market rates to acquire sufficient petrol for the journey to bring Cynthia to John.

Outside the pub, Fred gave full vent to the contempt he felt for her. Even so, he could find it in his heart to understand her incoherent explanation of her failure to see her husband. She said she loved him and swore she had not been unfaithful and only socialised with people to fill the monotony of the years of separation. She had met him, married him, and separated from him within just a few weeks, and had corresponded with him each week and looked forward patiently to his return. When she received War Office notice of his injuries - they had later informed her of two further amputations of his leg - she was fearful of the shadow of the man she had married and was in mental terror of the sight she envisaged of him, bereft of his leg. She could only think of him as the handsome, strong, virile man of their wedding day and dreaded seeing him differently.

Fred had hardly met her before, but noticed her nervousness, and could now fully appreciate the extent of her inherent lack of self-assurance. She was a woman who was lost without

224

the firm guidance of someone to reassure her, but he felt she was a fine person at heart. He waited as she went to the front door of a house strange to him, and as she opened it with her key she beckoned him to join her.

'This is my secret home I've got ready for John to come home to. Nobody knows about it, not even John. I've kept it as a special surprise for him. He sends all his letters to my parents' address,' she said.

As Fred looked around the small flat he could see the care and thought it had taken to build this cosy and inviting small home. She was just a nervous but loving child-woman and must learn to shoulder the responsibilities of adulthood, he thought, but somehow he felt she would surmount her fears now he had forced her into facing the future. She showed him all the little things she had, with almost childlike enthusiasm, prepared for John's eventual return home. In the tiny bathroom she had placed a shaving stick, brush and mug, new tooth-brush, toilet soap and even separate towels, ('I change them when they get dusty'). In the bedroom pyjamas were folded beneath the pillow. ('John likes to sleep that side') and a dressing gown was hanging behind the door. Even on the kitchen table places for two had been prepared.

The drawing-room was set out like a picture taken of a pre-war shop window display. By the armchair, which she said was to be John's, she had placed a pair of slippers.

Suddenly Fred became aware of her tears. She was looking at the slippers. He went over to embrace her. He, too, had suddenly realised she would only need one shoe.

'Don't worry too much, Cynthia. He will later get fitted with an artificial leg, and don't forget, Mrs Higgins, we are a family of survivors, and once John gets used to the fact that he has to go through life with a handicap, it will give him the strength to do better than many of those who have no infirmities at all, and I know you are going to help him do it,' he said.

'Do you think I can, Fred?' she asked.

'I'm quite sure. All you have to do now is tell yourself that you are, for the time being, in charge of him. You're the boss, and he must do as you tell him. Nag him, make him laugh and encourage him to forget what's happened to him, and let me tell you this, because I know better than most: a loving good woman is essential to the happiness and success of any man, no matter who he is. Success without love and happiness is worthless,' he said.

'I hope I can make him happy, but I don't know where to start,' she said.

'You silly girl, don't you realise you've already started?' he said, sweeping his hands over the small home. 'This is the most wonderful start that any man can have and he is going to be so proud of you, Cynthia. I know *I* am.'

'Thank you, Fred. You've made me feel different,' she said.

'Now, come along, get your things together and on the way back we'll have to think up a few white lies to explain to John why you haven't been to see him.'

'No, Fred. I'm not going to start off with lies. I'll explain to him in my own way later on when he will, I know, understand and forgive me,' she said.

He told her not to expect to see the man she last saw, although there had been a vast improvement since he first arrived back. His hair was beginning to assume its natural colour, his bandages had been removed from his head. And he was now able to use his crutches, pending the fitting of the artificial leg. He would no doubt be obliged to wait for a considerable time for that, as Roehampton Hospital was jam-packed with men bereft of limbs, and many had been measured before him.

They arrived at the hospital.

'Now, let me see you smile, Cynthia,' Fred said quietly.

'I want to cry' she said.

'You will! You will! But greet him with a smile,' he said as he led her into the room where John was sitting with Mary, who left them together, closing the door behind her.

A few weeks later John left Roehampton to join Cynthia at

her 'secret home' which he did not discover until she led him to the door. Her 'special surprise,' she told him.

Fred was forever ashamed of humiliating Cynthia in front of her friends, and told her so. She replied that he had made her into a responsible person. He was still ashamed.

# CHAPTER 14

The war in Europe was over when, one day, a man and woman knocked at the front door and asked for Mrs Inskip. Fred knew of no such person, but asked them to wait a moment while he asked his wife. Perhaps she might know a Mrs Inskip. Mary was eight months pregnant and about to attend the local ante-natal clinic when he called her to the door. At the mention of the name 'Inskip' Mary's face froze.

'No! I know of nobody of that name,' she said, 'my name is Higgins.' Indeed Fred had, with her agreement, had her name changed by deed poll in *The London Gazette* so that identical surnames would be on the Birth Certificate of the expected child. Under the Illegitimacy Act this also enabled him to re-register the child at a later date with full legitimacy should he be free of Lois and free to marry Mary, thereby removing the stigma of bastardy from his child. And so, when Mary said her name was Higgins she spoke truthfully, but not when she denied knowing the name Inskip.

The callers were from SSAFA, an abbreviation of Soldiers,' Sailors' and Airmen's Families Association, an organisation which dealt with social problems of members of the Armed Forces. They had, they said, called at her previous address where she had lived with her mother, requesting some property belonging to her former husband, a regular army corporal now serving in the Far East.

'Mrs Lucus, her mother, has given us this address as her present home,' said the man.

At the mention of the name Lucus, Fred knew at once that Mary had hidden something from him. He stood by her and bluffed the callers away.

Taking her arm he led her to the living room and asked her to sit down and tell him the truth about herself before they had met. She was pale and shaken, he could see, but he felt he must learn the truth.

Unbeknown to him she was married and was receiving a corporal's wife's allowance and would continue to do so until her husband divorced her, and when she would cite Fred as the co-respondent! She did not tell him, she said, for she had fallen in love with him and didn't want to lose him. She thought that if he knew she was married he would not be interested in furthering their relationship, so she lived the lie, allowing him to believe that she was free to marry him whenever he himself became free.

Unknowingly he had lived in another man's home, a man fighting the Japanese in Burma, and she had been drawing his money allowance. All this time her parents had not enlightened him because, as they said later, 'We didn't like the husband!' Her mother had sent the SSAFA people to the house firmly believing that Fred was at work, unaware that he had taken the day off feigning illness. And so another betrayal, albeit not as serious as that of Lois. But this time a child was to be born - his child!

'What property of his have you got?' he asked.

Reluctantly, very reluctantly, she told him of a Post Office Bank savings account. He demanded to see it. She made the excuse that it was at the headquarters office being checked. He never saw it. Fred was to learn of her worship of money.

Fred booked her into a private maternity home, engaging a private doctor to attend the birth; he wanted only the best of everything for his family and he had the money to provide a good standard of living.

Little Veronica was born to bring her father the Star which was to shine upon him for the rest of life. A lovely girl with blue eyes, flaxen hair and peaches and cream complexion, he loved her to the very depth of his soul. Each day she grew she became more and more precious to him and more beautiful. Mary mothered her with tender care and dressed her tastefully in the prettiest of clothes and as she developed to crawling and walking she filled Fred's heart with a joy he had never known.

Fred was thirty when she was born. His bank account was changed to a joint account with Mary, his purpose being to provide for her should death befall him, and to prevent Lois from benefiting from it.

It was time to lay foundations for the future. Fred started looking about for a fairly large house in a good residential area. He discussed with Mary his intention of eventually leaving the catering trade, with all its uncertainties and inclement hours (a bartender was required to work an average of sixty-six hours a week for a wage of two pounds ten shillings, the employers being well aware of the large amount obtained from tips). Fred was fed up with the trade's vicissitudes. Sometimes his meals were eaten standing, or consisted of a grabbed sandwich. Sometimes he got nothing at all.

Then Bevan introduced the Catering Wages Act in the early 1950s Fred's wages went up to four pounds ten shillings a week and his hours were reduced to ninety-six for a two-weekly period, and with tips the money was very good. But Fred wanted to get out nevertheless.

With the profits from his investment and interest on capital Fred was now better off financially than many of the people he used to serve, and in the summer of 1946 he bought a house in the best part of Streatham for cash. A slightly blast-damaged sixteen-roomed detached house. He turned it into three self-contained flats. No sharing of bathrooms or toilets, they would command high rents. He moved in after he had converted the five-roomed ground floor for his own use. Building materials were acquired by devious means, such was the demand for them in post-war-torn London.

But Mary began to want to live on a higher plane. She

wanted the housework done for her, and so a 'daily' was employed. She wanted the best clothes and the most expensive jewellery, and she asked Fred to sign blank cheques for them. Gradually luxuries became necessities and nothing seemed to satisfy her. A slight cold would lead to bronchitis requiring a private doctor to attend her, the National Health Service doctor being deemed beneath her station.

Fred had been raised frugally. Now fairly affluent, he was proud to provide her with a higher standard of living. But nevertheless, he hated to see waste. Rationing was still in force but Mary and Veronica lacked for nothing. Black market commodities were always available. Always recalling his days of want and hunger, it grieved Fred to see food thrown into the rubbish bin, especially bread. Often he secretly took it from the bin, sliced and toasted it, and then spread dripping or lard on it to remind him of those hungry days he was never to forget. He ate these secret meals with as much relish as he had when he did not have a food-laden larder at hand. Mary was disgusted when she caught him out one day, and would not even try to understand his explanations, so wedded had she become to her new standard of living.

To the neighbours, mainly upper-middle class, Fred was a mystery man. Most were snobs. It galled them to see Mary pushing the expensive bassinet perambulator, the daily woman arriving, the private doctor's car, and when they saw the television aerial being erected on the chimney their curiosity gave vent to much speculation.

A taxi would call for Fred mid-morning and a taxi would bring him home late at night. Most of the neighbours were professional and management class, but none could afford the new medium of entertainment which to some was itself a symbol of social status. There were no hire-purchase facilities yet, but Fred was able to walk into Keith Prowse on Kingsway and slap down a hundred and twenty-five pounds in cash, plus a further 'tenner' for the aerial and its fitting: for an HMV set which it took two men to lift, the only TV in the area! Princess

Elizabeth was to marry Prince Philip in Westminster Abbey shortly and the wedding was to be televised. Just everybody would have given their eye teeth for a television.

Mary lapped up all the new acquaintances' admiration for the baby Veronica and 'the beautiful pram,' and 'haven't you painted your house attractively!' 'isn't that a nice frock you're wearing!' compliments from new-found admirers, falling over each other to get an invitation to see the wedding.

Fred gave her strict instructions not to divulge the nature of his job to them. He couldn't care less if she invited the whole street, but he knew that kind of person well and, being the snobs they were, to learn he was just a cocktail bartender would give rise to Mary being considered not one of them, and that would result in more trouble for Fred. Mary was fast becoming snooty herself. Or at least she was acting like it.

'Tell them simply that I'm in catering and if they ask you where, *and* they will, just look at them but don't answer. They'll get the message.' In fact the son-in-law of his next door neighbour knew Fred well but didn't let the cat out of the bag. He was a CID officer stationed in the West End, and over the years he and Fred had had many a drink together. Being a policeman, he too was a student of human nature and knew the pettiness of the minds of these people. Douggie didn't tell.

Nanny Higgins, as Veronica called Rose, loved to stay with Fred in 'the palace,' as she named it, and he loved to have her there. She loved to play on the beautiful Challen boudoir grand piano in the large lounge with its Sheraton furniture, Persian rug covering the floor and high pale-blue fire place. The wide French windows, hung with tapestry curtains, opened onto a flower-filled garden with fruit trees dotting the large emerald green lawn. A long arch of red rambling and climbing roses stretched the whole length of the almost pure white crazy-paving path which ended at the far garden wall (Fred had secret memories of red roses); Tarquin, the larger than normal harlequin Great Dane dog, wearing his silver-plated wide collar, would sit beside Veronica whom he seldom

232

left, and Rose, as she played the piano. They were happy days for Fred, but he could not put from his mind his past.

Rose looked deeply into his eyes one day and said, 'Are you completely happy now, son?'

He could tell by that expression in her eyes that she was really telling him that she knew he was not, and as she gently squeezed his hand, she whispered softly, 'Do you remember, I told you a long time ago that you must wait for your complete happiness.'

'Yes I do,' he said.

'Then be patient, and God will make you happy and find your Will o' the Wisp for you.'

Fred wanted so much to be free of the secret torment within his heart. He wanted to love, and be loved as he loved and worshipped Veronica, and as he knew she loved him. She loved him simply with her heart and not for what he provided for her. He meant something to her and when her little arms were around his neck and her soft sweet lips kissed him as petals from a blossom she was a Gisselle. She was a Joan and a Maddy. She loved him because of him. Mary never loved him like that.

It was mid-winter. It had snowed for days. Parts of the country were cut off from others when Rosalina phoned one evening when Fred was home. Rose had had a stroke and 'that sod John hasn't been to see her for weeks.'

'Have you told him she's ill?' Fred asked.

'I sent a message but he hasn't bothered to come.'

'I'll order a car and set out straight away,' he said.

'Perhaps you won't be able to get through. The snow's very thick here,' she said.

'I'll be there,' he said, and rang off.

He could rely on the car hire man to take him. He always tipped him generously and he was at Fred's beck and call at all hours.

The main London-Dover road had been kept fairly clear of snow and only on nearing their destination was difficulty encountered; but in due course they pulled up outside John's house. Fred decided to see him before his mother to discover the reason for the estrangement. As he had rightly guessed, Rosalina was the reason. Her bossiness and bitchy habit of mouthing innuendoes to Cynthia and John when they visited Rose kept them away from the house, and John told his mother this. And, 'No! Rosalina's a liar! I haven't received a message from her. Do you think that girl would keep me away from Mum if I knew she was ill?'

All through the years when Rose lived in the cul-de-sac Fred had kept a key to the house and when she moved she gave him the new one.

'You never know when you might need it.'

He let himself into the small hallway and switched on the light, John following, walking stick in hand. He had long since been fitted with an artificial leg. Fred opened the door of the living room to find Sally, the newly married wife of Percy, Rosalina's elder son.

Sally was a very pleasant and likeable girl, and she was alone in the house tending Rose in an upstairs bedroom. Rosalina had found an excuse to disappear to a friend's house because, as Sally shrewdly put it: 'You scared the backside off her when you said you were coming - she's afraid of you.'

It struck Fred that this new member of the family circle was likely to be a god-send in keeping her mother-in-law in check. Sally, he could see, would not stand for Rosalina's tantrums.

Sally said she would like to creep upstairs first to 'See if Nan' - her name for Rose - 'was awake.' The doctor said it had not been a severe attack but if she slept on no account must she be awakened. She was awake and had heard Fred's voice. She looked pale and seemed to Fred, as he kissed her forehead, to have aged.

'Would you like to see John, dear?' he asked.

'He doesn't want to see me. My John never comes to see me,' she said so very sadly. Whatever lies Rosalina had fed to his beloved mother he knew not, but a sense of loathing filled his heart. What makes a woman like Rosalina tick? How could she live through life with her own flesh and blood holding her in disdain? Even her very own children were beginning to despise her.

'Mum, of course John wants to see you. He loves you, Mum, and he wants to come in here to see you.'

'Please, Freddie, where is he?' she asked as she tried to raise her shoulders from the pillows. Sally gently said, 'No, Nan. Doctor said you must rest, and not get upset. Come on darling, lie down.'

Sally was a kind young woman. Fred knew his mother would be in caring hands with her.

John knelt beside his mother, his head between her frail hands.

'Don't cry, Johnny boy,' she whispered, stroking his head, as she had so long ago. Poor Rose! Cursed with a selfish daughter but blessed with loving, generous sons, she did not believe that God intended us to live free of pain of heart. To Rose it was simply His will.

Rose recovered, but mainly by the kind hand of Sally and her grandson, Percy, who had temporarily moved into the spare bedroom.

Rosalina was too busy gossiping and minding somebody else's business.

Shortly afterwards, Rosalina's husband, with but a few days before the completion of his service, died of a heart attack. At his graveside she forbade the final salute to a man who had spent his entire adult life in the service of his country because the sounding of the 'Last Post' by a solitary bugler upset her. 'The sound of it always goes right through me.'

His body was barely cold before she found another, a widower, who should have been wiser, to marry her. It's an ill wind &c, for her marriage meant that, at long last, she relinquished her dictatorship of her mother's home.

John and Cynthia now moved into a larger house. With two sons and a daughter they needed it. John had surmounted his handicap and drove a specially adapted car. His success in his career was extraordinary. Firstly he became a clerk in a factory manufacturing soft drinks and soon rose to Departmental Manager. He later resigned to take the General Management of a large distribution company.

Bertie was happy now. He now earned a man's wage as a road sweeper and, with Rosalina now gone from the house, he and Rose were content together.

Veronica was five when Teddy was born after Mary's confinement to bed during eight months of her pregnancy. When he was about to be born Fred had arranged for a private ambulance to convey her to the same private maternity home as before and, after, Mary occupied the same private room as with Veronica, where she rested for ten days, attended twice daily by her private doctor.

Nine months before Mary had complained of severe abdominal pains. They were on holiday then, in the best hotel in a south-east seaside resort. Fred ordered a car to return them to London.

The doctor arrived that evening and attended her on subsequent days each morning and evening. Fred was becoming concerned about Mary's condition. The doctor told him he would like to get a second opinion, and asked if it would be in order to consult a Harley Street gynaecologist. The two doctors told him that she must remain in bed for the duration of the pregnancy.

The specialist fees were astronomical.

The doctors' bills, with the cost of the maternity home, the medicines, wages for the alternating women in the house during Fred's absence, their food and numerous incidentals amounted, in gold, to the weight of Teddy at birth, but to Fred he was worth every ounce.

Mary seemed to rather enjoy keeping to her bed. Fred had the television installed there and bought a small bedside radio. There was a bowl of fruit and sweetmeats, books, magazines and an electric push-button bell beside the telephone he had

had transferred. He had never heard of a woman being confined for as long but it was his responsibility, so he met it. But he often wondered how necessary all this was.

Three times Fred arrived home unexpectedly, placing the key into the lock quietly, not wishing to disturb Mary should she be sleeping, to find her standing in her night-gown at the hall telephone chattering away like a magpie. It did not occur to him to question her when she complained that 'it's an awful struggle to get out of bed to answer telephone when Mrs Batch is not here.' Mrs Batchelor was one of the ladies Fred paid a handsomely to remain in the house in his absence. Only later did he discover that 'Mrs Batch' had been cleaning the now-completed rentable floors above.

Installation of a telephone in a private house was at that time difficult. Priority was given to business premises and to the homes of company executives, but Fred, with a well-placed bottle of whisky and a few quid, strangely became a priority customer. To get an extension into the nearby bedroom was a little more difficult but, by good fortune, Mrs Batchelor's husband, Alf, had a brother working for the Post Office telephone engineers department who for a token gift was happy to add to the comfort of the expectant Mary by providing a telephone at her bedside.

But now baby Teddy (Fred knew he would in later life perhaps not wish to be addressed by his full name, Theodore) was safely at home for Fred to love and guide to manhood. As he grew in stature; as he matured from crawling to walking; as he learned to speak; and as he learned to know that his parents were important to him, he became a living part of his father. 'I've got a son! I've got a son! We call him Teddy!' Fred could have shouted his jubilation from the balcony of Buckingham Palace before multitudinous millions of people waving their salutations.

Is it not strange that in chemistry a father can love his children, be they of either sex, in a different manner? Is it not true to say the same for a mother? And yet children grow to believe that Dad always favours his daughter, and Mum always favours her son. Too late do they realise the utter stupidity of their beliefs.

The tragedy is that, in the passing of the years between childhood and parenthood, when all the squabbles and pettinesses turn to bitterness, the offspring only then realise how much their parents, each of them in their own different way, loved them: only when they, in their turn, become parents themselves.

Veronica and Teddy were no exception. Sometimes they fought as cat and dog. Teddy was five years younger. It was not easy to ensure equality between them. 'She's got this, and I haven't;' 'He's got that, and I haven't,' were constant thorns in the sides of their parents. With Fred away at work most of the day it was Mary who bore the brunt of their adolescent quarrels. She loved them equally, but Fred was at work at their bedtime, and usually in bed when they went to school, so he was unable to referee.

As they grew slowly to adolescence, he provided for all their needs. From him they could be sure of all reasonable requests being met. They gave him their love and they were his happiness, his reward for his labours. What he did not have was their every-evening nearness. The luxury of sharing the evening meal each night with them. To tuck them into bed and kiss them goodnight each evening. To sit at their bedside and read them to sleep and, on summer evenings, sit or play with them in the large garden he had landscaped. Only if he were fortunate enough not to be working at weekends, a rare occurrence, did he have that wonderful joy.

On such few occasions it was understandable that Mary should want him to take her somewhere away from the monotony of her daily routine. But *where*, other than to some establishment akin to that in which Fred spent his working life: restaurants, cabaret, dance bands were all a busman's holiday to him, while to Mary they were a pleasant respite from home. When he arrived back home Fred felt he has just completed another day's work. He just wanted to be at home with his kids.

Fred's love of home life (and well before the coming of his children) was the reason for his purchase of the house. This he had now completed in readiness for part-letting. That would bring in an income, enabling him not to have to work the very long hours he had done for so long; and enable him to leave behind the odious aura of the West End and all its artificiality, and to become a normal human being. He would be semi-independent and join the ranks of the 'extra ducks,' the waiters and bartenders who worked as casual staff at banquets, balls and other functions around town.

Fred intended working two or three days or nights only a week, and never at weekends and Bank holidays. Now he was independent.

Then the bombshell dropped.

The three upstairs apartments were ready. Five weeks earlier he had inserted an advertisement in the local paper and *South London Press*. His solicitor had drawn up documents to be signed by the prospective tenants and Fred left Mary to deal with applicants. But none, she said, were of the type she would like to see entering the house. Sometimes she said that nobody had applied to view. Housing accommodation at the time was at a premium and Fred had expected to be inundated with applicants. A seed of suspicion germinated in his mind. Then one day the brother of one of his colleagues called, to be told that the flats had already been let. 'A lady with an apron and with dark hair came to the door,' he said. The description fitted Mrs Batch and, furious, Fred took time from work to go home and admonish her.

Mrs Batch, a homely woman, was embarrassed.

'You had better ask Mrs Higgins,' she said.

'What does that mean?' he asked. Mary was out.

'I don't like to say, Mr Higgins. It's none of my business. I only do as I am told,' she said.

'Do you mean that Mrs Higgins told you to tell people the

flats were let?'

She didn't answer, but he guessed she had. But why?

Fred heard the front door open. He heard Mary and Mrs Batch whispering. He had never lost his temper with Mary before, although her new-found expensive tastes sometimes provoked him to do so.

'What's the bloody whispering about?' he called.

Mrs Batch, sensing a show-down, disappeared.

'I'm not having strangers walking in and out of my front door!'

Fred couldn't believe his ears. He had consulted her in every step. This was to be his security in later life, when perhaps the long hours of standing behind the bar would lead to the premature failure of his lame leg. And yet here she was standing before him righteously demanding he should not subject her to the indignity of allowing strangers - whose money was to support her and her children - to enter the same front door as she did.

'But why have you allowed me to spend so much money if you didn't approve?' he shouted.

'We'll be able to get four times as much as we paid for it if we sell it,' she told a stunned husband.

Was this a nightmare? Was he going insane? Could she not appreciate the benefits of long-term ownership or was her greed for ready money over-ruling common sense?

Quite by chance Fred discovered that Mary had opened a bank account in her own name. He had occasion to query a discrepancy in a bank statement during a discussion with the bank manager. He discovered there had been a clerical mix-up between the two accounts. The manager apologised, and , to save himself embarrassment, Fred allowed him to believe that he was fully aware of Mrs Higgins having a separate account.

But it shook him.

'Why shouldn't I have my own account?' she said, when he spoke of it.

Fred began to feel he was becoming entangled in a web. She

240

was beginning to make him feel it was necessary to seek her approval for any step he took, no matter what. A new Mary was emerging from the Mary he had been more or less content to settle down with, and he knew she would ultimately be the dominant of the two. The occasional oblique reference to her freedom to marry and his inability to do the same worried him at times. His children he loved to the depths of his heart and if she were to marry somebody else she had every right to take these illegitimate children with her. He had no legal right to them and it frightened him to think he could lose them should she wish to take them. The sword of Damocles was suspended above him. Life without his children would devastate him. How could she do it to them? They loved him, he knew, but they were children, and would soon forget him, and that he didn't think he would be able to bear.

Veronica's hair was now turning from silver to luxuriant gold and Teddy was growing more like Fred every day. She wouldn't hurt them, would she?

Mary loved the children, too, so she wouldn't make them unhappy? She was a good mother to them; they were more important to her than Fred. But to herself nobody was more important than she.

Fred was desperate. And in his desperation he engaged a private detective to snoop on Lois to get evidence for grounds for divorce. To free himself to marry Mary, and so hold on to the children.

Though Fred found that Lois was not without men-friends, he was unable to obtain proof of adultery. In the meantime every so often a plain-clothes court official would knock at the door with a warning for Fred to appear before a magistrate to contest her application for an increase in alimony. Over the years it went up and up.

Fred still took Mary to West End night spots, and they formed a slight friendship with the leader of a dance band who, he discovered, started telephoning Mary whilst he was away from home. Fred had an intuition that something might be

241

going on between them. Even if he was wrong it could be leading that way. So he took the bull by the horns. Her tears told him he had nipped this one in the bud. There were tears of fear of his leaving her, although she should have known he could never leave his children. He was sure nothing had happened, and that she had simply been flattered by the interest taken in her by the famous and, to her, glamorous man. But she should have seen how glamorous when Fred made the suave, black-pencilled moustached Romeo face up to Fred's confrontation over the matter.

There were many years of happiness between them, but Mary's love of money assumed more and more importance. What was left from her house-keeping money was hers and hers alone. Fred paid all the bills and the cost of the children's clothes and any other expenses, but Mary never lost an opportunity to unload him of any spare cash. It came to the point when he knew better than to let her know he was carrying money in his pocket. She would pick money up from, perhaps, a table, where he had emptied his pockets for some reason or another. Smiling, she would say, 'Do you want all this money to carry about with you?' It would then become her property to be shared with nobody, to spend as she pleased: on herself usually. And still she would not agree to let the flats.

He decided to try another avenue of escape from the dead-end monotony of his everyday existence. Fred had not told her of his new fear. He had been, up to now, the only man to have held the position of Head Bartender in the West End's two primary establishments; his name had become well-known, not only to the many in his profession, but to his customers, who ranged from stage and film stars to royalty, journalists and cabinet ministers. They all addressed him by his christian name. How could he keep this up?

Fred was employed in a famous Bond Street club when *it* happened. Perhaps he had become paranoid about Mary's selfishness. All he knew was that she didn't love him as she pretended. How could she, when she knew how much he depended on the house giving him his independence? And always he thought of the four women who had really loved him. They would have encouraged him.

Memories of Fred's youth and childhood would come flooding back. He would re-live those long-lost days of love and tenderness, his mind blank to all around him. Twice he emerged from vivid recollections of those days, to find himself surrounded by his colleagues and customers who had lifted him from the floor where he had collapsed behind the bar. Ashen-faced and completely exhausted he would sit in the chair of his small office to recover sufficiently to be assisted into a taxi and be driven home.

Mary, Fred knew, was not a woman to confide in, nor to expect to understand the torment of his mind. If only she would help him and say she did not mind others using her front door. So many quarrels they had had, he had given up any hope of her changing her mind. He felt trapped again.

Fred's employers had been kind to him. They gave him a week's holiday, and all went well back at work until he again re-lived those scenes from his youth, to find himself again surrounded by sympathetic colleagues and customers. He had already been to a private doctor in the West End who told him he had probably been overworking, and to take a rest. But Fred knew something had happened to him. He didn't know what, but knew its source lay in his ambition to become his own boss and Mary's frustrating selfishness. His employers, more embarrassed than he, told him that very reluctantly they must terminate his employment.

Fred could well appreciate their position. Customers were not likely to spend their time in a place where the head bartender was likely to suddenly pass out, bringing a sudden halt to the mood of gaiety, so they helped him into a taxi once more and gave him a bonus of cash and unemployment cards.

At Hyde Park Corner, Fred asked the driver to drive through the park towards Marble Arch. When they reached the bench seat where Joan had befriended him he stopped the cab and paid off the driver.

'Are you all right, guv'nor? You look a bit shaky.'

'Yes, thanks. I'll sit here a while and get some fresh-air,' Fred replied. As he sat on that same bench under that same old tree which had sheltered him from the rain in those far off days of hunger and destitution he thought of the kindness and compassion of a society-despised prostitute and of the intervening years. Tears filled his eyes as his thoughts turned to his children. Had God not given them to him? Had he not done so he would not have stayed with Mary, and he knew that she knew that. Had he not told her that often?

Mary was very kind and soft-hearted in many ways She was sociable, and obsessive in her kindness to animals. The children could not have had a better mother and he was grateful for that. She loved them deeply, and they her, but to him she was less than tender.

Mary's step-father had lost two businesses to the bookmakers, and as a child she had often witnessed punch-ups between him and her mother when he arrived home with empty pockets. For some reason, known only to herself, she proclaimed that Fred wasted money gambling on horses. Nothing could have been further from the truth. Yes, he did, like many men, have the occasional flutter but the highest amount during his entire life in a single bet was five pounds ten shillings, and then only after he had won two hundred and eighty pounds from a ten bob each-way accumulator. The five pounds investment realised a win of twenty-five pounds and, anyway, she asked for and got half of the accumulator winnings. He was never bitten by the bug. He had seen the demise of too many of his friends for that.

Later in life Mary became unpredictably addicted to the one-armed bandit, and it galled Fred to see her feed her money into that machine, but that was later. As he sat in the park that evening he tried to reason that perhaps her childhood and her step-father's behaviour had influenced her in holding on so firmly to money.

244

Mary was all for selling the house to make large profit and he knew he would ultimately have to yield to her but a sense of indignation overwhelmed him. 'She can go to hell! And when I am good and ready I'll sell it for my own purposes!'

Sometimes he loved her and sometimes he didn't. Sometimes she was considerate to him and sometimes she wasn't. Sometimes he wanted to kiss her and sometimes he wanted to kill her. But he guessed that this was the pattern of co-existence; even so, he hated it.

For a long time he sat there. He didn't want to go home and tell Mary why he had been fired. She wasn't anymore a woman to whom he could bare his soul. He thought of different excuses to give her as to why he had left. Too, his mind was plagued by the thought of another sudden lapse into unconsciousness. He knew the news of Fred Higgins getting the boot for fainting would soon spread through the West End bars and he could even now hear the shrill gossips piping away at the UK Bartenders' Club. How would he get another job, for God's sake? Damn it, he thought! He would go home and tell her he had chucked in the job, take a few days rest and then go 'extra ducking.' He had some good contacts and quite a few of them owed him favours.

It was a bonus for Fred to be with Teddy and Veronica for a few nights and put them to bed, all soft and warm after their baths, to kiss them good night and feel their arms around his neck holding him, giving all kinds of little reasons for keeping him with them before letting him tuck them lightly into their little beds. He wanted to be home every night like other daddies were, to kiss them good night and not come home late at night, when they were fast asleep, when he would stealthily creep up beside them to see in the half-light their darling little faces in dreamland. Weren't some men lucky, he thought! If only he could get a job outside the bar trade and lead a civilised family life he would be happy, even though he would have to take a large cut in income. It would pay the dividends of domestic normality. Perhaps his absence had been the cause of Mary's lack of nearness to him. She was a very attractive and vivacious woman. Men turned their heads in admiration; but for fifteen hours a day for six days a week she was alone with the children, apart from visits from friends.

Fred had often tried to discuss his dilemma with Mary. He had the aptitude to undertake a desk job, and indeed had been invited to do so. There were prospects for promotion in administration in catering companies and he had often proved his ability in that field. But Mary had got accustomed to a high standard of living, and voiced her wish not to have to start having to live 'like a bloody peasant.' Well, she might have to, he thought. But her luck was to hold for many more years.

Fred endured the shameful waste of the empty floors above, maddened by Mary's assurance that each year the value of property was rising. Of course it was, he knew that, but she failed to, understand his bitterness at having to watch his beloved children grow up without him. There were times when he found solace in the bottle but it did little to dim the pain in his heart.

Three times more Fred suffered attacks - and blacked out, once late at night when eating the meal Mary had left him before she went to bed. He had regained consciousness to find Tarky, the Great Dane, licking his face and whimpering. He felt dreadfully weak, as he always did afterwards. Usually fastidious in folding and hanging his clothes, he had left them in a heap and gratefully climbed into the haven of his bed. When she called him after the children had gone to school she blasted him for his untidiness, and 'were you sloshed when you came home last night?'

Fred yearned to tell her of his worry. One day he broached the subject.

'I fainted yesterday,' he said seriously.

'Did you say "fainted," Fred?' she asked.

'Fainted.'

'Drinking too much, I suppose,' she said.

'No, Mary, it's happened before.'

246

'Oh well, I shouldn't think there's anything wrong with you very much. Everybody faints sometimes. I have myself. You know I have,' she replied ... the first he had heard of it, and that was as near as he knew he would get. Mary didn't sit down and sympathise but carried on washing her underclothes in the kitchen sink.

Had it been Mary who had fainted it would have resulted in a visit from the private doctor, confinement to bed for days, and the constant service of Mrs Batchelor.

Fred was working for a film club when the opportunity came of going into business for himself. The administrators were nice people to work with, and the potential for widening the membership of the club was obvious. The entertainment was unique and its popularity was exemplified by the many names of stage and screen who were members. The premises stood on ground which was part of a complex then earmarked for demolition, and venues for a new location was being feverishly sought.

At long last a site was found for the building and work started. Of modern design, it was to be a showpiece of film entertainment; the only trouble was that the club was pathetically short of cash and was unable to provide the amenities and comfort members required.

Fred was popular with the members and he enjoyed his job; and when told that the Arts Council were loathe to subscribe the necessary capital to provide catering facilities and other vital social amenities, a plan began to form in his mind.

Mary's parents lived in a large house in Balham. Just the two of them occupied the ground floor, leaving the upper rooms vacant. Fred had craftily sounded out her step-father about his intention of letting the top floors and was somewhat amused when the 'old man' said, 'No, the old woman said she's not going to have strangers walking in and out of *her* front door.'

'It's a bit of a waste isn't it? If you turn the top half into a detached flat you could cop a nice rent for it. Get the gas and electricity channelled on to separate meters like I have done with my place,' Fred said.

'That's what I keep telling her myself, but she won't have it: she's like Mary, silly cows! They've got no bloody sense. I'm choked off with arguing.'

Fred was now working more sociable hours and could always rely upon the management to allow him the odd day off, should he tell them he had private matters to attend to. Now 'Nanny Inskip' was in the habit of making Wednesdays her regular days to visit her daughter and grand children; and it was a Wednesday that Fred stayed away from work.

She was a pleasant enough person but prone, as was her daughter, to nag her husband, and blame him for whatever disturbed her smooth-running existence. Perhaps a little more vehement than her daughter, she thought little of shying any heavy near-at-hand object at him to emphasise her displeasure, sometimes his dinner, should she know him to have spent his wages at the dogs. Mary out of earshot, Fred brought up the subject of her half-empty house and gleaned from her that she would more than welcome the permanent presence of her own kin to share her 'loneliness.' She agreed to his suggestion that he should bring the family together in one house and, it being to their mutual advantage, she also agreed to not yet discussing it with Mary.

Back at work Fred let it be known that he had a 'few bob' to invest, and appeared flattered and pleasantly surprised when the senior club official asked him if he'd be interested in putting the money towards the much-needed catering facility. He graciously accepted the kind offer, and after receiving written assurances confirming the agreement, dropped the bombshell to Mary of his intention of selling the house to raise enough capital for his venture. She ranted and raved at his decision but finally had to admit to herself that she could like it or lump it, and in this she was not going to get her own way. The worm had finally turned!

Fred informed an estate agent of the availability of the house to interested buyers, and applicants were told not to call at the house but to phone him at work for an appointment to view. He did not trust Mary not to turn people away.

Fred did not put the proceeds from the sale into the joint account at the bank. Knowing Mary's disappointment, he mollified her by giving her a not-inconsiderable sum to enlarge her own private account - the account he regarded with disgust, and said so. Fred knew she would never financially help him should he ever be in need.

Fred's venture was for a long time successful. He employed his own staff and his work was applauded by the ever-increasing number of members and officials who administered the organisation. Embassy and official government receptions Fred laid on with refinement equal to that of established hoteliers and catering companies. Mary was always eager to dress in her finery to attend the club as the concessionaire's wife, but was never prepared to help him should he be short of staff, nor to help him with the preparation of the special delicacies he sometimes made at home and transported to the club. But it filled him with pride to occasionally have Veronica to help him at the club and little Teddy to busy himself filling the shelves with bottles.

In the original agreement rental was fixed and provisions were made in respect of fluctuations of profits, the rental to be lowered or increased according to the failure or success of the business. But such was the success that the rental increased to an extent that Fred now considered to be exorbitant, and he came to learn that newcomers in the administrative hierarchy were plotting to squeeze him out.

Gone were the original men who had been responsible for the establishment of what was now the recognised venue of film connoisseurs, victims of the pressures in a power game. Fred was the last survivor. The lack of support he got from the administration told him he could not win. He lost a lot of money when he was finally obliged to relinquish the concession and return to the old life of wages and tips.

Mary didn't seem to be particularly disturbed at what she must have known to be a heavy blow to his ego. After he had settled down in a remunerative job which kept him away from home most of the week, a measure of normality settled upon the home, now a large house which they had moved into on the outskirts of London from Balham.

Fred would often sleep at his new job, a large select sports club of international renown where he would take Teddy to stay with him, returning home on Sunday afternoons. Too, the now youthful, getting-prettier-by-the-day Veronica would go there with him to serve soft drinks to teenage competitors in junior tennis tournaments. They were happy days for Fred, having his kids around him; and to know they were happy to be with him was the reward of his love for them. But his luck ran out again when he was obliged to leave. He told them he had quarrelled with the chief steward, but the truth was that he had been found face down in the cellar where he had collapsed.

Fred went home that afternoon in the summer and cried, and it was Veronica who put her arms around him in compassion. He was to remember all his life that simple, spontaneous act of love from his little girl, as he was always to call her. She was now over eighteen and held a post with an old-established company of Merchant Bankers in the City of London. She was an extremely intelligent person and was destined for success, and Fred loved her with his very soul. To him she was simply his perfect daughter and Teddy, five years younger, the perfect son.

It was when Fred had been working in the sports club, sleeping there most of the week, that Mary said she found it more comfortable sleeping alone: something she was to do for the rest of her life. He noticed that she had cooled towards him, but he did not press her for an explanation. For so long he had acquiesced to her wishes, rather than upset the children by quarrelling with her. Their happiness was paramount to him. To people outside, friends and relations, their behaviour

250

together radiated happiness, but beneath the facade Fred had been unhappy for a long, long time.

Mary sometimes reminded Fred that she was free to marry but that he wasn't. He invariably turned the other cheek. She would always win a verbal contest. However on one occasion that he was never to forget he succeeded in out-talking her, and she responded by using the weapon she knew would pierce his heart. She loudly told Veronica, who was present, that she was illegitimate. Fred realised that at some time in her life she must be told, but he hoped it would be when his dream of being free to marry Mary and legitimise her and her brother came true. He would present her with a new birth certificate and reveal all. But Mary had destroyed this hope and he hated her for it, not for shame brought on himself, but for the look of bewilderment on Veronica's face. How could she do it? He wondered if she really did have feelings for anybody but herself. If she loved Veronica why must she hurt her? What did she gain by knowing she had hurt him at the expense of shocking a sweet teenage girl, her own daughter? He knew he must suffer the lash of her tongue if Teddy were ever present when she was in another of her spiteful moods. She could see the effect her maliciousness had on him and he knew she would have no compunction in telling the boy the same thing, should she be so inclined. Veronica, to his peace of mind, did not hold it against him, but it did little to lessen his loathing of Mary.

Teddy and his father were very close to each other and Fred knew his son loved him by the many things he did and said. Fred was able to sleep at home on only one night a week and Teddy would always sleep in his bed with him in the spare room, talking and asking all the questions boys do of their fathers before he dropped off to sleep. Fred looked forward to going home but just to see his kids. When he arrived home each week he had seldom been in the house a few minutes before Mary asked him for house-keeping money as if she were broke. She never was, but pretended to be.

Veronica commuted daily to the City and met Stanley, a nice young man in the insurance world. They fell in love and Fred was not surprised when Stanley asked him for permission to marry his daughter. He told him of his intention of settling in Canada where he would go before returning for the wedding. Canada! How different Fred's life would have been had he himself settled there. Had it not been for the thought of leaving his mother and Maddy he would not have returned to England.

Preparations for the wedding were almost complete. Stanley returned from Canada to marry his bride, then to return there with her. Three days before the great day Fred was called to the phone. It was Mary. He knew at once by the tone of her voice that she had bad news for him. John had been found dead in the bathroom of his home!

Numbed with shock Fred tried to answer Mary, but the words would not leave him. As he sat down he felt his head swimming. He gripped the desk, resolving not to lose consciousness.

'What's wrong, Fred?' he heard somebody ask.

He was unable to speak as he made his way to the tiny room in which he slept. He unscrewed the stopper from a bottle of whisky, poured a tumbler almost full and drank it all. Feeling more self-controlled he phoned Mary back for details of his brother's sudden death. Evidently John had hopped from his bed to the toilet. The head wounds he sustained when he lost his leg had caused a clot of blood to damage his brain. Poor Cynthia had found him dead on the bathroom floor.

The ensuing five days were momentous. Wednesday, Veronica and Stanley were married. The next day John was cremated. The day after his little girl left him to journey to the other side of the world!

The large four-bedroom house was superfluous to their needs and although Mary said she didn't want to move she eventually did so and they shared a flat at the place of Fred's work. He had threatened to give her no money, the only weapon he had.

'You are very fond of telling me that I have no legal authority over you', he said. 'Well just let me remind you that you have none over me; and I'm not legally obliged to give you a bloody penny.'

Teddy was now learning the motor trade. He hated school, as some youngsters do, and unlike his sister had no scholastic ambitions. But he was very mechanically minded.

The reason Fred insisted that Mary moved was partly due to the fact that she had become very friendly with a woman neighbour whom he knew to have quite a reputation with the men. Mary drove a large distinctive car which was seen by a colleague of his parked outside a pub he used. Inside he had seen Mary and the woman in the company of two men. Teddy was present also, but Fred knew that she did not care about her son's opinion of her behaviour.

Then Fred discovered that Mary had alone accompanied a widower, the father of a friend of Teddy's, on an evening excursion. He had no idea where they went, but was anyway not interested. But he was interested in protecting his son. He wanted him to feel he could respect his mother and for once put his foot down and let her know that he was aware of what she got up to when he was away: 'If you think you can take advantage of me and get away with it, think again. Those days are gone and I'll sell the furniture if necessary and you can clear off!' he said.

Teddy was growing up and would probably go his own way within a few years. Fred reflected that when he was his son's age he was in Jersey and away from home, but he wanted a better start for Teddy who had not known want and poverty. Yes, he thought, want and poverty, and with it the love of a good mother whose happiness was in guiding and caring for her children, and not in her own well-being.

When Veronica and Teddy were young children and were growing up, Mary was all a mother should have been. Perhaps he was old-fashioned in his belief that parents should, throughout their lives, regard themselves as people to be respected by their children; and that they should practise what they preach. Veronica was luckily not there to see her mother's behaviour, but then perhaps Mary would not do anything if she were, and which she well knew might provoke her daughter's disgust.

Fred got his way but Mary was not happy to join him. The flat boasted two bedrooms, one very large, the other very small, but it was the larger that Mary demanded for herself, leaving Fred and Teddy to occupy the smaller. It was small to the extent that with two single beds the margin between them left very little space to manoeuvre. It was here that Mary shouted to Teddy from the larger room one night that he was illegitimate! Fred was anguished. Teddy took it well.

There were periods of harmony, sometimes quite long, but an explosive undercurrent pervaded that tiny flat. Fred learned to walk on egg-shells. Was he a man or a mouse? Such had the years with Mary shaped him! But he had the love of his children, and that was the golden harvest.

One day Rosalina phoned him to tell him of his mother's illness. She was now eighty-four and, as Fred kissed her forehead she whispered, 'Wait for your Will o' the Wisp, son.' And then she died.

Fred saw her again in her coffin. A wonderful old lady who had found her happiness in the happiness of her children. She looked so young. Fred recalled his father lying in the stench of the workhouse mortuary and subsequently in the peacefulness of the undertakers at Milton. By a strange quirk of fate, Rose died in the same now-modernised hospital as Bob. There were no workhouses now; they had been converted to area hospitals, but it was here that her husband died so long ago. Did God arrange that? Rose would be sure that he had.

Fred placed a single red rose beneath her folded hands and kissed her forehead before he said: 'Good bye, Mum,' and left the chapel.

Maddy was waiting for him outside. His dear Maddy!

Always her soft voice had comforted him, and now, 'We all have to go sometime, Fred, but it's nice to go and know you were loved,' she said.

'Yes darling.'

As if reading his mind she said 'Your children love you, I know, and you love them. And you will love someone like Aunt Rose loved Uncle Bob some day, you'll find.'

'I'm getting old, Maddy.'

'Don't give up, Fred. Someone's waiting for you to love them.' 'Yes, I'd like to love somebody like I loved Mum and Gisselle and Joan, but I've still got you, Maddy.'

The next month Mary's mother died. Fred knew she loved her mother and for the first time in years he held her close to him as she wept. He felt a compassion for the woman he was beginning to hate, and it took the loss of a loved-one to reveal to him that she had not completely lost all virtue. It rained on the day of the burial and as the mourners left the graveside Fred became incensed as the two grave diggers irreverently shovelled earth on to the grave below as Mary still looked in farewell at her mother's coffin. He saw her look of dismay, and snatched the shovel from the nearest man and tossed it at the other.

'You disrespectful bastards! Haven't you any thought for other people's feelings?' he asked quietly, and led the weeping Mary away. Later she thanked him.

'Sometimes I wonder why you put up with me.'

'So do I,' he replied, and went to his bed.

A year later Fred and Mary moved back into the house at Balham, Mary's step-father unable to withstand the loneliness. He had got rid of the tenants who occupied it, for non-payment of rent.

Fred's darling Maddy died three day's after they moved. He had not been told of her illness and wondered why. Sam told him that it was not realised that her condition was as serious as it was, and her death was a shock to all.

The four women Fred loved were now gone from him. He

felt a loneliness and isolation, and he searched his soul for a reason why. The only women he had loved during his whole life had now been taken from him.

Only as a youth and young man had Fred gone philandering. Other than for that, Lois and Mary alone had been the objects of his attentions, and it was only with Mary that he had ever wished happily to settle. He was never unfaithful to her, despite being cast from her bed. He had had plenty of opportunity to be. Indeed he had fought off one woman who, he was sure, would have attracted many men.

Her name was well known in London society. Wealthy, she owned a large villa in Palma, in the days before Majorca became a holiday resort for all classes of people. Fred had officiated at cocktail parties in her London home in Belgravia, and at her country estate in Gloucestershire, serving at several house parties that required him and the other catering staff to live-in for long weekends, sometimes longer. When once Fred was engaged elsewhere and could not be present at one of her parties she let the management know of her displeasure, and made it clear that he was to be in attendance at all her future functions. Fred was flattered to learn this but attached no importance to it other than that she must have been satisfied with his services.

It became the subject of much ribaldry among his colleagues that Fred was given one of the palatial rooms for his sole use; not to be shared with others (as was the lot of lesser fry). The head waiter was senior to Fred but was allocated a small servant's room and, rightly, he regarded this a slight to his status. Fred tactfully mentioned his embarrassment to the butler and asked whether there had been an error.

'No,' he said. 'Her Ladyship was quite clear in her instructions that Frederick was to be given a guest room.'

'Do me a favour and tell Mr Conti about it and I'll slip you an extra bottle,' Fred told him. (Fred was responsible for all wine and drinks to be consumed, and subsequently the figure of the amount used. This he had to submit to the hostess' secretary, who never failed to add a few bottles for his own personal use. But Fred had always, prior to obtaining his signature, stocked the butler with what was said to be his 'perks').

Conti, an Italian from London's Seven Dials, was typical of the head waiter of the day: a bombastic character who found it difficult not to waive his arms around in all directions to emphasise his point. His displeasure at discovering Fred's luxurious quarters was to prove no deterrent. His ranting and raving was to be overheard by her ladyship, and she did not beat about the bush when she summoned him to her butlers' pantry, and reminded him that he was a hired hand. If he did not care for her arrangements he could return to London forthwith. That was that! But Fred was still mystified at being singled out for special consideration.

At three-thirty the following morning he discovered why. He was awakened by the touch of a knee gently nudging him, and the smell of expensive perfume. It was her Ladyship! She began to eat him! Now over the years Fred had experienced the many foibles of women but her ladyship was something very different. Even Gisselle, with all her latin passion, was not to be compared with this. Fred was held in a ju-jitsu vice-like grip. His ears, nose, lips and neck were being bitten with the ferocity of a tigress. His back was being clawed as by a lioness. Groaning with discomfort, he tried to roll from her across the broad bed. Slapping her sharply with his open hands, he felt her gradually relax.

In the few seconds it took to cause Fred to believe she was bent on bringing about his early demise by mutilation, she told him in the most unladylike language she had been well pleased with her visit. But in the end he never regarded that episode as a break in his celibacy.

'Look what you've done to me,' he said wrathfully.

No 'your ladyship;' no 'madam' now. Cast aside were all formal and respectful observances of servant to lady.

'That was absolute heaven, Frederick,' she told Fred.

'To use your language, you bloody near slaughtered me,' he said.

Feeling the blood oozing from his back he said, 'You will have to help me bathe my back. Don't lay there. Come along quickly,' he told her.

He hurried to the bathroom and ran the water. Looking in the mirror he thought of how he could possibly explain away to Mary and his mates the cause of the bites and scratches. But most importantly to Mary! Her ladyship had the ready answer. Fred had been savaged by her two German sheep dogs. And he looked as if he really had been. His face and neck showed distinct teeth marks, his back claw marks more similar to an animal's than to a woman's. Who would ever have believed that a wealthy, educated, genteel lady was capable of causing such wounds to a humble bar-tender?

After she had plastered his back and helped him to dress his facial wounds she drove him back to London with three hundred pounds in his pocket and with an assurance that she would explain to his employers the unfortunate attack he had suffered from her two dogs, which she would have destroyed at once!

Back in Balham Fred picked up the threads of 'extra ducking' again, but was constantly on the look-out for something of a permanent nature.

Teddy was employed locally as a motor mechanic and Mary was now filling in her spare time as a casual waitress. She didn't need the money but Fred agreed to her wish to break the boredom of spending her evenings watching television, for now Teddy was finding other (two-legged) interests to keep him out of the house at night.

Fred's efforts in seeking a fresh start were rewarded when he successfully applied for a Civil Service post with the Metropolitan Police Force. A pensionable job, it entailed his working shift duties spanning day and night, but this presented no difficulty to him after his years of never knowing exactly when he would arrive home. He could hardly believe

258

his luck when he was asked to report for duty a fortnight hence to a police section house where he was to serve until his retirement. He never stopped thanking providence for releasing him from the treadmill of the past.

Eight hours a day or night, twenty days only in four weeks work, many evenings free and a long weekend from Wednesday to Monday night once every four weeks, extra pay for Bank Holidays and long annual leave, uniform provided. No longer a nobody, he had at last become a normal human being.

Three days before he was due to start work, while sitting at the dining table alone with Mary, he suddenly passed out and regained consciousness to find Mary rubbing his hands and looking very frightened. All through the years she had never witnessed the attacks he had undergone. The attacks always left him ashen-faced and exhausted and when she showed signs of being at a loss as to what she should do he told her not to bother as it would soon pass. Teddy arrived home shortly after, and Mary told him to get the doctor quickly. Then they helped him into bed.

It was the first attack that Fred had had in two years and as Mary stood by the doctor she heard for the first time how many years he had suffered. He too diagnosed over-work and Mary was content to accept his opinion; but Fred knew within himself that something of a more serious nature was the reason.

Fred felt himself lucky that the attack had not happened when he was at the new job and prayed that any future ones would occur when not on duty. He was not sorry that Mary had been present but all he got from her was the benefit of her expertise on medical matters, and not much by way of compassion.

'There's always something wrong with you,' she said.

What exactly she meant by that he didn't know, for the only occasion he had consulted a doctor was when he had his early attack, which she knew nothing of, and he had never been ill during all the years with her.

It was like a slap in the face when Teddy told him he wanted to leave home to take a small flat for himself. But even though Fred had seen this coming, this shock was none the lighter.

Fred was back to square one now - no kids, just two people yearning for love and companionship, and Mary was not providing either. Fred considered leaving her to find a small flat and start a new life from scratch, but he had never truly given up hope of legitimising his children. To him this was important, even in these days of well-known couples blatantly producing 'love children' with no intention of marriage. History is full of the tragedies of children born on the 'wrong side of the blanket,' children bearing the stigma of bastardy and utterly bereft of legal rights. Divorce laws were beginning to change and Fred would ask Mary to marry him simply to allow him to right the wrong he had never ceased to regret. He would rest his mind from his guilt.

Then Rosalina phoned him. Bertie was ill. He was in hospital. It was with dismay that Fred saw the emaciated figure of his brother. He had been ill for weeks and surgery had failed to stem the cancerous growth in his body, and yet his sister had only now phoned him, having been informed of his fast-approaching death.

Bertie was conscious and breathing faintly when Fred arrived. 'Hello Fred,' he said.

'Hello, Bertie, how are you?'

'Dying.'

'Don't say that, Bertie.'

'I'm glad you came.'

'Bertie, I didn't even know you were ill,' said Fred.

'She won't ever change,' Bertie said, meaning his sister.

Bertie closed his eyes as Fred took his hand. He didn't speak again and Fred realised that his brother had passed away. All the loved ones that he had grown up with were gone now. All except Rosalina: the only one of them lacking in compassion. And at home too, his loved ones were gone from him, but not for ever, and they were his anchor.

At Bertie's funeral Fred was to find Rosalina's children in a group with their partners, away from their mother. They had come, they told Fred, to pay their last respects to their Uncle Bertie, but did not wish to speak with their mother as she had been the cause of many rifts between them and had forbidden their children to associate with their grandmother. Bertie had been right when he said, 'She will never change.'

Mary found more time on her hands now that Teddy had gone. Fred understood her wish to find a job to occupy herself and he learned of a vacancy for a matron at a police station to be custodian of female prisoners awaiting court appearance. In no manner did she fit the general conception of the public's image of a wardress, for she was a very attractive and well-dressed woman and her young-looking features and figure gave the impression of a woman twenty years younger. She never corrected anyone who remarked that Fred was much older than she, nor tell them that the difference between their ages was a mere two years. She applied for and got the job. In it she found her forte as Fred knew she would. In that job it didn't suit to be soft and soft she was not. Her salary was good and her terms of reference akin to that of Fred's. Her shifts did not concur with his, which suited him fine usually. It meant that they did not spend much time together and both found other interests to fill off-duty time. Yet she was still the same old Mary with money. What she earned was hers and hers alone. No sharing of housekeeping expenses for her. He was the one responsible for all domestic bills and it was he who did the shopping and paid for it. Her wardrobe was far beyond her needs and her jewellery far from cheap. All the time her bank account grew.

Lois persisted in her periodic applications for an increase of alimony but Fred did not appear in court and accepted the magistrate's order without question. He did not wish to draw the attention of the police officers who were under the impression that Mary was his wife and had been for a long time. He decided to inform Lois of his intention of divorcing her under

261

the changed law of the separation of a couple. She had mellowed and made no protest, but was, after all the years he had paid her, resolute in her determination to squeeze as much as she could out of him.

'You'll still have to pay my money into the court,' she said emphatically.

'I know that. All I am saying to you is that I am going to apply for a divorce, and if you oppose it I shall exercise my rights and come back to the home I have supported for thirty-five years and make your life hell after I've chucked out your so-called lodger, so take it or leave it.' Fred meant it, and she believed him. She agreed to his terms.

Mary was outraged to learn of Fred's plan.

'It will appear in the local paper and everyone at work will know we're not married,' she said.

'Many years ago you deceived me over your marriage status, but I am being honest with you and you will not stop me,' Fred said.

'Why do you want a divorce anyway?' she asked.

'Because I want *you* to marry me.'

She thought this was hilarious and laughed.

Fred said, 'If you don't marry me I shall leave you to keep yourself, so it's your choice. Fred got his divorce, and two weeks later his nightmare - collapsing on duty - occurred.

Fred had gone to report for late turn - 2 pm to 10 pm - when he awoke to find a colleague's arm around him and hear a voice ordering an ambulance.

At the Casualty Department of the hospital Fred was once more told that he had merely fainted and was taken home. The following morning he was sitting at the kitchen table and blacked out again. That evening, in bed, he blacked out again, and with each attack he became weaker and weaker. Too weak to call for help . He managed to push the bedside table over to attract attention, the crash bringing Mary and Teddy who, by providence, had called at the house. It was Teddy, now married to Angela, who demanded an ambulance to take his father to hospital. And as they took Fred from the house he thought he was dying and would never return.

At the hospital Fred was taken to the Intensive Care unit where he was wired to electronic apparatus and closely attended by vigilant nursing staff and doctors. A few days later he was transferred to a neurology ward and then taken to another hospital where his brain was scanned; and then to a children's spastic hospital for tests, after being wired to a machine which recorded the impulses of his brain.

It was discovered that a lobe of his brain had been ruptured by blows to the head, causing a punch-drunkenness. Voice tests also revealed a slight slurring of his voice. There was not doubt in the minds of the specialists that his condition was due to his many boxing bouts. He had never been knocked out: they said it might have been better if he had. He was given tablets and told that he must regularly take them forever, and he was assured he would be free of any further attacks. The hospital was correct. It was only his forgetfulness in not taking them which caused another very minor attack. Gradually pills became part of his every-day routine. He would almost panic if he left home without them. They were carried in every jacket or suit in his possession.

Fred's fear of dismissal from his job proved unfounded, and when he returned no more was said. At long last Mary, now retired, agreed to marry him. Her quip: 'I don't mind making myself an honest woman now. At least if you snuff it I'll get a widow's pension to go with my police one,' was typical of her attitude towards him. But he cared not, and had learned to live with it.

Teddy, ever the joker, well understood the reason for the secrecy from neighbours surrounding the wedding plans. He agreed to use his large car to convey them to the Registry Office. As Mary and Fred emerged from the house they were amazed to see he had bedecked his car from radiator to windscreen with wide white ribbon, and later added a touch of black humour when he said to the Registrar after the ceremony, 'I bet that you didn't go to your Mum and Dad's wedding!' So now 'married bliss' reigned.

Fred's first task was to obtain new birth certificates for Veronica and Teddy, a task more complicated than he imagined. The records he thought to be lodged in the archives of Somerset House were now elsewhere, but after much leg work and many enquiries he held in his hand the two most prized documents ever published. His long ambition was realised. His children no longer bore the stigma he had sorrowed over. His shame was now pride. Mary said it was a lot of 'unnecessary rubbish - the kids were grown up and didn't care about it now.'

But Fred hoped they would understand his fatherly anxiety to right the wrong he had caused and it would perhaps show the depth of his love for them, if they had ever doubted it.

Fred was now past the official age of retirement of men in his work but such was his high standard he was granted repeated extensions to continue by the Commissioner of the Metropolitan Police Force.

Lois obtained a further raise in alimony when Fred received a letter from her sister informing him of Lois's death from cancer. He did not find it in his heart to rejoice but accepted the fact that now, simply, another burden had gone. The following month Mary complained of difficulty swallowing. Over many years Fred had heard so many cries of 'wolf' that he dismissed them after expressing sympathy. For a whole week she continued to complain and, as usual, retired to her bed with Fred waiting on her hand and foot, leaving it only to wash and use the toilet. He began to suspect that for once this was not an imaginary malady and called the doctor to examine her.

'I think she should go to the hospital for X-ray examination,' he told Fred and gave him a letter of introduction.

Having been X-rayed the hospital asked Mary to attend again for an internal throat examination. Fred, sitting in the waiting room, began to suspect the possibility of her condition being cancerous. The few patients who returned from the room where Mary was now undergoing examination were in a semi-stupor from mild anaesthetic and, from their conversations with friends, he gathered that he was in a section of the hospital dealing with patients suspected of having growths and tumours. Mary too had now returned in a semi-stupor and waited for the doctor to come to them. Fred heard the doctor tell patients to either 'come in for a few days,' or 'you are right: there is nothing there.'

Fred did not tell Mary of his fears for her. Throughout her life she had had a dread of cancer, he knew. It didn't matter to him that love had died between them. He must comfort her all he could. Thank God he had not left her to face the trauma of this illness alone. She was not a Lois.

Fred visited Mary daily and for the first time for many years kissed her forehead. Privately and in the quiet of their offices two doctors told Fred she had eight months to live. Bewildered, he left the hospital and sat on a bench overlooking the Thames, a stone's throw from the spot where Joan and his son had died. He cried alone and felt a terrible loneliness. If only Veronica was with him to give him the strength to overcome the next year of his life, but he must not tell her that her mother was dying. He must not tell Teddy and Angela, and their two lovable little boys must know that their Nanny was going back to Jesus.

Fred went home and drunk a bottle of whisky. It did nothing for him.

The next day Fred told his sergeant at work that he was retiring and told him the reason, swearing him to secrecy for fear of Mary discovering of her impending death by a chance remark by visitors. She underwent massive surgery in an attempt to remove the tumour in her oesophagus but it succeeded in providing only temporary respite. Veronica flew home from Canada and was happy to see what she believed to be the recuperation of her mother. Fred did not reveal to her that her farewell kiss to Mary was her kiss of goodbye.

Sometimes Fred wanted to tell Teddy the truth but knew it would prey upon his mind. His work entailed driving on the busy London roads where he must concentrate and not have the thought of his mother's terminal illness to endanger himself and others.

Mary wanted to go home, so ambulance transport for the tri-weekly treatment of radio-therapy was arranged. After each session she became ill for a few hours but this passed, and for a while it was thought that perhaps the therapy would greatly prolong her life. It was not to be.

To add to Fred's tribulations, his leg had unaccountably begun to give him pain, which slowly increased. His doctor told him he must accept the fact that the injury to it took place so long ago that nothing could be done now to put it right. He gave him pain killers. Mary steadily deteriorated. The nourishing liquid and light sustenance that Fred gave her she was having great difficulty swallowing. Her flesh seemed to disappear daily. Fred washed her, brushed and combed her hair, changed her night-dress and administered to her. During those months she became closer to him than she had ever done in their forty years together. When she sometimes wanted to speak of her selfishness and her lack of nearness to him he told her it was all his fault and not hers, but often she asked him to forgive her. He in turn asked her forgiveness and, as always, she won the verbal battles. Poor Mary, he knew, was sorry, but Fred could only tell himself that we are all imperfect. 'Know thyself,' God said. But can we really?

Ever more slowly it seemed she neared the end, and Fred wanted her suffering to be over. Despite her suffering, her face strangely maintained its beauty, while her arms, legs and body were mere bones covered with skin. Came the day when the doctor told her she must be taken back to the hospital 'for a few days.' He used the telephone in the adjoining room to inform the hospital and arrange transport.

'I'm sorry, Mr Higgins,' he whispered, 'but you know, don't you?'

Fred nodded and whispered his thanks. 'Yes.'

That night as he sat beside Mary's hospital bed she beckoned him to move closer to her. Her voice had now become a mere whisper.

'You've been good to me Fred. I'm glad you've not told the kids I'm going to die. I've always known and so have you. Please kiss me Fred.'

He gently kissed her lips and heard her tell him to go home and rest his leg. Through the glass door she feebly waved to him and then closed her eyes.

The next morning they phoned him from the hospital to say she had taken 'a turn for the worse.'

It was his old police sergeant who, at great speed, drove him through the busy traffic to her. They had moved her to a tiny ward which contained her lone bed. Her eyes were closed as he sat on the chair which a nurse had placed at the bedside. As he softly held her hand, her fingers momentarily tightened to his and then she died. Her head was turned in the direction of their meeting place of forty years before. Her face was now as beautiful as then. Why had they been forty wasted years, he asked himself and thought: No, they have not been wasted. They have given me my children and they have had a good mother. Me? I'm content to know it.

# CHAPTER 15

Why have I been so denied
A love for which I have for so long cried
For so many years
And with so many tears?
Who knows?
But ever has been a soft whisper
In my ear
Wait, wait, my son
And I shall guide you
To your Will o' the Wisp
Your Lydia

Veronica once more flew home. This time to attend Mary's funeral and to stay with her father to help him start a new way of life. She quite understood his wish to clear all Mary's clothes and personal effects from his flat, and filled numerous large plastic bags with countless feminine items of dress, shoes, handbags and such impedimenta. Cosmetics and toiletries, hats and other articles were disposed of, including a very expensive fur coat. Her jewellery was shared, apart from a few items which had been promised to Veronica, between her and Angela.

Mary left no will, and Fred became executor of her estate, and when he later gave the thousands of pounds from it to a hospice sheltering patients suffering with terminal cancer, he felt as a man who had unburdened himself of a life-long affliction; as a man weak from the thirst, who had plunged into a lake of fresh water! Goodbye and good riddance to the money - it had been the wedge that had driven them apart.

And so now, beyond the hope of finding a new Gisselle or Joan, he resigned himself to accept life as it presented itself.

Veronica suggested he might find painting an absorbing pastime - he had always wanted to paint.

Fred's leg was steadily giving him more pain and an old injury to his other leg was now showing the result of lack of medical attention since it happened. He had relied upon the strength of his stronger leg to compensate for the weaker, but now he could not walk without a stick. His doctor told him there was nothing to be done to help him but the pain from them was often excruciating and a bottle of whisky gave much more relief than his medication.

Fred found it necessary to employ a woman to do his housework and to shop for him. He began to feel himself vegetate and hated his helplessness. He wanted to visit Veronica in Canada but knew he would be unable to manage it alone. (He had previously flown to see her and Stanley some years before and knew what was required of his legs). So it was a Godsend to him when two young police officers he had worked with told him they would like to go with him to Toronto, and stay at his daughter's house. They would assist him on outings while there. It was an arrangement that was to prove full of fun. And to Fred, a much-needed relief from the monotony and drudgery of the previous two years. So they left a rainy London for the early-summer glory of a cloudless Toronto.

The two policemen enjoyed themselves, but always found time to help Fred into and out of Veronica's car, and they accompanied him to wherever he wanted to go.

Fred was somewhat surprised one morning when Veronica said, 'Come along, Dad, I want to take you some place special.' She helped him into her car.

'Where are we going?' he asked.

'Wait and see,' she replied. Veronica had always been pleasantly bossy and he knew he'd have to wait. She pulled up outside a large modern building. As he looked above the portico he realised she had parked outside the Toronto Orthopaedic Hospital. She had often said that she was sure that with modern medical techniques something could be done to improve his leg and alleviate the pain which she knew he endured. She had made an appointment with a leading surgeon who had successfully treated Stanley after a skiing accident in which he severely injured his knee.

The X-rays of both legs and hips showed a bizarre array of pictures. His pelvis was completely out of alignment, the left femur grotesquely above its correct position and his right knee devoid of cartilage - bone to bone.

'It's a wonder you can stand,' said the surgeon, 'but something can be done for you.'

He pointed to a glass cabinet containing artificial human joints.

'What you need is a totally new femur and knee, and it *can* be done,' he said.

He gave Fred a letter of introduction to a famous London teaching hospital.

'When you return to England, take the letter and, although I know there is a long waiting-list for the treatment, I am sure you will get it,' he said.

Veronica was as jubilant as Fred.

Fred was in the house of a special friend of Veronica's when he was introduced to a lady. As she turned her head to him his heart seemed to be stilled. He heard his host say, 'Lydia meet Fred.'

As Fred gazed into her eyes and looked at the softness of her features and expression he was looking at the four women his life had revolved around. Her face combined all the beautiful qualities of the four people he had loved and who had loved him, and he knew at once that his mother had led him to his Will o' the Wisp! She was many years younger than he, but to him it mattered not. In those few seconds he had found the heart that he knew was beating for him to find.

Fred fell in love with Lydia. He wanted to embrace her. He wanted to tell her he had found her at last. He wanted to tell her he loved her and would love her for ever, but she would think he was crazy. All the pent-up yearning of his heart wanted him to shout to the world that he had found his goddess. But who could he tell? Who would understand? They would snigger and laugh. They would think him crazy.

Fred wanted to stay in Canada, but how could he? He would become a laughing stock, and embarrass Veronica and Stanley. Also, of course, he had to return to England and await the surgery to his legs. But now he had found the love he had wanted for so long. It was his secret. He must tell nobody, least of all Lydia. If he told her, he felt she take care not to meet him again, and who would blame her? This stranger had fallen in love with her, and he so much older than she. No, he would keep his love to himself and be happy to fantasise about her. He could almost hear people saying, if they knew, 'Silly old sod!'

Fred did not see her again before he returned home, but her face and voice were ever in his mind. When he was admitted to hospital for what was to be the first of two operations to restore normality to his legs, the lady who brought him his mid-meal cup of tea was named Lydia, and she too was the daughter of a Polish father. She no doubt wondered why he smilingly insisted on kissing her hand before he presented her with something from his well-stocked bedside locker from among the presents visitors had brought. It became a ward and nursing staff joke to pull Fred's leg about his mythical sweetheart Lydia so far away in Canada. The Staff Nurse, Kim, would hurriedly come to his bedside and say, 'Hold on tight. Lydia's on the phone for you from Canada.' Then with a junior nurse she would quickly push him to the nurse's desk where he knew it would be his other sweetheart, his Veronica, on the phone.

Lydia was unaware that Fred knew a little of her background, craftily and casually gleaned from the host of the small party at which he had met her. Paul was her good friend: not in any manner attached other than in friendship. He was an Englishman and Fred had toyed with the idea of asking him to arrange an apparently casual meeting; but perhaps Paul would not want to.

The following year, a few weeks after his operation, Fred returned to Toronto, agog with the idea of meeting Lydia again. It was not to be. He met Paul on several occasions and asked of her, but never got the opportunity to open his heart to him, so again he returned home, filled with frustration.

The second operation to Fred's legs was more major than the first. Fred was administered many blood transfusions and drugs. His hallucinations included weird scenes of Lois and Mary striking Lydia with the chain suspended above his bed, and Joan lifting him and carrying him to Veronica and Teddy. To him the drug-induced fantasies were very real. His surroundings were foreign to him and he would call for help and see, in nurse's uniform, his mother and Lydia enter the room smiling at him, each approaching the bed and each to hold a hand.

Fred realised that the massive dosage of drugs given to him to alleviate his pain were causing his frightening dreams. He told the nurses to get the night-duty doctor. Now fully in charge of his faculties, he told the doctor that he would take no more drugs, but he would like his permission to partake of what he felt would help him to recover more quickly than all the pills in the drugs trolley - whisky! In his locker he had five half bottles that his friends had bought for him.

'You can have some whisky on one condition only.'

'And what's that, Doctor?'

'You give me a large one also,' he replied.

Fred made fast progress. The only pills he took were those prescribed to prevent black-outs. After five weeks and with the aid of two sticks he was taken home to his small flat.

Ten days later Fred was on a Jumbo jet over the Atlantic bound for Toronto. Christmas was approaching. His Canadian friends lifted his spirits. The sub-zero temperatures and every-day falls of snow did nothing to lower the warmth in his heart.

Fred had been in Toronto for four weeks and had just another six days to go before he was to return to England when he felt that Paul had finally got the message of his many requests of 'How's Lydia and why don't you bring her to see me?'

Paul phoned Fred and said that the next day he had arranged to have Lydia drive both of them to a newly-opened hotel which he wanted to inspect. Veronica and Stanley were at work and Fred was alone in the house when the door bell rang. Fred's heart was thumping as he opened the door.

No! Fred had not been imagining things when he had first seen all his loved-ones in her eyes and face. And although Lydia spoke with a Canadian accent, the intonation of her voice was reminiscent of all of them. In a strange and inexplicable way, Fred was still weak from the effects of the long surgery he had undergone, but his breathlessness was not due to that.

Fred suddenly realised that Paul was speaking to him.

'It's a brand new place, Freddie. It's called The Renaissance,' Paul said.

The Renaissance. The new birth.

So that Fred could stretch out his legs he sat in the passenger seat next to Lydia. She and Paul had helped him through the ice-packed snow to her car. She held his arm to steady him and eased him into the seat, gently lifting his weak leg into the car.

Fred wanted to touch her and hold her, and tell her of his happiness in being with her; but could only thank her. Seated at the wheel as she drove through the light snow flurries, he wanted the journey never to end. And when she solicitously helped him from the car on arriving at the hotel he knew that this woman would always be in his heart.

At the table they found they had much in common. She too was in the licence trade: his old job. Paul was host, but hardly ever did they allow him into their conversation. They were hardly aware of his presence.

When eventually they returned to the car a real Canadian blizzard was blowing: visibility nearly nil, but Fred was the happiest man in the world. Concentrating on driving on the slippery surface and through the blanket of snow Lydia took several wrong turnings. Fred delighted in each, while poor Paul became more and more agitated at the prospect of being late for his next appointment. As they found themselves in the bright glow of down-town Toronto, Fred boldly asked her to visit him at Veronica's house the next afternoon.

'Sure thing, Freddie! I'd like that,' she replied.

He could hardly believe his luck.

Veronica was peering through the glass panel of her front door as they arrived, worried at Fred's long absence.

'Thank goodness you're home! I thought you had been in an accident.'

Fred wanted to tell her that he had just spent the happiest day since his youth. He could hardly keep his excitement to himself. And that night he slept little.

Next morning Fred heard Veronica and Stanley leave for business. They would not be back until 5.30 in the afternoon. Veronica would phone him to enquire if he was in need of anything, but with the ice box filled with food and her cabinet well stocked with whisky there was no need to worry, and Lydia was coming at 12.30!

Fred prepared a large oval silver tray with delicate sandwiches, and all his old expertise was used in dressing them. Bottles were made ready for her arrival. 12.30 arrived, but Lydia did not. At 1.30 his spirits sank to rock bottom.

Fred phoned Veronica to ask if she thought Lydia was the type to stand him up.

'I don't know her very well, Dad, but I shouldn't think she would do that to you,' she said.

2.30 and no Lydia.

Fred poured himself a half tumbler of whisky and topped it up with beer but it did little lighten his misery. Then he heard the door bell. As fast has his sticks would take him he hastened to the door, silently praying it was Lydia and not a tradesman or a caller; and then, through the glass panel he saw a figure huddled in a heavy dark fur coat. Lydia!

At once they resumed their never-ending chatter. Never at a loss for words they ate the food and drank the plentiful liquor.

For years Fred had written poetry and lyrics to amuse himself. Mary had never shown any interest in them, although she wrote poetry herself.

During his long wait for Lydia Fred had written some verses on his usual writing material: kitchen paper. Lydia liked them and he composed some more about his 'Lady of the Snow.' He had never written a love poem nor a love letter to anybody in his whole life but with Lydia he knew he could write from his heart forever.

Fred knew she could not possibly love him. The difference of their two ages put that utterly out of the question, but he felt for her such a clean and fine tender love. He wanted to protect her from the hazards of the many years she had before her. If only he were just a few years older than she he would perhaps be acceptable to her, but he would not spoil this wonderful growing friendship by telling her of his love. She was happy with him and together the hours slipped by as minutes.

Fred would have loved to have sat and talked to her for the rest of the day but Veronica had arranged to take him to a party that evening. It would be two days before she came again to make him happy.

And so Lydia came to him again. Fred wrote more poetry for her. She had brought her small tape recorder with her.

'Please record the poetry for me, Freddie. I love the way you say it,' she said.

It was the beginning of all the love poems and love letters he was to write to her. I have never received a letter of love, Freddie,' she said in her adorable Canadian accent.

'And neither have I; nor written one. Do you mind if I write them to you, Lydia,' Fred asked.

She had arrived early that day and yet the hours again slipped by as minutes. Tonight she had to leave to prepare food for a meeting at the home she shared with two young men. 'They are like brothers to me,' she told him.

They were standing side by side replenishing their glasses when they gently embraced. He kissed her softly upon her warm cheek and knew the glow of her nearness. He almost blurted out his love for her then and there, but he thought it would spoil the beauty of their happy understanding. Just then they heard Veronica's key rattling the lock of the front door. His heart was beating with the ecstatic thrill he thought had left him long ago.

'Why don't you stay for dinner, Lydia?' Veronica asked.

'I'd love to,' and then explained her commitment.

'Why don't you take Dad along?'

'I'd love to. Would you like to come, Freddy?'

Need you ask, he thought.

'Yes please,' he said.

Armed with a bottle of scotch he found himself sitting beside her in her car.

It seemed so natural to hold her hand. Fred knew she liked to hold his, and at her home, after she had completed her preparations, she seldom left his side. Their hands would again entwine as lovers. How he loved her kindness. She seemed to know that she made him happy. When the guests left she took him to her room and showed him her dresser which contained her ornaments and small articles of sentimental value to her.

'Take anything you would like to keep to remind you of me,'

she said.

He didn't need anything to remind him of her, but chose a small piece of earthenware.

'The nicest thing I made in Pottery Class at school,' she told him as she wrote on its base, 'To Fred With Love, Lydia.'

Fred wondered if he was dreaming. Yet he knew he wasn't.

The day approached when he must return to England. Veronica had arranged a small farewell buffet luncheon in her house, inviting a dozen or so close friends. They were Fred's friends too; and although he included a little humour in his farewell speech, it was with sadness that he delivered it.

When Lydia arrived it was with a smile of possession that he introduced her, for none had met her. And as he hobbled around on his sticks he noticed that she got many an admiring glance.

Gradually they said their farewells. Tony and Isobel gave him a picture book of Ontario inscribed: 'Many Happy Returns.' Alan, who had been a London policeman and was now with the Toronto police, gave him a bomber jacket with a crest of the force and inscribed 'Fred.'

Two by two the guests departed leaving a pile of mementoes for Fred to take back to England.

Veronica and Stanley at last went to bed, leaving Lydia alone with Fred.

They sat together in the spot where they had spent many happy hours, and talked far into the night. Despite the sub-zero temperature of the early morning, frosting the windows of the kitchen, neither wanted to say goodbye. This friendship was more than just platonic. In it there was an unspoken depth of affection. As they gently kissed farewell Fred felt the pang of parting he had felt with the goodbyes he had felt with Gisselle and Joan. But with Lydia he did not experience the despair of utter finality of loss.

Veronica and Stanley said farewell to him at the airport, not suspecting that he had found the woman who had given him a new incentive to face the future.

At home Fred was sleeping off the jet-lag when the ringing of the telephone awoke him. It was Lydia!

'Hi, Freddie, did you have a good trip?'

'Yes, but I was thinking of you the whole time.'

'I was thinking of you, too, Freddie.'

'I love you, Lydia.'

'I love you too, Freddie.'

He knew that she told him that simply to make him happy. And it did. But he realised that she could not want to share the rest of her life with him as he did with her. That was Lydia: kind, sweet, compassionate. His Will o' the Wisp.

Lydia would be close to his heart for ever. He wrote to her regularly and sent her love letters and love poems. He wrote songs for her which he taped and sent to her. She told him she would never part with his correspondence, and would treasure it for ever. He wrote a song which he felt would convey to her the depth of his love, and taped it using his harmonica as music. He knew she spoke with truth, feeling and understanding when she told him she liked it.

> It's never too late for thoughts of love,
> It's never too late to dream,
> It's never too late to hold a warm hand
> And feel the magic glow of wonderland.
> It's never too late to see the stars
> Shining in smiling tender eyes.
> And it's never too late to live anew
> And not too late to share my love with
> you.

Fred would often speak to Lydia on the telephone. And always when he said, 'I love you, Lydia,' she never failed to say, 'I love you too, Freddie.' Fred was happy at last.